VARNEY
THE VAMPYRE;
or,
The Feast of Blood
A Romance.

I0614554

Book Four
Bride of the
Vampyre

Other works by James Malcolm Rymer

Phoebe; or, The Miller's Maid.
Moreton; or, The Doomed House.
Grace Rivers; or, The Merchant's Daughter.
The Black Monk; or, The Secret of the Grey Turret.
Don Caesar de Bazan. A Romance of Old Spain.
The White Slave. A Romance of the 19th Century.
The Black Mantle; or, The Murder at the Old Ferry.
Paul the Reckless; or, The Fugitive's Doom.
Jane Shore; or, London in the Reign of Edward IV.
Ada the Betrayed; or, The Murder at the Old Smithy.

VARNEY
THE VAMPYRE
James Malcolm Rymer

Book Four
Bride of the Vampyre

WILDSIDE PRESS
Doylestown, Pennsylvania

Varney the Vampyre;
or,
The Feast of Blood
Book Four:
Bride of the Vampyre
A publication of
Wildside Press

P.O. Box 301
Holicong, PA 18928-0301
www.wildsidepress.com

TWENTY-FIRST CENTURY EDITION

— "How graves give up their dead,
And how the night air hideous grows
With shrieks!"

Introduction

by Laura J. Underwood

I was all of sixteen and hot on the trail of literary vampires when I first heard about *Varney the Vampire*. The reference was in a book of vampire cinema, one of several I own even to this day. Yes, admittedly, I was a media child way back then. I cut my fangs on Christopher Lee's numerous appearances under the Dracula cloak. I read Stoker's Dracula, and then I learned there were other even older literary vampires out there. Naturally, like a good vampire hunter, I went in search of those undead who occupied the pages of tomes written before I was born. By the time I hit my twenties, I could recite the year, title, author and star of every vampire film and book on the shelves.

All this research was looked upon as pretty ambitious for a sixteen year old who did not know that she was a nerd. In those days, I thought of my pursuits as more intellectual, for by that age, I already knew that I wanted to be a writer. And where did a writer learn to write? Why through reading, of course.

What did I want to write in those days?

A vampire novel . . . or film. I don't think I was picky which media my story appeared in, so long as it was as good or better than the works of those who had written about bloodsuckers before me.

And this led me straight to Varney.

I was already familiar with LeFanu and Dr. Polidori's thin contributions to the lore. When I learned of James Malcolm Rymer's tale, this lengthy serial of blood lust and dark deeds, I was intrigued.

Finding a copy in print was another matter. I had already hounded the shelves of the local library without success (this was before I worked for them and was able to issue my own control over a bit of their collection development). But the librarian in charge could see that I was not going to give up on this quest, and she told me about something called "Interlibrary loan." If a copy of *Varney the Vampire* was available somewhere else, they would be able to borrow it for me.

The original had not seen print for many years, but Dover had issued a several volume set, and the library was able to borrow it from a university elsewhere. So imagine my surprise when I opened the first book and saw the print. Dover editions were literal facsimiles, which is to say, they looked like photocopies of old books and magazine pages, bound together so they had the ambience of the originals. This was not limited to Varney, I can assure you, as the owner of several of Dover reprints. This particular set of books had apparently been badly copied from something that reminded me of the OED. The print was atrocious, the books were several hundred pages each, and I only had a two-week loan period . . .

Fortunately, I had better eyesight and the patience of Buddha in those days, not a normal teen attribute. I had already, in that period of my life, read nearly every novel Dickens ever wrote, along with the ponderous works of Winston Churchill and the complete works of William Shakespeare, so I refused to be daunted by the print or the vast amount of it.

I just wasn't a visible presence in the house. It was in the summer, and I could take books out to the hammock and read undisturbed except for the occasional whine of my younger siblings.

From page one, I was mesmerized. Varney alternately invoked sympathy, disgust, and humor. On the one hand, he and his adversaries were both very much like the brooding, doomed variety of romantic protagonists the Bronte sisters and Thomas Hardy created in their darker works. On the other hand, there was a campy side to the tale. It was a nonstop adventure with a capital "A." Varney was no ordinary vampire. He went from desiccated corpse to nearly human, and during that journey, he gained enough humanity to see what an inhuman monster he actually was. While I was too young to ponder the "forbidden fruit" aspect of early Victorian literature, I managed to absorb the atmosphere and fun of the story, and added them to the literary knowledge that I had. Varney left an impression on my mind for a long time afterwards. Pulp could be fun and entertaining.

So here you have it, after all these years, *Varney the Vampire* is once more made available via several volumes (of which this is the fourth) through the kindness of the publishers at Wildside Press. Do I recommend that you waste time collecting and reading such a silly old classic with gothic pulp prose and Victorian morality when there are new Anne Rice and Laurel K. Hamilton vampires occupying bookshelves by the carloads?

I certainly do.

This kind of classic will live on forever, much like the undead themselves.

— Laura J. Underwood

Chapter CXVII.

THE PROPOSAL OF JACK PRINGLE TO TAKE ANDERSON TO THE WEDDING.

A circumstance now occurred which soon enabled Jack Pringle to console himself for the misadventure he had had, which he was delighted to think was not known to any of those persons with whom he came ordinarily into contact.

The pleasant circumstance to which we allude, was the reception of a letter from the admiral, and by the mere fact of his writing such an epistle to Jack, it would seem to be perfectly true that he really felt unhappy without the companionship of that worthy.

The letter was to the following effect: —

"Jack, you mutinous rascal, your leave of absence has expired, and you know you ought to have a round dozen when you come back to your ship; but as it turns out you may stay where you are, for a reason that I am going to tell you.

"There is to be a wedding at the very place where you are staying, between some odd fish, a Baron Something, I don't know who; but as we have been all invited, we are coming down the whole lot of us, and shall arrive on Thursday, so that you may look out from the mast-head as soon as you like, and you will see us coming with all sails set.

"No more at present from, you vagabond, you know who."

"What an affectionate letter," said Jack; "I know the old fellow couldn't do without me long — he is quite an old baby, that's what he is; and if I wasn't to take a little notice of him, he would be as miserable as possible. Hilloa! What cheer? Have you come back?"

These last words were addressed to James Anderson, who at that moment made his appearance in the cottage of the old seaman, he having just left the house of the Williamses, after the painful interview which we have recorded took place between him and Mrs. Williams, during which she had succeeded in convincing him that all his hopes, as regarded Helen, were crushed completely.

The appearance of deep dejection that was upon his countenance was such, as to convince Jack Pringle the nature of the business he had been upon, and he cried, —

"Come, come — cheer up, man. I guess, now, you have been looking after that sweetheart of yours, who is no better than she should be."

"I have, indeed," said James Anderson, "been to extinguish all hope — nothing now lives in my breast but despair. I shall proceed to London at once, to make my report to the Admiralty, as it is my duty to do so; and, after that, I care not what becomes of me."

"Stuff, stuff," said Jack; "I have got some news for you. My old admiral, that I take care of, has had an invitation to the very wedding, as I take it to be, of your old sweetheart."

"What! Is it possible — do you mean an invitation to Helen Williams's wedding with the Baron Stolmuyer of Saltzburgh?"

"Yes, I do; that's just what I do mean, and no mistake. Here is his letter which he has written to me to go, and I think I shall let the old fellow, for it will amuse him. Just read that."

Jack handed the admiral's letter to James Anderson, which he read with a great deal of interest, and when he had concluded, he said, —

"Mr. Pringle, a sudden thought strikes me, —"

"About ship," said Jack, "and begin again. I told you before not to call me Mr. Pringle — I cannot stand it. Call me Jack, and then go on telling me what your sudden thought is."

"Well, then, Jack, my sudden thought is this, that your friend the admiral might be induced, upon your representation, to let me join his party, and I would take care to conceal my features and general appearance so that I should not be known, while I had the mournful satisfaction of taking a last look upon that occasion of her who I have loved, before she becomes irrecoverably the wife of another."

"If you wish it," said Jack, "it shall be done. I'll undertake there shall be no objection on the part of the admiral; and as for the Bannerworths, they are good sort of people, and would do all they can for anybody, I am sure."

"I should take it as a peculiar favor; for although I feel now that my hopes are blasted, and I can have no possible expectation of beholding her with eyes of pleasure, I still wish to look upon her, that I may see if anything of regret is upon her countenance, of if she has quite forgotten the past."

"Say no more," said Jack, "but consider it as done. I'd take care though, if I were you, that she did not find me out; for I wouldn't let the finest woman that ever breathed — no, not if she was seven feet high, and as big as a hogshead — fancy that I cared so much for her as to go to her wedding after she had jilted me."

"She shall not see me," said James Anderson; "she shall not see me, you may depend; for, without doubt, the guests will be very numerous, so that I can easily keep myself in the back-ground, and look upon her face without her being at all aware of the presence of such a person at the ceremony."

"Yes, you can manage that; and, if I were you, just as I was going away, I'd give the baron a jolly good kick, and tell him you wished him joy of his bargain. I wouldn't do anything violent, you know, but a little quiet thing like that would just show them all what you thought of the business."

"A sense of my wrongs," said James Anderson, "should not extinguish a sense of justice; and I have no means of knowing that the baron is at all in fault in this matter."

"Oh, you are too nice by one half. If a fellow takes away my sweet-heart, hang me if I care who is at fault."

"Oh, but it is necessary that we should be just at all events; but still, Jack, accept my sincerest thanks for placing me in the way of looking upon Helen. I'd rather see that she was happy and contented with her lot, than I would observe evidences upon her face of any passionate regret. The former would reconcile me, by making me think I had made a great mistake in the object of my attachment; while the latter would leave in my heart a never ceasing pain."

"Gammon," said Jack.

"I fear I tax your patience, Jack Pringle, when I talk in such a strain as this."

"I'll be hanged if you don't. What do you mean by it? There is lots of women in the world. I have no patience with a fellow that, because one girl uses him ill, goes sniveling and crying about his feelings, and his agony, and his chest, and all that sort of thing. I should recommend a bottle of rum."

"Well, well, Jack, it may happen some day with even you, and then you may feel some of the mental agony of knowing that another has possessed himself of her whom you thought all your own."

This was hitting Jack rather hard, although James Anderson did not know it; so he said, —

"Ah, well, to be sure, there is something in that, after all, and I don't mean to say there ain't; but, however, keep up your heart, my boy, and there is no saying what may happen yet."

"Alas! There can nothing happen that can give me pleasure; all is lost now, and the only hope I can have, is to forget."

Jack would have written a letter back to the admiral in reply to the one which he had received, only that somehow or other he was not a first-rate penman; and as he said it was such a bother to know where to begin, and when you did begin, it was such a bother to know where to leave off, that, taking all things into consideration, he rather on the whole declined writing at all; and, as the appointed day was near at hand, on which the wedding was to take place, he thought it would do quite as well if he kept the look out which the admiral had suggested for the arrival of the Bannerworths.

As for the scheme of James Anderson to be present at the wedding, the more Jack thought of it, the more he liked it, because he considered that it afforded a chance, at all events, if not a good prospect, of as general a disturbance as any that had ever existed.

"Lor! What fun," he said, "if he would but kick the baron, and then if the baron would but fall foul of him, and the girl scream, and old mother Williams go into hysterics. That would be a lark, and no doubt about it; shouldn't I enjoy it above a bit. I'd give them a helping hand somehow or another; and then, who knows but the girl may have been regularly badgered by the old cat of a mother into the match, and may wish for all the world to get out of it."

There can be no doubt but that if Helen Williams, even at that last moment, chose to make any appeal, it would not be made in vain to Jack Pringle, who, with all his faults, and they were numerous enough, had in his heart a chivalrous love of right, and a hatred of anything in the shape of oppression, which nothing could subdue; and such qualities as these surely are amply sufficient to atone for a multitude of minor errors, which were more those of habit and defective education, than anything else.

It very much delighted him to think that the admiral and the Bannerworths were coming down to Anderbury, because such a fact not only prolonged his stay there, which he was pleased it should do, because he was really very much delighted with the place, but it at the same time threw him again into the company he so much liked; and his attachment to the Bannerworth family had really become quite a strong feeling.

He waited quite with impatience until the Thursday came on which the admiral had announced his arrival; and instead of being in the town, or on the outskirts, to watch for him, which would have been but a tiresome operation, Jack walked boldly on to meet them by the high road, which he knew they must traverse.

After he had gone about four miles, he had the satisfaction of seeing, in the distance, a traveling-carriage, manned, as he called it, with four horses, rapidly approaching, and Jack immediately produced a large silk handkerchief that he had purchased, which was a representation of the national flag of Great Britain. This he fastened to the end of a stick, and commenced waving it about as a signal to the admiral of his presence in the road.

At this moment, too, it happened, fortunately for Jack Pringle, as he considered, that a man came across a stile in the immediate vicinity where he was with a gun in his hand.

"Hilloa, friend," said Jack Pringle, "just let me look at that gun a minute."

"I'll see you further first," said the man; "you seem to me as if you were out of your mind."

So saying, he leveled the piece at some birds that were flying overhead, and fired first one barrel and then the other in rapid succession.

"Thank ye," said Jack, "that was all I wanted; and it will answer my purpose exactly; there is nothing like, when you display your flag, firing a gun or two. It's all right — he sees me, he sees me."

The admiral had actually been looking from the window of the carriage, although he had not expected to see Jack quite so soon; but the appearance of the handkerchief, which was made so much to resemble a flag, convinced him of the fact that Jack had come that distance to meet them; and when he heard the gun fired twice, he was quite delighted, and leaning back in the carriage, he cried, —

"Ah, Flora, my dear, it is a great pity that Jack is so given to rum, for he is a remarkably clever fellow. You would hardly believe it, now, but he has contrived to hoist a flag just because he sees me coming."

"Indeed, uncle."

"Yes, my dear, he has; and didn't you hear that he actually managed to fire a couple of guns, some way or another?"

"I certainly did hear the report, but had no idea that we were indebted to Jack Pringle's management for them."

"Oh, yes, I can see him a short distance ahead. He is lying to, now; and, if the wind wasn't against us, we should be up to him in a few minutes, but don't you feel it blowing in your face?"

Notwithstanding the admiral considered, which he certainly did, that the wind was a real impediment to the progress of the carriage, they did in a few moments reach to where Jack Pringle was waiting, when the admiral called out from the window in a loud voice, —

"Hilloa! What ship, and where are you bound to?"

"The Jack Pringle," was the reply, "from Anderbury, and to fall in with the Admiral Bell, convoy of the pretty Flora."

"There now," said the admiral; "didn't I tell you what a clever fellow Jack was? What shore-going humbug, who had never been to sea, would have thought of such a thing?"

"Well," said Jack, as he walked up to the coach window, for the postillions had been ordered to halt, or, as the admiral had expressed it, "to heave to," "well, here you are, all of you."

"Yes, Jack," said the admiral; "and I was just saying I thought you a very clever fellow."

"I am sorry I can't return the compliment, you poor old creature," said Jack; "I hope you haven't got yourself into any trouble since I have been away from you. What a miserable old hulk you do look, to be sure. There you go, again; now you are getting into a passion, as usual; what a dreadful thing temper is, to be sure, when you can't manage it."

Jack scrambled up behind into the rumble before the admiral could make any reply to him, for indignation stopped his utterance a moment or two; and, when he did speak, it was to Flora he addressed himself more particularly, saying, —

"Now, did you ever know a more ungrateful son-of-a-gun than that? After I had just told him that I thought him a clever fellow, for him to burst out abusing me at that rate! Now I have done with him."

"Oh, you may depend, Admiral Bell," said Flora, "that he don't at all mean what he says; and I am convinced that he entertains for you the highest possible respect, and that he is only jesting when he uses those expressions which would seem as if it were otherwise."

"Let's just wait," said the admiral, "till the wedding is over, and then I'll let him know whether a boatswain is to make a joke of an admiral of the fleet.

Chapter CXVIII.

THE BARON'S PREPARATIONS FOR THE MARRIAGE, AND THE WEDDING MORNING.

During this time neither Mrs. Williams nor the Baron Stolmuyer were idle spectators of the progress of the hours; but, on the contrary, they made the best possible use of the week which was to elapse before the marriage ceremony took place after Helen had given her consent to it.

Five hundred pounds in the hands of such a person as Mrs. Williams, will go a long way, and produce an amazing amount of show and glitter;

so that she managed, before the day on which the ceremony was to be performed arrived, to make quite certain that herself and her daughters would present a most dazzling appearance; and she thought it not at all improbable that even at the very church some meritorious individual might be dazzled into thinking of matrimony with one of her other daughters, upon seeing what a brilliant appearance they managed to present upon the marriage of Helen.

"I am quite sure that no harm can come of it," she said, "if no good does; and, at all events if no good is done at the church, the baron will soon be giving parties enough to bring out the dear girls to perfection, particularly as I fully intend we shall all live at Anderbury House."

Mrs. Williams considered this as a settled point, whether the baron liked it or not; and, knowing as she did the gentle and quiet disposition of Helen, she did not doubt for a moment of being permitted to rule completely over the domestic affairs of her establishment. All this was amazingly satisfactory to such a lady as Mrs. Williams, and the very thing of all others she would have liked, had she been looking out for what would please her in the marriage of her daughter.

We shall shortly see how these views and opinions were verified by the fact.

All the other preparations were left to the baron; and when he wrote a letter to Mrs. Williams, saying, that he would be ready by ten o'clock on the morning which had been named for the nuptials, and would send one of his carriages for the bride, Mrs. Williams was perfectly satisfied that all was quite correct.

There was no very good excuse for calling at Anderbury House; but, if she had then called, she certainly would have been astonished at the preparations which the baron was making for that day which was so near at hand.

It was quite terrific the expense he went to; and the gorgeous manner in which he fitted up one of the largest apartments in the house for a dance looked really like expenditure of the most reckless character, and such as indeed it must have required an immense fortune to withstand.

The walls of that apartment were hung with crimson draperies of a rich texture, and such beauty of design that they were the admiration of the very workmen themselves who were employed upon the premises.

Then the magnificent order he gave for a feast upon the occasion, and the wines he laid in, really almost exceeded belief; and such proceedings were indeed highly calculated to give people most exaggerated versions regarding his wealth.

He had indeed mentioned to Mrs. Williams, that he had silver mines on some of his estates abroad; and that fact to her mind was quite sufficient to account for any amount of money he might possess, because, to her ideas of geology and mineralogy, the discovery of a silver mine meant, finding a hole of immense width and depth, crammed with the precious metal.

But be this as it may, and whether the Baron Stolmuyer, of Saltzburgh, owed his wealth to silver mines, or to other sources, one thing was quite clear, and that was, that he had it.

And that was the grand point; for in a highly civilized and evangelical country like this, the question of how a man got his money is not near so often asked, as, has he got it; and it is quite amazing what liberality of feeling and sentiment is immediately infused into people by the fact of successful speculation of any kind; while failure immediately incurs the greatest of opprobrium and contempt.

And now the day was so close at hand, that Mrs. Williams got into a terrible flutter of spirits, and began really to wish it over; for she was completely ready, and each minute became an hour of impatience to her.

She was continually bothering the baron with notes and messages upon different subjects, and he had the urbanity to answer two or three of them; but he soon left that off, and the last half dozen, at the least, were, to Mrs. Williams's great mortification, taken no notice of at all.

Some of these notes were upon the most nonsensical points, and several of them, although they did not actually ask it, pretty strongly hinted that more money would be a very desirable thing.

The baron would not understand any hint, however, upon the subject; so Mrs. Williams became fully convinced that she must make the best of it she could, and put up for the present with the five hundred pounds she had already received.

But when the day had actually dawned on when the suspicious event was to come off, and, upon looking around her, she found herself surrounded by gay apparel and jewelry, she almost dreaded that even yet it would turn out to be some delusion, or a dream, for she could scarcely believe in the reality of such glory and magnificence belonging to her.

But facts are stubborn things, and, whether for good or for evil, are not likely to be got over; so, when she looked out of the windows and saw that a bright morning's sun was shining, and that the life, animation, and bustle of the day was commencing, she told herself that it was, indeed, real, and that she had reached very nearly the summit of her desires and expectations.

"Yes," she exclaimed; "I shall be mother-in-law to a baron; and I dare say I shall have at least twenty servants in Anderbury House to command and control continually."

A more gratifying reflection than this could not possibly have presented itself to Mrs. Williams; for if any one thing could be more delightful than another, it certainly was that kind of petty power which gives an individual a control over a large establishment.

After she had arisen on that eventful morning, she did not allow her establishment many minutes' repose; but, in the course of half-an-hour, all was bustle, excitement, and no small share of confusion.

And while she was thus energetically pushing on her preparations, let us see what the Bannerworths are about, now that they have fairly arrived at Anderbury, and are in readiness, probably, to be present at the ceremony.

By Flora's intercession, a peace was established between Jack and the admiral; and the former took the latter down to the old seaman's cottage, in order to introduce him to James Anderson; and on the road he made him acquainted with the particulars of the young man's story; at the same time informing him of the wish that Anderson had expressed to be permitted to join their party.

"Oh, certainly," said the admiral," certainly; let him come by all means, although I must say that he ought to leave for London, at once, with his dispatches, or at all events with the news that he had lost them. However, I am not on active service; and, therefore, have no right to do anything more than advise him in the matter."

"Oh, he will go," said Jack, "as soon as he has seen his sweetheart, and perhaps kicked the baron; for though he said he wouldn't, I live in hopes yet that he will be aggravated enough to do it."

The admiral liked James Anderson so much, that he not only promised him he should go to the wedding under cover of the general invitation which he, the admiral, had received, but he proposed, likewise, that he should come home with him at once and be introduced to the Bannerworths; and by home he meant the inn at Anderbury, where they were staying.

The young man expressed himself highly gratified at this invitation, and at once accepted it, so that they walked towards the inn together, and began to make preparations for their appearance at Anderbury House.

Flora and the Bannerworths, as well as Charles, received young Anderson very graciously, and they each expressed to him their sympathy for the painful situation in which the baron's marriage was placing him.

Flora and Charles Holland, as may be well supposed, could both feel, and feel acutely too for any one crossed in his affection, as poor James Anderson was; and it certainly much damped the satisfaction they had in going to what everybody told them would certainly be the most brilliant wedding that had taken place in that part of the country for many a year.

"Let us hope," said Henry Bannerworth, "that you will find some other, Mr. Anderson, who will be more worthy of your esteem, than she who has treated so lightly your affection and her own faith."

"I know not," said Anderson, "whether to accuse her not; for who knows but after all she may be the victim of treachery, notwithstanding the apparent powerful evidence that has been given to me by her mother?"

The Bannerworth family were determined, and so was the admiral, that they would bestow what credit they could upon those who had so kindly invited them; and, accordingly, when they started for the Hall in the handsome carriage which had brought them down to Anderbury, they certainly presented a rather showy and attractive appearance.

But still when they reached the entrance to Anderbury House, they found that theirs was by no means the only equipage of the kind that was there to be seen; for although both the entrances were open for the reception of guests, they had to wait a considerable time before they could get up to either of them.

One hundred and fifty guests, sixty or eighty of whom kept equipages, were calculated to make some little degree of confusion; but when the Bannerworth family fairly got within the house, everything else was forgotten in their admiration of the brilliant arrangements within.

The richest carpets were laid down that money could purchase, and servants in gorgeous liveries ushered the guests into an immense hall, in which the marriage ceremony was to take place, and which was decorated with a splendor that was perfectly regal.

And here a new set of domestics glided noiselessly about with various refreshments upon silver salvers, and the place began rapidly to fill with such an assemblage of wealth, and beauty, and rank, as perhaps scarcely ever had been congregated in one place before.

But among those whose beauty attracted much attention, we may need well reckon our friend, Flora Bell, as she was now properly called, and whose sweet countenance was the cause of many a passing observation, couched in the most flattering terms.

It wanted yet an hour to the time of the ceremony being performed, and the Bannerworths, as they saw that their companion, young Anderson, was in a painful state of excitement, all sat down in the deep recess of a large window to wait the coming of the bride and bridegroom.

"I don't think, Mr. Anderson," said Henry, "that your coming here at all was a well advised step; but since you are here, you should muster up resolution enough not to betray any feeling."

"I will not betray it, although I feel it," said Anderson. "Rely upon it, that I shall look much firmer, and act much firmer when she whom I wish to see is actually here, than I do at present — I am enduring suspense now, and that is the worst of all."

"I do wish," interposed Flora, "that you had seen her whom you love before this ceremony, for in that case, although you might have endured the pang of finding that she was willing to call herself another's, you would have been spared the pain of this day's proceeding."

"I wish to Heaven I had seen her; but I knew not how to arrange such a meeting; and when I was shewn, in her own handwriting — which I knew too well to doubt — a consent to be the wife of another, I no longer had the spirit and the perseverance to ask to see her; and it was an afterthought that made me wish to look upon her face once more before I left her for ever."

"What," said Jack Pringle, suddenly making his appearance, "is he gammoning you with his feelings?"

"Oh! so you have got in, have you?" said the admiral.

"So I have got in — why, what do you mean by that? Of course I have got in; wasn't I invited? I do think you get a little stupider every day; and, in course of time, you won't know what you are about. I should not be surprised to see you take out your handkerchief to blow your eye instead of your nose."

Latterly, Jack, when he made one of these speeches, always walked away very quickly, leaving the admiral's anger to evaporate as best it might; so that he escaped the retort which otherwise he might have received.

Chapter CXIX.

A RATHER STRANGE CIRCUMSTANCE AT THE BARON'S WEDDING.

At length, the hour came, so anxiously looked for and expected by all the Baron Stolmuyer's guests; and the great clock which was in one of the turrets of Anderbury House proclaimed that the minute had arrived when all was presumed to be ready for the union.

All eyes were directed to a large table that was placed at one extremity of the hall, and covered with crimson velvet, and at which the ceremony was to be performed.

The Bannerworths were a little forward, so that they commanded a good view of everything, and James Anderson was completely hidden from observation behind the bulky form of the admiral. Now, a small door opened, and an archdeacon somebody — who had been engaged, as you would engage a celebrated performer, at some theatre, to perform the ceremony — made his appearance, accompanied by several ladies and gentlemen, whom he had brought with him to partake of some of the baron's good things.

In a few moments, from another doorway, came the bride, accompanied by six bridesmaids, but she was covered with such a massive lace veil from her head to her feet, that not the slightest vestige of her countenance was visible.

But, still, Flora thought that, as the bride first came in, she heard from beneath that veil a deep and agonized sob; and she remarked the circumstance to Charles, who confirmed her opinion by at once saying, —

"It was so, and I don't think it at all likely that we should both be mistaken."

There was a slight murmur of applause and admiration among the assembled guests as the bride took her seat by the table; for although there were many there who had never seen her face, there were likewise many who had; and even those who had not, could not but perceive, by her graceful movements and the delicate outline of her figure, that they were looking upon a creature of rare beauty and worth.

It was astonishing that the bridegroom should be late, and the audience who were present began to be indignant at such a fact, and whispered together concerning it in language not very flattering to the baronet, who, had he heard it, would have found that he must mind what he was about, or his rapidly-acquired popularity would soon be at a discount.

Minute after minute thus passed, and Mrs. Williams, who was attired in a richly flowing garment of white silk, embroidered with flowers, began to be in a most particular fidget.

"Where could be the baron — good God! where is the baron?" and some one or two said, "D — n the baron!" When suddenly the door at which the bride had entered was again flung open, and two servants in rich liveries made their appearance, one standing on each side of it. Then there was heard approaching a slow and measured footstep, and presently, attired in a court suit of rich velvet, the Baron Stolmuyer of Saltzburgh appeared in the hall, and marched up to the table.

He had but just time to execute half a bow to the assembled multitude, when Admiral Bell called out in a voice that awakened every echo in the place, —

"It's Varney, the vampyre, by G-d!"

Yes, it was Varney — the bold, reckless, audacious Varney, who had thus come out in a new character, and, with vast pecuniary resources, acquired Heavens knows how or where, was seeking to ally himself to one so young and beautiful as Helen Williams.

We do absolutely and positively despair of giving an adequate idea to the reader of the scene that followed.

Ladies shrieked — the bride fainted — Mrs. Williams went into strong hysterics, and kicked everybody — Jack Pringle shouted until he was hoarse; while Varney turned and made a dash to escape through the door at which he had just entered.

James Anderson, however, by springing over a table, succeeded in clutching him by the collar behind; but Varney turned on the instant, and lifting him from the ground as if he had been a child, he flung him among a tray of confectionary and wine, and from thence he rolled into Mrs. Williams's lap.

Following close, however, upon the footsteps of Anderson in pursuit of Varney had been Henry Bannerworth; but he accomplished nothing, except to strike his head violently against the door through which Varney escaped, and which was dashed in his face, and immediately bolted on the other side.

"He is a vampyre," shouted the admiral — "I tell you all he is a vampyre — Varney, the vampyre, and no more a baron than I am a broomstick. Stop that d — d old woman from making such a noise."

"It's the bride's mother," said somebody.

"What's that to me?" roared the admiral; "it don't make her a bit less of a nuisance. I offer a hundred pounds reward for Varney, the vampyre; and there must be some people here that know the house well enough to catch him."

"Do you mean a hundred pounds for master, sir?" said a great footman, with yellow plush breeches.

"Yes, I do, you hog in armor," said the admiral.

The footman rushed through another doorway in a moment, and then Jack Pringle jumped upon a chair, and, waving his hat, cried, —

"Hurra, hurra, hurra! Three cheers for old Varney! I'll tell you what it is, messmates, he is the meanest fellow as ever you see; and as for you ladies who have been disappointed of the marriage, I'll come and kiss you all in a minute, and we'll drink up old Varney's wine, and eat up his dinner like bricks. My eye, what a game we will have, to be sure. I am coming —"

At this moment the admiral gave such a kick to one of the hind legs of the chair, that down came Jack as quickly as if he had disappeared through some trap door.

"Hold your noise, will you," said the admiral, "you great brawling brute!"

"I'll settle him," said Mrs. Williams, who had suddenly recovered; and had not Jack suddenly made his escape, it is highly probable she would have make him a regular scapegoat in the affair, and that he alone — for Anderson had pretty quickly escaped her — would have felt the consequences of her deep disappointment.

The confusion now became, if anything, worse than at first, for many of the guests who had looked on apparently quite stunned and paralyzed at what had taken place, now recovered, and joined their voices to the general clamor.

Some, to rush out of the place, took the opportunity of going through the different rooms; while a number, who had heard of the wide-spread fame of Varney, the vampyre, and who were utterly astonished to find him and the baron one and the same person, joined in the pursuit, with the hope of taking prisoner so alarming a personage.

No one knew for some time what had become of the clergyman, until Jack Pringle saw a human foot sticking out from under the table, upon which he took hold of it, and with a pull dragged the archdeacon somebody fairly out, to the great horror of some very religious old ladies who were present, who considered that an arch-deacon must be somebody very wonderful indeed.

"Hilloa! Mr. Parson," said Jack; I suppose you thought it was your old friend the devil come for you before your time; but cheer up, I know him; it's only a vampyre, and that's nothing when you're used to it."

Jack did not seem at all to think that it was necessary he should assist in the capture of Varney, and probably the real fact was, he did not care whether Varney was captured or not, so he walked to one of the tables which were loaded with refreshments, and knocking the neck off a bottle of champagne, he gave a nod to Mrs. Williams, saying, —

"Come, old girl, take something to drink. That red nose of yours looks as if you knew something of the bottle. It's only me, so you needn't be shy. Ah, it's devilish good wine, though. I do give old Varney credit for getting up the thing decently, which he certainly has, and no mistake."

"Who has seen my daughter? Where is my daughter?" cried Mrs. Williams, as she looked about her in vain for Helen.

"You needn't trouble yourself, ma'am," said the admiral; "she has just walked off with a little fellow of the name of Anderson, who, although he was no match for Varney, the vampyre, I think will turn out to be one for your daughter."

Mrs. Williams was thoroughly thunder-stricken, and she sat down in a chair, and commenced wringing her hands, muttering as she did so, —

"Oh, that I should have lived to see this day. Oh, that I should have existed to be so — so —"

"Jolly well humbugged, ma'am," said Jack Pringle, "with a vampyre, instead of a baron; why, lord bless you, ma'am, nobody in their senses would have taken old Varney for a baron; why, he is a regular old blood-sucker, he is, and a nice family you would have had; but, however, if you are fond of him, you can marry him yourself, you know, now; and I shouldn't at all wonder, but he will consent, for a man will put up with any d — d old cat, when he finds he can't get a better."

"Good God," said Mrs. Williams, "I think I know your voice now; ain't you Admiral Green?"

"Avast, there," said Jack; "I ain't anything of the kind; they calls me Colonel Bluebottle, of the horse-marines."

"The what?"

"The horse-marines. Didn't you never hear of them, ma'am?"

"I certainly never did. But don't try to deceive me, sir; you are Admiral Green and if you will, my dear sir, spare me a few minutes of your valuable time, I shall be able to explain to you —"

"What?" said Jack.

"Why, that really — you will scarcely believe it — but really, Admiral Green, my daughter Julia is, although I say it, one of the best of girls."

"Oh, I dare say she is, ma'am; but I don't know as that much matters to me."

"Excuse me, Admiral Green, but it really does, and you must know — of course it's quite between ourselves this — that she happened to see you when you did me the honor of calling upon me."

"Did she really?"

"Yes, my dear admiral; and, do you know, ever since then she has been positively raving about you; and as you were good enough to say, the baron should not stand in the way of your affections, allow me to recommend Julia to you."

"Oh, that's it, is it!" said Jack. "Well, ma'am, I should not have said no, only that you ain't half particular enough for me!"

"Not particular! Oh, good God."

"No, ma'am, you ain't. Here you would have married one of your daughters to a vampyre, and how do I know what other sort of odd fish you might bring into the family."

"But, my dear Admiral —"

"Oh! gammon. I tell you what, now, I will do — I don't mind standing something devilish handsome, if you will marry old Varney yourself."

"What! the baron that was, and the vampyre that is? I marry him! Oh, dear, no, I really could not — that is to say, how much would you give, Admiral Green?"

"Ah!" said Jack, "I knew it. Who says, after this, that women won't marry the very devil himself, if they only have the chance. And now, Mother Williams, I'll just tell you what you have done. The fact is, I took a fancy to you myself, and that's why I came here at all today. I meant to have proposed to you, and if you had only said you would not have the Baron Vampyre for any money, d — n it, I would have had you myself, and settled a matter of £15,000 a-year upon you."

"Oh, gracious Providence! what do I hear?"

"Just what I says. I'm a man of my word, ma'am, and would have done it."

"Mrs. Williams was so affected at the chance she had lost, that she quite forgot to look after Helen, but was actually compelled to indulge herself with a glass or two of something strong and powerful, which she said was sherry, but which somebody else said was brandy, in order to recover from the faint feeling that would come over her.

After this, Jack thought he had had about the bitterest revenge upon Mrs. Williams that it was possible to achieve, and he was quite right as far as that went. The old admiral, too, who overheard some part of the colloquy, was quite delighted with it, and again told himself what a clever fellow Jack was, and quite a wonderful character in his way.

"Ah!" he said, " one would have to sail a tolerable lot of voyages before finding anybody as was exactly Jack's equal; and I'll be hanged if I don't forgive him for the next piece of mutinous conduct he is guilty of, on account of the way he has served out that horrid old Mother Williams; for in all my life I never saw a woman I disliked more. Stop, what am I saying? Did I really forget Mrs. Chillingworth, the doctor's wife? That was too bad."

Chapter CXX.

THE HUNT FOR THE VAMPYRE IN THE SUBTERRANEAN PASSAGE.

*T*he information that had been given to Mrs. Williams respecting her daughter and James Anderson having together left the great hall of Anderbury House, was perfectly correct.

The voice of Anderson, whispering words of affection in the ear of Helen, was sufficient to arouse her from the state of syncope into which she had fallen; and when she recovered and looked in his face, the expression of joy which her countenance wore, at once dispelled all his doubts.

"Helen, dear Helen!" he whispered; "are you, indeed, still, in heart, mine?"

"Still, as ever," she replied.

"Come with me; I have much to tell you; and we need not heed the thoughts and feelings of the throng that is here. If you can walk, place your arm in mine, and lean upon me, and we will get out of all this trouble and confusion."

Helen was but too glad to avail herself of such an offer, and she accordingly at once did so; and leaning for support upon that arm, which, of all others, she most loved to bear upon, they together passed out of the great hall, through one of the numerous doorways leading from it.

Being both of them quite ignorant of what may be called the topography of Anderbury House, they went on till they came to a small but very elegant apartment, in which a table was laid with wines, and some costly refreshments, which, from the fact of an extremely clerical-looking shovel hat being upon one of the chairs, there was no great difficulty in coming to the conclusion that this had been a reception-room, got up purposely for the reverend gentleman who was to perform the ceremony of marriage between the baron and Miss Williams, and in which he had refreshed himself prior to the performance of that dreadfully arduous task, for which, no doubt, as all persons are, he was so very insufficiently paid.

A glass of wine, which James Anderson poured out for Helen, tended much to recover her; and then he said to her in accents of the greatest affection, —

"Helen — Helen! is it possible that you really so far forgot me, as to promise your hand to another?"

She burst into tears as she clung to his arm, saying, —

"I know you cannot, you ought not to forgive me. I did promise; but I did not forget you; and if you know the cruel persecution to which I have been subjected, you would pity, perhaps, as much as you condemn me."

"You did not know that some days since I wrote you a note."

"Me a note? Oh, heavens! no — no. What became of it? To whom did you entrust it? Oh! James, had I but thought you were near me, do you think that for one moment I would have yielded, even to the representations which were made to me?"

"I see it all," he said. "Your mother has carried on this matter with more tact than candor and honesty of purpose. I do not condemn you, dear Helen; and no one shall ever disturb you in your possession of a heart which is wholly yours."

"And can you forget —"

"All but that I love you I can and will forget, Helen."

"I do not deserve this noble generosity, for I ought not to have yielded, James. I feel that I ought to have clung to the remembrance of your affection, and found in that an abundant consolation, as well as abundant strength, to resist the whole world."

"Say no more, dearest, upon that head; but let us, to the full, enjoy the happiness of this meeting, without the drawback of a single doubt."

"We will never part again."

"Never — never."

"But, James, what was the meaning of that sudden exclamation, from one of the guests, as regarded the baron?"

"You allude to Admiral Bell proclaiming him to be a vampyre; and, I must say, it fills me with quite as much astonishment as it can you. I did hear a strange story of that sort from a sailor a short time ago, but I looked upon it as a mere superstition and paid no attention to it. You know what it means, I presume, and that a vampyre is supposed to be a half-supernatural creature who supports a spurious and horrible existence, by feeding upon the blood of any one whom he can make his victim."

"If this horrible superstition," said Helen, with a shudder, "be true, what a dreadful fate have I escaped!"

"It surely must be some error of judgment; but still, dear one, you have escaped a dreadful fate, a fate worse than any vampyre would have inflicted upon you — the fate of being united to one whom you cannot love."

"Yes," said Helen; "that is, indeed, an escape; but how came you, of all persons in the world, a guest here?"

"I came, Helen, under cover of a general invitation, with a most worthy family, to whose kindness I feel myself much indebted, and which empowered them to bring with them whom they pleased. My wish and object was to take one last look at the face I had loved so well before I left you for ever."

"Oh, Heavens!" said Helen, "and I was so near being sacrificed while you were by. Even now I shudder at the dreadful chasm; I feel that you ought not to forgive me."

"Say no more — say no more; all that, Helen, is now past and forgotten, and I can well imagine how your mother would torture you with supplications, because she believed this man to be rich, and consequently the sort of person, above all others, as most desirable for her to have as a son-in-law. We will only consider that a great anxiety and a great danger has passed away, and we will not stop to ask ourselves what it was."

"Ever good, and ever generous," resumed Helen, as her head reposed upon her lover's breast.

"Oh," said Jack Pringle, as he popped his head in at the door; "I beg your pardon, you are better engaged; but we are going to have a grand vampyre hunt through the house, and I thought you would like to join in it, perhaps."

"Stay a moment, stay," cried Anderson. "Do you mean to tell me, really, that this is the person who gave your friends, the Bannerworths, so much trouble and inconvenience?"

"Yes, I do," said Jack; "lor bless you, he is quite an old acquaintance of ours, is old Varney; sometimes he hunts us, sometimes we hunt him. He is rather a troublesome acquaintance, notwithstanding, and I think there are a good many people in the world, a jolly right worse vampyres than Varney."

"I have no cause to hunt him," said Anderson, "and so, therefore, I feel certainly more inclined to decline, than otherwise, engaging in such a transaction."

"Don't mention it," said Jack; "you are a deuced deal better engaged, and there needs no excuses."

Jack was quite correct as regarded the projected hunt for the unfortunate Varney in Anderbury House; for the liberal offer of reward which the admiral had made to any one who would secure him, was calculated to stimulate every possible exertion that people could make upon the occasion; so much so, indeed, that the Bannerworths, after a brief consultation among themselves, thought that for the protection of Varney it would be much better that they should find him, than now leave him with the character that had been given him as such a dangerous member of society.

The servants, and some of the guests, even, had gone very systematically to work for the purpose of taking Varney prisoner; for, in the first instance, they had secured all the outlets from the house, so that, as the footman with the yellow plush continuations remarked, he must jump over the cliff if he wanted to get away.

The admiral and Henry agreed with each other that they would be foremost in the search, in order to protect Varney from any violence; for although this conduct of his might be considered as very bad, and an outrage upon society in passing himself off as a baron, and endeavoring to effect an alliance with a young and innocent girl, yet they, the Bannerworths, had nothing to complain of in the transaction whatever.

Consequently was it that they felt an inclination to defend Varney from personal violence.

And this was, to a certain extent, to be dreaded, because Anderbury being so short a distance from Bannerworth, it was not to be supposed but that some news of the mysterious appearance of the vampyre had reached the ears of almost every one who happened to be present at the baron's wedding.

And although these persons might be supposed to belong to a class of society not likely to commit acts of violence, yet there was no knowing what, in the excitement of the moment, might be done.

While the search went on, Flora was introduced to Helen Williams, and remained with her, commencing a friendship which lasted afterwards, to the great advantage of Helen, for many a year.

The Bannerworths would have been pleased and interested at going over Anderbury House, under any other circumstances than the present one, for truly the baron had made it a most magnificent abode.

By judicious additions to the antique furniture which had belonged to it when he took it, he had made some of the apartments look gorgeous in the extreme; and while he had not disturbed the character of the decorations, he had certainly shown a very fine taste in adding to them.

But their minds were by far too much occupied with considerations connected with Varney to pay much attention to his house; and, as they traversed room after room in search of him without finding him, they began to think that, with his usual good fortune, he had contrived entirely to escape.

The servants, who knew the place well, perhaps better than Varney did himself, searched for him in almost impossible places, until it began to be the general opinion that he must have escaped.

They were standing by a large bay window, which commanded a view of the gardens, when one of the servants suddenly exclaimed, —

"I see him — I see him; there he goes," and pointed into the garden, where, for one instant, Henry Bannerworth, as well as the admiral, saw Varney, in his rich suit of wedding apparel, dart from among the bushes, towards a summer-house that was in the garden near at hand.

"Tis he, indeed," said Henry. "Let us get down instantly, or he may yet effect his escape."

"No, no," cried one of the servants, "he cannot do that; the garden wall is too high, and the men are stationed at the gate. It's quite clear to me what he is about. Look at him; he is going towards the old passage that leads to the sea shore."

"Then he will escape, of course," said Henry, "for no one can hope to overtake him."

"Don't you be afraid of that, sir," cried the servant; "one of my mates has gone round to the beach to watch, and he won't let the door be opened that leads out on to the sands, so he cannot get away by that mode."

"In that case, then, we have him completely entrapped, and, as you say, he cannot escape. It must be the madness of positive desperation that induces him to go to that place."

"Let us be off at once after him," said the admiral; "that is our only plan. Come on at once. The sooner we get hold of him the better, for his own sake as well as for ours."

Thus urged, they all proceeded towards the garden, in which was the mysterious, well-like entrance to the subterraneous passage, which formed so great a feature in the estate of Anderbury, on the moment, and which, at the time that Varney had taken the mansion, had evidently formed to him one of its principal attractions.

To the admiral and his party, as well as to several of the guests, who joined from motives of curiosity in the pursuit for Varney, this place was perfectly new, and it certainly, to look down it, did not present by any means an inviting prospect; for although it sloped sufficiently to take off the absolute appearance of being a downright hole in the earth, yet, beyond a few feet in depth, the gloom had something positively terrific about it.

"Well," said the admiral, "I've been into the hold of many a ship, but never one that looked half so gloomy as this, I can say. What do you say to it, Jack?"

"It's no use saying anything to such places," said Jack. "The only way, if we want to catch old Varney, which I suppose we do, is to pop down it at once and done with it; so come along, I won't flinch if it was ten times worse. Come on, admiral, let's go down after the enemy."

"I cannot say it's exactly the kind of place I admire," said the admiral; "but, howsomedever, if one must go down it, who shall say that Admiral Bell flinched from it? Come on, all of you. Let all who will follow."

The passage did not look a very inviting one; and it was found that the courage of the guests began to cool down wonderfully when, instead of rushing from apartment to apartment, in search of Varney, the vampyre, they found that they had to encounter the gloom and darkness of that underground abode.

Out of the positive throng which had been pursuing Varney, only four, in addition to the admiral and the male portion of his party, ventured to descend into that black-looking place.

"What!" cried Jack, "have we got such a lot of skulkers whenever we come to close quarters with the enemy? Well, shiver my timbers, if I didn't expect as much from a lot of land lubbers, who don't know what they are about any more than a marine in a squall. But who cares? Come along, admiral; and, if we do have all the fighting, we shall, at all events, have all the glory."

"I hope there will be nothing of the one, at all events," said Henry; "for my intention is rather to save Varney from injury than to injure him.

"We must have lights," said the admiral. "I don't mind going down into a queer place to look for Varney, but I must have the means of seeing what I am about when I get there."

"They will be here, sir, directly," said the big footman, who from the first had made himself conspicuous in the pursuit of Varney; that is to say, ever since the reward of £100 had been offered by the admiral to any one who would take him prisoner.

And in a few moments, some of the links, which were always kept in the kitchen of Anderbury House, for the express purpose of descending into the subterraneous passages with, were produced and lighted. By this time, too, the four guests had decreased to three, and two of those seemed to hang back rather a little; while one of them seemed disposed to make up as much as possible for any deficiency of courage on the part of the others, by declaring his intention of ferreting out Varney, let him be hidden where he might.

"I am with you, sir," he said to the admiral, "let this place lead where it may; for I have heard so much about vampyres, and really am so curious to know more about them."

"You don't believe in them, do you?"

"I cannot say that I do, sir. But, at the same time, when we hear such well authenticated cases brought forward about them, it is very difficult, indeed, to say at once, that one has no belief in such things."

"Well, you are right enough there; and if you knew as much about Varney, the vampyre, as we do, I think you would be a little puzzled to know what to say about him; for I'll be hanged if he don't puzzle me above a bit, and I don't know now what to think of him."

Chapter CXXI.

THE DEATH OF THE INQUISITIVE GUEST. – THE ESCAPE OF SIR FRANCIS VARNEY

*T*he guest who was so valorous, and so very impatient for the capture of Varney, would have preceded everybody in descending to the passage cut in the cliff, but Henry Bannerworth thought not only was it more particularly his concern to do so, but that as he knew Varney better, it was desirable that he should go first.

He thought there would less likelihood of any mischief by adopting such a kind of procedure, for he did not anticipate that Varney would willingly do him any injury; while, as regarded what he might do if any stranger should attempt to seize him, that was quite another affair.

"You do not know him as we know him," said Henry, to the guest. "He is a dangerous man, and in all respects such an one as your prudence might well induce you to keep clear of. Allow me to precede you, therefore, for the sake of preventing the probability of the most unpleasant consequences."

This argument appeared to have its effect and to damp a little the ardor of this individual, which it might well enough do, without casting any imputation upon his courage whatever; for, after all, he could have no strong motive in the pursuit of Varney, since he was in a line of life which would have prevented him, even if he had been the sole captor of Varney, from taking the reward which the admiral had offered for his apprehension.

The sudden change from the daylight, and all the noise and bustle which had animated the scene above, to the silence, the darkness, and the strange atmosphere which reigned in the underground region, could not fail of having some effect upon the imagination of every one present.

This effect would, of course, vary in different individuals, being the greatest in those of a highly excitable and imaginative turn of mind, and the less in those who were of a more matter-of-fact kind of intellect. Probably, Henry Bannerworth felt more acutely than any one else the full effect which such a scene was likely to produce, and he was profoundly silent upon the occasion for some time.

Under even the most extraordinary circumstances, the descent into such a place must have affected the mind to some extent, for it seems like leaving the world altogether for a time, and bidding farewell to everything which we have been in the habit of enjoying and thinking beautiful.

No one ever thought of accusing Admiral Bell of being very imaginative; but, upon this occasion, although he was the first to speak, what he did say, showed that he had felt some of those sensations to which we have alluded.

"How do you feel, Henry?" he said. "I'll be hanged if I don't seem as if I were going into my grave before my time."

"And I, too," said Henry; "but I rather like the solemn feeling which such a place as this inspires."

"Gentlemen," said the tall footman with the yellow plush what-do-you-call-em's, "gentlemen, I think, after all, that I somehow will go back again. I don't seem, actually, in a manner of speaking, to care to catch the baron, somehow; so, if you please, gentlemen, I rather think I'll go back."

"Why don't you say you are afraid, at once, John?" said the admiral.

"Who, me, sir? I afraid? Oh, dear, no, sir. It would take a trifle, indeed, to frighten me, I rather think. Oh! no, no, sir you mistake me. It's my feelings — it's my feelings, sir."

"Why, what the deuce have your feelings to do with it?"

"Everything in the world, sir. Haven't I drank his beer, sir, and haven't I eat his beef, and his bread, and his *tatoes*, sir, and shall I now hunt him up among his own ice-wells? No; perish the thought — perish the blessed idea. Perish the — the — the — good bye, gentlemen."

With these words, the chivalrous footman gave up all idea of continuing the chase for Varney, the vampyre, and turning quickly, so as to stop the possibility of his hearing any further remonstrance, he went from the place with great speed.

Still, however, with the departure of this individual, whose courage from the first had had about it a very suspicious color, they were in quite sufficient strength to have accomplished the capture of the vampyre, if they could get hold of him, and always provided he was not sufficiently armed with powers of mischief to their number, by taking perchance the life of some one of them.

There was one circumstance connected with a search for anybody in that strange region, which spoke much in favor of a successful result, and that was that the passage was narrow, and that there were no hiding-places except the ice-wells, to explore which, at all events, could not be a very difficult task; and as they proceeded, they felt certain that they must be driving Varney before them.

Before they had got very far, Henry Bannerworth thought it would be advisable to announce to Varney the precise intentions of himself and the admiral, always provided he were equally peaceably inclined, and within hearing of what was said to him.

He accordingly raised his voice, inquiring, —

"Sir Francis Varney, you no doubt recognize, by my tones, that it is Henry Bannerworth who speaks to you; and therefore you may feel convinced that no harm is intended you; but you are implored to come forth and meet your friends, who, from former circumstances, you ought to know you can trust."

There was no reply whatever to this appeal, and when the echoes of Henry's voice had died away, the same death-like stillness reigned in the place that had before characterized it.

"He will not answer," said the admiral; "and yet, if the other end of this passage be guarded as it is said to be, he must be here. Let us come on at once — I have no wish of my own to stay in this damp, chalky hole a moment longer than may be absolutely necessary."

"Nor I," remarked Henry; "so let us proceed, and it will be necessary that we keep an accurate watch upon our progress, for I am told that there are ice-wells here of great depth, down which you may fall and come by an awful death when you least expect, unless you are very cautious in looking where you tread."

"There's no doubt of that, sir," said one of his guests. "This place is considered to be one of the most curious that Anderbury can boast of, and I have been told that there are ice-houses, in which all kinds of provisions may be kept with ease and safety in the most violent heat of the summer months."

After a few moments they came upon one of the ice-wells, which yawned terrifically before them, and had they not been very careful and watchful upon the occasion, one or more of them might have been precipitated down the well, and the loss of life must have been the result.

"I scarcely think," said Henry, "that ordinary caution has been used in the construction of these places, or they never would have been left in such a state as they are now in. The ice-well, you perceive, lies directly in the very pathway?"

"Yes," said the admiral, "it does seem so, Master Henry; but if you look a little closer you will perceive that at one time there has been a wooden bridge exactly over this chasm."

"Ah, I do, indeed, now perceive such has been the case."

"Yes, and that made the place both safe and convenient; for no doubt there was a means of lowering down any baskets of wine or other matters that required a low temperature."

The admiral was perfectly right in his supposition, for that was just the way in which the ice-wells of Anderbury House were constructed; and now, since the bridge had been broken down, there was but a very narrow pathway, indeed, by which the well could be passed, unless it was jumped over, which might be done by any active person.

They would not pass this ice-well without an examination of it, and that was accomplished by lying down upon the rough pathway of the passage, and holding a light at arm's-length down it, when the bottom was clearly visible.

"He is not there," said Henry, who was the person who made the experiment; "he is not there, so we must pass on."

They accordingly did so, until they came to another such ice-well, and then the guest which had shown such eagerness in the chase, and accompanied them so far, went through the process of stooping down the chasm to ascertain if it contained anything unusual beyond the debris of broken bottles, old flint-stones, &c, which might fairly be expected to be there.

"Do you see anything?" inquired Henry, as the guest seemed to be looking very intently over the precipice.

He was about to reply something, for some sound came from his lips, when he suddenly, as if he had been impelled to do by some unseen power, toppled over the edge and disappeared, torch and all, into the abyss below.

"Good God!" cried Henry, "he has fallen."

"Good night," said the admiral, with characteristic coolness; "I suspect, my friend, that your career is at an end."

"Listen! for God's sake, listen!" cried Henry; "does he speak?"

There was a strange scuffling noise, and then a low deep groan from the bottom of the ice-pit, and then all was still; and from the character of the sound, Henry was of opinion that this well was of much greater depth than the former one, which he had so successfully examined.

"He has met with his death," said Henry.

"Don't be too sure," said the admiral; "we must have a good stout rope, and somebody must go down; if nobody likes the job, I will go myself."

"If ropes are wanted," said one of the other two persons who were present, "I can show you where they may be found, for I was at the inquest on the body of the man who was found dead in this place some time ago, and I marked that the ropes by which his body had been got out of one of the ice-wells were left where they had been used."

"That, then," said the other, "is further on, and nearer the beach."

"Yes; lend me the light, and I will get the rope as quickly as I can; for I don't think, as well as I can remember, that there is another well between this one and that which is nearer the beach entrance."

This was done, and for a few moments Henry and the admiral were left in darkness while the ropes were being searched for. It was a darkness so total and complete, that it did indeed seem like that darkness which it requires but a little stretch of the imagination to fancy it can be felt.

"Henry," said the admiral — "Henry!"

"Yes; I am here."

"Were you ever in such a confounded dark hole in all your life?"

"Scarcely, I think, ever. It is certainly tremendous, and it is a grievous thing to think that a life had been sacrificed, as no doubt it has, in this adventure."

"Ah, well! we must all go to Davy Jones's locker some day, you — But — but don't lay hold of me so!"

"I lay hold of you! I am not near you, sir."

"D — n it! who is it, then? Somebody has got hold of me as if I were in a vice. Stand off, I say! Who are you?"

"Varney, the vampyre," said a deep sepulchral voice; "who warns you, and all others, that there is abundance of danger in visiting here, and nothing to be gained."

Almost as these words were spoken, Henry suddenly found himself whirled round with such force, that it was only by a great effort that he succeeded in keeping his feet, and he felt convinced that some one had passed him. Who could that one be but Sir Francis Varney, the much dreaded vampyre?

In the next moment the light glanced again upon the walls of the subterranean passage, and the admiral cried, —

"He has escaped, unless some one stops him above. But let us think of nothing else at present, but to find out if the poor fellow who fell down here be alive or dead."

Henry descended by the assistance of the ropes, and found the adventurous guest quite dead. They raised the body from the well, and conveying it, as best they could, among them, they arrived, after some troubles on account of their burden, in the gardens, and, finally, in the great hall of Anderbury House, on a table in which they laid the corpse.

It was quite evident now to the admiral and to the Bannerworths that Varney had escaped, so they could have no desire to remain at the house, over which Mr. Leek was running like a madman, wondering what he should do. Flora had invited Helen Williams to accompany her to the inn, so that the whole party of the Bannerworths went away together, with the one addition to it of that poor girl who had so narrow an escape of becoming the vampyre's bride. Horrible destiny!

Chapter CXXII.

MRS. WILLIAMS VISITS THE BANNERWORTHS AT THE INN. –
THE MARRIAGE OF JAMES ANDERSON WITH HELEN.

*L*et us fancy now, after all these singular circumstances had taken place, the Bannerworth family, with James Anderson and Helen Williams, seated in a comfortable room at the inn at Anderbury, where they had put up when they came to that place, in pursuance of the invitation they had received from Mrs. Williams.

And that lady, probably could she have foreseen what was about to occur, would have taken most especial pains to prevent such an invitation from ever reaching such a destination; but she had fallen a victim to her own love of display, and not being content with inviting people whom she did know, she must, forsooth, give them a *carte blanche* to bring with them people whom she did not know at all.

And this it was that she had been horrified by what had taken place, and had had all her brightest visions of the future leveled with the dust.

When Jack Pringle told Mrs. Williams that he believed she would quite willingly have sold her daughter to a vampyre, he was right; for she would have done so, always provided that the vampyre, as aforesaid, had a good property, and was able to convince her of that most important fact. The only person of all the little party that was assembled at the inn, who looked pale and anxious, was poor Helen, and she certainly did look so; for when we come to consider her novel position we shall not wonder at it.

She had thrown herself completely upon the consideration of strangers, and was severed from all those natural ties which ought to have for ever held her in their gentle bondage. But this conduct, or rather the conduct of that one who ought to have protected her though all trouble and anxieties – her mother – had been such as to deprive her of the feeling that she had a home at all.

Flora saw that her guest, as indeed she considered Helen, looked sad and dejected, and she made every effort within her power to rescue her from such a state of things.

"Do not despair of much happiness," she whispered to her; "but rather thank good fortune, which, at the last moment, rescued you from one whom you could not love. Be assured that now you will enjoy the protection of those who will soon be able to prevail upon your mother to look with a favorable eye upon any new arrangement."

"I am much beholden to you," said Helen — "very much beholden to you, and I feel that I ought to congratulate myself upon my escape. But my heart does feel sad, because the state of things, to avoid which I made myself a sacrifice, may now ensue in all their terrors."

"My dear," said the admiral, who overheard her, "don't you believe any such rubbish as all that. I have no doubt you have been regularly persecuted into the match with the supposed baron, and you would, perhaps, have found out afterwards that one-half of the things you were told, to induce you to consent, had no foundation but in somebody's active imagination."

"Do you think so, sir?"

"Do I think so! To be sure I do. Now, I dare say you were told how, if you married the Baron What's-his-name, you would be doing something wonderful for all your family."

"Yes — yes."

"Oh, of course; I can see through all that clearly enough; and I tell you, my lass, that you have had a most fortunate escape, and that there is, and shall be, no reason on the face of the earth why you should not be married to the man of your choice. He has been to sea, and so, of course, he has finished what may be called his education. If he had been on shore all his life, you might have doubted about the prudence of having him; but, as it is, it's quite another matter."

"Sir, I thank you for your kind advocacy of my cause," said James Anderson; "and I shall ever consider, as one of the most fortunate accidents of my life, the meeting with Admiral Bell."

"Oh, don't say anything about that. I know some of the people at the Admiralty, and when you go to make the report of how you have been shipwrecked, and how you lost your dispatches, I will give you a letter of introduction, which, I dare say, won't do you any harm."

"Indeed, sir, this is more kindness than I ought to expect."

"Not at all, my boy — not at all. Don't put yourself out of the way about that. Only I tell you what I would do. You need not take my advice unless you like; but, if I were you, I'd be hanged if I moved an inch anywhere till I had made Helen Williams my wife."

"Can you suppose," cried James Anderson, while his eyes sparkled with delight — "can you suppose, my dear sir, that such advice could be other than most welcome to me?"

"And what do you say, Helen, to it?" whispered Flora.

"What can I say?"

"You can say yes, I suppose?" said the admiral.

Helen was silent.

"Very good," added the admiral. "When a girl don't say no, of course she means yes; and you can make sure of your prize now you have got her, Master Anderson. Let's see; you manage these affairs with what you call a special license, don't you?"

"Yes, uncle," said Flora; "that is the way. You seem to know all about it, and I almost suspect you really must have had some experience in those matters."

"I experience, you little gipsy! — what do you mean? I never was married in all my life, and I don't intend to be."

"Don't make too sure, uncle. But, despite all that, no one could more warmly second your advice to Mr. Anderson than myself."

"Very good. For that speech I forgive you. And now, Mr. Anderson, just come along with me, for I want to say a few words to you which nobody else has anything to do with."

When the admiral got James Anderson alone, he said to him, —

"Of course you are without funds, so it's no use making any fuss of delicacy about it. I have no doubt but that, with my interest, I shall be able to get you into an appointment of some sort; but, in the meantime, I beg that you will not cross me in my desire to serve you; and mind, I take your word of honor to repay me, so, you see, there is no obligation."

"Sir, this noble generosity —"

"There, there — that's quite enough; for the fact is, it ain't noble generosity at all, so hold your tongue about it, and be so good as to let me consider that as settled. Here are fifty pounds for you, which will enable you to go to London like a gentleman, and to conduct your marriage either here or there, as you may yourself think proper, and as your bride may consent."

"Sir, I would fain make Helen my own here."

"Very good. I don't pretend to understand how to manage these things: but set about it as quickly as you can, and don't be deterred by anybody."

This short but, to James Anderson, deeply interesting conversation, because it relieved his mind from a load of anxiety, took place a few paces from the inn door only, so that they returned at once; but scarcely had they joined the rest of the party, and were considering what they should order for dinner, when one of the waiters of the establishment came to say, —

"If you please, there's a lady who wants to come in. I asked her her name, but she won't give it; but she says she must see everybody."

"The deuce she must!" cried the admiral. "What sort of a craft is she?"

"Sort of a what, sir?"

"My fears tell me," sobbed Helen, "that it is my mother."

The admiral whistled, and then he said, —

"I suppose we shall have a breeze; but the sooner it's over the better. Let the lady come in; and don't you be afraid of anything, my lass. Why, you look as pale as if you expected — here she is."

The door was flung open, and Mrs. Williams made her appearance. Anger was upon her face, and it required but a small amount of penetration to perceive that she came fully charged with all sorts of reproaches. Helen trembled and shrunk back for she had an habitual fear of her mother, which the imperious conduct of that individual had induced in the mind of so gentle a creature as Helen from her very childhood.

"Well, madam," said Henry, stepping forward; "to what are we indebted for the honor of this visit from one who has not the courtesy to wait for an invitation?"

"Oh! I expected this," said Mrs. Williams, with a shivering toss of her head; "I quite expected this, I can assure you — of course. But I'll pretty soon let you know, sir, what I came about. I have come for my daughter, sir. What have you got to say against that?"

"Nothing, madam; if your daughter chooses to comply with your request."

"Helen!" screamed Mrs. Williams. "Helen! I command you to come home this moment!"

"Mother, hear me!" said Helen. "Consent to my happiness with one whom I can love, with the same readiness that you would have seen me the bride of one for whom I never could hope to feel anything in the shape of affection, and I will accompany you home at once."

"Oh, dear, yes — of course. Consent to ruin — consent to nonsense! Consent to your marrying a scapegrace who cannot even keep himself — far less a wife! No, Helen; you cannot expect that I should ever consent to your marrying such a poor wretch."

"But don't you think," said Henry, "that any poor wretch is better than a vampyre?"

"No; I do not."

"Oh! very good, then," said the admiral; "if that's the lady's opinion, what can we say to her? And, as for commanding Miss Helen, here, to go home, I command her to stay."

"You command her?"

"Yes, to be sure. Ain't I an admiral? What have you got to say against that, I should like to know? I shall take good care that James Anderson is no poor wretch by getting him some good appointment; and, as your daughter is of age, old girl, and so can choose for herself, you may as well weigh anchor, and be off at once, for nobody wants to be bothered with you."

"Do you mean to say you are a real admiral, and have nothing to do with the horse-marines?"

"Nothing whatever, ma'am. Good day to you — we are all waiting for our dinners, and don't feel disposed to talk any more; so be off with you."

Mrs. Williams seemed to be considering for a moment, and then she said, —

"Oh, gracious! a mother's feelings must always be excused. I almost think that — just to please you, admiral — I will consent."

"You will, mother?" exclaimed Helen.

"Why, in a manner of speaking," said Mrs. Williams, "I should not mind; but it's quite, you see, a dreadful thing to think of, when we consider what an expense I have gone to in all these matters, and that I have not had so much as one farthing from the baron, although he did say he would pay all the cost I might be put to."

"From resources which, in course of time, industry may procure me," said James Anderson, eagerly, "you shall be repaid all that you can possibly say has been expended for Helen."

"Ah! well, then, if Admiral Bell, here, will say that he will see me paid, I consent."

"Very well," said the admiral; "I'll see you paid. If you had acted generously in the matter, you should have been a gainer; but, as it is, you shall be paid, and we decline your acquaintance."

Mrs. Williams began, from the tone and manner of her daughter's new friends, to suspect that it would have been more prudent on her part if she had behaved in a very different manner towards them, and complied with a good grace with their wishes; for, as regarded the baron, anything in the shape of a more extended connection with him was clearly out of the question.

But she had gone almost too far for reconciliation, and, although there was no such thing as denying the genius of the lady, she was, for a few minutes, puzzled to know what to do. At length, however, she thought it would not be a bad plan to be suddenly quite overcome with her feelings, and make a desperate scene.

Accordingly, to the surprise of every one, and the consternation of the admiral, she suddenly uttered a piercing scream, and commenced a good exhibition of hysterics.

"D — n it!" cried the admiral; "what does she mean by that? Come, come, I say, Mother Williams, we cannot stand all that noise, you know; it is quite out of the question!"

"Let us all leave the room," said Henry, "and send Jack Pringle to her. I have heard him say that he has some mode of recovering ladies from hysterics by throwing a pail-full of salt water over them, and then biting their thumb-nails off."

"The wretch!" exclaimed Mrs. Williams, suddenly recovering. "The wretch! I'd let him know soon enough what it was to interfere with my nails!"

"Oh! you are better, are you?" said the admiral.

"What's that to you?" shrieked Mrs. Williams. "I'll go at once to a lawyer, and see what can be done with you. I look upon you all with odium and contempt!"

"Ah! words easily spoken," said the admiral; "and just like young chickens they commonly go home to roost."

Mrs. Williams darted an angry look at the whole party, which she intended should be expressive at once of the immense contempt in which she held them, and of her determination to have vengeance upon their heads, which double-dealing look, however, had no effect upon them of an intimidating character, and then she bounced from the room.

"My dear," said the admiral, turning to Helen, who he saw was affected at the proceeding. "My dear, don't you fret yourself. Your mother cannot make us angry; and, as far as regards her own anger, it will all subside, and then we will forget that she has said anything at all uncivil to us. So don't you fret yourself about what is of no consequence at all."

"You may depend," said Henry, "that such will be the fact, and that in a very short time you will find that your mother has completely recovered from her anger, and will be as pleasant with us all as possible. I grieve to say so to you, but the fact is, what you must perceive, namely, that, as regards your mother, your marriage is merely a matter of pounds, shillings, and pence, and when she finds that the baron's fortune cannot be had, she will content herself with reflecting upon the prospects of Mr. James Anderson, who, if he do well, will soon be quite a favorite."

It was humiliating to poor Helen to be forced to confess that this was the correct view to take of the question, but she could not help doing so at all: and, after a time, she did not regret having sufficient moral courage to resist the command of her mother to return home.

In the society of him whom she loved, and upheld and encouraged, too, as she was by Flora, who was just about the best and kindest companion such a person as Helen could have had, the minutes began to fly past upon rosy pinions, and the remainder of that day she confessed, even to the admiral, was the happiest she had known for many a weary month.

The Bannerworths and James Anderson fully expected another visit from Mrs. Williams on the morrow, but she did not come; and, although they had expected her to do so, her not coming was no disappointment, but, on the contrary, a matter for some congratulation.

But no time was lost; and, as James Anderson was really most anxious to get to London to report himself at the Admiralty, and as that was an anxiety in which the admiral much encouraged him, so that as it was quite an understood thing among them all that the marriage of the fair Helen should take place before he again left her, a special license was procured, and the ceremony arranged to take place at nine o'clock in the morning, on the second morning after the strange and exciting occurrences at Anderbury House.

This marriage was conducted in the most private manner possible; because, as it had been so well known throughout the whole of Anderbury that Helen Williams was the chosen of the great and rich Baron Stolmuyer of Saltzburgh, who had tuned out to be such an equivocal character, the news of her marriage with any one else would have been sure to have created a vast amount of pubic curiosity.

All this they escaped by fixing the hour at which the ceremony was to be performed at an early hour in the morning, and trusting no one out of their own party with the secret.

Of course, from what the reader knows of the gentle and timid disposition of Helen Williams, he may well suppose how glad she would have been to have had the countenance of her mother at her marriage, notwithstanding the conduct of that mother was certainly not what should have entitled her to the esteem of any one whatever, not excepting her own child.

But this was a feeling which, when she came to consider the new tie she was forming, was likely soon to wear away; and, although, while she pronounced those words which were irrevocably to make her another's, the tears gushed to her eyes, they were far different from those bitter drops she had shed when she considered that, beyond all hope of redemption, she was condemned to become the bride of the baron.

When the ceremony was over, they all went back very quietly and comfortably to the inn, and, after a good breakfast, and many healths had been drank to the bride, James Anderson, according to arrangement, took his departure for London, leaving Helen in the care of the Bannerworths until he should come back to claim her, as he now could do, despite all the plots and machinations of Mrs. Williams, who, as yet, was in a state of blessed ignorance as to the fact of her daughter's wedding, and who had not quite made up her mind as to what she should do next in so delicate and troublesome a transaction.

Chapter CXXIII.

MRS. WILLIAMS TAKES THE INITIATIVE, AND NEARLY CATCHES AN ADMIRAL.

*M*rs. Williams, when she reached home after what must be called her very unsuccessful attempt to make a disturbance, and to do the grand at the inn where the Bannerworths were, set herself seriously to think what would be the best course for her to adopt in the rather perplexing aspect of her affairs.

The few words she had used at the inn, indicative of her censure of all the proceedings, had been of rather a strong and energetic character, so that she had a very uncomfortable suspicion upon her mind that she would find it rather a difficult task to pacify her daughter's new friends.

The offer which the admiral had made to repay to her any expense she had been at, impressed her with a belief that he surely must be in possession of what, to her, was the most delightful thing in the world, and comprehended all sorts of virtue, namely, money; and of course her feelings became instantly most wonderfully ameliorated.

"I'm very much afraid I have been too precipitate," she said. "I really am afraid I have, and that ain't a pleasant reflection by any means. What can I do to get good friends with them all, and particularly the dear old gentleman who promised to pay me?"

This was the problem which Mrs. Williams presented to her mind, for the captivating idea of actually having been paid 500 pounds by the baron, and thus sending in a bill of the same amount to the admiral, took wonderful and complete possession of her.

This was, indeed, she considered, a masterstroke of policy, and all she had now to consider was, the means of getting on such good terms with the admiral that he should neither question items nor amount of the account she intended to send him in.

"If he only pays the 500 pounds as well as the baron has paid his, I shall not come out of the transaction so badly," said Mrs. Williams.

While she was in this state of perplexity, she was sitting by the window of her dining-room, which commanded a view of the street, and, as she sat there, she was much surprised to see Jack Pringle, who she still had a lingering suspicion might, notwithstanding his disclaimer of the title, be Admiral Green, on the other side of the way, making various significant movements of his hands and head, as if he had something of an exceedingly secret and strange mysterious nature to communicate to her, Mrs. Williams.

This was quite sufficient to call for that lady's most serious attention, and accordingly she walked graciously so close to the window that her aristocratic nose touched the glass, and nodded to Jack, after which she beckoned him across the way, after the manner of the ghost in Hamlet, upon which Jack, with a nod, came across the way forthwith.

In another moment Mrs. Williams opened the street-door herself, and said, —

"Mr. What's-your-name, have you got anything to say to me?"

"Rather," said Jack.

"What is it, then — pray what is it, Mr. What's-your-name?"

"Don't call me What's-your-name, ma'am, any longer; my name is Jack Pringle."

"Mr. John Pringle, I suppose?"

"No such thing; nothing but plain Jack, ma'am; so you see you are mistaken. But I have got something to say to you, ma'am, as you ought to know."

Any one who had known Jack would have seen, by a certain mischievous twinkling of the eyes, that he had on hand what he considered one of the most excellent of jokes in all the world, and was about to perpetrate what he thought some famous piece of jollity. What it was, we shall quickly perceive, from his communication with Mrs. Williams.

"Well, ma'am," he added, "you know Admiral Bell, I believe?"

"Oh, yes — yes; certainly, I do."

"Well, I don't know as I ought to tell you, Mrs. W., what I'm going to tell you; but, first of all, the old admiral, what with prize money, pay, and one thing and another, is so immensely rich, that he really don't know what to do with his money."

"How dreadful!" said Mrs. Williams; "I think I could really suggest to him some few things to do."

"Oh, he is so desperately obstinate, he will listen to nobody; and, you see, as he never married, who as he got to leave it to? At least that's what we have been all wondering, for I don't know how long; but now what do you think we have found out, Mrs. Williams?"

"Well, that's very difficult, of course, for me to say. Perhaps you will be so good as to tell me."

"You ought to know. He has fallen in love, ma'am — actually in love, for the first time in his life. Yes, he has actually fallen in love, Mrs. Williams; there's a go."

"And with one of my daughters! It's with Julia — I did mention her to him, and I thought I saw a curious expression come across his face. Of course, I'm quite delighted to hear it; for, with the feelings of a mother, I like to get my girls off hand as well as I can; and, as Admiral Bell is so very respectable a person, I can have no sort of objection in the world."

"There you go, again," said Jack; "you are quite mistaken, I can tell you. You never made a greater blunder than that in all your life, Mother Williams — excuse me, ma'am, but that's my way."

"Oh, don't mention it — but where's the mistake, my dear sir?"

"Why, just here, ma'am — just here. The admiral is not so young as he was twenty-five years ago, and he ain't quite such a fool as to think that a young girl can care anything for him. But he is in love, for all that. Only you see, ma'am, it happens to be with somebody else."

"Good gracious! Who is it? — and why do you come to me about it?"

"Because it's you."

"Me! me! oh, gracious Providence, you don't mean that! In love with me! The rich old admiral — he cannot live long. How much money, take it altogether, do you really think he has got? I declare you have taken me so by surprise, that I don't know what I am saying. Of course he will propose a very handsome settlement."

"You may depend upon all that," said Jack; "but the odd thing is, you see, ma'am, that although he is quite over head and ears in love, he won't own it, but walks about like a bear with a bad place on his back, doing nothing but growl, growl, from morning till night."

"Then how can you tell," said Mrs. Williams, "if he never said so?"

"Oh, he does say so. He mumbles it out to himself, and we have heard him say, —

" 'Damn it all! that Mrs. Williams is the craft for my money; but what's the use of me bothering her about it? — she wouldn't have an old hulk like me, so I won't say anything about it to anybody.'"

"What an amiable idea!"

"Very, ma'am, very; and what I have come to you for now is to say, that if you have no objection to the match, you might as well make the old man happy, by letting him know, in some sort of way, that you wouldn't be so hard-hearted as he thinks, but would have him if he would say the word."

"How can I express how much obliged I am to you, Mr. Wingle!"

"Pringle, if you please, ma'am, is my name; and as to being obliged to me, you ain't at all, and I'll tell you how: you see, I and the admiral have sailed with each other many a voyage, and I have a sort of feeling for the old man that makes me, when I see that he has a fancy, try my best to gratify him; and, without thinking of anybody but him, I've come to you just to tell you what I know about the affair, and I must leave it to you to do what you like."

"Still I am very much obliged to you. What if I were to call and ask for a private interview with the old man?"

"A good idea," said Jack. "It was only the other day I heard him say you was his pearl, and the main chain of his heart, I can tell you, and ever such a load more. He will be taking his dinner at four today, and after that he usually takes a sleep in an arm chair, in a room by himself, and if you like to come then, you will catch him."

"Be assured, my dear sir, I shall be there punctually to the minute. You will be so good as to receive me, and introduce me to him, and, perhaps, it would remove some of his timidity if I were to let him know that I was aware that he had called me his pearl, and the main chain of his heart."

"Of course it would," said Jack. "You put him in mind of it, ma'am, and if you find him back'erd a little, don't you mind about giving him a little encouragement, because you know all the while he really means it, so you need not care about it."

"Well, Mr. — a — a — Bingle, all I can say is, that I feel very much obliged to you indeed, for letting me know this matter; and my great respect for you and for the old admiral will, I assure you, induce me to consent to what you propose. — A-hem! of course I have many offers, as you may well suppose, Mr. Cringle."

"Damn it," said Jack, "I've told you before that my name is Pringle, and if you can't recollect that, just call me Jack, and have done with it — you won't forget Jack, I'll be bound. Call me that, and I shan't quarrel with you about it, ma'am; but don't be inventing all sorts of odd names for me."

"Pray excuse me, my dear sir, I certainly will do no such thing; and at three o'clock, I hope I shall have the pleasure of seeing you. I believe it's the Red Lion where you are staying?"

"Yes, the Red Lion Inn; and at three I shall be on the look out for you, ma'am, you may depend; and I only hope you won't mistake the admiral's bashfulness for anything else, because, I assure you, he is mad in love with you, but don't like to own it, ma'am; so just you bring him out a little, and don't you mind what he says."

Mrs. Williams duly promised she would not mind what the old man said, and, from what we know of that lady, we are quite inclined, for once in a way, to give her credit for sincerity in that matter, and the greatest possible amount of candor.

As for Jack, when he left her house, and had got fairly round the corner and out of sight, he laughed to that excess that several passers-by stopped to look at him in wonder, and had he not ceased, he certainly would have had a crowd round him in a very few minutes longer, that would have perhaps thought him out of his senses.

But after a few minutes, the explosion of his bottled-up mirth had subsided, and after giving a boy, who was the nearest to him of the admiring spectators, a good rap on the head, he walked to the inn.

Jack would have been glad to have told some one of the capital joke he was playing off at the admiral's expense, but he was afraid of being betrayed; so he wisely kept the secret of the forthcoming jest all to himself; although Henry Bannerworth and Charles Holland might both, after such a thing happened, or even during its progress, have a good laugh at it, it is not to be supposed, entertaining as they did so great a respect for the old admiral, that they would have lent themselves to the perpetration of such a joke.

As may be supposed, Mrs. Williams was all flutter and expectation, and the idea of at length mending her decayed fortune by an union with the old man, who was reported to be immensely rich, and who had already reached an age when his life could not be depended upon one week from another, was one of the most gratifying circumstances on record to her.

No possible plan could have been devised which was so likely to chime in with her humor as this, and if she had been asked in which way she would like to make money, it would have been that which she would have undoubtedly chosen.

"Now," she thought, "I shall, after all, make an admirable thing of this affair, there can be no doubt. I shall, of course, soon be a widow again, for the old sea monster cannot live long. I shall insist upon a very liberal settlement indeed, and then I suppose, while he does live, I must keep him in a good humor, so that he may leave me, at all events, the bulk of his property when he dies, and then I can live in the style I like, and make everybody die of envy."

To excite an extraordinary amount of envy was the very height of felicity to Mrs. Williams, as, indeed, it is to many people of far greater pretensions than that lady; and we cannot help thinking, when we see gaudy equipages and all the glittering and costly paraphernalia of *parvenu* wealth, that the great object of it is to excite envy far more than admiration and pleasure.

"There are the Narrowidges, and the Staples, and the Jenkinses," thought Mrs. Williams. "Oh! I know they will all be ready to eat their very heads off, when they hear that I am married, and that, too, so well. Oh! they will die of spite, and particularly Mrs. Jenkins. I am quite sure she will have a serious illness."

These were the kind of triumphs upon which Mrs. Williams felicitated herself, and pictured to her imagination as the result of her marriage with the admiral, which she now looked upon as quite a settled thing; because, if he were willing, she felt perfectly sure that she was; and, therefore, what was to prevent the union from taking place?

What pleasant anticipations these were! Really, we can almost consider them, while they lasted, as sufficient to counterbalance any disappointment which was likely afterwards to take place; and the hour or two which Mrs. Williams devoted to the gorgeous dream of wealth she so fully expected to enjoy, were probably the most delightful she had ever passed. And certainly so far she had to thank Jack Pringle for giving her so much satisfaction, although, as will be seen, she did not feel towards him any great amount of gratitude on the momentous occasion.

Mrs. Williams, no doubt, still thought herself quite a fascinating woman; and when she had failed in guessing that it was to herself that the admiral was, according to Jack's account, devoted, it was not that she entertained a modest and quiet opinion of her own attractions, but from the force of habit, seeing that so long a period had elapsed without her having an admirer, that she could not believe she had one then, until actually assured in plain language of the fact.

And now, about half an hour before the appointed time, the lady arrayed herself in what she considered an extremely becoming and fashionable costume, and started to keep her appointment with Jack Pringle, who, in her affections, now held quite a pleasant place, and towards whom she considered herself so much indebted for the kind information she had received at his hands.

The distance from any house in Anderbury to any other, was but short, so that Mrs. Williams was within the time mentioned, when she reached the door of the Red Lion; but she was gratified to find that Jack Pringle was there, apparently on the look out for her, because it showed that nothing had happened to alter the aspect of affairs, but that the chances of her becoming Mrs. Admiral Bell were as strong as ever.

"I'm glad you have come," said Jack. "They got over their dinner rather quick, and that's a fact; and the old man is fast asleep as usual, so you can commence operations at once."

"A thousand thanks — a thousand thanks, my good friend, and you may depend upon my gratitude."

"Hush! never mind that," said Jack; "I don't want nothing. This way — this way, ma'am, if you please."

Chapter *CXXVI.*[1]

THE ADMIRAL IN A BREEZE. – A GENERAL COMMOTION, AND JACK PRINGLE MUCH WANTED, BUT NOT TO BE FOUND.

*T*o say that Mrs. Williams was on the tiptoe of expectation, is to say very little that can convey a good idea of what was her real condition, nervously speaking, as she followed Jack Pringle up, not the principal, but a back staircase of the inn, toward the room where the admiral took his nap, which was

"His custom always of an afternoon."

The fact is, that Jack had a great dread of Mrs. Williams being seen by any of the Bannerworth family, because they all knew her; and the nice little plot he had got up for the purpose of holding out the admiral to ridicule, while at the same time he enjoyed the immense satisfaction of having some revenge upon Mrs. Williams.

Hence was it, that, like many a great politician, he went up the back staircase instead of the front, in order to avoid unnecessary observation and remark.

By good fortune, as well as good management, Jack met nobody, but succeeded in reaching the room door, within which the admiral was sleeping, in perfect safety.

"Now, ma'am," said Jack, "don't you be backerd in going forerd, cos,

---

1 Editor's Note: The chapters of *Varney, the Vampyre* are misnumbered in the original at this point. Chapters 124 and 125 do not appear in the 1847 reprint edition of *Varney.* Whether it existed in the original publication in 1845-47 or in the 1853 printing is unknown. There are no gaps in page numbering in the 1847 printing, so either the chapters were really lost, or an error occurred in numbering the chapters.

as I tell you, the old man is dying by inches for you, and I don't see why you shouldn't have his half a million of money, as well as anybody else. Ah! and a good deal better, too, when one comes to consider all things."

"Thank you, Mr. Pringle, thank you. I really don't know how to express my obligations to you, upon my word. You are so very kind and considerate in all you say."

"Oh! don't mention it, ma'am. Walk in, and there you will find the old baby. I shouldn't wonder but he's disturbing his old brains by dreaming of you now."

Jack opened the door, and Mrs. Williams glided noiselessly into an apartment, where, seated, sure enough, in an easy chair, with a silk handkerchief over his face, sat the admiral, fast asleep, enjoying that comfortable siesta, which he never for one moment imagined would be disturbed in the manner it was about to be.

"Well," said Mrs. Williams, "there he is, to be sure, just as Jack Pringle said, — asleep, and no doubt dreaming of me. I must make sure of the old fool in one interview, or he may slip through my fingers, and that would not be at all pleasant after counting upon him, and taking some trouble in the matter."

But although she made up her mind that nothing should be wanting, upon her part, to make sure of him, yet she debated whether she ought to awaken him or not; for she well knew that many old people, especially men, were very irascible if they are awakened suddenly, and from what she had already seen of the admiral, she could very well imagine that such might be the case with him.

This was getting rather a quondary, out of which Mrs. Williams did not exactly see her way; and yet the proposition that the admiral was to be, and must be, awakened in some way, remained as firmly as ever fixed in her mind. And then, too, the idea — a very natural one under the circumstances — came across her that each minute was fraught with danger, and that, for all she knew, the yea or nay of the whole affair might depend upon the promptitude with which it was concluded.

What, if, she asked herself, some of the odious Bannerworth people were to come in and find her there — of course they would awaken the admiral at once, and in consequence of their presence, she would lose all opportunity of exercising those little blandishments which she meant to bring to bear upon him.

This was positively alarming. The idea of all being lost, prompted her at all events to attempt something; so Mrs. Williams thought that the mildest way of awakening the admiral was by a loud sneeze, which she executed without producing the least effect, as might have been expected; for the man who had many a time slept soundly in the wildest fury of the elements, was not likely to awaken because somebody sneezed.

"Dear me, how sound he sleeps. A — hem! — hem! A — *chew!* — a — a — hem! — A *chewaway!*"

The admiral was proof against all this, and Mrs. Williams might just as well have spared herself the trouble of exciting such an amount of artificial sneezes, for the admiral slept on, and it was quite clear that something much more sonorous would be required for the purpose of awaking him.

"How vexatious," she thought; "how very vexatious. But there's no help for it. Awakened he must be, that's quite clear; and if fair means won't do it, why, foul must."

Acting upon this resolve, Mrs. Williams hesitated no longer, but, approaching the sleeping admiral, she dragged the handkerchief off his face, and its passage over his nose, no doubt, produced the tickling sensation that induced him to give that organ a very hard rub, indeed, and start wide awake with an exclamation that was much more forcible than elegant, and that consequently we need not transfer to our pages at all.

"Oh! admiral," said Mrs. Williams, assuming a look that ought at once to have melted a heart of stone; "oh! admiral, can you, indeed, forgive me?"

"The devil!" said the admiral.

"Can you, indeed, look over the fact, that in my anxiety to see that face, I took from before it the envious, and yet fortunate handkerchief that covered it? It was my act, and upon my head fall all the censure, my dear, good, kind admiral."

The old man rubbed his eyes very hard with his knuckles, as he said, — "I suppose I'm awake."

"You are awake, my dear sir. It is, indeed, no dream, let me assure you, that disturbs you, but a living reality. You are awake, my dear sir."

"Why — why, what do you mean? I begin to think I am awake, with a vengeance; but who are you? Hang me if I don't think you are old Mother Williams!"

"Oh! my dear admiral, you are so facetious — so very facetious; but can you for one moment fancy, my dear sir, that I am insensible to your merit? Can you fancy that I could look with other than indulgent eyes upon a Bell?"

"Upon a what?"

"A Bell — an Admiral Bell. Indeed, I may say — with a slight but pardonable alteration of a word — an admirable Bell. My dear sir, your pearl speaks to you."

The admiral was so amazed at this address, accompanied as it was by most languishing looks, that, with his mouth wide open, and his eyes preternaturally distended, he gazed upon Mrs. Williams without saying a word; from which she inferred that he was beginning to see that she was aware of his attachment to her, and was thinking of how he could best express his gratitude for her taking the initiative in the matter.

Thus encouraged, then, she spoke again, saying, as she advanced close to him, —

"Oh, my dear sir, what a thing the human heart is. Only to think now, that from the first moment I saw you, I should whisper to myself — there — yes, there is the only human being for whose sake I could again enter into that holy state from which the death of Mr. Williams released me."

"Why, good God!" said the admiral, "the woman's mad!"

"Oh! no — no. The world — the horrid, low, work-a-day world, may make invidious remarks about us, but your pearl will recompense you for all that, and in the sweet concord of domestic life, we shall never sigh for more than we shall have, which will be, of course, if I understand rightly, a large income — I don't know how much a year, and if I ask, it is only out of curiosity, my dear sir, and nothing else. Love — absolute and beautiful love, is all I ask."

"Hilloa!" roared the admiral; "Charles! Henry! Jack! Where the devil are you all? D — n it, you are all ready enough when I don't want you; but now, when I am going to be boarded by a mad woman, you can't come one of you. Hilloa! help! Charles! Jack, you lubber, where the deuce have you taken yourself to, and why don't you tumble up when you are sent for?"

"But, my dear sir, why need you trouble yourself to call so many witnesses to our happiness? Let us be privately married in some rural church."

"Privately d — d first, I'd be," said the old admiral.

"Oh, then, it shall be a public alliance, if you wish it," exclaimed Mrs. Williams, as she made up her mind to clinch the affair at once by a *coup de main;* and advancing to the admiral, she flung her arms around his neck just as a door at the other end of the apartment opened, and Charles and Henry, with Flora, made their appearance, and looked with the most intense astonishment at the scene before them.

"Well, uncle," said Charles, "I certainly should not have expected this of you. I am astonished, I must confess."

"Nor I," said Henry; "why, admiral, I had no idea you were so dangerous a personage."

Mrs. Williams, when she saw what arrivals had taken place, gave a faint scream, and released the admiral, and then she added, —

"Oh, admiral, how could you hold me so when you hear somebody coming? How shall I ever survive such a scene as this? My character will be gone for ever, unless I am immediately married to you, and I have no doubt but that all your friends will at once see the propriety of such a step."

"I do," said Charles.

"And I," said Henry.

"And I," of course, said Flora.

Mrs. Williams burst into tears when she saw this unanimity of opinion; but the admiral's face got the color of a piece of beet-root, and he was only silent for a moment or two, while he was made the subject of these cruel remarks, until he could sufficiently recover to speak with the energy that did characterize him when he really began.

We are not exactly in the vein to transfer to our pages the violent expletives with which he garnished his outburst of passion, and our readers, if they recall to their minds a large amount of nautical oaths, can have no difficulty in supposing that the admiral uttered every one of them with a volubility that was perfectly alarming.

"D — n it! do you mean to kill me, all of you, or to drive me mad? (Five oaths in a string came in here.) Do you want to cut me up, you — ? (Three horrible epithets.) What do you mean by setting this old woman upon me? Whose precious idea was this, I should like to know, to put an elderly she-dragon upon me, whom I hate and be — (ten oaths at least) when I was enjoying a comfortable nap?"

"Hate!" exclaimed Mrs. Williams; "did you say hate, you old seducing villain! when you knew you said I was your pearl, you hoary-headed ruffian!"

"That's a thundering crammer," cried the admiral; "you said it yourself; and as for hating you, d — n it, if I don't do that with all my heart."

"And is this the way I'm to be treated before people? Oh! you wicked old sinner, I understand you now. Your intentions were not honorable, and now you find that my virtue is proof against your horrid old fascinations, you want to pretend that it's all a mistake."

"Really," said Charles, "we must confess, uncle, that we found Mrs. Williams and you — ahem! — rather loving, you know; and the gentleman on these occasions is usually asked to account for such things, I take it."

"Of course," said Mrs. Williams; "I'll bring an action against the admiral, and I shall call upon you all to be witnesses for me. Oh! you old sinner, I'll make you pay for this!"

"We certainly can all be witnesses," said Flora, "that the admiral called for help; and when we came we found Mrs. Williams holding him fast round the neck, to which he seemed to have the greatest possible repugnance."

"That's right! hurrah! That's the truth, Flora, my dear. That's just how it was. This horrid old woman come all of a sudden and laid hold of me after awakening me, and then I called for help. That's how it was."

"But these gentlemen," said Mrs. Williams, appealing to Henry and

Charles, "will swear quite different."

"Oh, I beg your pardon, Mrs. Williams," said Charles; "if we are brought forward to swear anything, we must be correct; and, therefore, we shall have to say just what this lady has stated; and perhaps your best plan will be to go away and say no more about it; but consider that you have made a mistake."

"A mistake!" screamed Mrs. Williams; "how could I make a mistake, when Mr. John Pringle, who knows the admiral so well, told me that he was dying to see me, and in love with me to never such an extent, only that he was afraid I would not have anything to say to him on such a subject."

The admiral drew a long breath and sat down. Then, clenching his hand, he shook it above his head, saying, in a voice of deep and concentrated anger, —

"I thought as much. D — n it, if I did not. It's all that infernal scoundrel Jack Pringle's doings, I find. It's one of that lubberly, mutinous thief's tricks, and it's the last one he shall ever play me."

"A trick!" screamed Mrs. Williams; "a trick! You don't mean that! Ah, me! what compensation shall I get for the dreadful circumstance which has made me confess the secret of my heart! What shall I do — oh, what shall I do? When shall I hope for consolation! What sum of money, even if you, my dear admiral, were to offer it to me, would be a sufficient balm now to my wounded heart?"

"Madam," said Henry, "it seems that you have been imposed upon, and made the victim of a practical joke, which we nor the admiral can have nothing to do with; and the only consolation we can offer to your wounded heart, is, that we will keep the secret of your attachment most inviolate."

"What compensation is that to me? I'll bring my action for breach of promise of marriage, if I don't get something, and that something very handsome too. It's all very fine to talk to me about your mistakes; I'll be paid — ah, and paid well, too, or I'll make the whole country ring again with the matter."

"Madam," said Charles, "I dare say the admiral don't care one straw whether the country rings again or not, and you can do just as you please; but since you have commenced threatening, you will, I hope, see the obvious propriety of at once leaving his place."

"I will leave this place, but it shall be to go direct to my solicitor, and see what he will say to a lone woman being treated in this way. I'll swear that he called me his pearl — and if that don't get me a verdict and most exemplary damages, I don't know what will. We shall see what we shall see, and, in the meantime, you wretches, I leave you all to contempt. Yes, contempt."

"Stop a bit, ma'am," said the admiral. "It's quite plain to me that

you don't mind how you earn a trifle, so that you do get it; and now
I'll tell you, that if you find out that rascal, Jack Pringle, and give him
a good trouncing for his share in the business, you may come to me for
a reward."

Mrs. Williams, whatever might have been her personal feelings on
this head, did not deign to make the least reply to this intimation, but
suddenly cried —

"I want to see my daughter."

"She is not here at present," said Flora; "and, if she were, she is Mrs.
Anderson now, and therefore would of course decline accompanying
you to your home — and she is only waiting some arrangements of her
husband's, prior, most probably, to going to London with him."

This speech brought to the recollection of Mrs. Williams, that the
admiral had promised her all the expenses that she had been at contin-
gent upon the broken-off marriage of her daughter with the baron, and
she began to consider that her action for breach of promise of marriage
against him might fail, and that, if it succeeded, it might not bring in
half so much as the amount of the bill she could by fair means get out
of him.

These considerations were of great pith and amount, and they had
their full effect upon Mrs. Williams; so, instead of bursting out with
any further reproaches, she sat down and commenced a softening
process by a copious flood of tears which she had always at command.

"Oh," said the old admiral, "you may well cry over it, old girl. I
suppose you really thought you had hooked the old man at last, eh? But
never do you mind, you may make a good thing of it yet, if you get
hold of that scoundrel, Pringle, and serve him out well. I'll pay for that
job more willingly than for anything else I know of just at present."

"Don't speak to me of that brute, my dear sir," sobbed Mrs. Williams.
"It's a very cruel thing, of course, to be used in this way, and, as it's all
a mistake on my part, I hope you will excuse and look over what has
happened. I am sure I should be the last person in the world to trouble
anybody with visits who did not want to see me; and so, I dare say, we
shall only meet once again in this world."

"Once again, madam! What is the use of our ever meeting again?"

"It would look decidedly disrespectful on my part, if I were not to
hand you the bill myself for the little matters that you were kind enough
to say you would pay for on account of what I had expended on Helen's
projected marriage with the vampyre baron, you know, admiral."

"Oh, ah! I recollect now. Well, well; I don't want to go back from my
word, and as I did promise you, why, I will pay you; but as I don't want,
on any account, the pleasure of your company again, you will be so
kind, ma'am, as to take this twenty-pounds note, and keep the change."

This the admiral thought liberal enough; for his idea of matrimonial preparations consisted of a new dress or two, or so, and which twenty pounds ought fairly enough to cover; and he thought he would do well enough by overpaying Mrs. Williams, as he believed, with that amount.

When Mrs. Williams recovered from her surprise, not unmingled with indignation, into which this most audacious and, to her, extraordinary offer threw her, she spoke with a kind of scream, that made the old admiral jump again, as she shouted in his ears, —

"What! twenty pounds? Are you in your senses? Twenty pounds! Why, my bill will be, at least, five hundred pounds."

"What?" roared the admiral. "Are you in your senses? D — n it, ma'am! you may swallow your bill; and you had better do so, for all the good it is likely to do you; for, if I pay a farthing more, may I be hung up at my own yard-arm. Why, you must think that a British admiral is another name for a fool."

"Then I tell you what," said Mrs. Williams — "I tell you what, you stupid, old, atrocious sinner — I tell you, I will bring my action against you for breach of promise of marriage; and I'll swear that, before your gang of people here came in — who, of course, will swear black is white, and white is crimson for you, because, I believe, you are the father of them all — that you first asked me to live with you, and when I refused, you said you would marry me by special license tomorrow."

"Madam," said Charles, "now that you think proper entirely to forget that you are a lady, allow me to beg of you to retire; because it is quite impossible, after what has happened, that I should hold any further conversation with you."

"Yes, Mrs. Williams," said Henry, "I hope you will perceive the propriety of at once leaving."

At this moment a note was handed to Henry, who, upon opening it, read aloud, —

"The Baron Stolmuyer, of Salzburgh, presents his compliments to Mr. Bannerworth, and begs to state that Mrs. Williams has received from him the sum of five hundred pounds for expenses to be incurred on account of the wedding of her daughter; and he hereby fully empowers Mr. Bannerworth to demand of Mrs. Williams that sum, and to devote it to the service and uses of Mr. James Anderson, of whose existence the baron was not aware when he made his proposal to Mrs. Williams for her daughter, whom she sold to him, the baron, for that sum."

"Hilloa!" cried the admiral; "what do you think of that, Mrs. Williams? I don't know what you will say to it; but I know very well that I should consider it a shot between wind and water."

"I trust," said Henry, "that you will now still further see the propriety of leaving here, and of letting this matter completely rest; because it strikes me that the more you investigate it, madam, the more it will turn out greatly to your disadvantage."

"I don't care a pin's head for any of you, nor half a farthing," cried Mrs. Williams. "The baron gave me the money, and he has no power to get it back again, as you know well enough. I'll bring my action, and my principal witness shall be Mr. Pringle, who came to my house, and who, if put upon his oath, will be obliged to swear —"

"That it was all a lark," said Jack, popping his head just within the amazingly short distance that he opened the door, and then he disappeared before a word could be said to him.

Mrs. Williams who, notwithstanding all her threats, seemed to have a lingering impression that she was victimized in the transaction, had all the ire of her nature aroused at once by the sight of Jack, and she at once rushed after him, leaving the admiral and the Bannerworths not at all lamenting her loss.

Jack had no idea that he would be followed by anybody but the admiral, and to distance him he knew there was no occasion to run; so, when he had got down to the hall of the hotel, he subsided into a walk, until he heard a tremendous scuffling of feet behind him, and, upon looking round, saw Mrs. Williams in full chase, and with an expression upon her countenance which plainly enough indicated that her intentions were not at all of a jocular character.

"The devil!" said Jack; "if here ain't Mother Williams coming full sail, and at fourteen knots an hour, too, with a fair wind, I'll be bound. Never mind — a stern chase is a long chase, so here goes."

As Jack uttered these remarks, he dashed onwards at tremendous speed; but the sight of him again, had inflamed Mrs. Williams's wrath to madness, and she made the most incredible exertion to come up with him, so that it was really wonderful to see her.

But Jack, being less encumbered by apparel than the lady, would have distanced her, but for an unlucky accident, that gave her a temporary mastery. The fates would have it, that a baker with a tray upon his head, containing sundry pies, was coming up the street, and as people do sometimes, when they are mutually anxious to pass each other without coming in contact, they dodged from side to side for a few seconds, and then, of course, ran against each other as if they really meant it, with such force, that down came Jack, and baker, and pies, in one grand smash.

In another moment the enraged Mrs. Williams reached the spot.

To snatch up the only whole pie there was left, was to the lady the work of a moment, and to reverse it upon Jack's face, was the work of another moment; and then, in the vindictiveness of her rage, she stamped upon the bottom of the dish until his head was embedded in damsons, and he was nearly smothered.

From the window of the inn the Bannerworths and the admiral saw all this take place, and the delight of the old man was of the most extravagant character, exceeding all bounds, while the Bannerworths, for the life of them, could not help laughing most heartily.

"Now, you wretch!" said Mrs. Williams, "I hope this will be a lesson to you. Take that — and that — and that, you sea-snake! you odious tar-barrel!"

As she spoke, she hammered on the dish till it broke, and that was for Jack the best thing that could have happened, for it gave him a little air, and by a frantic effort he scrambled to a sitting posture, and commenced dragging the damsons out of his eyes and mouth. Mrs. Williams then thought it was high time to leave, and so muttering threats, to the immense amusement of a crowd of persons who had assembled, she walked away, leaving Jack by no means delighted with the end of the adventure, and to settle with the infuriated baker as best he might.

It was no small additional mortification to Jack to look up and see the admiral and the Bannerworths at the window of the hotel, enjoying his discomfiture, and laughing most heartily at his expense.

Chapter CXXVII.

A CHANGE OF SCENE AND CIRCUMSTANCES. – AN EVENT IN LONDON.

*T*he recent events which followed each other so rapidly, were strangely concluded by the sudden and mysterious disappearance of Sir Francis Varney. That he should thus have eluded all, was aggravating to a very large class of people, who seemed to insist that he should have come to some notable catastrophe.

"Had he only been killed," they argued, "we should have known the last of him."

Of the truth of this there could be no doubt. When a man is dead and buried, you do, as far as human nature serves, know the end of him;

but this great fact does not always come within the knowledge of men, who sometimes, contrary to expectation, drop off themselves, and instead of knowing the end of somebody else, why, somebody else knows the end of them.

It is a well known fact, that as some die before others, that it does sometimes happen that those who wish to see another out, may be seen out themselves; besides, taking the question of longevity aside, it does not follow, because we so wish to come to the conclusion of an affair, that its author may but change the scene, and transport it elsewhere, and the good and curious lieges become defrauded of their self-satisfying knowledge, viz., the end of the affair.

Of course it was an aggravation, to know that there was an interesting and highly exciting affair gone off, and they were not allowed to peep into that mystery, the future; but so it was — they were not gratified.

Some were of the opinion that he had departed this life in a mysterious and unsatisfactory, because secret manner, and that was why nobody could tell anything about it.

But there were other opinions afloat, and among others, that of the admiral, which was pretty general, which was, that he had very likely disappeared from that part of the world to seek in some other place the renovation his system required, by means that were natural to him, but hideous in others to contemplate or think of.

This was generally the received opinion, for it was universally admitted by the wise people thereabouts, that he must at certain times recruit himself.

The opinion thus entertained by all who lived thereabouts, became less and less absorbing; other matters began to be thought of, things began to flow into their usual channel, and a subsidence took place in the turmoil and excitement consequent upon the presence of the vampyre.

About this period, while these parts were regaining their original serenity and calmness, and while the vampyre was looked upon as an awful and fearful episode in the life of those who lived there, there happened in London a circumstance that it is necessary to relate to the reader, inasmuch as it is very important, and bears strongly on our story.

Not far from Bloomsbury-square, which, at the period of our story, was a very fashionable place, and in one of the first streets thereabout, was the house of a widow, whose name was Meredith. She had been the wife of a man in good circumstances, but at his death she was left with a house filled with furniture, some little loose cash, and several daughters, marriageable and unmarriageable, this being all Mr. Meredith had to leave.

There could be but one way of obtaining a living — at least, but one that suggested itself to her, which was to turn lodging-house keeper of the better sort. Her children had been well educated, that is, sufficiently so, to pass off in life, in decent society, without any particular remark.

As she was well calculated for the object she had in view, it was no wonder that she succeeded in her undertaking, and appeared to do very well.

About this time an arrival occurred at an hotel not very far from this spot, which caused a communication to pass to Mrs. Meredith, who had been recommended lodgers from the hotel, when any of the inmates desired to be accommodated, and wished for a place with all the comforts of a home, and domestic attention.

"Mrs. Meredith," said the head waiter of the hotel, "I wish to have a word in private with you."

"With greatest pleasure, Mr. Jones," said Mrs. Meredith, who was extremely civil to the waiter; "will you be pleased to sit down."

"I have not the time, I thank you — I have not time; but I have run over to you to inform you we have an old invalid colonel at our place, who seems as if he did not know what he wanted; he wants some kind of lodging — he don't like the hotel — whether there is some genteel family, whose kind attentions would soothe his disorders, and, I suppose, his temper."

"Oh, poor gentleman," said Mrs. Meredith; "how unfortunate he should suffer — is he rich?"

"Yes, I believe so — very rich, he's a colonel in the India service; he's been a fine man, but he has had some hard knocks. I have seen more rickety matters than he before today, and he will do very well. I told him I knew where there was a lady who occasionally admitted an inmate to her house, which was a large one, but she must be satisfied that her lodger is a gentleman.

"'Has she any family?' he inquired; 'because I hate to go where there's nobody but the lady of the house, because she can't always attend upon me, read to me, and the like of that.'"

"Goodness me, what an odd man!"

"Yes, but he pays well; a retired colonel — large fortune. You know that these East Indians expect I don't know what; they are even fed by beautiful young black virgins."

"The wretch!"

"Oh, dear, no; it's the custom of the country; so, you see, he's been humored, and it will be necessary yet to humor him, if you mean to have him for your lodger. I expect he'll only be troublesome; but, when they pay for trouble, why, it's all profit."

"Very true," replied Mrs. Meredith; "is he a single man?"

"Yes, oh, yes; I believe he has never been married; has had so much to do in India, that he had nothing to do with marriages."

"Where does he come from?"

"India. I believe he had a very fine palace of his own, at Put-tytherapore, so I'm told. Lord, he seems to think nothing of these parts — but he's an odd man; however, as he pays well, he'll make a good lodger anywhere."

"Well, you may tell him, Mr. Jones, that we have a fine suite of rooms for his accommodation on the first floor, and bed rooms — every attention he can wish. You know our terms, Mr. Jones, I think — but I may as well tell you — five guineas a-week."

"Five guineas a-week, eh?"

"Yes; that is moderate, when you come to consider what a trouble and an expense it will be to get such things as will please the palate of an Indian."

"It is a trouble, certainly."

"And, besides that, he will have such a place and furniture as he seldom meets with in London; besides, from what you say, there will be little trouble in attending to him by myself and daughters, and you know I have several."

"Exactly — exactly; that is the thing he seems to desire; you will, therefore, have a preference over any one else who may have anything that he wants — a kind of domestic hearth; he has none of his own, you see."

"Has he no friends?"

"None living, I dare say; besides, he would hardly like to trust himself along with relations, who would poison him for the sake of his money; and, if he have any living, he may know nothing of them, where they are, or anything else, and they would be as strangers to him, for he would not be able to recognize them — but I must go now. Five guineas — that includes all?"

"Yes; all, except wines and liquors, you know."

"Very well, I'll let him know; and, perhaps, you'll be in the way, in case he should come round this evening to examine the place."

"Do you think there is any chance of his coming in tonight."

"Really, I cannot tell; he may, or may not, just as he pleases — he is an odd fish; but, good Mrs. Meredith, I will talk to him."

The waiter left; and Mrs. Meredith sat in her parlor, which was her own private apartment, which she and her daughters usually retired to and received their own friends. Here they remained, in some degree kept in continual expectation; nothing was said, for some time, by either mother or daughter, for there was but one at home at that time.

"Do you know, Margaret," she said, "we are likely to have a new lodger?"

"Indeed, ma?"

"Yes, my dear; he is a fidgety old man, a colonel from India; he is vastly rich, I am given to understand, and will require all the attentions of a relative. He will pay very handsomely; in fact, my dear, he will keep us all with a little care and management."

"Well, ma, the men ought to do so, the creatures! — what are they for, if they don't. I'm sure, if ever I come to marry, which I am sure I shan't, and if I found that he didn't find me in all I wanted, wouldn't I lead him a life! — I rather think I would," said the amiable child; "I'd never let him know peace night nor day. It would be useless for him to tell me misfortune had deprived him of means; that would do for me. Oh, dear, no; a married man has no right to meet misfortunes; indeed, he deserves to be punished for having a wife at all under such circumstances."

"A very proper spirit, my dear; but you must never let such a thing as that pass your lips, because it would be very likely to cause you to lose a chance; the men are so fastidious now a-days, and they think they win us, when we angle for, and catch them."

And this lodger, ma?"

"Oh, he's, as I told you, a rich old East Indian."

At this moment, a coach drove up to the door, and a tremendous double rap was played off upon the door, as if it had been committed by a steam-engine; so loud and so long was the application for the admittance, that both mother and daughter started.

"Dear me, that must be him," said the mother; "yes, a coach and all — there — there, I declare."

"What, ma?"

"Why, look at that girl next door out in the balcony; there's Miss Smith — that girl is always trying to attract some person or other; and the men affect to believe that she is beautiful; for my part, I think a girl of seventeen ought to have more modesty."

"The hussy!" said the young lady, contemptuously.

The servant now entered to inform her that a gentleman had called about the apartments.

"Ask him up stairs," said Mrs. Meredith; and she prepared to follow the colonel so soon as she heard he was ascending the stairs, which was a slow job to him, as he walked lame, with a gold headed cane.

When Mrs. Meredith came to the room, she saw a tall gentleman; his height was lost, on account of him stooping; he wore a green shade over one eye, and he had one arm in a sling; besides which, as we have before related, he was rather lame.

"Not so bad as I thought for," muttered Mrs. Meredith, to herself, as she curtseyed to his salute.

"I have been recommended to seek here a lodging, ma'am. I do not know if I am correct in believing you have such as I want."

"This, sir, is the sitting-room; it is a very handsome one, and above what is visually offered at a lodging-house. The fact is, sir, the house was never furnished for letting, but for our own private occupation; there-fore, it has all of the comforts of a private residence."

"That is what I chiefly want. You see, I do not care to undertake the trouble of setting up an establishment myself. I am alone, I may say; therefore it is I seek such a lodging as comes nearest to what I should myself choose if I were to make a home of my own."

"Precisely, sir. There is the back drawing-room, and a bed room up-stairs."

"Oh, very good; I need, I presume, make no inquiry as to what kind of table you keep; the best, I dare say. I was informed of the price you asked."

"Yes; we consider that quite moderate, sir."

"I dare say," said the Indian, looking about the place with an air of curiosity; "I dare say."

"Yes, sir; you see the advantages we offer are much above the usual run. Besides, you are an invalid, and will require extra attention."

"Yes; there is much truth in that; I have used to it, and therefore you will see that I bargain for it; but, at the same time, you will not find me difficult to please, I flatter myself; but we shall know more of each other the longer we are together."

"Certainly, sir. I can assure you, that should you take the apartments, nothing on my part, or my daughters', will be wanting to make your stay agreeable."

The stranger examined the appearance of the room, and the others, and then, after much conversation with them, he agreed to take the lodgings, and to come into them on the morrow, as he was extremely particular as to well-aired beds, and should require them all to be re-aired.

"And now, madam, before I finally agree to come in, will you show me the means of escape, if any, in case of fire. I am anxious about that; I have read so many calamities arising from that cause of late in London that I am somewhat nervous about it, though I am so much of an invalid that I should hardly be able to avail myself of it."

"You shall see, sir," said Mrs. Meredith; "we have ample and safe accommodation in that respect. You see, here is a pair of broad steps that lead up to that door — a trap-door; and here is another, that opens upon the leads at the top of the house."

The colonel made shift to walk up, and to look over the house-tops; there was a sea of chimneys and pantiles, at the same time they were all easy of access on this side of the street; so there was no danger from fire, and each house there was similarly provided.

"Well, madam, I think I may say that this affair is concluded. I will leave you my card, and, if you think proper, you can obtain what information you desire of me at the hotel."

"I am quite satisfied, sir," said the landlady, as she took the card that was proffered her, and also a bank-note which he offered her, in token of his taking possession of the lodgings.

Mrs. Meredith curtseyed, and the colonel left the apartment, and descended the staircase with great deliberation, for he could not go very swiftly; he was lame, and one arm was up in a sling, and therefore he had not the free use of his limbs.

As he came down the stairs, and when near the mat, Margaret, the eldest daughter, came out and passed into the back parlor, for no other ostensible purpose than that of seeing the stranger, whose eye was instantly, but only momentarily, fixed upon her; but it was enough; they both saw each other, and had a glance at the features, and Margaret disappeared.

The stranger stepped into the coach, and, as the door was being shut, he looked up to the windows of the next house, where the young lady, nothing daunted, still sat at the window; and so little was she interested with her neighbor's affairs, that she barely bestowed a momentary glance upon the coach or its occupant, whose solitary optic took notice of her, and then the

Jehu drove away with his rumbling vehicle.

"Well, I never saw such impudence, in my life!" said Mrs. Meredith, as she came to the windows-windows, which happened to bow outwards, and gave her a better opportunity of watching her neighbors to the right and left of her.

"What is the matter, ma'?" inquired her daughter.

"Why, there's that minx still up yonder. I declare if she didn't stare at the colonel; he saw her, and noticed her, too. Well, I wouldn't have had her there today for a trifle; he will think he has got into a bad neighborhood, seeing her so bold. Really, now, she lays herself open to all kinds of imputations. I do not mean to say any evil of her; but, really, if she will do that now, what will she not do by-and-bye? I am sorry she has no one to advise her better."

"I am sure she is old enough to know better," rejoined the daughter. "I am quite sure she's no beauty, and, if she wants to catch any of the men, she won't be successful in that manner; unless, indeed, she doesn't care whom she picks up with."

"Oh, that is, I fear, too often the case with young girls with weak intellects. But did you see our new lodger, my dear?"

"Yes, ma'."

"And what did you think of him?" inquired Mrs. Meredith, with an amiable whine, and a gentle rubbing of hands.

"Think, ma', think — what can I think of a man whom I have hardly seen, ma'? He only passed me; I could not recollect him again if I tried."

"Ah, well, my dear, you know best. I can always recollect people whom I have once seen? He is a very fine man — at least, he has been; he has lost much of his height, for he is lame, and stoops much; but still he has been a handsome man."

"One eye, only, ma', I think."

"Yes, my dear, one eye, as you say; but I think a remarkably keen one, too. He's quite the gentleman, too; he's been used to command, you can see that. These military men have an air about them that you cannot mistake; and even this gentleman, though, you see, wounded and lame, yet he has the air of an officer about him."

"He may have, ma'; but, you know, if he have the air of a general, with nothing else, it would buy a very poor dinner."

"So it would, my dear. You certainly are an extraordinary girl, Margaret, a very extraordinary girl, and will be the making of your family. Only suppose you should marry this rich colonel, what then, eh? I only say, suppose you were to marry him? — because it isn't certain, yet — well, wouldn't that minx next door think you were lucky? She would bite her nails in anger."

"Yes, she would, ma'; but it may never happen. But, if she thinks to get a beau that way, she's much mistaken. I am sure she will get insulted."

"No wonder. But, Margaret, my dear, you must do your best to please this gentleman; he wants to have people about him just as if he had his own home. He has no friends or relatives; who knows what may happen yet?"

"No, ma'; we don't know what may happen, and I will do my best to please him; but I shan't court him, you know, ma'; he must do that."

"Yes, certainly, my child, he must. No; you mustn't appear anxious about it; but merely say you are pleased to have his good opinion, and you must be a little coy of everything else; for there are times when such old gentlemen are easily entrapped. But I must set about having things aired and put into order for his arrival tomorrow."

Chapter *CXXVIII.*

THE NEW LODGER. – A NIGHT ALARM. – A MYSTERIOUS CIRCUMSTANCE.

*I*t was not until late the next day that Mrs. Meredith heard anything of her new lodger. All she had heard was that he would be there during the day, but whether to breakfast, dinner, or tea, she could not tell which, and now she was waiting with expectation, if not anxiety; but, at the same time, she knew she was quite sure of her lodger, because she held his bank-note.

It had been a dull day; there are many such in London, and therefore that was no singular circumstance. It was one of those dull, leaden-colored days of which you can predict nothing with certainty, or even a chance of being right; it was rather squally at times, and at others a west wind blew; not cold – at least, not particularly so; but, yet, notwithstanding the heavy appearance of the sky, there was a clear white light that made every object look more disagreeable than ordinary.

The landlady and her daughter were both on the *qui vive*, as it is called, looking out for their new lodger, whom they expected the more immediately as the evening drew on, for there was less likelihood of his coming in the middle of the day than towards the evening, and less after evening had set in than before, for he was an invalid.

It was, they thought, just about the time when he must arrive, when there could only be the uncertainty of a few minutes. The whole house was in order; nothing was left to chance; Mrs. Meredith herself had gone over the whole place, and took especial pains to find all sorts of fault with the unfortunate drudge who did the work, of course, aided by the mother and daughter; but such aid was distressing, because she had to wait upon both, and do her own work as well.

However, all was in readiness, and they were looking out at every coach from between the blinds. The sound of wheels was enough to cause them to start, when suddenly a coach drove up to the door, upon which had been carefully packed several leather boxes and portmanteaus.

"Here he is," said the daughter; "here he is."

"Yes; and, as I am alive," said Mrs. Meredith, as she cast her eye upwards towards the next house, "as I am alive, there is that girl again. I do believe that she does it on purpose. It is done to aggravate me, and to attract attention from the men. The hussy!"

There was now no time to lose, the knocker at the door giving pretty clear indication that instant attention upon their part was requisite, and up jumped Mrs. Meredith and her daughter Margaret. Immediately the servant opened the door into the passage, the coach door was opened, the steps let clattering down, and Colonel Deverill entered the house.

"Will you walk into the parlor, colonel," inquired Mrs. Meredith, "until your boxes are all in, and you see they are all correct? There is a good fire."

"Thank you, madam," said the colonel, with some difficulty walking along. "I am scarcely so well able to walk as I was yesterday."

"Ah! colonel, you must have suffered much. But I am glad the parlor is so handy — it will save you the walk up stairs at present, until you are quite recovered from your fatigue. Pray be seated, colonel, by the fire. The man shall bring them in, and lay them before the door."

"Thank you," said the colonel, and he sat down in a large easy chair, having first dropped his cloak, which was a large blue military cloak, lined with white, with a fur collar, and looked extremely rich and handsome; beneath which he wore an officer's undress frock, covered over with a profusion of braid.

The boxes and portmanteaus were brought in and laid down so that the colonel could see them; and, when that was done, the coachman made his demand, which excited an exclamation of horror from Mrs. Meredith, and a declaration that she thought hackney coachmen were the greatest impostors and extortioners under the sun. There never was such a set as hackney coachmen — never!

"Saving lodging-house keepers, ma'am — axing your pardon for saying so. Not that I means any offence, only I lived in one once, and ought to know summat."

The colonel, however, made no remark, but, pulling out an embroidered purse, which appeared to full of gold, he paid the man his demand.

"Thank you, your honor; you are one of the right sort, and no mistake." So saying, the coachman walked away, jinking the money as he walked along the passage, until he came to the door where the girl was standing, and then, giving her a knowing wink, and jerking his head backwards, he said, —

"They are a scaly lot here, ain't they, Mary?"

"Mary!" screamed Margaret.

"Yes, miss."

"Shut the door, and come away form that insolent fellow."

Slam went the door, and then the servant went down stairs, and the door-door was immediately closed, and the colonel was given into the tender mercies of the lodging-house keeper; for, though she pretended that she merely offered a genteel and presentable house for such as desired it, and could afford to pay for it, she was, in every sense of the word, a lodging-house keeper.

The colonel, however, sat very composedly in his chair, and gazed at the fire in silence; and from time to time he gazed at the mother and daughter with his one eye; he had not lost the entire use of the other, but had a green silk shade over it. He watched what went on, and replied cautiously to what was said to him, but appeared inclined to silence, and occasionally abrupt in his conversation; but this they attributed to the habit he must have been in, when abroad, of commanding.

"Will you take tea at once, colonel, or at what hour do you choose to have it?"

"I will take it at once. I am tired."

"What will you take, sir?" inquired Margaret, at one end of the table; and, placing herself in an enticing posture, she awaited the answer, expecting to be looked at.

"Coffee," said the colonel, abruptly.

There was a pause; but Margaret said nothing more, and set about doing such little matters as appeared to be an employment. But it was a mere deception — it was all done; nothing had been left undone; they had taken care of that, as the servant knew full well.

However, there was little that passed of any peculiar character on that occasion, for the evening passed off very calmly and comfortable, the colonel giving his opinion somewhat dogmatically; but that, of course was submitted to, as he was a military man and had much experience, and, moreover, he was a rich man — quite a nabob.

It is astonishing, as a general rule, what people will submit to when it comes from those who have riches at command. That fact alone seems to stamp all that is foolish and absurd, coming from such a quarter, with sense and worth.

It is in vain for any one not blessed with property to talk; his talking is nothing in comparison with what falls from the lips of the man who has property. You are talked down, and if you are obstinate, and won't be talked down, why, you are a disagreeable fellow, a dissatisfied man, and your neighbors ought to set their faces against you.

Thus, through life, he who does not submit to the wealthy, is always run down, and there is every disposition, if possible, of running him off the road altogether, no matter how great the injustice against him, and the enormity of the conduct of others; they are, as they think, justified, because he is not a genteel person; in fact, he is not evangelical.

The evening passed over, as we have said, in calmness and quiet, and Mrs. Meredith appeared to be well pleased with her lodger; and, at a moderately early hour, they separated and went to bed. The colonel retired, after taking leave of them, to his own room, complaining he was in great pain, and scarce able to walk, and so cold, he was nearly benumbed.

"This climate," he said, "is so cold, so moist, and altogether so uncomfortable, that I cannot understand how it is people ever endure it. Indeed," he continued to Mrs. Meredith, "there must be some great difference between rich and poor in their conformation, else they couldn't stand it."

Of course, Mrs. Meredith assented to the proposition, as she would have done to any other, no matter what proposition, that had been so urged by such a person.

Thus it was with the colonel, who appeared very well satisfied with his lodgings; and all parties, for so short a time, were well pleased with each other.

*T*he night was dark, that is to say, it was one of those nights in which neither moon nor stars showed themselves; no sound was heard through the streets, save the heavy step of the guardian of the night, or the midnight reveler, who might be finding his way homeward boisterously, and with scarce enough sense to enable him to take the right path.

There were clouds enough to have intercepted the moon, but there was a kind of light that was spread through them that you saw when you looked up, but which aided not the traveler below; but, then, there were countless lamps that illumined the streets.

At that time there was a man creeping over the house-tops. He had gained the housetop of Mr. Smith, the house in which resided Miss Smith, who had given so much offence to Mrs. Meredith by sitting so much out in the balcony. He stooped in the gutter, and looked cautiously around; no human being was within sight; he was alone, and no soul saw him.

Cautiously he crept towards the trap-door — it was bolted; but that was soon obviated — no sound, however, could be heard. The soft, but rotten, wood gave way under the steady pressure exerted upon the door, which at length opened.

He paused a moment or two, and listened carefully for several minutes. Then he entered the loft slowly and noiselessly, keeping as low as possible, so that he might run no risk of being observed by any one who might be passing the house, or who might be up by accident in any of the opposite houses, in consequence of illness, or any other cause.

There was a lower trap-door through which the figure passed. There could be no difficulty in passing, because that was always kept open, as it was considered to assist in ventilating the house; and then the intruder stood within the house.

He then drew himself up to his full height, and paused for some moments, as if considering the next step he would take; but then he descended to the second floor, on which were placed what are called the best bedrooms. He paused at one, gently tried the handle, and finding it turn, and the door open, he gave one look towards the stairs that he had just descended, and then he entered the apartment.

All was yet still; no sound met his ear, save the breathing of the sleeper within, who lay in a sweet sleep, and was as calm and unconscious as the blessed; perfect rest and forgetfulness had steeped the senses of the young girl, who lay in ambrosial sleep. One arm was thrown outside the clothes, and revealed, in all its symmetry, a snow-white bosom, heaving gently to the throbbing of the heart.

The intruder gazed at the young girl for some moments, and clasped his hands with trembling eagerness, and a ghastly smile played upon his terrible features, while a fearful fire shot from the eyes of one who thus disturbed the slumbers of the living.

He approached the bed, and took the hand within his own, and then the sleeper awoke. It would be impossible to describe the look of terror and horror that sat on the young girl's face.

She could not scream, she could not utter a sound; her whole faculties appeared to have been bound up for a short time. She could not even shrink from the horrible being who approached her, she was so perfectly horror-stricken with that truly horrible countenance, the glance of which seemed as if it would destroy the power of speech for ever. She shrank now, but could not move.

The creature crept closer. It seized her hand, and held it within its own; but even that could not awake her from the trance she was in. She felt a horrible sinking feeling, as though she must sink through the very flooring of the house, and yet she could not stir.

It appeared as though, so long as the hideous face was opposed to hers, so long she was unable to move; it was a species of fascination; however great the horror felt, yet there was no help for it. She could not ever shut her eyes; that boon was denied her.

What she saw cannot be described. It is by far too horrible for pen to describe. The wild horrible insanity that appeared in the eyes of the creature, with their peculiar cast, was indescribable; the only light that entered the room, at that moment, came from a lamp below, and illumined only the upper part of the room above the window sills.

The creature then stood in relief against this light, a horrible dark object, whose glaring eyeballs were too terrible ever to be forgotten.

Then, again, while he with one hand held hers, he passed his other hand up her arm, and then felt along the soft, white flesh with its cold, clammy fingers, as if it were feeling for something, or greedy of the velvet-like substance.

Still keeping the eyes fixed upon the hapless and helpless girl, he drew the arm towards him, and, leaning upon the bed, suddenly plunged his face on the arm, and held and seized it near the middle with its teeth, and then it made an attempt to suck the wound.

This, however, broke the charm, horrible and complete as it was; for the creature's hideous countenance was lost to her sight, as he plunged his face to her arm.

Shriek followed shriek in quick and rapid succession. The whole house was alarmed by the terrible shrieks that came from the apartment. She struggled, and by a sudden effort, she disengaged herself from the grasp of the fiend, and rolled, wrapped up in the bed-clothes, to the other side of the floor.

The monster still pursued her with greedy thirst for blood, and had picked her up, and again placed her on the bed, with more than mere human strength, and again sought the arm he had been deprived of by the sudden effort of the young girl.

"Help! help! Mother! father! help! help!"

The shouts rang through the house, awaking the affrighted sleepers from their repose, in a manner that may be called distressing.

It is distressing in the midst of a large city to be awoke, in the dead of the night, by loud and urgent cries of distress. It is such a contrast to the dead stillness that reigns around, and when the first cries are heard, it creates a terror and surprise that takes away all power of action.

It was not till the cries had been heard a second time that the inmates aroused themselves; the fact was, they were fearful of fire. The moment that idea floated across their minds, then, indeed, they started up, and the father of the young girl, hearing the fall, at once rushed to the room of his daughter. He arrived but in time; the hideous monster, being affrighted by the footsteps approaching him, turned from his blood-stained feast, and hid himself beneath the drapery, as the father entered the room.

"Mary," he said, "Mary! Mary! what means this — what can be the matter — are you hurt — how come you in this disorder?"

"Oh, God! that thing from the grave has been sucking my blood from my veins. See — see yonder — he moves! Watch him — note him, father!"

Believing she raved, her father paid no attention to what she did say, but continued to regard her with sorrow and regret, for he believed it to be a sudden attack of mania; but seeing the curtains move, he turned his head, and at once divined it to be the cause of his daughter's alarm.

The glance was but momentary; but he saw the figure of a man who was escaping from the apartment by the door by which he had at that moment entered.

"Help!" he shouted — "help — thieves — murder!"

And as he shouted, he rushed after the figure that was flying towards the top of the house. By this time the house was filled up with people, and the noise up stairs had caused the servants below to rise confused and thoroughly terrified by the sounds they heard, and the cries of their master.

At that moment, one of those watchful guardians of the night passed by the house, and was immediately hailed by the unfortunate people below, who were afraid to go up stairs to offer any assistance, lest they might be knocked back again, which fear stopped all aid from below.

"Hilloa! what's the matter now?" inquired the worthy guardian of the night.

"Oh, I don't know — goodness knows. You had better go up and see. I'll come up after you. Don't be afraid; I'll come up after you, if you'll go first."

"Stop a moment while I spring my rattle," said the worthy functionary; who thereupon gave an alarming peal upon his instrument, and then he entered the house, with instructions to the servant to run down stairs and let any of his party in that might come up.

Then the guardian of the night hastened up stairs with all the haste he could, and came up just in time to pick Mr. Smith up, who was lying stunned at the foot of the stairs.

The fact was, Mr. Smith had pursued his adversary too quickly, and finding he could not get off, he turned round and felled him to the earth, like an ox. It was just at this juncture when the charley came up stairs, and in another moment Mr. Smith recovered.

"What's the matter?" inquired the watchman; "is the house on fire."

"No, no; the vampyre — the vampyre!"

"Eh — what? Never heard on 'im afore — never seed him."

"Quick — quick! he has gone up stairs. Quick — after him!" said Mr. Smith, as he ran up the stairs, and was quickly followed by the watchman and some others who now crowded about, having had time to dress themselves and come to Mr. Smith's aid; and they now crowded to the house-top, for they saw the trap-door was unfastened, though it had been hastily pushed to. This they opened, and then looked on the house-top, first one way, and then another.

"He ain't here," said the watchman, "and we mustn't expect to find him here; he wouldn't wait for us, you may depend upon that. We had better search along the house-tops till we see him, or find some of the other traps open, and then you may guess where he has gone."

"The difficulty is, which way did he go?" said Mr. Smith.

"Oh, I saw him go that way," said another watchman, who came up stairs, having been first attracted by the sounds of the rattle, and then, looking up at the house, he saw the figure of a man stealing, with great rapidity of motion, across the house-tops.

"There I lost him, then," he said. "I didn't see him after that spot; but he may have gone further, for all I can say to the contrary. But we shall soon see."

"This trap-door is open," said the other watchman, as he pulled aside Mrs. Meredith's trap-door, which had only been pushed to. "We had better go in here, and see if he isn't gone somewhere into the house, and hiding himself until all is quiet, and then he will make off if left alone."

Chapter CXXIX.

THE UNSUCCESSFUL PURSUIT. – MR. SMITH'S DISAPPOINTMENT, AND THE TESTIMONY OF MRS. MEREDITH.

Mrs. Meredith and her daughters had long sunk into deep sleep before the events just narrated took place in her neighbor's house. There was a perfect stillness; the whole house appeared as though there were no living soul within it, all was so still and quiet.

Presently, however, there was a terrific sound; it was like that of a human being falling and bumping down stairs, and then there was a great deal of shouting and calling, and Mrs. Meredith opened her eyes and trembled in her bed, while her daughter Margaret, who upon the occasion slept with her, was likewise as frightened.

"What is th – that?" she stammered, with some difficulty.

"Oh, hear, I cannot think. Thieves – murderers, I dare say. Oh, merciful Heaven! what shall we do – where shall I go? We shall be murdered!"

Both females trembled in their beds, and were quite unable to move, breaking out in a profuse sweat from fear; and yet the noise came nearer and nearer, and there were many persons evidently in the house; their numbers were so numerous that they evidently didn't care to conceal themselves.

The fact was this: when Mr. Smith and his party found the trap-door open, they descended into the house, the watchman leading the way; but in going down the ladder, his foot slipped, and he came with a dreadful thump on the landing, and fortunately he rolled up against the servant girl's door, instead of down stairs. The door flew open, and the girl was too terrified to speak for some moments.

At length the watchman having got up, he made for the bed, upon which the girl jumped up, and began to scream out for help in piteous tones.

"Come, come — don't be frightened," said the watchman; "get up and show us over the house."

"Well, I'm sure!" said the girl, who had recovered some of her assurance, for the coat, stick, and lantern of the watchman at once assured her that she was in no immediate danger whatever. "Well, I'm sure! to think of coming in a female's room in this manner. You ought to be ashamed of yourself, you old wretch, you ought!"

"No names. If you don't get up and show us over, and call your master —"

"I ain't got a master."

"Well, your mistress, then — we will go ourselves, and we'll soon make short work of it. Come, come, no nonsense. We will dress you ourselves."

"You monster! Go out of the room, can't you? Have you no decency left you? I'll get up; but I'll lay a complaint before the lord mayor, and he shall tell you a different tale to this. I'm ashamed of you, and so you ought to be of yourselves."

However, during this energetic remonstrance, she contrived to shuffle on some things, and when she was ready, she came down to her mistress's door, and then began to hammer and kick at it, saying, —

"Oh, Mrs. Meredith, here's sich a lot of men in the house. Do come out, mem. I don't know what's the matter; but they'll break into your room, as they broke into mine."

"What do they want, Mary?"

"Don't know, mem."

"There is some one escaped into your house that has broken into the next house, and your trap-doors on the roof were open."

"Gracious me!" said Mrs. Meredith — "gracious me! Show them over the place, Mary. We will get up in a few moments, and come to you. Margaret, my dear, get up; some housebreakers have got into the house, and we shall all be murdered in our sleep if we don't find them. Oh, dear, dear! what will become of us? What will our new lodger say to this disturbance?"

Margaret made no reply, but began to dress herself, while the party began their search; and Mr. Smith hastened back to his daughter, to understand the nature of the attack that had been made upon her, and whether she were any better than she was when he left her.

However, when he came to hear what was the real cause of her terror, to find the marks on her arm, and the certainty that nothing had been lost or moved, he was perfectly staggered, and hastened back after the party he had left, to make some further attempt to follow the miscreant, and to discover, if possible, his retreat, and bring him to justice for the vile attack he had made.

When he returned, he met Mrs. Meredith coming out of her room, she having hastily dressed herself, followed by her daughter.

"Oh! Mr. Smith — Mr. Smith, what is the meaning of all this disturbance? Here are a number of strange men, who have forced themselves into my house, and whether their object is our property or our lives, we cannot tell. What can I do, Mr. Smith?"

"You have nothing to fear, ma'am."

"Nothing to fear, sir! Why, is not such an occurrence something to be feared for its own sake alone?"

"Yes, ma'am, it is very disagreeable, I am willing to admit; but I presume you would not give refuge to a vampyre?"

"A what, sir?"

"A vampyre, madam. I know not how to explain it to you, but I have to assure you my daughter has been attacked in her sleep by the midnight blood-sucker from the graves. Oh! God, that such a thing should happen in my family. I would not have believed it, had the same been related to me from anybody else."

"It must have been the night mare," suggested Mrs. Meredith.

"Would to Heaven it had been so; but I came to her assistance, and saw him as he fled from my daughter's bedside, and I followed him to the roof, and he was lost on your house, and your trap-door was open, and we presumed he went in here."

"The door was bolted when we went to bed last night," said Margaret.

"Yes," responded her mother; "we always have that bolted every night, for it is our only protection from that side of the house; but no one can be here; we have no man in the house save our lodger, and invalid and quite a gentleman."

"Can we see him?"

"I should think not, because he is an invalid; he's a colonel in the East India service, and will, no doubt, be very angry at such a distur-bance, and much more so when he finds he is wanted. I am really much shocked at this disturbance, which is the more unfortunate as it is the first night he has slept here."

"I must see him."

"Must, Mr. Smith — must! I cannot permit anything of the kind to be said in my house. I give you permission to look for him over the house, but I can't give any such permission with what my lodgers possess — it is not in my power to do so if I had the inclination."

While this was going on, the house had been rummaged over and over, and then a party of them, with Mr. Smith, came to the colonel's bedroom; a close traveling cap and a dressing-gown were found on the mat before the door.

"Oh!" said Mr. Smith, as he picked it up, "this appears very much like what I saw the figure was dressed up in — something like robes, and this would serve the purpose."

"Ah!" said the watchman, "we shall have him now."

"But the gentleman is an invalid; he can hardly walk up stairs, much less can he be scrambling over house-tops," said Mrs. Meredith. "You must surely all have been dreaming. Something has disagreed with you, and the result has been visions of which you can of course find no trace."

"Not quite that, either," said one of the watchmen, "for we saw him getting away, and he made for your trap-door, where I missed him. I could not see any more of him among the chimneys, or something of that sort, but I thought he came in here, and found your door open."

"And you saw him come in?" said Mrs. Meredith.

"I can't say I saw him come in," said the man; "I couldn't see through a brick-wall and a stack of chimneys which were in the way, but I felt certain he must have come in here."

"Well, this is very strange — very singular."

"The dressing-gown, too," said Mr. Smith, "is dusty and dirty all over — at least in places where it appears to have come in contact with anything dirty — possibly the roof of the house; certainly something of that sort has happened. It looks very much like it."

"And the cap sits close to the head; that is dirty."

"But it is dry dirt," said Mr. Smith, "and of the same character; we had better see this lodger of yours, Mrs. Meredith, and with your permission I will knock."

As Mr. Smith spoke he gave two or three loud knocks at the door, which were not answered for some time. But they were speedily repeated, and then a peremptory voice exclaimed, —

"In the name of goodness, what is the meaning of all this disturbance? Is the house broken into, or is it a resort for thieves? Be it as it may, if I am disturbed in this way, and you don't instantly get out of the way and make less noise, I'll fire through the door. I have loaded pistols by my side, and I will not submit to this shameful disturbance."

A the sound of these words, the two watchmen were much disturbed, and immediately stepped back so hastily as nearly to overthrow Mrs. Meredith and her daughter; but Mr. Smith, after a step or two backwards, resumed his place by the door, and exclaimed, —

"I have not come here, sir, to be frightened; some strange circumstances have just happened, and I must beg you'll open your door to explain them."

"And who the devil are you?"

"My name is Smith, sir. I live next door, and my daughter has been attacked by a vampyre. I know not what nature the creature must possess, but it has shocking propensities — there are evidences at your door which make it appear he has got into your room."

"It would be very foolish in him to so anything of the sort," said the colonel, "for, in the first place, I will not suffer annoyance in any shape; and besides, I have loaded pistols for his reception. Wait till I am dressed, and then I will come out to you."

"I am sure the colonel will be very much offended by this conduct, which is very shameful; people's houses broken open and entered in this manner, and people's rest broken so. I am quite ashamed of my neighbors — quite."

"Really we have strong suspicions — strong grounds of suspicion, too, against that lodger of yours; look at that dressing-gown and cap, the open trap-door, and all — really I can't help thinking there is something very suspicious in all this."

"Yes," said the watchman; "I know there's nobody else in the house. I've been all over it, and it's very strange to me if he ain't the man."

"Well," said Margaret Meredith, "it seems as if you are most willing to accuse those who are quite incapable of doing what you accuse them of. This gentleman was barely able to get up stairs without assistance; besides, he could not have gone up stairs without some one being awoke by the noise. It's my opinion that it is a piece of impertinence altogether."

"So I think, my dear," said Mrs. Meredith.

"I am a father, Mrs. Meredith," said Mr. Smith, "and I have my daughter's safety and happiness at heart. I am sure there's much, too, very suspicious. You wouldn't like your daughter's blood sucked out of her arms. I am sure I don't, nor does she."

"Oh, botheration!" said Margaret; "who ever heard of such stuff? I'm sure I never did, except in some book of improbabilities, and nothing more; but here is Colonel Deverill."

At that moment Colonel Deverill opened the door, and then retired a little into his room, saying as he did so, in a very angry voice, but, at the same time, endeavoring to be courteous, —

"You can come in, now; but I am quite at a loss to understand the nature of this disturbance; the house don't appear to be on fire; and that is the only contingency in my mind that will justify such a disturbance. What is the matter, Mrs. Meredith?"

"I can hardly tell you, sir. I have been disturbed by finding a party of people in my house; it is most amazing to me how they came in."

"I will tell you, sir," said Mr. Smith. "My daughter has been terrified by the appearance of some one in her bed-room, who attempted to suck her blood from the veins of her arm. I don't know what to say about it."

"I am sure I don't," said Colonel Deverill; "but I must say it's a most unpleasant affair for those who have nothing to do with it. It is a pity your domestic afflictions should call you out in this manner; take my advice, sir; go home, else you'll catch cold."

"You may repent making a jest of this —"

"I never repent anything, sir. I regret I am so unnecessarily disturbed; and it appears to me, your intrusion here is most unwarrantable."

"Is this your dressing-gown, sir?"

"Yes, it is."

"Well, then, how did it come here, and in this state?" inquired Mr. Smith, triumphantly.

"I don't know — I didn't put it there; but I suppose it must have fallen accidentally; it would not have been thrown there willingly," said the colonel, deliberately.

"Well, I don't know," said Mr. Smith, "but it strikes me you've been on the tiles this evening."

"My good sir, if you don't leave my apartment, it may happen I may forget my pains and lameness, and fling you out of the window. If this had happened in India instead of here, you would have had a particularly sharp knife inserted between your ribs, or have been thrown into a well. But I know nothing, of this matter, which appears so strange, as to be beyond all reason; neither experience nor common sense at all throw any light upon the matter; be advised, sir, and retire, and allow honest people and invalids to sleep the night out."

Mr. Smith looked very blank, and, unable to comprehend all that had passed, he could not tell what to think; he could not urge the matter further, for he was met by real contempt and perfect self-assurance on the part of the colonel, who moved about the room very lame, while his hand was in a sling, and a green shade was placed over his eyes.

"You see," said Mrs. Meredith, "you must be very entirely mistaken. Colonel Deverill, we are sure, is quite unable to run about over house-tops, even had he the inclination to do so, which is really absurd. It must be at least a great mistake on your part."

"Yes, I am sure, too, Colonel Deverill could not have left the house without our knowing it; indeed, it is a very silly affair, and has been a great nuisance, to say the least of it. I wonder Mr. Smith doesn't know better than to break into peaceable people's houses."

"But I did not do so."

"How came you here, then?"

"I followed some one else; the place was open; and yet you say it was shut at night, and you usually kept it so. How do you account for that?"

"I cannot do so, unless some neglect took place, or else you must have forced it open."

"Oh, no, ma'am," said the watchman; "I can swear Muster Smith didn't do that; it was open, and I found it so, so there's that to be accounted for; and then there's the togs a lying outside here, that's to be accounted for; so, you see, it's a werry suspicious case."

"You are a very stupid fellow," said the colonel, "a very idiot, if you imagine people are to be held responsible because a dressing-gown happens to fall down. I do not know but I shall proceed with this matter myself; it seems to me you have committed a trespass, to say the least of it. I can pledge my word, as a man of honor and a soldier, I have not left my room; indeed, these ladies know I could not do so; and their testimony would be ample in a court of justice, and to a gentleman."

"Yes, that is no more than the truth," said Mrs. Meredith, who was by no means pleased with the disturbance; and because she had no sympathy for the young lady who sat in the balcony to the annoyance of herself and daughter.

"And I can bear witness to the same," said Miss Meredith. "I think it is quite time Mr. Smith returned to his own place, and see what is the matter there; perhaps the person he saw may have passed him, and gone back again into his own house."

Mr. Smith lingered, looked wistfully, as if his doubts were not cleared off; but yet the testimony was so clear and so strong, that he could not dispute it; and, however unwillingly he was compelled to acknowledge, there were some matters that he could not dispute, though he was unable to solve them; and he and those with him returned from their unsatisfactory search.

Chapter CXXX.

A BREAKFAST SCENE. – A MATCH-MAKING MOTHER.

*T*he next day there was some anxiety on the part of Mrs. Meredith, to ascertain how far her new lodger might have been disturbed by this event; and in what temper of mind he felt upon the occasion. It is usual in all lodgings, to have some little regard to the lodger's comforts for some days, perhaps a week or two, and then things are allowed to take their chance; and if the lodger complains, he gets for an answer, that they take a vast deal of pains to oblige him, and intimate that he is a peculiarly lucky man for having become a lodger at that place; and you would have been worse off if you had gone elsewhere, which, of course, you don't believe, though they tell you so.

It is an old and favorite saying, that a new broom sweeps clean; and, in time, an old one becomes very nearly useless. So it is with lodging-house keepers; the longer you remain, the more inattentive they become, until you get wearied, and are compelled to leave, and then you get some scurvy insolence, and your landlady eventually believes she is an ill-used woman.

But, in the present instance, Mrs. Meredith had other hopes and fears than those of a mere lodging-house keeper. Not that she had formed any plan in her own mind; but she had some floating idea that there was seldom such a chance turned up, because the colonel had evidently no relations; and who could tell what, in the chapter of accidents, might happen?

"I am quite grieved," she said to her daughter, "it should have happened this night. What could be the meaning of the disturbance, I can't think. Now, it's very tiresome things will happen so cross as this, that I don't know what to think of it."

"It really appears as if it was done on purpose."

"It does; but I am sorry for it, because it would seem as though we were liable to some kind of interruption at all times, for they generally expect attention at the first, if at no other time; and he may think this is a bad beginning, at all events."

"But we shall convince him that we shall not treat him neglectfully, ma'."

"No, my dear; but these Indians are strange-tempered people, and when they once take a fancy, there is no knowing what they may do; and there is no knowing what a dislike taken at such an occurrence might produce, and likes and dislikes are taken without rhyme or reason."

"Yes, ma', so they are; and that is the reason why you took such a dislike to young Willis, for he was as nice a young man as I have seen."

"Nice, my dear — nice! I don't see why he was nice, unless it was because he was presumptuous, and had no money," said the amiable parent.

"He was not rich, ma' —"

"He was positively poor, Margaret," interrupted the mother, "and therefore it was absolutely necessary to discourage such persons; for, if they do no good, they are sure to be productive of mischief; for their hanging about, you know, deters others from coming forward who have means."

"He was very handsome."

"'Handsome is as handsome does,' my dear. You'll find that is a motto through life, that will carry weight at any time. All the good looks in the world would never put a gown on your back, or a sixpence in your purse, recollect; besides, he was not handsome."

"You are prejudiced against the young man. Not that I care anything about him, though he was a very agreeable and nice young man; so it's no use in saying that he wasn't."

"Well, my dear, it doesn't much matter; this is a matter of opinion. What do you think of our colonel? He is a fine man, and a rich one besides."

"He is tall, I admit, but stoops a great deal; is very lame; one eye much worse than the other, and one arm in a sling. Well, I can't see much beauty in all that; much out of repair, you must admit, ma'."

"Yes; Colonel Deverill has seen some service, and his misfortunes are so many points of honor; they are like so many medals which speak of his worth. Besides that, he is a most gentlemanly and pleasant man. I don't know that I ever spoke to a more fascinating man."

"That might be at times; but then that was evidently a constraint upon his natural temper, because he every now and then broke out abruptly about something or other, which proves that he has an abrupt and imperious temper, not to say savage and snappish."

"There you are clearly unjustifiable, my dear Margaret. The colonel, you see, is a military man, and used to command, and therefore it is a very usual occurrence, and not a matter of disposition at all; but what can that matter when you come to consider his wealth?"

"There is certainly room for congratulation there," said Margaret.

"Indeed, my child, there is room for congratulation; and I am convinced there is happiness where there is a fortune, for that will obtain all you want, and, when you obtain all you want, what can you be otherwise than entirely happy? — therefore, riches are happiness."

"Yes; there is much truth in all that, ma'," said Margaret; "and all I hope is, that I might obtain a fortune; then I would make you comfortable, ma'."

"I am sure you would, Margaret. My whole life has been spent in shifts to maintain you and bring you up in a manner that would enable you to become a fortune; which, thanks to my care, example, and precept, you are fully equal to at any moment it may become your lot."

"Yes, ma'; I feel that I was born to command, and the lady of a colonel would not be a bit too high in rank for my ambition or deserts."

"Indeed, it would not, my dear; but now listen to me. You know, my dear, I never plan anything but what is for your benefit. Now, I am given to understand that Colonel Deverill has no relatives at all, and I think hardly any friends, and we can make ourselves quite necessary to him — in fact, perfect friends to him. He will look upon us as his nearest relatives, and he may take a fancy to you, as you may easily induce him. Old men like flattery, there is no doubt, and that kind of flattery which is called attention. Wait upon him most assiduously, and read to him, and all that kind of thing, my dear."

"Yes; I know, ma'."

"And then, dear, if you mind what you are about, the colonel and all his wealth may be yours before six months are over, or I am no witch."

"Hush! I hear him stirring."

"He's coming down stairs; there he is in the drawing-room; I hear him over head. Go up stairs, my dear, and inquire when he will choose to have his breakfast."

"Yes, ma'," said the young lady, who betrayed an extraordinary desire to obey her parent, a matter not equally to be said of all young ladies, nor of this one upon many occasions; but, then, this was one that was quite agreeable to her own feelings, which explains the secret.

Colonel Deverill had, indeed, descended, and was seated in the drawing-room, with his feet on the fender and his head leaning on his hand, and his elbow on the table, when Margaret entered. He appeared to be thoughtful and unwell; he had, perhaps, passed a bad night, or the interruption had robbed him of his sleep, which to an invalid was the more severely felt.

Good morning, colonel," said Margaret, advancing. "I hope the disturbance that so inopportunely took place, did not have the effect of destroying your night's rest."

"Indeed, it did do so to a very great extent," replied the colonel, "though not entirely; but still it makes one very poorly, gives one the headache, and causes a sense of lassitude and fatigue to oppress the body, which, added to the weariness incident to such cases, makes one very uncomfortable."

"I am sorry you have been so discomposed, and so is my ma'. She really is grieved; but you see, sir, it was a matter so entirely beyond any control, that she cannot be blamed for it, though it happened, most unfortunately, at a time when it was least wanted, or most to be avoided."

"True — very true. I can imagine all that. I am not unjust enough to blame you for it. I could no more help it than you could, and I dare say you were none the better for such a disagreeable disturbance; I am not, I am very certain.

"No, sir, I am not. When would you please to breakfast?"

"As soon as I can have it," replied the colonel.

"You can have it at once."

"Then be pleased to let me have it. I have the use of but one arm entirely; may I beg your aid in making tea for me?"

"With pleasure, sir."

Margaret immediately left the room, and informed her mother of what had passed upon the occasion; and when the breakfast was laid, and all things ready, Margaret Meredith sat down with Colonel Deverill to breakfast. Before, however, they had gone far, he inquired if she had breakfasted.

"No, I have not."

"And your mother — has she breakfasted?"

"No, sir, she has not."

"Then give her my compliments, and I shall be glad to take breakfast in her company too; for I am very poorly this morning, and company is agreeable."

This was soon effected, and in a few minutes more they all sat down, the colonel being duly waited upon by Margaret and her mother; the latter being employed in aiding the former to pay great attention to their host; for they breakfasted at his expense, as a matter of course.

"It was really a most unfortunate occurrence, that of last night," said Mrs. Meredith; "very unfortunate; because some people have a difficulty in sleeping in a strange bed; and when once awake, they cannot easily, if at all, get asleep again, and that I had great fears might have been your case."

"Not precisely," said the colonel; "but the fact is, I have seen so much hard service, that I can sleep anywhere without any effort of mine; but when one has suffered from wounds, the heats of climate, and the terrors of imprisonments in Indian prisons, one's health becomes so shattered, that one's rest is not so good as it ought to be — but that is no one's fault."

"It is a grievous misfortune," said Mrs. Meredith.

"Yes," added Margaret; "and I think there is not enough gratitude in the country towards those who so nobly defend us in our homes; to do which they must not only brave danger and death in the field of battle, but all the evils that spring from climate, insidious diseases, brought on by the exposures and hardships of a soldier's life; and then when they see them return to their own country, with wounds that ought to bring honor, glory, and sure profit, they are omitted and neglected."

The colonel sighed deeply, but said nothing.

"My dear Miss Meredith, will you fetch me my keys? — I left them in the bureau."

"Yes, sir," said the amiable young lady, who arose, and left the room.

"Your daughter is an amiable girl, Mrs. Meredith," said Colonel Deverill. "She reminds me of one who is now dead, and at whose decease I left England for India; the country became insupportable to me at that time, but she now recalls all the feelings and aspirations of youth."

"Ah! she is an amiable and good girl — though I am her mother; yet I must not do her less than justice, because it is usual to consider it partial or silly of a parent praising her own child; but she does deserve all that can be said of her."

"It is a blessing. There was the same class of beauty, and the same amiable and sensible deportment. Oh, dear! those days are gone by, indeed!"

"Who knows but they may return?"

"It is doubtful; more than doubtful — certain. I am an old man, now, Mrs. Meredith, — an old man. Yes; I have deserved some thanks at the hands of my country; and I am rich — yes, Mrs. Meredith, I am rich — very rich, I believe I may say."

"That is some reward."

"It is. But I cannot recall the past — I am no longer young — I have no young wife by my side — to soothe my pillow — to attend to my wants. No; I am an old man, as I said before, and cannot expect the attention of the young and beautiful."

"But, Colonel Deverill, you are not an old man; and as for your wounds, they are honorable."

"But my shattered constitution —"

"May be mended by care and attention, doubtless; and I am sure, while you are here, you shall want no attention we can possibly bestow."

"I thank you, Mrs. Meredith — I thank you," said the colonel.

"I only regret the disturbance you suffered last night," said Mrs. Meredith. "I am afraid want of proper rest has made you melancholy.

I knew not of such a thing, neither was I at all aware of the fact of the trap-door being open — indeed, I can't understand it."

"Nor I, ma'am. I do not clearly understand what they said; they talked of some young lady being strangled or assaulted in her sleep."

"Yes, colonel. It was in her sleep, and I cannot help thinking it must have been a dream; however, if it were not, I do not know what to think of it."

"Nor I," said the colonel, thoughtfully.

"They talked about a vampyre, and said Miss Smith had been seized by the arm; and the creature had attempted to suck the blood from the veins."

"Dear me, what a strange affair."

"Very, sir; but I never heard of such things only in books; but, goodness help us from such strange unearthly beings — have you seen any in your travels, Colonel Deverill? You have traveled in hot countries, and have seen them, I should imagine."

"Not I, Mrs. Meredith; I have seen strange things, but I never saw a vampyre, though I have heard of such things; indeed, there are many disgusting things in creation, and that is one of them. But what could be the reason they should come to that young lady above any other, I cannot conceive."

"Nor I, sir."

At this moment Margaret returned, having recovered the keys, which were not wanted; only the watchful mamma thought there was an opportunity for a little tender gag relative to the amiability of the young lady, and, therefore, it ought not to be omitted.

Moreover, she saw there was no necessity for leaving them alone yet; there would be plenty of time yet for that, and she felt assured there would be ample opportunity for the progress of the suit she now confidently anticipated must take place; for she saw, however prompt and ready the colonel might be from habit, yet there was a good deal of the willing mood about him.

"His health and weakness," she thought, "causes that; and now, while his health lasts this way, he may be secured; or, at least, the foundation laid upon which we may build our hopes. He shall want no aid of mine to help him on that way."

"Have you been long in England, colonel?" she inquired.

"Not very long."

"The voyage homeward must have been very tedious."

"It would have been, but I did not come that way. I crossed into Egypt, and came to the Mediterranean, and thence to Italy; so I varied the scene, and traveled at leisure, and got here a month before the vessel I was to have come by."

"Oh, that was much more pleasant."

"Decidedly so; and then I came to the hotel; not that I had not all proper attention paid me — but then there is no sociality there; men only surround you with whom you can hold no converse whatever."

"Certainly not, they are menials."

"And of the lowest class. However, I sought out such a place as this, where I wished to have some of the domestic comforts around me, that I might have had, had I a home of my own; some one to whom I could speak more seriously; for I am debarred the affectionate regard of near and dear female relatives."

"You must look upon us in that light, Colonel Deverill; as persons who are anxious and desirous of causing you to forget these wants by our assiduity and attention. I can speak for my daughter as myself; she will do all in her power to render your stay comfortable."

"She is young and beautiful."

"Ahem!"

"And doubtless will change such occupations to those of a more endearing character. Well, it is as it should be, and I am selfish to feel jealous. I wish I was young myself — but, enough of this. I have to express my obligation to you for the ready manner in which you came forward to speak of my being in my room last night, when that man was here and the watchmen."

"Mr. Smith?"

"Yes, that was the man; they would not have taken my word for it; however, I hope to be able to remain here until I find myself sinking to the grave; and those who act as you have began to act for me, I must and will remember at my death and afterwards."

"I do not act with such a motive, Colonel Deverill."

"No, no; I am well aware of that; but that renders it a duty in me. However, we will say no more now; I am even wearied out."

Chapter *CXXXI*.

MRS. MEREDITH'S FRIEND. – EXCHANGE OF SERVICES, AND COMPACT.

*T*here could be no doubt in the minds of both mother and daughter that there was something much resembling a moral certainty concerning the fate of the retired colonel. That he must marry was evident – he was to all intents and purposes resolved to do so. He talked of a home and domestic comfort, and all that kind of thing; therefore it would be easy to entangle him in the meshes of love; the snares of passion might be successfully set, and they would be sure to be productive of some sport, and even a stray colonel might be caught, one who, having had enough of the wars of man, might now be considered to become a fair object of attack in those of Venus.

However, there appeared much in the colonel's circumstances and disposition that laid him open to the attacks of designing matrons and maidens. He seemed to appreciate female company – was particularly well pleased with female attentions; perhaps his health required their aid more than that of any other; and he had evidently been in love, and lost the object of his earliest affections.

One great thing in Margaret Meredith's favor was, the colonel had taken it into his head that she much resembled this lady, whoever she was; and this fact, no doubt, had opened his heart towards her; and he felt a kindly, and perhaps a warmer feeling, towards her. This, they calculated, would greatly assist them in their efforts to circumvent the colonel, and cause him to capitulate upon matrimonial conditions.

"There never was so good a chance," said Mrs. Meredith, in the course of a day or two after the above scene; "there never was such a chance as the one you now have."

"What, with the colonel, ma'?"

"Yes, my love, you may depend upon it, that is a very safe speculation.

Why, he must be immensely rich. I am sure that some of the jewels I have seen on his fingers must be worth thousands of pounds. He is a very rich man, there can be no doubt."

"Yes, ma', he is very rich."

"And you will have many fine things that you have never dreamed of. Why, you will have a carriage; I should think he would never refuse you that trifle."

"He has not one now."

"Yes, that is true; he would never use it himself; and that accounts for it. But when he has a wife it is quite another matter; and one which you can easily manage when you are a wife; you can do more then than you can now. Besides, you'll see how the money is spent; and it must all go through your hands, you know; that can't be helped."

"No, I dare say not; but, ma' don't you think, when he dies, there will be a loss of the pension? and that would be a serious loss."

"It would; but then you will have a pension as an officer's widow, besides all his vast property, without any trouble whatever − with nobody to contradict you; that is, if he were to die; but I think he will not do that; he does not, at times, appear so old as one would think; and yet, he is very pale; but that, I suppose, is caused by his long residence abroad in hot climates, and being exposed to the weather of all kinds, attended by wounds and sickness.'

"No doubt he has suffered much; but he has obtained a handsome fortune, which pays for a great deal, you know, said Margaret.

"Undoubtedly, by dear; by-the-bye, have you heard how that affair of Miss Smith was ended, and why they came in here in such a manner?"

"Oh, it was a very shocking affair; there were some marks in her arm, which I cannot understand; it does seem very extraordinary to me, but she says she was awoke in the night by some monster sucking her blood."

"Dear me! who ever heard of such nonsense?"

"I cannot but think there must have been something in it; and, yet, what could have been the reason for them all to utter a falsehood, I don't know. There was, you know, the father, then the watchmen, all of whom said they saw it; at all events, they appeared to have some idea that it must have been done by some one in our house; the dressing gown and that appeared to bewilder them."

"Did they say they thought so still?"

"No; they did not do that, we spoke so positive; and I saw when I went in to see her, she was much terrified at what had occurred, and could not get up; she had a physician to attend her, who will not hear of anything that she says."

"Well, I think he is right."

"But the whole family appear to side with her, and insist that it was no robber who made the attempt; for nothing was gone, nothing was attempted in the shape of robbery; nothing was touched nor moved; therefore, there could be no common motive, they said. Well, at all events, they have made somebody very disagreeable in the family, and they had better have been quiet, but they are a disagreeable set, and I shall not go in again."

"You are right; my dear; they would be glad to push that minx of theirs in here, and get an acquaintance with the colonel. No, it will be safest to keep them apart; we will have as few female visitors, my dear, as possible; not that I think you run any chance of rivalry, but, you know, men are such uncertain things."

"To be sure they are, ma'." replied Margaret.

"Well, then, if we have no female acquaintances, you see we cannot possibly run any risk, and the matter will not be so protracted, because everything depends upon things being smooth and uninterrupted; he will be the more ready to propose and push the matter to a point."

"Do you think him a likely man, ma', to marry?"

"Certain of it, my dear, quite certain of it. I know a marrying man as soon as I see him; the colonel is decidedly a marrying man, he talks of home, domestic comfort, and all that kind of thing; and when men do that, you may be sure, if you are cautious, to catch such an one."

"Well, I will try."

"Do, my dear; it will be worth your while, it will make all our fortunes. I wonder what his money is invested in."

"I should like to know that," said Margaret.

"And so should I. Do you know, I have been thinking of that myself more than once. It will be necessary to find it out, and yet it is so delicate a matter, that I think you had better make no attempt to work it out of him. Let the affair take its own course at present."

"But I can hear all."

"Then you will act wisely, my dear, very wisely, prudently; but do no more — hear and see all, and say nothing — of course, I mean upon that subject alone. Now, if we proceed cautiously, we shall be sure to gain our object; I will take some method of obtaining the information I want at some future time, because it will be well to have him caught before we begin to pull tight the line; or, at least, before we begin to make any inquiries respecting his means he must give us some cause to do so."

"I dare say we shall know something by accident some of these days; perhaps, at the hotel where he comes from, something may be learned by inquiry."

"Possibly there may, my dear; but I do not like to go there. At all events, they can know but little, for he has not been long in England, and would hold but little communication with such people. We must have some better plan than that to go upon, else we shall never be successful, except at the cost of some cross in our hopes we would rather have avoided."

"Well, ma', you shall do as you like in this affair. I am sure you will do what is right and best for the occasion; besides, one plan is better than two."

"You are right, my dear. I am, however, resolved to have a visitor."

"A visitor, ma'?"

"Yes, my dear; only Mr. Twissel, the attorney."

"Oh, I know who you mean now; but why do you have him? He is a very funny sort of an acquaintance, especially if he is to meet the colonel."

"I wish him to meet him, my dear, for that reason. He will be able to get out of him, by some means, what he has got his money locked up in. A hint will serve him, and he can make inquiries, and learn it all, and then he will, if we are successful, have a good thing of marriage settlements, and so forth. Besides, I will make an agreement with him that he shall have a sum of money for his trouble."

"That will be a very good plan, certainly."

"Exactly, and you needn't be seen in it at all; so I think we shall be all very fairly put in the way of doing well. I shall go out this morning, and call upon Mr. Twissel, and have some conversation with him. He used to have some business of your father's to do, and has had much of his money, as well as a good word now and then."

"Dear me, who is that? There is a double knock at the door, ma'. How vexing it will be to have any one come here. I shall hate the sight of any one coming in now."

"Can't you see from the window who it is, my dear?"

"No, ma'."

"Then we must wait until the servant comes in."

The words had hardly been uttered, before the servant entered, and said that Mr. Twissel wanted to speak to Mrs. Meredith, if she was at home.

"God bless me! — send him in," said Mrs. Meredity, after the first surprise was over; and then, turning to her daughter, she said, "Talk of what's-his-name, and you are sure to see some of his friends. If I had wanted him to come, he would not have been here."

"Very likely, ma'; and yet you do, and he is here."

At this moment Mr. Twissel made his appearance, and entered the parlor. Having saluted the ladies, he proceeded to lay his hat and cane on the table, saying, —

"Mrs. Meredith, I dare say you are surprised to see me, after so long an absence."

"My surprise is not greater than my pleasure, Mr. Twissel. I am very glad to see an old friend of my husband's. Pray sit down, sir."

"Thank you, I will. I am glad to see you look so well. I need not ask how you are, and your amiable daughter too; she appears charming."

"Yes, Mr. Twissel, we are in tolerable good health; not often better."

"Do not let me disturb you, Miss Margaret," said Mr. Twissel, as she rose to leave the room.

"Oh, no, sir, not at all. I have something to attend to, if you will excuse me."

"Certainly, certainly. I hope I shall not be any cause of putting you to any constraint and inconvenience; at the same time, I shall not detain Mrs. Meredith long."

"Oh, we don't intend to lose you suddenly," said Mrs. Meredith. "Anything I can oblige you in I shall be very happy to do so, if you point out the how."

"Then I will proceed to do so at once," said Mr. Twissel; "I will do so at once. You see, when your late husband died, or before, he gave me several debts to collect."

"So I understood," said Mrs. Meredith.

"Exactly; I see you understand me. Now, those debts I was to collect myself for my own benefit, he having, when he died, owed me a considerable sum of money. He assigned them to me, and I accepted them as payment of his debt due to me."

"I understood such to be the case, and at that point the matter was considered as settled; was it not, Mr. Twissel?" said Mrs. Meredith.

"It was so, and is so now, as far as I know now; but I want some few papers which it is possible may be somewhere in your possession, to enable me to secure the payment of them; and without those papers I shall not be able to enforce attention. Now, I want to know if you will oblige me with them if you have them by you?"

"I will certainly look and make any search I can for them, and if I find them you shall have them, certainly. But, now I have disposed of that, will you do me a favor?"

"Certainly, with pleasure."

"Well, then, Mr. Twissel, you see, there is a certain rich lodger of mine who pays certain attentions to my daughter Margaret," said Mrs. Meredith.

"I see," said Mr. Twissel.

"Well, then, he had made no positive offer yet; but we have certain expectations, you see, and in case those expectations become realized, I want to be in such a situation as to know at once what I shall do in such a case — what ought to be done."

"Very good, my dear madam; very good."

"Now, we only know from report, and from appearances, that he is rich; we feel quite convinced of that — he could not well be otherwise," said Mrs. Meredith; "but we are anxious to know in what kind of stock or property he is likely to have invested it."

"Yes, I see. Well, then, all you have to do is to learn what you can from himself or his friends, and then make inquiries respecting the truth of what you hear. I should be very happy in assisting to make such inquiries, or in any way you may point out."

"I am very much obliged to you; but, Mr. Twissel, it is a very delicate subject for females to touch upon, and, moreover, it is worse, considering how my daughter is likely to be in connection with him."

"It is a delicate matter, certainly."

"Well, now, what I wanted was this; if you would on some occasion — I would let you know beforehand, — call in and take some tea, or whatever meal happened to be at hand, and get into conversation with the colonel, and get this matter from him —"

"Oh, he is a colonel in the army, then?"

"Yes; but returned, in bad health, from the Indies. He has come only recently."

"Aye, aye, I see; you have a nabob, I see. That will be a very handsome settlement for your daughter, my dear madam; a very handsome settlement."

"Yes, it will."

"Well, it is handsome; but there are drawbacks, you see."

"Oh, age, and ill health."

"Exactly; they are drawbacks, you see, that are not always to a young female's taste."

"No, no; but, then, my daughter is a reasonable young woman, Mr. Twissel, and would not object to a good fortune because there was a kind, though, perhaps, elderly, gentleman for a husband. Oh, dear, no, sir, I have no apprehensions of that character; she will be good and obedient, especially when she knows that it is all for her good; besides that, you see, the colonel, though an invalid, is not so very old, and is a most pleasant, and, I might say, fascinating gentleman to converse with; so that she can have no personal objection; and, besides, from what I can observe, I have reason to believe that the colonel is by no means disagreeable to her."

"Then I am sure it is a very handsome prospect for her, and one that might have been long in happening to one who had a better fortune to aid her."

"Yes, indeed, it might."

"Well, then, if I can aid you, command my services."

"In this respect you may do me much good, but I do not, as it will be some little loss of time to you, desire you should do so for nothing. If we succeed, and all is comfortable, you shall have a hundred pounds soon after the marriage — say three months."

"Very well. I am quite willing to accept the terms, and should I be wanted at any time, perhaps you will let me know as long before as possible."

"I will do so."

"And then, when I next come, perhaps you'll be able to hand me the papers, and be ready to sign some agreement which I will get ready for the purpose."

"Very well, I will do it."

"I am much obliged to you," said Mr. Twissel; "however, I suppose, when I am introduced to the colonel, I am only to come in as an old friend of the family?"

"Exactly so; that will be by far the best character to assume, because you may be anything; besides which, when matters come to a point proper for interference, you can do so the more easily, and with more effect, and he also will be less inclined to quarrel; and at the same time he can have less objection to do so, which, you see, is a little better."

"I see," said the attorney, rising; "and now, as we have settled this business so far, I will bid you good afternoon, as I have some business elsewhere this evening, which I must get finished."

After exchanging greetings, the attorney quitted the house of Mrs. Meredith without further remark.

Chapter CXXXII.

THE EXPLANATION, AND THE PROPOSAL. – A TÊTE-À-TÊTE.

A week or more had passed away since the visit of the attorney to Mrs. Meredith, and yet the latter saw not a sufficient reason why she should send for her friend. Things were not ripe yet; the colonel had, it was true, been melting gradually; but then to progress ever so little, was a great point in anything – no matter what it is – something gained.

Mrs. Meredith, however, by no means lost sight of her object; she had that steadily in view, and worked for it every day; and her daughter was no less assiduous – she was attentive and humble, waited upon

Colonel Deverill with the affectionate assiduity of a daughter; while, on his part, he sighed and said, what a happy man he must be, who should have her for a wife.

It was arranged one day, when he appeared to be more than usually tender, that the mother should be out that evening, and see some of her friends, and break the news a little to some of them; a pardonable vanity in the lady, for it was not in accordance with her position in society that her daughter could expect such an offer as the one she daily expected.

The lady did as she had agreed, and left the house, while Margaret went to the colonel's sitting-room when his bell rang, and hoped he'd excuse the absence of her mother, as she had gone out to see some friends whom she had not seen for some time.

"I am happy in having you attend to me, Miss Margaret. I cannot be attended to better. I am afraid, as it is, I am a terrible annoyance to you."

"Annoyance, colonel! far from it — very far from it; and I do hope you do not mean what you say, else I shall fear I have unwillingly given you some cause for your opinion, which I shall the more regret, as you are yourself so kind. I assure you it gives me great pleasure when I know I can do aught to alleviate the misfortunes, or satisfy the wishes of any of my friends."

"And do you reckon me one, Miss Margaret?"

"I hope Colonel Deverill will not consider me too presumptuous in looking upon him as something more than a mere casual friend or acquaintance."

"Casual acquaintance, Miss Margaret — casual acquaintance!"

"Well, friendship, if you allow me to say so."

"Friendship!" repeated the colonel, with a deep drawn sigh; "I would I could claim a yet warmer title than a friend. I could then hope for some of those pleasures which are denied a solitary man like me — I should then have those whom I loved to soothe my death-bed, and whom I could benefit by worldly wealth, could I, Margaret, think I could claim a feeling stronger than that of friendship."

"Oh! Colonel Deverill, how can you talk in this strain? Indeed, you — you are too good — dear me, I do not know what I was about to say."

"Miss Meredith," said the colonel, taking her hand with gentleness, and tenderly pressing it, "I am seen to a great disadvantage; I have been many years fighting for my country, and I have not had time to cultivate those sweet and tender emotions such as I feel at this moment."

"Yes, you must have suffered much," said Margaret.

"And now, when I return again, I am somewhat the worse in appearance; but my heart is as warm as ever it was, and I am more than ever alive to the charm of female society. It is that unreserved interchange of thought and good offices which attaches me to life, and makes me live even with hope. Do not dispel this day-dream of mine, Margaret."

The colonel paused and pressed her hand to his lips, while she appeared confused and irresolute, and was unable to withdraw her hand from his, but at length she sank trembling into a chair.

"My charming creature, may I suppose this emotion is caused by excess of feeling — that — that — in short, I am not wholly indifferent to you?"

"Oh, colonel! I'm really unable to speak!"

"My beloved girl, I am loved; yes, I see it — oh, happiness!"

Midst these broken sentences, the colonel contrived to slip his hand round the young lady's waist, and he pressed her close to him. For a moment she forgot his proximity, and remained passive; but suddenly and quietly disengaging herself, she said, —

"Pardon, me, Colonel Deverill; I had forgotten — I was unconscious — a weakness came over me, and —"

"You love me!"

"If you have become acquainted with that which was a secret, sir, you must use it as such; but you must not talk in this strain to me; promise me, colonel, and — and — I will see about the tea immediately."

"May I speak to your mother?"

"Colonel Deverill can do as he pleases. I have no secrets from my dear mamma."

"I will — I will, and Heaven bless you for saying so much. I may say you are not averse to me, and that, with her consent, I shall not despair."

"We will say no more, Colonel Deverill," said the cautious maiden.

"You shall command me — you are the arbitress of my fate," said the colonel, who had become warmer and eulogistic to a degree.

Much more, however, passed between them; the ice was broken, and they conversed more freely; for when they began the tea, much was said that did not partake of so warm a character as that which had already passed; but it, nevertheless, partook of the same purpose.

"When I am married," said the colonel, "I should like a carriage. I have no use for one now, as I could but very seldom ride; but when I had a wife, then I should wish for her accommodation as well as my own; but which do you prefer, country or town life?"

"There is much of comfort and quiet in a country life," said Margaret; "and yet I am not entirely wedded to country life — there is much of pleasure in London."

"So there is; and where you have no resources of your own, or in your own house, it is preferable; but when such is the case, London loses all its charms, or a great part of them."

"So it does," said Margaret.

"However, I am partial to both. I should like a partial town and country life."

"That, indeed, would be the very greatest delight one could experience; to live sometimes in one place, and sometimes in another."

"So it would."

"By the way, if we kept a carriage, which I would do," said the colonel, after a pause, "it would be a very excellent thing to enable us to travel about in."

"Perhaps you have been to some parts, and like them better than others."

"Yes, I have been to a good many parts; but I cannot at this moment speak of them; but we would look out for some place that would be more agreeable than others."

"Perhaps you have some place of your own you would like to live in?"

"No, — not exactly; these things are not of one's own choice, and not empty; and, therefore, are useless as residences."

"Certainly. Besides, you must be near enough to come to town for business purposes."

"Yes, I must, but that needn't be often," replied the colonel; "but where there is plenty of means, there is no fear of not getting what we want."

"No, indeed, there is not."

"And one thing alone would repay me for the hardships I have endured, the misery I have suffered, and the misfortunes I have experienced in all my marchings and counter-marchings; my sleeping in the open air by night, and scorched by the sun by day."

"And what may that be, colonel?"

"Why, the power it gives me of conferring happiness and wealth upon you; for, in the natural course of events, you will outlive me."

"Oh, for mercy's sake, don't talk of that, sir."

"But it is a matter that I can think of calmly enough; and, as a soldier, I have ample occasion, I can assure you."

"Indeed! I dare say you must have."

"I can remember, on one occasion, especially, which I will relate to you, if I do not weary," said Colonel Deverill.

"On, no — no! I cannot be weary," said Margaret.

"Then I will tell you. I was ordered to march some troops to attack the stockade of Puttythempoor, a very strong place."

"Was it a town?"

"No, merely a place of strength, where the enemy had gathered together in great numbers; and here we were determined to attack them. The stockade was a very strong place; and there were strong and high timber fences, with large mounds of earth and bags of sand, all tending to make the place one of great strength," said the colonel.

"What a place it must have been!"

"Yes; it was very strong. Well, my party did not amount to more than fifteen hundred men strong, while the enemy, with the advantages of the defense, were more than three thousand, giving them a vast superiority over us; but we were not to be daunted by that; we were determined to make a dash, and, from the character of the men I commanded, I had no fear of the result. We were sure to make our way among them, and then we were sure of the result."

"How dreadful!"

"Well, the men were divided into three bodies — five hundred each — and these into divisions of one hundred each, the one to support the other. We had no guns, and were therefore compelled to depend entirely upon our luck in the assault."

"Goodness me! I wonder how you could think of it with anything like case or comfort. It would make me all of a freeze!"

"Oh, Margaret! when the soldier is in the field of battle, he must get the better of all feelings, save those of honor."

"It is too true!" said Margaret, with a sigh.

"And then," said Colonel Deverill, "we, having arranged our plans, and settled who was to take the command, if I had the mischance to fall —"

"Good Heavens!"

"Well, I say, having done all this, we were resolved to make a dash at the point, and take the place by assault. To do this the more effectually, we were resolved to make the attempt in three different places at once, so as to divert the enemy's attention, and to place them in a cross fire, and thus take them the more easily.

"This plan was carried out to the letter, and we made the attack; but the enemy defended their stockade so vigorously, and what with the strength of the place, and the determination of the enemy, we were for some time repulsed — at least, held at bay.

"This would never do, I thought. I must mount the breach myself; for, if my division was held at bay, I had fears of the rest; they might meet repulses also, which would occasion the loss of our whole party, which would have been sure destruction; not defeat alone, but imprisonment, and possibly death from ill-usage, or from malignant disorders."

"What fearful scenes!"

"I ordered my men to keep close and follow me. We made a dash at the stockade three abreast, and up we went. By Jove, it was fine work — a brave sight — a sight I can never forget while I have remembrance left me. We got up the stockade Heaven knows how, and were over it in the space of a minute; but the impetuosity of those who came first was not seconded by those who came after; it was easy enough to get down among the Indians, but it was very hard to get up; and while our friends were getting up, we were exposed to the strength of hundreds — only four men to as many hundreds for several minutes."

"Goodness, how dreadful! Were you not all killed?"

"Except for myself, they were all killed. Each received a dozen wounds, and I should have met with the same fate, but for an Indian officer, who, seeing me surrounded and thrown down, saved my life from the fury of his men; but, in a minute after, I was free — my own men came down by dozens, and the blacks were swept off by the hundred.

"At that moment, too, there were our other parties just appearing over the other parts of the stockade, so we had now plenty of assistance.

"The blacks now on all sides fell in numbers before the fire, and the place was our own; and a hearty cheer was given that made the woods re-echo again."

"Were you not glad the danger was over?"

"The danger was not over, though we thought it was; for suddenly the earth heaved up with a tremendous explosion, and many of our poor fellows were blown up into the air, and I myself was completely knocked over and smothered in dirt; however, it was dry, and we were soon put to rights again. I was picked up, and nothing more happened."

"What was the cause of your disaster?"

"Oh, a mine the scamps had sprung as they were retiring, hoping to do us more mischief than they did; however, we beat them off, and they lost many men on that occasion, and did not show themselves again, but made the best of their way through the woods and jungle by some paths that we did not know, and hence we did not follow them further."

"It must have been dreadfully dangerous."

"Yes, life was the game we played for, and it was won and lost often enough, during that war; but we must expect it should be so."

"But you are now safe."

"Yes, I am now safe, and, I may say, happy. I have had some knocks, and am none the better for them bodily; but then I have had them well paid for, so I must not complain. I have now but one object to attain before I die."

"And what may that be, colonel, if it be no secret?"

"It is not to you, Miss Meredith," said the colonel; "it is an early day — a day on which I may claim you as my own; then, indeed, I shall have lived and accomplished something; an object worth living for, and, may I say so, worth dying for."

"Ah, I hope you may live many years yet, colonel — many years of life and happiness, to enjoy the fortune you have so gallantly won. Indeed, I think no fortune ought to give so much joy as the soldier's."

"And why, Miss Meredith?"

"Because there is none so arduously won; won often with bloodshed, and even life; it ought, indeed, to give great and lasting happiness."

"If I obtain my wishes, I shall be the happiest man in the universe; and I would go through all I have gone through over — aye, twice over, and that is no little — to have such a reward as the one I now seek — it is the crowning happiness of my life."

"You are very kind to say all this —"

"Aye, but I mean it. It is no common compliment," said the colonel; "I mean what I say, most earnestly. Do you believe what I say? I am not used to the pretty speeches of young men who make love — perhaps I ought; but I am an old soldier, and am but little used to these ways; however, I have spoken my mind, and I hope you will not allow any one else to injure my cause."

"Anything you have said, Colonel Deverill, has been of too serious a nature for me to think of anything save the object itself. Your conduct has been that of a gentleman, and I should be wanting in respect to myself, and courtesy to you, to think otherwise than seriously of it," was the wily reply of Margaret.

"You have my own thoughts," said the colonel.

"There is my ma'," said Margaret, as the knocker and bell sounded.

"You will do your utmost with Mrs. Meredith for me, and I will beseech her myself," said the colonel; "I hope she will take things in a favorable light."

Chapter CXXXIII.

MRS. MEREDITH'S CONSULTATION WITH MR. TWISSEL, AND HER RESOLVE.

*M*rs. Meredith's arrival was very opportune, for it broke off the interview; and Margaret descended to the parlor, where her mother she knew would repair the moment she had freed herself from her dress. Margaret was now left alone for a few moments. She felt all the exultation of success in a strategy, and all the exhilaration of spirits that such a prospect of wealth and riches floating before her eyes, and all the natural consequents upon such possessions would give rise to.

"I shall be rich," she thought. "Aye, I shall not only be rich, but very rich — I know I shall. Well, he is old — no matter; better be an old man's darling, than a young man's slave. Yes; I shall know how to use wealth. I shall be able to spend a little of his countless hoards, and he will not thwart me, I am sure. He will be too fond — too doting, by far. I shall be indulged like a spoiled child, I am sure."

Margaret smiled at the thought of what length the colonel might not be induced to carry his fondness for her.

"He will not set any value upon what will give me pleasure. I am sure he will give me all I ask. I have but to ask him for what I want, and he must comply. I am sure he is too easy — too quiet and generous to make a moment's hesitation."

The colonel, too, was left to his reflections, but as to what they were we know not. He sat long, silently gazing at the fire.

Mrs. Meredith now entered the apartment, and, looking at her daughter, she said, —

"Eh! something been said, Margaret? I can see by your eye that the colonel has said something to you. Am I not right, my dear?"

"Yes, ma'; you are right."

"Well, my love, and what did he say? I am dying with curiosity."

"It will be quite impossible to do that; but he has been quite explicit enough, without any hesitation at all, or any reserve — quite candid and open."

"He has offered?"

"Yes; he wishes for your consent; for I told him I could not possibly decide without your consent and countenance. He did not disapprove of that, only he wished to propitiate you in his favor, and begged me to let him have the satisfaction of knowing that he had my good wishes, and that I could look upon him in a warmer light than a mere friend."

"Which I hope you did?"

"Yes, ma'. I let him imagine that I was not indifferent to his good opinion; but, at the same time, I would not commit myself, but left him to infer a good deal. I think I know, ma', how to manage such an affair well — I may say, very well."

"Exactly, my love. I was sure you would."

"Yes, ma'; I should think I did. For when I found he had proceeded a certain distance, I was resolved that he should speak out plump at once; and when I found he paused, I paused too, and he was compelled to explain; but he betrayed no unwillingness, or anything like hesitation at all, but he has fairly proposed himself to me."

"And you have not committed yourself?"

"Not in the least."

"Very well. I must be cautious, too not to do so; because I must have some conversation with Mr. Twissel, so that we may proceed in a safe manner, and not commit ourselves in any way as we shall repent of afterwards."

"How do you mean?"

"Why, child, you would not marry the colonel if he was not a rich man."

"Not exactly; though I must admit, ma', he is a very nice man — a very nice man, and I should be entitled to a widow's pension, if nothing more, and that I might not have under some circumstances; even you yourself have been left worse off, you see."

"Yes, my child; but circumstances alter cases. I had a better prospect when I first married, else I would not have done so, you may depend upon it. However, we can always retrace our steps, and he cannot. But I will get Mr. Twissel to come and see into matters a bit for us."

"Well, ma', you shall do as you think fit — only, take care not to throw away a good chance because you have greater hopes."

"Has he said anything about his property?"

"Not a word, except it was to intimate it was large, and he had won it very hardly, with great danger; but he did not say what it consisted of. Of course I could not ask."

"Oh, dear, no."

"But he intimated he would keep a carriage, and a country house, as well as a town house, besides several other matters, which makes it plain enough he has been used to plenty; besides, as he spoke to me in describing some scenes in India, he appeared so much animated that I am sure he must be what he appears to be, and what he says he is."

"Ah, well, I think myself it is all quite right, and that we shall have nothing to repent there; but we will let all go on but the naming of the day — that must not be named, for, if we do, we shall not be able to retract."

"Oh, no, we shall not have any occasion to do that, I think; but I dare say he will speak to you tonight, as there is time at supper especially."

"No doubt. You may as well retire early, so that you may be absent, and that will give us greater liberty to talk than if you were present, my dear. I wish Mr. Twissel were here; but it can't be helped; and when he does come, I must have some conversation with him, and I must, in the meantime, learn what I can for him to inquire about afterwards."

Thus resolved, Margaret went to bed early, leaving her mother to attend upon the colonel, who sat looking at the fire without any change of posture since the last time he was seen by the girl; but Mrs. Meredith caused him to break the steady gaze and deep thought he was indulging in.

"I hope you have been quite well, colonel, since I left?"

"Yes, quite well, Mrs. Meredith."

"What would you choose for supper?"

"Margaret —"

"Eh?" said Mrs. Meredith, amazed.

"I beg your pardon; I did not know you were near — at least, I did not know I spoke at the moment; but, pray, what did you desire to know?"

"What you would have for supper, sir?"

"Oh, whatever you have at hand; some of what we had for dinner — I think I should like it as soon as you feel disposed to have it. I am ready — quite ready."

"Then it shall be had at once, sir," said Mrs. Meredith; "I will order it up immediately, for it is later than I intended to have stopped out; but the hours so soon ran away, and there were so many motives to forget the time that was flying so fast."

The supper was soon laid, and the colonel and Mrs. Meredith alone sat down to it, at his earnest request. Indeed, they used to have meals much in common; for the colonel professed to be very fond of female company, and was desirous of their company, which they translated into a desire for the presence of Margaret herself.

The supper was laid and over before the colonel said anything; but appeared to be absorbed in deep thought, from which it was difficult to arouse himself. But at length, after looking around once or twice, and not seeing Margaret at table, he said to Mrs. Meredith, —

"I hope I have not driven your daughter away."

"Oh, no, sir; she complains of headache, and has gone to bed somewhat earlier than usual."

"I fear I must lay the blame on myself."

"She did not say you were the cause," replied Mrs. Meredith, "of her ailment; and, therefore, I think you must be free from blame; for she would have said so, if it had so happened. She generally speaks the truth in such matters, at least, and, I believe, in every other."

"No doubt; but I have been speaking upon a subject that concerns my own happiness to her, and perhaps the excitement may have caused her some evil of that sort. She would not, perhaps, name it to you, Mrs. Meredith; but I will. You have been a wife yourself, and know that a few candid words are better, and more to the purpose, than a long desultory courtship."

"Yes, sir; it certainly is so."

"There is some difference, too, in our ages," said the colonel. "I have not overlooked that matter, at all events; but I hope that will be no cause of impediment or objection."

"It cannot be, sir, in such a case as your own, for instance."

"Well, then, I have proposed for her husband. I wish to make her my wife. I am yet hale and hearty, and have some few years yet which I could wish to pass in happiness, and which I will use to make her happy. And if I die early, I have ample means of providing for her — of leaving her a most handsome and ample fortune. Not more than she deserves; but possibly more than she might have thought of seeking."

"Certainly, sir."

"Then I wish for your consent to our future happiness."

"You may have my good wishes," said Mrs. Meredith.

"You are very good," said the colonel; "and I trust your daughter will live long to make you happy by making her own apparent to you."

"Of course," said Mrs. Meredith, "this is rather a sudden affair; you will not think of hurrying it to a conclusion, but permit her to become acquainted with you, and to know her own mind."

"Certainly, I do wish it pushed on to a conclusion; but not so much so as to cause any dissatisfaction. I am anxious to call he wife. My feelings are those of an ardent lover."

"I do not dispute it."

"Still you and she must be the best judges of all this. You will not, I hope, punish me by compelling me to a longer probation than you are compelled to put me to. I am not like a young man who has a fortune, or rather a living to earn; but I have one ready, a handsome one, and my wife will be a lady of fortune when I die."

"Do not think of dying at such a moment, sir."

"Why, it is not desirable," said the colonel, who did not deem it necessary to carry the conversation on any further that night; thinking, possibly, enough had been said for the first occasion of revealing his passion, and he, no doubt, considered his success signal.

The supper then passed off in the usual style, and Mrs. Meredith left the colonel, and wished him good night, with feelings somewhat akin to triumph, and returned to her own daughter's room, there to cogitate and sleep upon what had that evening taken place.

*T*he next day she determined to send to Mr. Twissel, and arrange the meeting she desired; and, at the same time, she resolved that she would not push matters to the extremity, of making a point of knowing what his property were, for she might lose all; she was convinced that the colonel must be a man of large property; how could such a man live if he were not.

That was a speculation she could not help indulging in. She knew that a man in Colonel Deverill's line of life was quite able to support himself; besides, the jewels he had about him were worth a large sum of money; putting all things together, she considered it was not worth while to lose so good, so excellent an opportunity as the present for making a brilliant, at least, an excellent settlement for her daughter, and a home for herself.

"There can be no fear," she muttered; "there can be no fear; her widow's pension will be a better support to her than the livelihood of some."

Mr. Twissel was sent for; and, the papers she desired to find for him, she was fortunate enough to discover, and laid them by at once. The attorney came willingly enough, and was well pleased when he was informed of the success of the search after the papers, and produced the bond, by which she agreed to give him one hundred pounds for his assistance in the marriage affair.

However, he did not seem to agree with her, that she should not be over particular about the colonel's property; he thought that there must be some inquiries made respecting it, to ascertain if there were any or none.

"But," suggested Mrs. Meredith, "the colonel is a kind, but a proud man, and he would, probably, take great and deep offence at any inquiry being made into his pecuniary affairs."

"Hardly, my dear madam; don't you see, love would be strong enough to counter-balance that; he would make some allowance for paternal anxiety and love."

"There is much reason in all that; yet I have heard so much of these nabobs, that one is afraid to lose a good chance by inadvertently touching their weak points; for, the kind of society and company they have, theirs is so different to what they find here."

"Yes, that is very true; but we should like to know that it is true. What service has he been in — I think, though, you said in the East India Service?"

"Yes."

"Well, then, I will make some inquiries at the house; they will answer my inquiries, and no one will even be the wiser for it; they will, at least, tell me if there is such a person in the service, and, perhaps, I can learn something more."

"Very well, that may be done. Will you come round with me to tea this evening, as I will contrive to bring you in the presence of Colonel Deverill, whom you will then see and converse with? I am not sure of it, but I will try to do so."

"I will be here," said the attorney; and, in the mean time, I will make the necessary inquiries."

They parted upon this mutual good understanding; and the attorney, in high spirits, for the papers were of great value to him, and the promised reward was a stimulus to a greater exertion on behalf of Mrs. Meredith and her daughter, for he thought he could do business for the Colonel, after this affair was settled – such an opportunity of increasing his connection did not offer every day.

Mrs. Meredith redoubled her assiduity about the person of Colonel Deverill; and, at the same time, lost no opportunity of putting her daughter forward; nor was that daughter a bit disinclined to take such opportunity as was offered her, of making the most of herself on this occasion, to appear amiable, and in some new and languishing position, or to perform some new service for the colonel.

Chapter CXXIV.

THE INTRODUCTION. – THE ATTORNEY'S FIRST FEELER.

When the attorney had left the house he proceeded upon some business of his own, and then he proceeded to the India House for the purpose of making inquiries after the colonel, for his friend Mrs. Meredith. In the course of the day he did go to the India House, and, upon making some inquiries, he was sent to a particular department of the house where he saw two gentlemen.

"Pray, sir," said one, "what do you want?"

"I wish to make some inquiries concerning a Colonel Deverill, who is employed, or was serving, in the Honorable East India service."

"In what part was he serving?"

"In India," said the attorney.

"But, to what presidency did he belong?"

"That I do not even know. He has been many years away from England, I understand, and some of his friends have not heard from him for many years, and they are desirous of finding out whether he is dead or alive; and if so, where he is."

"There is a Colonel Deverill returned this year from India."

"Indeed! Do you know anything of him?"

"Nothing more than he has retired from the service on his half pay, some time before he came home, on account of his wounds."

"Is he rich?"

"I can answer no such question."

"I am a solicitor, and do not ask the question from an improper motive."

"You may not, sir, but we cannot answer such a question. We have no inquisitorial knowledge of the private circumstances of those gentlemen who have served in the company's army; but, you put it to your won sagacity to consider how far it would be probable for a man so placed, as regards rank and opportunity, in India, without making money."

"I see; certainly – he must."

"And yet, you know, there are means of getting rid of money."

"To be sure. I see."

"Not that I have any idea that such can be the case; indeed, I should be disposed to believe the contrary, seeing the colonel must have been wounded long since, for the last engagement must have been some few years since."

"Thank you. I will report what I have learned. You do not know where he can be found at this time?"

"No, indeed; we have no information."

This being all he could learn, he left the India House, and as it was now about time to return to Mrs. Meredith, he at once went back, and having seen all his business transacted, he had now leisure to go there, and in a short time he arrived, and at once related to her all that he had heard respecting the colonel, from the first to the last word of it.

"Well," said Mrs. Meredith, "that, at all events, is very satisfactory."

"Yes, it is something," said the attorney, "to know your man; but, as the clerk said, he might have spent it, that is to say, dissipated it."

"Oh, it's impossible; he's been an invalid a long while now."

"Ah! there's no knowing what might be done in these cases. Who knows what he may have done – gambled and diced it away, and entered into extravagant speculations, which may have turned out ruinous bubbles."

"Well, well, Mr. Twissel, we won't say much about what might be," said Mrs. Meredith; "we won't care about them; but I am very much obliged to you for this trouble. It is, however, a very satisfactory thing to know he is what he represented himself to be."

"Yes, that is a very great point gained."

"His veracity having been found unimpeachable in one point, may be presumed to be so in another," said Margaret. "It appeared to me to be extremely probable, if not quite certain, he is what he appears to be,

I am glad that all is so far good."

"Be that as it may, it will be more satisfactory to know what his property really consists of, and how much there is about it."

"No doubt; but it would not be worth while to risk anything on that account; he might imagine we were mercenary, and that would disgust him altogether."

"That's what I am fearful of," said the mother.

"We may not yet have occasion to ask him any question, or to make any inquiries of him at all, for we may be able to worm it all out of him."

"That is true," said Mrs. Meredith. "Dear me, there is the bell. Go, Margaret, and say we have an old friend come to tea; perhaps he will excuse you — he may give the invitation we desire."

Margaret at once departed, and proceeded to the colonel's room, and began to wait upon him as usual; but he saw there was but one cup placed.

"Are you not going to take tea with me, Margaret?" he said. Am I to be a prisoner, and put in solitary confinement for the evening?"

"Why, colonel, Mr. Twissel has called to take tea with my mother, and as he was a very old and particular acquaintance of my father's, I do not like to put a slight upon him."

"He is a gentleman, I presume?"

"Oh, yes, colonel, he is a member of the profession of the law."

"Oh! Well, will you ask him to tea with me? As we shall be both united, I hope your friends will soon be mine; there can be no great objection to our acquaintance beginning earlier. I am not fond of being entirely alone," .

"If we shall not be intruding upon you, sir," said Margaret, "I dare say my mother will. I will tell her of your kindness immediately," .

In a few moments Margaret returned to her mother and the attorney, to whom she related the invitation she had received from the colonel, and instantly clutched at the idea of going to the colonel to tea, the thing, of all others, she most desired to do, and, at the same time, she had calculated upon it; for the colonel appeared to be wholly dependant upon them for society, which he appeared to be passionately fond of there, especially Margaret.

"That is just fortunate. Now, Mr. Twissel," said Mrs. Meredith, "you will be cautious, and do not make any open attempt to discover what may be the peculiar species of property he holds; it may do much mischief, you know."

"I am at your mercy," said the lawyer; "if you say so, I will not make any attempt, though I must tell you, Mrs. Meredith, that you will be to blame if you allow your daughter to marry without some inquiry being made; and if he mean well, he will take no offence."

"You may do what you can without broaching the subject to him. Still I think we have heard enough to set all doubts at rest."

"I'm a professional man, my dear madam, and know what the world is, and have had much experience in these matters; however, as I think there is much probability in all he says, why, you shall see I will not do anything that will offend the nicest delicacy."

"That will be all we want, Mr. Twissel; and now come up stairs."

"Mr. Twissel, Colonel Deverill — Colonel Deverill, Mr. Twissel, an old and dear friend of my late husband, sir, who has called to visit us."

"I am very happy to see the gentleman," said the colonel, but with the air of a man who is conscious of his own superiority, and that he is committing a condescending act. "Will you please to be seated. Excuse my rising, sir; I am an invalid, and am lame; but you are welcome."

"I am much obliged," returned the attorney, bowing. "My good friend Mrs. Meredith has made me intrude upon you, else I had not done so."

"You are welcome, sir," again repeated Colonel Deverill. "Pray be seated; I have seen but little company, and am glad now and then to converse with any one. Will you oblige me, Mrs. Meredith, with making tea for us? Your services are really invaluable."

"Ah, Colonel! you are really too good."

"Not at all. I'm afraid I'm too much in the rear of the march of courtesy since I left England, as our habits and manners in the East are very different to what they are here."

"Ah! I dare say they live in a style of regal magnificence and splendor," said the attorney.

"Yes; more so than you may at first imagine, and more so than in appearance; so much so that it is difficult for the law at all times to take its course. It becomes a mere dead letter, and the matter usually ends in some indignity being offered to its servants."

"Indeed, sir! that was dangerous."

"Not at all. It was an attorney, who having deputed some one to serve a process, and finding that he could not, imagined that it was the fault of the process server, and he determined to make the attempt himself, being well assured that he could succeed. However, he found himself mistaken, for, after several disasters, that he was led into purposely, he was well pumped upon by some slaves, and thought himself lucky in escaping with life."

"That would never have been permitted here," said the attorney.

"No, possibly not; but there are not the distinctions between classes here that there are there, and things are not on the same scale, either living or attendance."

"And yet, people who have passed their lives there, come to this country at last, they do not like it well enough to remain there. They come back to the land of their birth, where none of these things exist to fascinate them."

"Yes; they many live and die there – very many; but, at the same time, those who do return, do so because it is the land of their birth – because they love the country, and because they go there merely to make fortunes to come here and spend them."

"They don't like the kind of investments, perhaps?"

"They usually do so, and it fetches a high price – a very high price, and is considered equal to the stocks of the Bank of England."

"That is first-rate stock, and on dividend days the place is usually surrounded with strangers, who come to town for the purpose of receiving their incomes; indeed, it is quite an interesting sight to strangers. Have you ever witnessed it? It is well worth the while to go and see it."

"I never trouble myself anything about it," said the colonel; "but I must be going there, by the way, tomorrow. I must have a coach."

"Do you know the routine of the banking business? It is confusing to one not used to it."

"I know enough for my own purpose."

"Didn't you find London much altered," inquired Margaret, anxious to give a turn to the conversation, as she thought this attorney's conversation would appear as if it were much too pointed – "when you first returned to England, and came to live here again?"

"I cannot say much about that," said the colonel; "because I was not in a condition to twist about like many men; I am lame."

"Exactly; that must have deprived you of much of the pleasure one feels in surveying old places and well remembered spots."

"It was," replied the colonel; "but in a place like London, alterations and additions are not so extensive as to cause any alteration in general features, so as to make it perceivable at once. It is only when you come to examine localities that you notice it. You improve and alter parts, but the town is the same, and there is no doubt this appears the work of steady growth, and not any one of sudden effort; indeed, the very additions to it have a character which stamp it as being London."

"There is much truth about that," said the attorney.

"It is the same all over the world, and only in those places where the extent is but small, than any great alteration makes a conspicuous and general change, and gives a new character to the place."

As this conversation passed between them, the attorney making one or two delicate allusions to property, and asking his advice respecting some purchases he wished to make. To all which the colonel made but short and direct answers, and of such character, that it was difficult to carry on the conversation upon that topic, at least, and both mother and daughter looked beseechingly at him, so that he was compelled to resist, and found himself completely baffled by what appeared the colonel's pride.

"Well, Mrs. Meredith," said Mr. Twissel; "I have done my utmost with this Colonel Deverill, and I can make nothing of him — nothing at all, I assure you."

"You cannot form a bad opinion of him?"

"No — no. He is at one moment one of the most agreeable men to converse with, and the next moment he is frigid and severe; perhaps pain, or perhaps contempt for any one else, may induce the alteration in his manner, and no allusion to himself does he make."

"Don't you think he is quite the gentleman, and a man used to good society?"

"Yes, I cannot doubt — he has the air of all that he says; but he is going to the bank tomorrow; now, I wonder if it is to receive dividends."

"I dare say it is," said Mrs. Meredith; "I have very little doubt of that, and yet I should very much like to know; it would settle one's mind — not that I would run any risk about the matter. I would not have him offended for the world; it would be willfully destroying a chance that is so good, that we never can expect it to again occur, therefore we must not lose it."

"Certainly not; I will undertake the matter myself," said the attorney, "so that there shall not be any risk in a miscarriage, whatever. I will take care that nothing shall be done that will be at all likely to reach his ears, or that will be displeasing to him."

"We will trust to your prudence, Mr. Twissel."

"You may do so safely, and depend upon my caution in this matter. Now I will be at hand in the morning. If I am not here before he goes out, send for me, and let me know the hour; if there is not time to reach here send me the number of the coach; I will post off to the bank and there await until I see him come there."

"I will send to you, then," said Mrs. Meredith; "I think that a very good plan."

"But what will it do for you if you do see him enter the bank, that will tell you nothing, and I cannot see the utility of it," said Margaret; "many people go into the Bank of England, who do not go there to receive any money for themselves; so that would be inconclusive."

"It would," said the attorney; "but you must remember, I can enter too, and ascertain to what portion of the building he goes, and I can learn how much he received, if any — but I must bid you good-by; for the present; do not forget to send to me at the first blush of the affair, and then much subsequent trouble may be saved.

Chapter CXXV.

MR. TWISSEL'S MISADVENTURES. – THE CONSEQUENCES
OF BEING FOUND IN THE BANK WITHOUT GIVING A
SATISFACTORY ACCOUNT OF YOUR BUSINESS THERE. – AN
UNPLEASANT DILEMMA.

*T*he peculiar position of Mrs. Meredith and her daughter Margaret, in some measure, and to a great degree, tied their hands, and caused a corresponding desire to know more than was told them; at the same time, they were fearful of giving any offence to their new and wealthy lodger. They were both avaricious and designing. To make a good settlement was the grand object of their lives, and to that object they would sacrifice themselves — at least, sacrifice Margaret, who, by-the-bye, would consider it no sacrifice at all, but a great stroke of good luck.

However, they could do nothing of themselves; they saw there was a great, and glorious chance for the future; they felt they had entangled the colonel; they felt he had become a victim to their snares, and they were unwilling that they should run any risk of a failure of their plans.

"If we offend him, he may consider us avaricious and designing," they argued; "and that might prove too strong an antidote to even an old man's love, and the prize might be snatched out of our hands, and we might not only lose a rich husband, but a good lodger also."

These considerations induced them to act more warily and cautious than the attorney, Mr. Twissel, who was anxious at once to seize the bull by the horns, and come to an explanation, and thus save himself much labor and time, for the sooner there was an explanation the better; and he did not apprehend the result that they did; he believed it would only appear proper caution on the part of a mother.

They had different opinions; and, between the two, there was an indecisive policy adopted, which occasioned delay and uncertainty.

There was no doubt but the colonel meant matrimony; his infirmities were of no consequence. It was not the man, but the money, that was wanted, and which was sought with perseverance and constancy. They appeared negligent of money matters before the colonel; and, when he paid them, which he did regularly, he always appeared to have money about him, which, of course, increased their respect, and gave them increased confidence in him.

"It is all very well, ma," said Margaret, "but Mr. Twissel must not offend Colonel Deverill; he is evidently a man much above him; his actions and manner are such, that at once stamp him immeasurably his superior; now, as regards this property, there can be no doubt but he must have enough."

"I think so, too, my dear; but it would be a dreadful thing if it should turn out otherwise in the end; it would really be very dreadful; I should never survive it."

"Nor I mother."

"What is to be done? — I declare I am at my wits' end."

"There is no fear, ma; do you not remember that Mr. Twissel himself has found out that he is Colonel Deverill, and that he has retired from the army of the Company?"

"Indeed, my dear, that is correct; I had forgotten that — quite forgotten it; but it may so happen he has no money at all; he may have spent it."

"He does not appear to be extravagant," said Margaret; "he has retired upon his half-pay, which you know must be a very good living, and I am sure of a widow's pension, if nothing more; and, besides, I am sure, from what he has said, there must be money."

"Well, I think so, too, my dear," said Mrs. Meredith; "and I think it will be better that things should go on as the colonel desires; to lose him would be horribly aggravating."

"So it will, ma, because I am sure he will do justice. It is not like as if we had money, too, and were as willing to have our affairs investigated, as we are to investigate his."

"That is very true, my dear, very true; and Mr. Twissel does not seem to know that; that I will tell him when I see him; by the way, I must send to him, to tell him the colonel is going out in about an hour. If he can find out anything, without compromising us in the affair, why, he may do so, and welcome; for, you must acknowledge, it will be all the more satisfactory."

"Yes, yes, I admit that; but I would not willfully lose a good opportunity."

"I must now send off to him. Mary must go, and that, too, as quickly as she can; for I shall want her back again very soon, so she must run."

"Then, the sooner she goes the better," said Margaret.

Mary was sent to Mr. Twissel, who happened to be at home at the time, and judging that Mary had been a good time on the road, that there would be no time to go to Mrs. Meredith's house, and then follow the coach, so he determined to go to the bank at once, so that he would be there in time to see the colonel descend and enter the bank, into which he would follow him.

He sent word back to Mrs. Meredith that he would go on, and see her as soon after as he could; and then he made the best of his way towards the bank, where he arrived in good time — indeed, half-an-hour before the colonel, who did not set out so soon as he intended.

"Now," thought Twissel, "if he were to turn out all right, why, I shall be in good fortune; but if bad, it would be laid upon my shoulders. They shall not say that I have not given them attention enough for their money; and if I don't do something, they will say I haven't earned my money; and though I can enforce payment of the bond, yet it may hurt my future prospects with regard to my future connection with the family, which I hope to make a profitable one in the long run."

Filled with these thoughts, he determined to watch with due caution for the arrival of the colonel, on the other side of the way.

It was some time before the coach drove up, which it did after a considerable lapse of time, and then Mr. Twissel crossed over, and placed himself in a position by the lamp-post where he could obtain a good view of any one passing in and out of the coach.

"'Tis he," he muttered, as he saw the colonel step out of the carriage, and walk into the bank very leisurely and quietly, leaning upon his stick, and walking lame. He watched him into the bank — he saw him go some distance down the passage, and then he muttered, —

"Now, I will follow him up closely."

And, after a moment's pause to permit some one to pass him, he then darted down the passage into a kind of yard; but no, he could not see him; he was not there; and yet he was so lame, he could not have got out of sight so soon as all that.

"He's gone to the dividend-office," he muttered; "I shall find him there," and away he posted to that department; but he could not find him, he was — he was not there. Then what could have become of him? That was a point he could not solve.

"Well, this is very odd," he muttered; "very odd."

He paused to think over the matter; but that did not aid him. He was in the dark but thought it was no use in waiting in any one place, so wandered about from office to office, until he came to the body of the place, when he waited until some one came up to him, and touched him on the shoulder. He turned round, and at once perceived it was an officer.

"What do you want with me?" inquired Twissel.

"What is your business here?" returned the officer, by way of reply.

"I am here upon my own business. I am at a loss to understand what you mean by asking me such a question in a public place. What can you mean by it? I was never asked such a question before, and cannot see why you should do so now."

"Excuse me, sir, I have ample warrant for what I am doing."

"Have you? Then state it."

"Easily. I have followed you about this last half-hour, and you have been wandering about the place for some time, and looking about you in a manner that has excited a good deal of suspicion, to say the least of it; and I must have some satisfactory explanation."

"You can have that," replied Mr. Twissel, very much annoyed; "you can have any explanation you can require. I am very sure I came here on my own affairs; what other explanation can you require?"

"Your affairs may be ours also, and the explanation you have given will be just enough to justify my taking you into custody — so if you have no more to say, I must request the favor of your company; that's my card of invitation; do you hear, sir?"

"Yes, I do; I am an attorney-at-law, and you may depend upon it I will not be content without punishing you for this indignity — I came in here because I saw a friend call, to whom I wanted to speak."

"Where is he?"

"I don't know," said Twissel; "I have missed him."

"Very likely, and your friend will miss you for a short time; for you must come with me; — you have been found here without being able to give any account of yourself."

"I tell you I came in here to see Colonel Deverill."

"Well, what do we know of Colonel Deverill? We don't know anything about him, nor you either; you must come with me. We are obligated to be very particular when we see strangers walking about with no object whatever in view — it is very suspicious."

"But I tell you I am a respectable attorney — a professional man. I had no bad object in view."

"That may be as you say; but you must come with me."

Seeing there no help for it, Mr. Twissel resigned himself into the officer's hands, and followed him to the station-house, where he was examined by the inspector, at the place where he was taken.

"Well, sir," said the inspector, "this may be all very true, but we must have some proof of what you assert; then we can let you go."

"I'll have a complaint against you."

"You may; but you must prove not only that what you say is true, but that there was no cause for suspicion, and that you were not loitering about the bank, as the officer asserts you were."

The attorney thought that it would be quite unnecessary to get into the public prints, because it would not do for him to make use of

Colonel Deverill's name; and that he had already done. What was he to do? he had got into a very disagreeable scrape, out of which he must now get in the best manner possible, and which he could not see his way clear to do.

"What do you want me to do?"

"Give us some proof that you are the person whom you represent yourself to be," he replied, "and then we can let you go at once."

"Then I will give you my card," said Twissel, producing his card-case.

"That is no proof," said the constable. "A man might have robbed you of your card-case, and you would have some one passing himself off for yourself."

"What shall I do, then?" inquired Twissel.

"Send for some one who knows you, or send for your own clerk — that will do."

"That I can do at once," replied Twissel; and he at once wrote a note to his clerk, and gave it unsealed into the hands of the constable, and asked if there was any one who would go with it.

"You can send a messenger; there are many who will do that if you pay them for it," replied the constable; and in another minute, for the sum of half-a-crown, a messenger agreed to take the letter to his office, and deliver it to his clerk, and wait for him.

This was done, and until that time he was locked up in a cell, where he had a light certainly, but in which he had no other comfort at all; but in about an hour and a half there was the prospect of a relief; for he saw his clerk come into the station-house, and with him the messenger, who came to the constable and said that was Mr. Twissel's clerk.

"Do you know Mr. Twissel?" inquired the constable.

"Yes, I do; he is my employer."

"Then point him out," said the constable.

At that moment, Mr. Twissel was brought in, and he at once pointed him out to the satisfaction of the constable, who, with an admonition, consented to the enlargement of Mr. Twissel, and in answer to his threat of future investigation, said to him, —

"You see, sir, the bank is such a place, that we are compelled to keep all persons out who have no business there, and it must not be a place where people meet who have no particular bank business to transact; do not wait about, then, for the future, sir, else you may run the same danger."

Mr. Twissel left the station-house with a feeling very much akin to anger, and he walked home with a very disagreeable feeling. He felt that he had been baffled, and had been also much ill-used, and very much affronted.

"Where could he have got to?" he murmured. "He must have turned in some of the offices — confound him! I wish he had taken it into his head to tumble. I am sure he ain't no good; if he were, I should not have been placed in such an unpleasant position."

Suddenly he recollected that there was no necessity for his going home, unless there had been anything happened since his departure; and upon being informed that such was not the case, he determined to alter his course, and proceed to Mrs. Meredith, and relate the misfortunes that had befallen him.

"And if that don't satisfy her I have her interest at heart, why, nothing will."

And he left his clerk, after giving him some directions, and then turned off towards Bloomsbury-square, where he arrived just before tea time.

Chapter *CXXVI.*

AN EVENING WITH COLONEL DEVERILL. – THE STRATAGEM OF MRS. MEREDITH.

*M*r. Twissel seated himself by Mrs. Meredith's fire, not at all pleased with what he had anticipated and expected on that day, and yet well pleased that there was an end to it; but, at the same time, he had conceived a dislike for the colonel, of which the reader can easily guess the reason. The colonel had received him rather haughtily, and he was annoyed at it, and he was resolved that he would do him no service; and now, the indignity he had received was so vexing, that he knew not on whom to wreak his anger — at all events, it gave him a great dislike to the colonel, which would require a considerable time to overcome.

He sat there, waiting for Mrs. Meredith, who was then engaged somewhere else; but it was not long before she entered the apartment in which Mr. Twissel sat meditating upon his misadventure, and considering in his own mind what would be the best course to pursue.

"Oh, Mr. Twissel!" she said, "I hope you have not been waiting long for me."

"Not long, ma'am."

"And how have you got on today, Mr. Twissel?"

"Rather indifferently indeed," said Twissel, with a groan; "I may say very indifferently indeed. I have had plenty of incident — I may say of adventure — I ought to say misadventure, which appears to have dogged me step by step in this affair."

"Indeed! I am amazed at that," said Mrs. Meredith.

"You would be more so if you knew all."

"Tell me what has happened, Mr. Twissel," said Mrs. Meredith. "I am anxious to hear to hear what can have happened to you of this character. I hope it did not happen in consequence of your doing anything in this affair of Colonel Deverill's."

"Indeed it did, Mrs. Meredith," said the attorney, solemnly. "I have been sedulously engaged in this affair, and I have been seriously inconvenienced by it."

"I regret it very much."

"But you could not have helped it, Mrs. Meredith," said Twissel. "You could not have helped it at all. I know that very well, there fore there is no blame attached to you. You are free; but I have suffered, nevertheless. I have suffered."

"Dear me, how sorry I am, to be sure."

"Yes, ma'am, but it can't be helped. I was taken into custody as a suspicious person, and had some difficulty in getting my release from custody."

Mrs. Meredith lifted her hands and her eyes to express the amount of astonishment she felt.

"Yes, Mrs. Meredith. I followed the colonel into the Bank of England, and there I saw him enter, but by some wonderful means he suddenly disappeared. I missed him, and could not again obtain the slightest clue to him. I did not again set eye upon him, and while endeavoring to regain the track, I was taken into custody for loitering about."

"Indeed. Then you have learned nothing about the colonel?"

"Nothing at all. I missed him. I saw him going into the bank, and that was all."

"Well, he has come back, and appears to have received money. I should think there could be doubt as to where he got it from."

"It is a mystery."

"Indeed. I should hardly think it possible, as you saw him go in. What would he go there for but for money matters? It seems clear enough to me. I have no doubt in my own mind — everything appears to be straightforward and plain."

"Indeed," muttered the attorney; "there is much truth in that. I have had a straightforward intimation that I have been considered a suspicious person."

"I regret it very much; but here's Margaret."

At that moment Margaret entered the apartment in which her mother and Mr. Twissel were seated. There was an air of triumph in her eye when she entered, and her mother at once divined the cause; but she said nothing, and waited until Margaret spoke.

"Ma," she said, "it is tea-time, and the colonel expects you up stairs; and if you had any friends, he hoped you would not deprive him of your company on that account, but bring them up stairs to tea. He is particularly good-humored to night."

"Curse him," involuntarily exclaimed the attorney, as he heard of the good-humor the colonel was in, and he had so much cause to be vexed himself.

"Will you come with us, Mr. Twissel?"

"I will, thank you, ma'am. I am very tired," said Twissel, as he thought it would afford him some opportunity of discovering something that would enable him to be revenged, and at the same time do a seeming service to the other party.

"At all events," he muttered, "it will give me a change of making a more intimate and useful acquaintance with him. I must do something or other, and I may as well make a good thing of it as well as a bad one. That wouldn't be bad policy."

"Then you had better come up at once," said Margaret, "for the tea is waiting."

Thus urged, Mrs. Meredith and Mr. Twissel followed Margaret, and walked up to the drawing-room, where the colonel was, as before, seated in an easy chair, with the green shade still over one eye, and his arm carried in a sling, though he did not appear to have lost the entire use of it, and by his side was his stick, a valuable Malacca cane, with which he walked, and his lame foot was supported by an ottoman.

"Well, sir," said the colonel, "I have the extreme felicity of meeting you again; be seated. It is a very charming day, the most comfortable that I recollect since I have returned to England."

"It is remarkably fine,:" said the attorney, shrugging his shoulders, and giving a suspicious glance towards the colonel, as if he thought there was a latent smile lurking upon the colonel's countenance; but he could not detect it, and yet he felt very much aggravated.

"There is, even in this climate," continued the colonel, "some decent weather; but then, when matters go on happily and cheerfully, then the climate appears more genial and kind."

"Strange that it should be so," said Mr. Twissel; "but I can't help thinking he looks more provoking than ever I saw in my life."

As he muttered, the colonel said, —

"What did you say, sir?"

"I merely said that we, who are used to it, look upon it in some other light than that of a merely negative character; that is, we look upon some of it as positively good — nay, we are apt to call it beautiful, especially when it continues fine."

"Continues fine!" said the colonel; "does it really continue fine in this climate?"

"Why, one would think, colonel, you have never been in this country before, to hear you talk; and yet you are a native of this country."

"Yes, I am; that is, I believe so; but I have spent so many years in Asia, that I am more a native of India than this country. However, I believe what you say to be correct; but, you see, the slightest change of weather affects my wounds, when you could not believe any change that had taken place; or, at all events, the change would be so slight as to cause no difference to you, and yet, even before that comes, I feel the approaching change."

"I day say you do, sir; but it must be unpleasant in the extreme."

"It certainly is; and I have found it so. Mrs. Meredith, I hope you enjoyed your walk; did you go far?"

"No, Colonel, I did not; else I had not been back so soon. By the way, how do you feel after your walk, or, rather, ride? I had not time to ask you before."

"Oh, I am very well; I enjoyed it much; but I must take another the day after tomorrow," said the colonel. "That is, another ride; for I cannot walk far."

"Do you intend going far?"

"To the South Sea House," replied the colonel.

"To the South Sea house," repeated the attorney to himself, as he sipped his tea; "he has some of the stock on his hands. Well, I dare say that is likely; people belonging to these companies generally prefer them to any other stock. However, I will follow him there, and see if I can't do better. I will tread upon his heels but what I will find out something this time, at all events."

"Are you acquainted with that stock?" he inquired, after a pause.

"What the South Sea Stock?" inquired the colonel.

"Yes."

"Not much; but I believe it to be a good, steady stock — a very good investment; it will pay you a better interest than the funds."

"But is it as secure?"

"Well, that is a very difficult thing to answer," said the colonel; "but I think is safe enough. I have that opinion of it that I do not object to hold it."

"That, of course, is the best answer one can have to its presumed security."

"Yes, I have a good opinion of it, and do not object holding it, as I said before; and that is the best opinion that can well be offered. Have you any?"

"None, sir; but I have a friend, who wanted to purchase stock of some kind, or to place money out to advantage, and I wished to learn a little more concerning it."

"I do not mean to say there is no better; but when you have once invested your money, you do not like to change the stock."

"Certainly not; it is unadvisable," said the attorney, "unless you have some specific reason for so doing at the best of times. You are the loser by the expenses."

"Well," said Mrs. Meredith, "I am very glad to see you are so well after your journey."

"Journey, do you call it? Why ma'am, I cannot call anything less than some few hundred miles a journey; anything less is a mere bagatelle."

"Dear me, colonel; what journeys you must have traveled."

"Indeed I have, madam; some of hem beautiful and romantic, and some of them dreary, and some terrible, from the obstacles that opposed us, and others, from the nature of the ground that we had to go over, and the dangers attendant from fatigue, climate, and the enemy."

"It must be a terrible thing; females in those parts are out of the question."

"Oh! dear, no; there are ladies, and English ladies, too, who live there for years, and who follow their husbands; movements with the camp, and who undergo all the dangers and fatigues merrily and cheerfully, and even put some of the best of us to the blush for fortitude."

"Well, I am glad we have a good character, even so far off as India."

"It cannot but be expected but the mothers of such men can bear fatigue and hardship, else; their sons could never be what they are. However, we have many examples of heroism in India, not of men only, but women also."

"Then there are many interesting points for us to hear explanation about India," said Margaret; "I love to hear such things, especially from those who have been there, and mixed up among the people who live here, and who have had much experience with them."

"I hope we shall have ample time to talk over many such matters," returned the colonel, "for to me it is pleasant to speak of the past, and relate all I have seen, known, and taken part in, in a place so distant from us all, as our Eastern empire."

"Indeed, I love to hear them," said Margaret.

"I am afraid she will keep you pretty constantly employed in relating all that you have ever seen, colonel," said Mrs. Meredith; "she's a strange girl, and has many fancies that way; she fond of the wild, irregular life that you describe; she would have made an excellent soldier's wife, I am sure; she's so fond of that kind of thing."

"I hope she will do so now, madam: and that she will have less of the fatigue and danger that fall to the lot of a good many, for I candidly tell you it is one thing to hear these things talked of, and another to bear with them. Plains of burning sand, and want of water, mountainous regions covered with snow, and no means to obtain warmth and shelter, — these are things exciting enough in a narrative, and yet heartbreaking to experience."

'Oh!" said the attorney; "there can be no doubt it's much better in perspective, than it is to experience. I can easily imagine when you hear of battles and sieges, how they wish they had been there; and how much would have been done by our individual exertions. But, dear me, that's as different from being shot in the beginning, and so seeing none of the fun that was to follow. Lord bless my heart, being put out of the way in that manner, positively makes me nervous, I do believe. I could be hanged before I marched up to the breach."

"Fortunately, all men are not of that opinion, else we might all of us be murdered in our beds, and no one to protect us," said Margaret, contemptuously.

"It is necessary," said the colonel, "that some men should be born for one purpose, and some another. Some are poltroons from their birth, and require better men to take care of them, while others win honor and profit on the field of death and danger, and snatch triumph from the hands of death."

'Exactly," said the attorney; "half a loaf is better than no bread; and half a man is better than no man at all; and I believe that many of them leave the field of battle, leave it in a very little better state. Now, I should not care for life upon such terms; it must be such as is worth living for, and such I do not consider life, when one is rendered a cripple all one's life."

"Well," said the colonel, "we all have out different ideas upon that subject; but I rather think the state would be nothing without the profession of arms, and the lawyers would grace the lamp-posts, if I might judge from popular opinion."

"Popular opinion is nothing in this country upon such matters," said Twissel, contemptuously.

"It amounts to something," retorted the colonel; "and you would say so, I imagine, if you felt it clinging to your throat in the shape of a halter, administered by the *canaille*."

"Why," said Mrs. Meredith, "I dare say it isn't always expressed so forcibly, and Mr. Twissel does not hold it of any importance, so long as it is not expressed so loudly as that."

"Certainly, Mrs. Meredith; that is my meaning; for an illegal act committed by a contemptible portion of the population becomes of importance."

"So it does," said the colonel; "that is easily verified."

"But still we may be thankful to those who bravely fight and die, that we may be here in ease and quiet, and free from danger, and able to enjoy our lives and homes in peace."

"That is true," said the attorney; "the one part of a nation cannot do without another; all are necessary, and produce a powerful kingdom, and not only powerful, but rich and intelligent."

"No doubt of that," said the colonel.

Tea was now cleared away, and some wine was placed upon the table, and the colonel took a few glasses of some rare wine, of which he offered the attorney to drink, and the latter willingly accepted, and found it some of the best he had tasted; and he continued to taste it until he got quite talkative, and, to the pain and mortification of Mrs. Meredith, began to talk in a strain that would in a short time have done them much discredit and mischief.

Mrs. Meredith, however, always full of expedient, soon devised on that had the effect of putting an end to a scene she feared would come to an unpleasant act, if continued in; and therefore, left the room for a few minutes, and then when she returned, she said, —

"Mr. Twissel, you have been sent for; you are wanted immediately."

"I — I sent for?"

"Yes, sir, you are wanted."

"Nobody knew I was here. Oh, yes, I told my clerk as I came along, confound him! Just as I was so comfortable, too."

"We can finish this another time," said the colonel, pointing to the bottle.

"Yes, thank you. Good night, Colonel Deverill."

"Good evening, Mr. Twissel."

Mr. Twissel quitted the drawing-room, vowing vengeance to himself against the brute of a clerk of his, who should dare to come and interrupt such an agreeable evening. It was most horribly provoking. He could have called down the vengeance of the universe upon the head of the offending mortal who had come for him, and in this mood of mind he entered the parlor.

"Where is he — where is he?"

"Where is who?" inquired Mrs. Meredith.

"My clerk — the man who came for me."

"Listen, Mr. Twissel," said Mrs. Meredith; "I have called you out. No one has been for you; but I had no other means of calling you out, as I wanted to speak to you."

"Well," said Mr. Twissel, half surprised and half vexed, "what do you want to say to me now I am here."

"I want to impress upon you the fact, that the habits of the colonel lead him to retire about this time, and I feared you, not knowing this, might stop beyond the proper moment, and so took this method of telling you what I am sure you would like to know."

Mr. Twissel could not object; there was something reasonable in it, and yet he was at heart vexed, and could not help saying, —

"I should have thought the colonel would not have been so pleasant and so talkative; if he had not been comfortable, he would have said so."

"Oh, dear, no, he would not have done that, even if you had remained till daylight; he has too much courtesy towards a stranger to do so."

"Very well," said Twissel, "I will be gone. However, I will take care and not forget the South Sea House the day after tomorrow. You must make the best of it you can, and let me know when he is likely to go, so that I may not lose any chance."

"Certainly not. I'll do as I did before," said the lady.

"Do so."

"And I hope you will meet with better luck than you met with before."

"I hope so too," said the attorney, gravely. "However, here I am, and I'll do all that I can do for you. Good by, Mrs. Meredith — good day — good night."

"Good night," said Mrs. Meredith, and the attorney left the house, to their inexpressible relief, for he was growing very talkative and very troublesome too, for the misfortune was, he more than once touched upon forbidden topics.

Chapter CXXVII.

THE DIFFICULTIES TO BE ENCOUNTERED IN THE CHOICE OF A BRIDESMAID.

"Well, Margaret," said Mrs. Meredith, when they were alone in their own apartment — "well, and how have you got on with the colonel?"

"Oh, very well indeed, ma'."

"I am glad of it. Has he proposed anything new to you, my dear, or has he said anything more to you of a particular character? Has he said anything respecting property? That is what we want to know pretty well, and that is the only point that can be more than usually interesting to us."

"No, ma', nothing about property. I could not expect he would say anything to me, and I hardly expect he would to any one at all. You see, he is no doubt a rich man."

"Well, and he would not consider it at all necessary to say anything about it to any one; that it is so peculiarly private, and has nothing to do with any one; and he does not imagine that we require anything of the kind. I am sure if the thought entered his mind, he would at once satisfy us upon the subject. I cannot speak to him about it, because, having none, I am really not entitled to do so. That's my opinion upon the subject, though Mr. Twissel, I dare say, has a different one to me; indeed, he generally has one of his own."

"Yes, you may depend upon that; but I have been thinking the matter over, and I am sure he is what he says he is. But what did he say, my dear?"

"Why, he insists that I shall name an early day."

"Insists! my child. What does he mean?"

"Merely in a good-natured, though urgent manner. Indeed, he wishes me to make up my mind and have him at once. If I'll consent to have him, he'll obtain a special license to solemnize the marriage here in this house, or at church, which I like best. Which shall I consent to, ma'?"

"Well, my dear, I think you may as well be married at home; it will be so much more fashionable than going to church."

"It will be much more trouble, and will hardly seem like a marriage, I think, if it is not done at a church. What do you think?"

"It will make more noise," said Mrs. Meredith, "if it is done at home; and yet nobody can say a word about it if it takes place at church."

"So I think, now; so I think."

"Well, what did you decide?"

"I did not decide upon anything," said Margaret; "I declined to do so upon the moment, but said I would think about it, and after a few words, I promised I would let him know the next time he spoke to me about it, which should not be before tomorrow afternoon."

"Very well, my dear. A becoming reluctance will never hurt your cause; you have done quite right, and I have no doubt but he will feel more pleased with you than if you had at once consented upon his first asking."

"So I thought, ma," sad Margaret.

"But you must not carry that too far, or it may defeat its own object, when next he asked you, you must affect a great deal of emotion —

trembling and blushing, and all that kind of thing, which you can do very well; or if you should distrust yourself, you can practice it a bit before a glass. I did it when I was your age, and I did it well."

"Yes, ma', I can manage all that well enough; but what time shall I name?"

"Well, that must in some measure depend upon the humor you find him in. If he be very pressing, you may shorten the period; if he appear distant, lengthen it; but if there is any danger, take him at his word at once, and have no delay. It will not do to lose a chance; he must not be allowed to get off in that manner; and you must declare your confusion to be so great that you hardly know what you say, but, as he is so very pressing, you will give in to his wishes, and you may name any day you like best; and then he is caught, you see."

"I understand that clearly; but what time would you, as a medium time, give, which I out to lengthen or shorten as occasion may seem to require?"

"Well, my dear, about a fortnight."

"Ah, that was on my own tongue, too. Well, then, I should not have done wrong in naming three weeks or a month, which I felt disposed to say at first."

"No, no, but you need not make it more than three weeks, unless you see any fitting occasion, or any necessity for so doing," said Mrs. Meredith.

*A*fter an amiable council the mother and daughter held, having for its object the entanglement and speedy marrying of the unfortunate East Indian colonel, they both indulged in balmy sleep, and slept till morn. The colonel himself said no more about the object of the previous day's conversation, when the amiable mother left the daughter alone with the colonel, who appeared as if actuated by clock-work; when the hour of his forbearance had passed, he again spoke of the matter.

"Miss Meredith," he said, "my impatience will, I hope, be excused, on the score that my love is ardent; and I have already waited as long as I promised. You know to what I allude."

"I am afraid I must say I do, Colonel Deverill," said Margaret; "but will you not grant me more time to consider this matter over? Remember, it is a serious matter."

"Of that there is no doubt," said the colonel; "but I do not feel the same doubts you do, for I only feel how much I can do for your happiness, and how willingly I will do it."

"Of that I can have no fear."

"Then why not consent at once? Consent to have the man who loves you who dotes upon you, and who will do all that an ample fortune can enable him to do for your welfare, and your future prosperity and comfort. Consider all that."

"I have considered much; I don't know that I need consider more than my present happiness; the future will take care of itself; at all events, we can do no more than to deserve to do well, and to succeed in all our undertakings — to deserve to be happy."

"And do more you cannot; and who is there that can do as much?"

"We all endeavor to do so."

"I hope we do so, though I am sure there are many who might do better; but, to return to my hopes, when will you consent to become mine — say the day on which I am to be made happy; and, if you really love me, make it as short as you can."

Margaret appeared to hesitate, and hung her head, trembled, and the blushes mounted her cheek; the colonel caught her in his arms — and pressing her to his bosom, he said, —

"Come, come, my own Margaret say when shall I be made happy."

"Oh! Deverill," she sighed, as she hid her face; "what shall I say — you are so urgent; shall I say a — a fortnight; and yet that is, — too — too, soon."

"No — no, not at all — not at all; thank you, dear Margaret, thank you."

"I — I — I fear I have said too much; forgive me —"

"Nay, nay, no more about it; I will be content; tomorrow I will go to the city, and then I will purchase the wedding-ring. I will obtain a license, and then we shall be ready against any contingencies; and on our wedding morning, I will have some jewels ready for you. I have given them some orders, but they take a long while in getting ready."

"Oh, you are too good."

"Not a bit — only just," said the colonel; and he appeared as though he were quite satisfied with his conquest, and looked very well pleased with the success he had met with in the prosecution of his suit. It was a settled thing now, and he was, or professed to be in ecstasies.

"Mother," said Margaret as she entered the room, "it is all settled at last; I have given my consent, and the day is named."

"Indeed! I am glad of it. When will the day arrive — what day is it?"

"This day fortnight."

"This day fortnight! well — well, that will be a very good time — very good time, indeed; we shall have a very busy time of it, for we must make the most of our arrangements between this and then; for we must get you in a fit out; but if you have a dress to appear in, that is as much as I shall be able to afford you, for my means are so short."

"I know all that; but he has promised me jewels, which he has ordered, but which will take some time in making; but he expects them to be ready by our wedding-day. Come, now, this seems to me to be a very handsome provision."

"Very, my dear; very fortunate, too, because you see the furniture was becoming somewhat less new and fine that it was; that would have compelled me to lessen my terms; so we should have gone gradually back, and, perhaps, been obliged to seek some other mode of living."

"But you have some money by you?"

"That was reserved in case of extreme misfortunes, and I cannot realize that immediately; however, it would only put off the evil day; but we are saved that, now — we have caught a rare good fish — we have only to land him, that is, get some little to be done before we pull him ashore. We must keep up the farce; but, I tell you, we must not be guided by Mr. Twissel, though he is of great use."

"No, ma', we must not; I have thought on that."

"And yet I do not like to give up the idea of finding out first what he may have in the shape of property, though I am sure it would do no good; yet, to have one's curiosity satisfied is something gained. Still, I am not so curious that I must be satisfied at the expense of our prospects."

"No, ma'; I am sure I want badly enough to know all about it, but I will restrain my curiosity until I find out by means and at a time when no offence can be taken; or, if it be, why it's of no consequence, and I don't care anything about it, because I shall have a right to speak for myself."

"Certainly, my dear, that is a very proper spirit — a very proper spirit, indeed; but then he won't interfere with you much, except it is to want you to be always at his elbow."

"Ah, I won't mind that, because, you see, he may make a will; but I'll take pretty good care that nobody comes in between him and me."

"Exactly; you have no relatives on his side to tease you, or give you any trouble; therefore you have all plain sailing before you."

"I have; and now, I suppose, it will not be too much to speak to one's bridesmaids?"

"Ah! my dear," said Mrs. Meredith, with a shake of the head.

"What's the matter, ma'?"

"Ah! my dear, there is the difficulty; you know how easy the colonel has fallen in love with you; how sudden that has all come about, and how short a time the courtship has continued."

"So much the better, ma'."

"Certainly, my love; but it should make you cautious — very cautious, how you act with bridesmaids, because you don't know what may happen with such old people as the colonel — they are dreadful, some-times and you don't know what they will do. They will fall in love with anybody; it is quite shocking to think of it; but it don't so much matter, only you see he may take a violent fancy to some one, and then you may lose by the whole affair."

"How so, ma'?"

"Why, suppose he takes a fancy to one of the bridesmaids? — you don't know what may pass between them."

"Certainly not."

"Very well; then he may make a will to reward her, as he would call it, and then you lose so much, which is a clear robbery, as I call it."

"So it would be, ma'; and yet, after all's said and done, I cannot tell what else we are to do; some female friends we must have; and the only precaution we can take will be to get some one as ugly as I can, and then keep her away as much as possible."

"The latter is the only effectual method, for ugliness is not always a safeguard, for men have got such tastes, and what we think extremely plain, they, by a perversity of taste, will persist in believing to be interesting, at least, if not pretty. I have known so many instances; besides, I do know that even ugliness itself is no safeguard."

"Indeed, ma'!"

"No; I had an instance of that — I may say two — even with your father, who took a fancy to two of the servants, one after the other. I am sure there was nothing in the hussies to attract any attention; but then men will be men, and you can't help it."

"We must get rid of them."

"Yes, that is all you can do; but whom did you think of having?"

"There are the two Miss Stewards —"

"They are called pretty. I heard a gentleman say so at the last party we went to, so that I think decidedly bad policy. I know the men's taste very well, my dear, but it is different to what we call taste; I don't know why, but it is so."

"Well, ma', if the Misses Steward won't do, what do you say to the Misses Brown? They are anything but even passable; besides, they are pitted with the small-pox, and very light hair, almost carroty — they are anything but fascinating."

"That may be all very true, my dear, but you know the Misses Brown sing, they are called good figures, and dashing young women, and they are very bold, which might tempt many people, especially when they are looking about for sweethearts."

"Yes, that is very true; then there are the Misses Smith — they are very young — much too young to be at all likely to cause men to have any fancy for them."

"There, my dear innocent girl, you are entirely wrong — most entirely wrong."

"Indeed, ma'?"

"Yes, my dear, you are innocence itself, because you have been brought up at home; but, look here, men are the nastiest creatures alive — why, some of them would fall in love with a girl sixteen or seventeen years old. Aye, more than that, — I have seen some of them married at that age."

"Oh! I am shocked," said Margaret, as she lifted up her hands in amazement at this description of the vices of men. "Ah! well they may say at church, 'And there is no good in us.'"

"Indeed, my dear, you are quite right, and so is the Prayer-book — but it is as I tell you; beside, men never forget these things; they will remember faces they have seen for a year or two, and then they will begin their games."

"Dear me, ma', what shall I do?"

"That is the difficulty, my dear. I would not have unfolded this book of vice before you, had it not been necessary for your happiness."

"Oh! fiddle de dee ma' — it's the money that I care for; it ain't the colonel, poor old cripple. He may do as he pleases, as long as I get the gold."

"Well, my dear," said the careful mother, who felt the sedative effects of this speech, "well, my dear, but you know they do waste their means in these affairs, and that most outrageously, sometimes, to cause a ruinous effect upon their home."

"Oh! but he's too much of an invalid."

"Do you know, Margaret, I think the colonel is more of an invalid from habit than reality. Sometimes, when nobody's looking, he can walk and use both feet alike, and even use his left hand without any trouble at all."

"Do you really think so?"

"Yes, but I don't mean to say it is all sham. Oh, dear, no, but long habit, and the laziness of these rich Indians is so great, that there is no knowing its extent. I don't believe they would eat, if it wasn't for their being hungry."

"What is to be done?"

"I will tell you, my dear. Have Miss Twissel and her friend."

"Miss Twissel and Martha Briggs," exclaimed Miss Meredith with a giggle. "What a fright!"

"So much the better, my dear — so much the better. It is just what you want — the very thing above all others. Have a fool and a fright, and you can drop their acquaintance whenever you like, and I think there can be no danger of the colonel's falling in love with them. At least," added Mrs. Meredith, with emphasis, — "at least, upon such an occasion."

"Very well, ma'. Let it be Miss Twissel and Martha Briggs. Goodness me, how I shall be attended upon this occasion — it will be quite laughable. I mustn't let the colonel see them before the morning arrives, else he will be sure to laugh at them."

"Ha! ha! ha!" laughed both mother and daughter at the idea of the two frights, as they called them, being bridesmaids; and in high good humor they both retired to rest for the night, to dream of the forthcoming occasion.

Chapter CXXVIII.

MR. TWISSEL'S MISFORTUNES, AND HIS RESOLUTION NEVER TO GIVE IN.

*T*he next day after that on which the conversation respecting the choice of a bridesmaid took place, was the day on which the colonel was to visit the South Sea House.

Early that morning he ordered a coach to be in attendance, and left the house, saying that he would be back in time for tea; that he had to make several purchases, and transact some necessary business that would occupy him until that time. He kissed Margaret, and whispered in her ear that he should call and see about the jewels, and urge the jeweler to get them ready.

"These people are so dilatory," he said, "that, unless I worry them, they will disappoint me of them; and I would not be without them on the occasion of our marriage for a trifle."

"We must not set our happiness upon such things," said Margaret.

"Ah, what self-denial you can exert!" said the colonel, playfully.

"No; my happiness is not fixed upon such objects as those, and, therefore, it is no trouble to renounce them when it is necessary to do so."

"I hope there will be no need. I believe there will be none; but good bye till teatime, and then we shall pass a pleasant evening together."

The colonel left the house, and no sooner had he done so, than Mrs. Meredith wrote a short note to Mr. Twissel, informing him of the colonel's departure at a much earlier hour than she had anticipated.

"Here, Mary," she said to the drudge.

"Yes, ma'am," replied the domestic.

"Just run as fast as you can to Mr. Twissel with this note, and don't let the grass grow under your feet. Do you hear?"

"Yes, ma'am."

Away went the drudge as fast as she could to the man of law, and arrived there out of breath; and having gone there fast, according to orders, she thought herself at liberty to take her own time in going back, which she performed to perfection.

Mr. Twissel cursed himself for this unexpected departure; but there was no time for deliberation. He crushed on his hat, took a coach, and drove as hard as the mysteriously-kept-up cattle cold carry it, and was fortunate enough to see the colonel go by in another. He jumped out, paid the jarvey, and then made a rush after the colonel, whom he saw going up the steps.

Determined that he would not be outdone this time, he rushed through a crowd of men who were near at hand, and jostled them so, that they gave him more oaths than was consistent with courtesy, and one of them desired to know if he were running after himself or anybody else.

Heedless of this, he pushed on, and trod upon a bricklayer's foot so hard, that the man gave a great shout, and, by way of retaliation, brought his heavy hand down so hard upon the attorney's hat, that the article of wearing apparel was forced below his chin, much to the detriment of his vision, which was totally eclipsed.

In an instant he was struggling with his hat, and yet was unable to release himself from the durance in which his head was held; but he found this was not all he had to contend with, for he felt himself pushed and hustled about in a strange manner, till he was thrown on a door step, and then he was suddenly left to himself, with no soul near him.

"Upon my word, this must be done on purpose, I do verily believe," said Mr. Twissel, as he at length succeeded in wrenching his hat off his head, after many violent efforts; but even then it was at the expense of the lining and skin off his nose, which was a very disagreeable affair, after all.

Mr. Twissel, for a moment or two, stared round him, and wondered where he was, until, at length, upon some examination, he found himself round the corner.

"Oh, I must have got hustled round the corner — yes, yes, I see how it is; it's a down-right conspiracy of theirs — there can't be two minds."

But then, again, he thought what conspiracy could there be necessary to marry a girl without money? If she had money, he could have understood it, but not as the matter stood — that was quite impossible. It was an impenetrable mystery.

As these thoughts passed through his mind, he was sitting on the step of a door, and, seeing the blood trickle off his nose in vermilion drops upon the pavement, he felt for his handkerchief to wipe the injured feature, and stop the bleeding.

But, alas! it was not in this pocket, nor in that; it was not in his hat — he never carried it there; if he had, his head would never have reached the crown of his hat — that was quite certain; it would have been better had he done so.

But, as it was not about him, where could it be? He knew that he had had it before he left home on this errand; the truth, however, was not long before it came across his mind like a flash of light. He had got among a gang of London thieves, who had hustled and robbed him of his handkerchief.

This was suggestive of other matters, and he, in consequence, put his hand to his watch-fob, but also that was gone, too. He gasped — felt his breeches pocket, and then he sank back, for he found his garments had been slit open by some sharp instrument, and his purse had fled.

"D — n!" said the attorney, in a fury; but this subsided in a moment. The loss he had felt, and the pushing about he had experienced, was too much; he felt weakened and disheartened, and paused to think upon what he should do, and which way he should go.

"It's no use giving in," he muttered; "no use at all. I must go on. And yet, I had better go and see if the coach is gone, for if it is still there — and it can't have gone away yet — I'll yet go in and see if I can find him."

He walked round the corner, much shaken with what he had received in the way of knocks and kicks, but when he did get round, he saw the coach was gone. There was, however, a ticket-porter at hand, and he determined to go and ask him a few questions.

"My friend," he said, feeling in his pocket; "do you know a Colonel Deverill?"

"No," said the man; "never heard of him — where does he live?"

"He came in here just now."

"Ah, did he?" replied the man, kicking a piece of orange peel off the pavement; "I don't know him."

"Do you recollect a hackney-coach coming up to the door just now, with a lame gentleman, who got out?"

"Yes; with a green shade over his eye."

"Yes — that was the man."

"Oh, well, I never seed him afore — I don't know him — he didn't stop a minute."

"Oh!" said Mr. Twissel, and then he turned away, and walked towards his own house. However, he felt in his pocket for some money; a small sum in silver was loose in his pockets, and this he had saved, and he determined to treat himself to some brandy-and-water, for he was really much knocked about, and terrified and nervous, so he went into the first public-house he came to.

This was a low house, the parlor of which was situated a long way back, and he walked in and threw himself into a seat.

"Well, well; here I am. This is disaster the second. Well, who would have believed I should have met with such misadventures as those I have just gone through? There's a fate in it. I am sure this is an unlucky business altogether — of that I am certain. I got into the watch house on the first occasion, but now I am worse than that; I have been knocked about and robbed of money and goods — fifteen pounds in my purse — confound Colonel Deverill, I say."

"What will you take, sir?"

"Eh?" inquired the bewildered attorney, who forgot that he had entered a public-house, and the waiter was desiring to know what he wished to have.

"What will you like to take, sir?" inquired the waiter, again.

"A glass of brandy-and-water, and a biscuit."

The man left the room, and Twissel retired within himself to contemplate the evils he had suffered, and those he was likely to endure.

"Well, I never thought I was in such a thing as this. Who would ever have believed it? None, I am sure — no one could. Confound them! I'll give it up as a bad job, and a bad job it has been for me, I am quite confident of that."

"Brandy-and-water, and a biscuit," said the waiter, laying down the articles enumerated, and Twissel gave the necessary cash, accompanied by the customary gratuity, which ranges from ten to twenty-five per cent upon the money paid for the articles purchased.

We have often thought this a most exorbitant tax upon those who require accommodation. If people cannot pay their own servants, they ought not to keep them; to be sure, you are told you need not pay anything — it is entirely voluntary, and that they do not wish it; but you only obtain a flippant answer, so as to attract every one's eyes in the place, and the end of it is, if there is much business, you don't get any attention at all.

"Well, I won't give in," said Mr. Twissel, with a thump on the table; but he had drank nearly two-thirds of the brandy-and-water.

"No, I won't give in."

He swallowed down the remainder, finished the biscuit, and leaned back in his seat, and then he began to talk to himself.

"I will not give in; after all that has passed, it would be a shame to be done, robbed, beaten, and kicked; and then give in — nonsense! I will go through the whole affair, and that shall repay me in the end. I'll lay it on the thicker for this."

This was a comfortable resolution on the part of Mr. Twissel, and which appeared to please him well, for he smiled quietly, and then rose much refreshed and left the house.

This last allusion of Twissel's was consolatory, and had an intimate connection with certain imaginary charges he would make to the Deverill family when he got the business; but as that was a matter buried in the womb of futurity, we will not follow him in his speculations.

"I won't give in," he said, as he walked on, and thrust his hand into the slit that had been cut in his trousers to extract his purse; but this only confirmed him in his resolution, and he uttered again and again, "I won't give in."

"I won't give in," he murmured, as he sought the knocker of Mrs. Meredith's door. "I won't give in — I'm not a man whose resolution is easily shaken. Oh, dear, no; I'll tell my good friend, Mrs. Meredith, all my troubles, and then ask her what she thinks of me — if I ain't an indefatigable friend, one who will never sink under difficulties.

Chapter **CXXIX.**

MRS. MEREDITH HAS A CONVERSATION WITH MR. TWISSEL. – THE ANNOUNCEMENT, AND THE INVITATION.

When the servant answered the knock, Mr. Twissel learned, to his severe disappointment, that Mrs. Meredith was from home; and he was about to turn from the door, after leaving his name, when the girl said that her mistress had left a message, the purport of which was, that if he, Mr. Twissel, was to call, she would feel obliged by his awaiting her return, as her absence would be but short, and the subject upon which she wished to see him was one of particular importance.

Mr. Twissel was shown into the parlor much about the same as usual; but he himself was somewhat of a different state. He himself was considerably disgusted with his share of the business; but, as we have before stated, he was resolved never to give in; no, he was resolved to carry it on to the end.

"It must come to a wind-up somehow or other, and at some time or other; but, at the same time, as I have taken so much interest in that I am resolved to see it out, I won't lose all I have lost for nothing; it shall be with me a neck or nothing affair; and, however aggravating it may be, you will have a greater chance in the long run of coming off victorious."

Several minutes passed away, and still Mrs. Meredith came not. At length the attorney began to grow somewhat impatient, and he looked around the apartment, as if to find some object to pass away the time until her arrival. On a table in the center of the room lay several books, and he opened one or two of them for the purpose of ascertaining the nature of the contents. The title of one of them attracted his attention; it consisted of a collection of tales of the supernatural, and he opened it upon a legend called "The Dead Not Dead." It possessed considerable interest, and Twissel was soon lost in its details. It ran as follows: —

The moon, with her train of glittering satellites following with silent grandeur in her wake, is sailing, in lustrous glory, through the heavens, and shedding such a flood of light over the face of nature, that the mountains and trees look as if some mighty hand had tinted them with silver.

Our scene is a rocky pass amidst the stupendous Apennines — one of the wildest, and yet most beautiful of that romantic region.

At the foot of a tree, and on a spot on which the rays of the moon fall with all their power, sits a young man, who is evidently watching over what appears to be a dead body that lies prostrate at his feet. His head is resting on his hand, and he is regarding the form before him with mingled fear and determination.

Hark! he speaks! What are his words?

"For full an hour have the rays of yonder luminary poured their radiance upon the ghastly features of my dead master, and yet there is no effect visible. Surely he must have been laboring under some fearful delusion of mind, and the dreadful compact of which he has spoken had existence but in his imagination. I certainly had some little faith in the existence of those scourges to mankind — vampyres, but now, I am inclined to think, my faith will be terribly shaken. In God's name, I hope it may."

The moon rose higher and higher, until, as she reached her zenith, everything was so bathed in her gentle light, that scarcely a shadow was thrown around, save by the tall pines that were scattered here and there upon the face of the rocks.

Suddenly there was a movement in the form of the dead man — a spasmodic jerk of the whole muscles of the frame, as if a galvanic battery had been applied to it; and then the eyes slowly opened, though at first there was but little or no expression in them.

The young man started to his feet with an exclamation of horror, and stood glaring upon the form with fixed and protruding eyes, his limbs trembling, and every feature distorted with mental agony.

"Holy mother of God!" he murmured, in a low tone, "he moves! he moves! The terrible compact is too true."

At this moment, though there was not the slightest appearance of a cloud in the whole heavens, mutterings of thunder were heard, and the lightning was seen playing around the tree-tops with a pale and sickly glare. The young man, so intensely was his attention fixed upon the corpse at the foot of the tree, did not notice this phenomena; and he was at length horrified at beholding a ball of blue fire dart from the air, and glide into the ground immediately at the head of him whom he had named as his master. Then there was a loud explosion, and a glare of light so broad and strong that the watcher of the dead was obliged to veil his eyes with his hands, and he could scarcely tell for some moments whether he were deprived of his sight or not.

When he opened his eyes again, it was with a start of surprise, for, before him, with his arms folded on his breast, and regarding him with a calm and untroubled countenance, stood his master; while the moonlight streamed out upon the landscape, and as great a silence as when he lay in death upon the ground reigned around.

"Oh, signor," he at length stammered, in broken tones — "my vigil has been one of the most terrible —"

"Silence, Spalatro," said the resuscitated one, in a deep and hollow voice — "silence. Not a word, now or henceforth, must pass your lips respecting what you have seen to night. Breathe but a syllable of what I am to a human being, and naught on earth shall hide you from my vengeance."

Spalatro bowed before his master in obedience, while his frame gave a shudder of horror, as he regarded the deathly appearance that still lingered in the signor's features.

"Spalatro," resumed the signor, after a slight pause, "you have rendered me great and faithful service, and your reward has been proportionate; but there is yet another service which I would seek at your hands. The Lady Oriana, for the possession of whom the Signor Fracati and I have fought, and for whose sake I received the wound which deprived me for a time of life, is at Florence, and at present ignorant of the mishap that befell me. The Signor Fracati and yourself are the only persons who are aware of it. He will carry to Florence the news of my death; and, on my re-appearance before the Lady Oriana, what tale can I invent to satisfy her? No, no — he must not reach Florence — he must never look upon the Lady Oriana again. You, Spalatro, wear a poniard, you have a powerful hand — and you know well where to strike. Rid me of this hated rival, and wealth shall be yours."

Spalatro stood rooted to the spot while the signor spoke, and an expression of mingled horror and disgust crossed his countenance as the latter proceeded. When the signor had concluded, he stepped a pace or two back, and in a tone full of indignation, said, —

"Signor Waldeberg, I am no assassin; my poniard is yet guiltless of shedding human blood. I saw you receive what was thought to be a mortal wound in honorable combat with the Signor Fracati, and in these arms I beheld you sink in death. You had extorted from me a promise that after a certain lapse of time I would convey your body to this vast solitude, and lay it where the moonbeams should fall upon it; for that then life should once more revisit you. All this I have done, and faithfully; I feared to fail in my promise, for I knew the penalty you would pay if you failed to fulfill the conditions of your compact. But, signor, I am now no longer bound to you; you have commenced a fresh existence, which you would baptize with blood; you have passed the portals of death, and I will no longer serve you. I will seek another service and another master, who will require less at my hands, though his pay may be lighter. Farewell, signor, and better thoughts to you."

Spalatro turned upon his heel as he spoke, and with a hasty wave of his hand was leaving the spot, when the signor drew a pistol from a belt that was fastened round his waist, and, exclaiming, "He knows too much respecting me to be suffered to live," fired it full at the head of the young man. The latter uttered a yell of agony which echoed loudly amid the awful silence, and fell lifeless on the earth. When the smoke from the pistol had cleared away, that lonely spot was deserted save by the body of Spalatro, whose blood, streaming upon the ground, reflected the moonbeams with a dull red glare.

When the morning sun broke over the mountain tops, its rays fell upon the form of the still insensible Spalatro. It was but seldom that any footsteps, save those of the wolf or the goat, left their impress on those rocks, and it was almost a miracle that the body of the unfortunate man was not left a prey to the former.

About an hour after daybreak, the bells of a string of mules were heard in the distance, accompanied by the cheerful song of the muleteer. A short time sufficed to bring the cavalcade to the spot, where lay the body of Spalatro, and the muleteer, with a cry of alarm, brought his train to a stop. Finding that life still remained, the humane mountaineer raised him from the ground, placed him across one of the mules, and then hastened forward to the next inn, which, however, was at some miles distance.

On arriving there, he found that the only apartment was occupied by a signor and his daughter, who, however, when the condition of the wounded man was made known to them, instantly relinquished it to him, and, after seeing his wounds looked to, ascertained that no mortal result was to be feared, and giving orders that he should want for no attention that money could procure, they pursued their journey.

It was many weeks before Spalatro recovered, and when he did regain his strength, he learned, with a feeling of deep gratitude, that the lady who had been so instrumental in his recovery was no other than the Signora Oriana. In an instant a vow was upon his lips that he would save her from the power of the fearful monster, whose only mission now on earth, seemed but to destroy the most beautiful of nature's creation. With this purpose fixed in his mind, he one morning bid adieu to the residents of the little inn, and set off on his self-imposed errand.

*S*ome days after the scene we have described as occurring on that lonely mountain pass, a report reached Florence, where the Signora Oriana was then staying with her father, that the Signor Fracati had met his death at the hands of a bravo, and that his body had been discovered stabbed in innumerable places. The grief of Oriana was intense, for she held the signor in great estimation, and she would have had but little hesitation in bestowing upon him her hand, if her father's consent could but have been gained to the union. Signor Vivaldi, however, had been captivated by the great wealth, personal appearance, and captivating manners of the Signor Waldeberg, and he had fixed his mind upon him becoming the husband of his daughter.

Weeks passed away, and the memory of the murdered Fracati was gradually fading from the mind of Oriana. The respectful yet warm attentions of Waldeberg won upon a young and innocent heart that had always felt a slight esteem for him, and as she knew that her father's happiness in a great measure depended upon her consent to the union, it was at length given with a freedom that brought joy to the old man's heart.

It was arranged that the ceremony should take place at a chateau belonging to Waldeberg, in the neighborhood of Lucca, whither it was resolved at once to proceed; and for this purpose Signor Vivaldi and his daughter, accompanied by Waldeberg, left Florence for that city.

As they were passing through the gates, a monk, with his cowl drawing carefully over his face, stepped hastily up to the carriage window, and, thrusting a letter into the hands of Oriana, as hastily disappeared.

With some surprise, she opened it and read it, and then a paleness overspread her countenance, and she sank back in her seat almost insensible. Her father snatched the paper from her trembling hand, and hastily glancing over its contents, with a look of anger, handed it to the Signor Waldeberg.

"See, signor, what some meddling fool, envious of your happiness, has done to alarm my daughter's fears. Does he deem us so grossly superstitious as to believe in such children's tales?"

The signor took the paper, which he found to run thus: —

"SIGNORA, — A grateful heart warns you. Wed not the murderer of Fracati — wed not him who, once returned from death to life, seeks but your hand to provide a victim for the purpose of prolonging a hateful existence. If you despise this warning, at any rate, postpone the ceremony but for seven days from hence, and then his power of injuring you will have departed from him."

"Do you know the writer, signor?" asked Vivaldi.

"It is evidently the handwriting of a servant of mine, whom I dismissed for insolence some few weeks since," returned Waldeberg, a shade of vexation evidently passing across his brow; "and he now takes this means of endeavoring to obtain his revenge. But I will take means of having him punished."

They now endeavored to soothe the agitation of Oriana, but the incident seemed to have taken a firm hold upon her imagination, and, in spite of all their efforts, she found it impossible to shake off the effect it had upon her.

The chateau, the place of their destination, was at length reached; preparations were instantly commenced for the celebration of the marriage, which was to take place, by the Signor Waldeberg's express desire, on the sixth day from that on which they had left Florence. As the day drew near, the spirits of Oriana grew gradually depressed, and a slight feeling of dread seemed to steal over her, whenever she found herself in the presence of her lover. Her father questioned her as to its cause, and then she confessed that the mysterious warning she had received preyed deeply on her mind. It might be a superstitious weakness, but she could not repress it; and she requested her father, however reluctant he might be, to consent to put it off for at least another day.

The entreaties of his daughter, though he laughed at her fears, prevailed upon the old man, and he gave his consent to her request; but when he mentioned the alteration in the time to Waldeberg, the countenance of the latter underwent a complete change to the hue of death. No prayer, however, could prevail upon the old man to recall his consent to his daughter's wish, and the signor departed evidently in a state of the greatest despair.

That night the Signora Oriana was missing from her chamber, and though the strictest search was made for her, not the least trace of her presence could be found. The grief of the father and the lover knew no bounds, and there seemed to be no hope of consolation for them.

*I*t is the night of the sixth day — that day against which Oriana had been so mysteriously warned. In a large vault, far beneath the chateau, and lighted by innumerable torches, that threw a red and smoky glare around, stood the beautiful Oriana and the Signor Waldeberg. The former was pale as marble, and an expression of the most intense despair was upon her countenance.

The signor, resolved that she should become his wife before the expiration of the six days, had torn her from her chamber, and immured her in that fearful place, with the hope of forcing her to become his bride; but Oriana revolted at such usage, and feeling more convinced than ever that the warning she had received had its foundation in truth, had resisted alike his persuasions and his threats.

The hour of midnight was fast approaching, and before an altar that stood at one end of the vault, was an old and venerable priest, with an open book in his hand. Waldeberg drew Oriana towards him, and forced her to kneel at the foot of the altar. She entreated — she supplicated — she appealed to the priest; his only answer was a solemn shake of the head, and then he proceeded to read the marriage ceremony. Waldeberg took her hand — but she suddenly flung it from her, and uttered the most piercing screams that echoed fearfully amidst those cavernous places. Still the priest read on, and despite her emotion and her agony of terror, Waldeberg regarded her with a cold and determined gaze.

"Faster! faster!" he muttered to the priest, "or all will be lost!" and he glanced anxiously around the vault.

At the moment, striking fearfully on the silence, came the sound of the turret clock telling the hour of midnight. On the first stroke, the most fearful sounds the human ear ever listened to filled the place — strange indefinite shadows flitted around, filling the air with a rushing sound, as if of mighty wings — the altar changed to a heap of human bones — the priest to a ghastly skeleton. Then came darkness, terrible and distinct; and Oriana swooned upon the damp floor.

When she recovered, she found the day had broken, and the sunlight was streaming upon her face; while her father and the young man whom she had seen wounded at the inn on the mountains were stooping over her in alarm.

The inhabitants of the chateau had been alarmed in the dead of the night by a terrific storm, which had thrown into ruins a part of the castle, and a vast chasm had been made in the foundations, disclosing the vaults, the existence of which had been until then unknown.

Beneath the rich vestments of Waldeberg, and lying in a heap on the ground, were the remains of a human skeleton — all that was now left of the guilty being who had thus paid the penalty for failing in complying with the conditions of the fearful compact into which he had entered with the unholy powers of darkness.

It was many months before the mind of Oriana recovered its strength, and when it did, she entered a convent of Ursuline nuns, and endeavored to forget, in the consolations of religion, the fearful trial she had undergone.

*T*wissel laid down the book which he had been reading, and fell into a strange kind of musing, in which the vampyre, Waldeberg, and the East India colonel were strangely mixed up together. From this reverie he was awakened by a rap at the street-door, and then, in a few minutes afterwards, Mrs. Meredith entered the room, exclaiming, —

"Well, Mr. Twissel, you always come in luck's way."

"Indeed!" said Mr. Twissel, involuntarily thinking of what he had that morning undergone, as well as what he went through a day or two before; and, for the life of him, he saw not what might be called luck, unless it was that species known as ill-luck.

"Yes, Mr. Twissel, you are; you've just come in time to hear the news."

"What news, ma'am — what news? If you'll be pleased to enlighten me upon that subject, I shall be better able to understand what you allude to."

"Why, you see, the colonel has been so pressing, that my daughter has been induced to name the day. Yes, Mr. Twissel, she has named the day — not a distant day either. He begged and entreated you don't know how hard, which, at least, shows how much he meant it."

"Well, truly, it is news, Mrs. Meredith," said the attorney; "but, at the same time, it is what I expected, though not just at this juncture. The fact is, there is but little can be said against Colonel Deverill; but, at the same time, there will be but little said for him. I am by no means sure that there will be any property found. If he were a man of money, he would not hesitate to lay his circumstances open."

"He is too proud a man for that."

"Well, it may be all very well to attribute it to that cause. However that may be, there can be no doubt you have a right to do as you please, and I bow to you decision; but, still, I do so, having expressed my opinion to the contrary, being very suspicious of him. But, as I said before, you are entitled to do what you please in the affair; I have no right to do more."

"My daughter and I have been considering the matter over and over again, and we have come to the conclusion that it should take place, and she has consented that it should take place in about ten days' time, when we shall expect to have your company, Mr. Twissel."

"I am obliged to you, and assure you my opinions upon this matter are not at all personal. I will meet the colonel, and I will be present with you all on that happy occasion with much pleasure; and I hope it will be a fortunate and happy marriage."

"I hope so, too," said Mrs. Meredith; "and I have every reason to believe so."

"That is good," said the attorney.

"And now, Mr. Twissel," said Mrs. Meredith, "what did you do this morning at the South Sea House? I could not send to you so early as I could have wished, as I did not know he was going till the coach was ordered, and he went away almost immediately. I then sent Mary to you; I don't know at what time she came to you, but at all events she was not back here until late."

"She must have got to my place in good time, if she only started after the colonel had left this house," said the attorney.

"I am very glad of that, at all events; but what success did you have?"

"Success, indeed," said Mr. Twissel, with a shrug of mortification. "I have only succeeded in getting myself into a very serious difficulty, and the colonel has eluded me again. I can't understand it all. I don't know what to think; but I am sure of this, that I have been in a series of disasters ever since I undertook to follow him about, and I have discovered nothing concerning him."

"What has happened to you today, then?" inquired Mrs. Meredith.

"Oh! as for that, what seems to be but natural in itself; and, therefore, it may be said not to be connected with him; indeed, though that were really the case, yet there is so much concurrent action, I cannot divest myself of the idea that it is a fatal affair, as far as regards looking after him."

"Then don't do so any more, Mr. Twissel."

"I'll never give in," said Twissel.

"Well, but what need you trouble yourself more about the affair? I assure you we're all well satisfied that Colonel Deverill is Colonel Deverill, and that he had property; that being the case, I am sure you have nothing to trouble yourself about, or to blame yourself for."

"I am conscious of that," said the attorney, rubbing his knee. "I have done all I can; and I have given my advice — I hope I have done my part."

"Yes, you have," said Mrs. Meredith. "I am quite satisfied; but what has happened to you?"

"I will tell you, my dear madam — I will tell you. I have been assaulted, knocked about, robbed, and my faculties all confused, and no use to me. I have lost my handkerchief, watch, and purse; and I have had my trousers ripped open; and I can't tell what besides. I am safe, however."

"Well, that is right, at all events; but it is most annoying to me that you should be subject to those terrible accidents. I can't understand the meaning of it."

"I can't," said the attorney.

"But why should you, more than any one else, be subject to these misfortunes? I can't understand it at all, Mr. Twissel. Perhaps you do something or other unusual on such occasions, which had been the cause of such terrible trouble."

"Not that I am aware of," said Twissel; "but the fact is, I don't know of anything peculiar in my appearance or behavior, that should cause this disaster. But I am sure of this, that there is nothing more singular about me, than what there usually is; and why it should only attract notice on these occasions and no other, I cannot tell."

"Nor I. Well, I suppose it must have been there was some other circumstance, independent alike of him and you, that had caused this disagreeable affair."

"Perhaps there might be."

"Well, now, Mr. Twissel, there's another affair I wish to speak to you about; or, rather, it's a thing my daughter Margaret should speak to your daughter Elizabeth and Miss Martha about. You see, as they are not very often together, I thought it right to speak to you first."

"Yes, ma'am — go on, pray."

"Well, my Margaret is to be married in a few days. Now, we don't want relatives at all; and I was advising her to beg your permission to have the two young ladies whom I have named, as bridesmaids, and who will be of essential service to my daughter."

"I have no doubt but they will feel very much gratified with the proposal; and one could not have been better devised than this one to please them."

"Then, will you invite them to come here, and spend the evening with Margaret and yourself, Mr. Twissel, the first evening you find leisure and inclination?"

"Well, I have destroyed today, so far as a business day, by drinking brandy-and-water early, and I may as well finish it in an agreeable manner."

"That is very good; we shall expect you to tea this evening."

"You may," said Mr. Twissel; "if you are not otherwise engaged. I may as well do all that is necessary, so as to have as little to do, by-and-bye, as possible. Has the colonel come home?"

"No, not yet; I did not expect him to come home so soon as this, but he will be back in a very short time, now, I dare say."

"Then I will bid you good bye, for it will be unnecessary to meet him in this plight; indeed, he might think I paid him no respect to do so; and besides it will be better, altogether, that he should not see me so soon, lest he should have caught sight of me in the city; which, indeed, I think wholly impossible, for I only had a distant glimpse of him."

"Then, good bye, sir; I shall see you and the young ladies."

"Both — my daughter, and her young friend, Martha."

Mr. Twissel arose, and left the house to return to his own house, and get his daughter prepared for the visit, and her friend also, while Mrs. Meredith and her daughter, Margaret, consulted together, as to what would be the best method of doing honor to the occasion of the forthcoming marriage.

"You see, my dear," said Mrs. Meredith, "we cannot very well invite our own friends, because they are such a greedy, rapacious set; they would sooner spoil a good chance for us than let us have it unmolested; they are by far too greedy — no, no, they must not come — they will think themselves injured if they cannot share the harvest."

"And all will be lost."

"To be sure; and, moreover, we could not shake them off when we wanted, and which we must do very soon, for the colonel will never abide them."

"No, ma' I think not, indeed — they are decidedly low people, who are genteel only of a Sunday; it will never do to have such people about us."

"Oh, dear, no."

"Here is the colonel come back; see if that girl has got the water hot, he will like his tea early; I am quite sure she hasn't got it ready — what a provoking girl that is, to be sure. She does nothing all day; I must get rid of her."

"Yes; but she is very ugly."

"That is one great recommendation in her favor," said Mrs. Meredith; "one very great recommendation; it ensures domestic peace, to say the least of it, and there's not so many followers usually. Now, however, we must do the best until we have one; but here he is."

At that moment the colonel entered the house, and proceeded at once to the drawing-room, having first divested himself of his hat and cloak in the passage. Up stairs was a good fire and an easy chair, with ottomans for his feet, and a comfortable well furnished apartment it was.

Mrs. Meredith followed him up and entered the room after him, to inquire what he would like done next; and with her assistance, he took his boots off and put on a pair of splendid slippers, and reposed with a groan of satisfaction on the chair.

"I think, Mrs. Meredith," he said, "that the best thing I can have will be some tea. Where is Margaret? when she is at liberty, I wish to see and speak to her."

"She will be here in a few moments, colonel," said Mrs. Meredith; "I will send her to you."

"No hurry for a few moments," said the colonel.

"Something about the jewels, I'll be sworn," said Mrs. Meredith, to herself; "I wonder what he has in that parcel; a present, I dare say."

Mrs. Meredith sought Margaret, and related what the colonel said, with his desire to see her, and that young lady at once proceeded to the drawing-room.

"Oh, my dear Margaret," said Colonel Deverill, "I see you are pleased to see I have returned; your very eyes tell me so. Come here to me, dearest."

"Ah, my looks, I am afraid, say too much."

"Not at all — not at all," said the colonel; "I love to see them, especially when I know they are sincere, when they come from the heart, you know; I love to see innocent and heartfelt satisfaction beaming from such a face as yours."

"Oh, colonel, you are really too complimentary; not that I think you don't mean what you say, but your partiality is too great to allow you to judge as a stranger would."

"I do not desire to judge as a stranger would; it does not give me any satisfaction. To look upon you with the eyes of a lover, is a privilege I most desire, and very soon with those of a husband; then my happiness will be complete. How I long for the days and the hours to fly by — they cannot go too fast now; by and bye they may pass as slowly as you please — that done, then I am quite content, because I shall pass them happily, rapturously."

"Ah, you are so kind-hearted, so good, that I can never repay you."

"Do not seek to do so, you will only make me the heavier in debt; but come, there is a small parcel, with a few trinkets I have purchased; the jewels I spoke of are in hand, and they will be ready in time for our marriage."

"Nay, do not think about them — not to disturb yourself, colonel; I am quite content if I am dressed as befits the occasion; but I am really obliged to you for your present, whatever it may be; and I may as well tell you I have thought — indeed, I have said as much — I should like to have a couple of female friends to visit me on that occasion."

"Yes, my dear, you may depend upon it, I shall be the more happy when I know you are so too; but no matter, ask whom you please; as far as I am able, I will make them welcome and happy. I suppose, however, you are alluding to your bridesmaids."

"I am," said Margaret.

"I shall be most happy to see them, or any friend you may desire," added the colonel.

"And will you have no one on the occasion?" inquired Margaret; "won't you have somebody to keep you in countenance upon the occasion?"

"No," said the colonel, "I shall not; I have no friends with whom I am intimate enough, that I know of, at this present moment; there may be people in London, with whom I have been, in India, intimate with, but I do not know for certain; but time and accident will turn up old friends, and I have not the desire to seek for them; but if we must have some one, I do not know whether Mr. Twissel would not do quite as well, if he would come, and your mother had no objection."

"I am sure she would not. Mr. Twissel was an old friend of my father's, and, consequently, he would be no stranger at all to the family; besides, it is daughter, and her friend, Martha, that I have invited upon this occasion; have I done wrong?"

"Not at all, it could not have happened better; I am sure they must be very worthy people, and any one whom you please, or they know, that you feel disposed to invite, do so, with the confidence that whatever pleases you on the occasion, will please me."

At that moment there was an alarming rapping at the door, which caused them to pause a few moments; then they continued their conversation until the servant announced to Miss Meredith, that Miss Twissel, her papa, and her friend, Martha, were come.

Chapter CXXX.

A PLEASANT EVENING. – THE BRIDESMAIDS.

"*I* know how that is," said Margaret, before she left the drawing-room; "that was through my ma'. I dare say she has invited them to take tea with her tonight. I should not at all wonder about that. I have not seen them for some time. They keep a great deal at home, and visit but little. They are playful, homely girls, but good-hearted, and that is why I prefer them to more fashionable friends, whose goodness of heart I cannot rely upon. They are insincere."

"You are very right; but you will, I hope, let me see your friends, and unless you have family matters to speak of, perhaps you will take tea up here with me. I shall be all alone if you do not; so, you see, I am speaking from selfish motives; but do not think I shall be at all hurt if you do not see fit to accept the invitation for them."

"I will accept it for them cheerfully, and shall be much surprised if they do not do so too," said Margaret, as she walked towards the door, and then left the apartment, to proceed first to her own room, and there to examine her present, before she sought the visitors to give them their invitation.

The parcel contained some handsome laces and other matters, beautiful and expensive, such things as she could wear, and excite the envy of others; which was, of all things, and usually is of women in general, the most enchanting thing in all the world, and gives intense gratification.

After admiring for a moment or two the beauties of the laces, she could not help involuntarily exclaiming, —

"This will be beautiful, so very becoming, and so much above anything else that can be brought by my bridesmaids. I shall be a queen amongst them; indeed, they will but set me off to the utmost advantage. I shall be the glory of the occasion."

Having secured her new acquisition from inquisitive eyes, by locking it up in her drawers, she returned down stairs, and then entered the parlor, where, truly enough, as she had imagined, there was Mr. Twissel, Miss Twissel, and Miss Martha, all of whom were dressed out for the occasion.

There was some truth in what Margaret had said to her mother, that the two intended bridesmaids were not likely to induce any one to fall in love with them. They were oddities of the first water. Miss Twissel had light brown hair, bushy eyebrows, a straight masculine nose, a mouth that turned up on one side, and one of her eyes had a gentle inclination to gaze at her nose, while her complexion was increased by a vast quantity of sun freckles.

Then, as for Miss Martha, she was another beauty of a similar class; hooked nose, with one eye paying undue attention to the auricular organ, while the other was somewhat injured by a blank appearance; her hair was red, and she was pitted by the small-pox to a fearful extent.

Such were the two friends whom Miss Meredith had chosen for bridesmaids, with the laudable view of putting no temptation in the way of the colonel, which Mrs. Meredith, her mother, most strenuously advised, as she had experience of the men.

"My dear Miss Twissel, and you, Martha!"

"Ah! Margaret, God bless me, who could have imagined, above all things, what I have come about. What can you be thinking and doing? here you've no friends to help you. I see you have done it all yourself. What can you think of people? you have no mercy."

"Aye," said Martha, "there's no doing anything while you are about. No one else has a chance, but you must tell us all about it."

"Yes, yes, I will tell you all about it; and more than that, you shall see the colonel if you please."

"That is what we should like, above all things."

"Oh! it is a colonel, then — a rich Indian colonel. Upon my word, you will have to be presented at court next."

"He! he! you are joking me now. Well, never mind, I shall joke you some of these days. You may depend upon that; my turn will come next, and then I won't forget you. But seriously, there are more unlikely things may come to pass than that."

"Well, now; I dare say. Who would have thought of that, now? But then you are so lucky, you see; only think what might have been the case if the colonel had been a young man! why he might become as great a man as the Marquis of Granby. Why, you'd have been a marchioness then. Well, bless my heart, how things do come about!"

"Well, you had better come up to the drawing-room," said Margaret, "and see the colonel, who is waiting tea for us all. Come, ma'."

"Yes, my dear, I am ready. Mr. Twissel, will you come?"

"If you please," said Mr. Twissel, "if you please. We shall now soon have the pleasure of seeing an end to this affair; for, as it is to come off, why, when it is over, it will be all the better. Expectation is always a time of uncertainty and anxiety — at least, to most people."

"So it is, Mr. Twissel, so it is; and I am not without my share of it; for, in the first place, human life is short, and circumstances may alter cases; so I am anxious to see it over, and offer no impediment in the way of the completion of the marriage."

"Certainly, you are quite right; having made up your mind to permit the marriage to take place, why, the sooner the better."

They were all now introduced to the colonel, who was very polite and courtly, which in some degree embarrassed the young ladies, who were compelled to put on, as they expressed it, their best behavior, and so did not become quite so familiar. However, that did not spoil the harmony of the meeting, for the young ladies considered there was more respect paid to them, and the less they were able to appreciate the politeness with which they were treated, the more they believed themselves honored.

They were well enough pleased, and the conversation turned upon various matters, while Mr. Twissel was uncommonly attentive to the colonel; indeed, he watched him most narrowly, every turn and every expression, as if he were resolved to ascertain, by constant surveillance, whether there was any foundation for his half-inspired doubts respecting him; and also as to whether it were possible that he could have had any hand in the disasters which he had on two several occasions suffered.

But yet he could see nothing — nothing at all that gave him the slightest pretext for persisting in his suspicion. He appeared the same easy, careless individual, who would not trouble himself to consider whether he was watched or not, or whether his actions were the subject of other people's thoughts, or whether they were unnoticed, it mattered nothing to him.

"It is singular," he muttered to himself, "very singular, how it could all happen by accident, and only at moments when I was watching him. I can't tell; and yet the occurrences were of that character, to another they would seem wholly unconnected, and I am unable to connect them, save by fancy; but he looks not a very old man, but rather like one who has the full use of his faculties. He is singularly pale, to be sure, and yet, at times, he does not appear so old, nor does his arm and leg seem quite so bad at others; perhaps it varies, according to circumstance, weather, the moon, or unforeseen changes."

He remained cogitating very quietly by himself; he was thoughtful, and could by no means divest himself of the idea that there was something more than common about the colonel.

"He don't seem so blind with that eye as he might be," he muttered; "but there is no use calculating about an Indian; they have got such luxurious habits and fancies, that if he fancies one of his eyes is in any degree weak, he will wear a shade for its preservation. Well, he is entitled to do so, but he ain't so old as they imagine. And that will be no detriment to him or to them; so much the better, unless they reckon upon the colonel's death, which would hardly be an object to them, seeing that it could bring them no more; indeed, it would diminish their income. But he is a tall man now, and, if he did not stoop so much, would yet be a fine man."

These thoughts passed through his mind, time after time, during the whole evening; while the colonel himself was at times conversing in the most refined and courtly language, and doing much towards amusing them with anecdotes of the places he had seen, and the battles he had fought.

"You would be surprised," he said, "to hear that, in India, there are places so cold that they more resemble the Polar regions than central Asia, of which we only used to think of as being one of the hottest regions in the world, filled with wild animals and numerous serpents."

"Certainly, we hear more of that than anything else — the yellow fever, the cholera, and all these kinds of things, caused by exposure to the heat."

"So they are; but it is only in the plains, and not on the high table lands and mountains, where you gradually meet with more temperate climates, many of which equal northern Europe for salubrity; and, further up, you come to frozen regions."

"Indeed! that is a phenomenon."

"Oh, dear, no; the altitude of the plain, and the exposure, make the sole difference. I remember once, I was sent with some other regiments to chastise some of the hill tribes."

"Under whom was that?" inquired the attorney.

"General Walker," returned the colonel; "he was a very able general, and we performed some extraordinary marches under him, as well as some service."

"Oh, indeed!" said the attorney; "what might have taken place?"

"I will tell you an incident that did take place; and not relate more scenes of carnage that we passed through in the execution of our duty than shall be actually necessary. We had, on one occasion, to storm a city; on another, a fortified town; it was strong, and well protected by nature and art.

Well, we arrived there, and the gates were closed against us; guns were brought to bear, and men appeared on the walls. We expected, of course, a sharp time of it, and being only the advance guard, we halted for the main body to come up with us; and, after having summoned the garrison to surrender, we put posts and watchers for the night, not expecting to do anything upon that occasion; nor did we expect the main body up with us till the middle of the next day, they having sent word on to me that they would not be up in consequence of some accident to some part of the train, which would have to be repaired; but a portion of the troops would advance a stage nearer to me, in case of an accident, upon which I could retire for support, or send to them to come up as the exigencies of the moment should most require; but they did not anticipate any movement at all. Nor did we; the fact was, we had made a forced march of it; and had got over more ground than we had expected, and our main body did not think we should have been so near the scene of action as we were.

However, a counsel of war was held amongst the officers; and it was resolved that we should attempt nothing without the assistance of our comrades, as the place was very strong, as I have before told you.

Well, sir, half the night was over, and we lay fast asleep, having had a hard — very hard day's work of it, — so hard that we could sleep sound on the bare earth; we were all suddenly awakened by a loud explosion, which shook the very earth under us; and, upon starting up, and rushing out of our tents, we saw the earth and air illumined by the explosion of, as we afterwards learned, and guessed at the moment, one of the enemy's powder magazines.

In another minute we found there were plenty of falling missiles, with the debris of the magazine, and the mangled corpses of the men who were near it.

There was an instant order to muster the men; everybody knew what was meant. They were all ready in a few moments — indeed, we slept by our arms — fully accoutered, so it did not take long to be ready for action.

We were ordered to form in divisions and bodies, and as there was ample breach made by the explosion there, I was ordered to mount the breach, and enter the town for the purpose of assault.

We did this. We marched down upon the breach after some difficulties, and were fairly in it; but had our commanding officer known any of the difficulties; he would not have incurred the responsibility of ordering us to advance, for the ruins we had to scramble over were dreadful, and, had there been light, we could every one have been picked off by the enemy.

Darkness was our friend, and we got into the town with a comparatively trifling loss, and when our men got together they began to tell a tale, for their volleys were well directed upon the enemy, who were drawn up in masses, and whose fire directed ours. We were not completely exposed to their fire, for the same objects that exposed our men, as they were surmounted before reaching the enemy, protected them from immense volleys of musketry.

However, we carried the point, and at that moment another explosion took place in some other part of the town, which illumined all around for a moment or two, and then came masses of bricks, and stones, and timber, killing friend and foe. For a while we were staggered; we did not know what to think of this affair. We knew not whether we had an enemy to fight, or even where he was. We were completely at a standstill.

But this did not last long. The defenders fled, and left us masters of the field. We remained under arms all that night, till daylight.

Glad were we, indeed, when daylight came; we were fatigued, so much so that our men could scarcely stand in the ranks. Then parties were sent out to look after the wounded, who had been left in all imaginable situations. It was at such a moment that I was discovered; my leg was shattered by a musket bullet."

"And you lay bleeding all night?"

"Yes. Not exactly bleeding, for I had sense left me to bind a ligature over the wound to stop the effusion of blood, which would have killed me in a very short time. However, there was no necessity to lose my leg, but it has made me permanently lame."

"I see you are so, sir," said Twissel; "but do you never feel it worse at some times than at others?"

"Yes, I do. There are times when I do not know that I have received a hurt at all; but sometimes I suffer a little, and am a little more lame in consequence."

"It was fortunate," said Twissel, "it was your leg, for it might have been your head, you know, and that would have been a death-blow to your fortune."

"Yes," said the colonel, mildly; "I might have been killed, as you observe; but at the same time I should have done my duty, which in these cases is all we looked to. I might have saved a better man, who had a wife and family — I had none."

Conversation now ran on the forthcoming event, and Mr. Twissel was invited by the colonel, and the whole party were well satisfied with each other, and parted very good friends, with the promise of meeting again before the propitious morning which was to unite the fates of Margaret Meredith and Colonel Deverill.

Chapter CXXXI.

A NEW CHARACTER. – MISS TWISSEL'S VISITOR. – THE INVITATIONS.

*N*othing could exceed the smoothness and easiness of the course of things in the wooing of Margaret Meredith; all things appeared so well ordered. People were all of one mind; and it is needless to say that the young lady was elated. She was elated, and we might not be out of the way in saying she was elated overmuch, and knew not how to keep the exhibition of her joy within proper bounds; she could not help showing she was to be the lady of a colonel.

Mrs. Meredith, too, was well pleased. What could she do but feel proud at the change that was about to take place? She would go to watering places in the summer, and remain in town during the winter; they would lead a very fashionable life — they would be of the elite, and all their acquaintances they would be compelled to cut, or, at the most, only speak to them when they were unseen by any others.

It is astonishing how a change of circumstances produces a change in our habits and feelings; how it happens that those who were considered respectable acquaintances suddenly become the objects of our aversion, and we begin to devise all sorts of methods for evading recognition, or of speaking to them when we can avoid it.

This arises merely from the change in one's circumstances, which causes us to look for something much beyond what we have been used to; but, unfortunately, it brings ingratitude often in the train of its consequents.

"My dear," said Mrs. Meredith to her daughter Margaret, "we really cannot know the people at the corner house over the way, who invited us to their parties."

"Oh, dear, no, we cannot think of it; but we must get rid of them the best way we can. You see they will not be quite the thing for us when we come to have our change of circumstances, you may depend upon it; it will become necessary to weed one's acquaintance."

"Yes, that must be done." said Mrs. Meredith.

"And the sooner we set about it the better; for the more intimate we continue now, the more trouble will there be of getting rid of them afterwards."

"Certainly; we need not accept of their invitation for tonight."

"Oh, dear, no; I have dismissed the whole affair from my mind, and there is no need even of thinking of it any more. I shall not even think of sending them an answer; the consequence will be, they will be angry, and expect we shall go and apologize, and when they find we don't, but that we try to get rid of them, they will be baffled, and the whole affair is settled."

"That is a very good plan, my dear. Then, you know, there are the Morgans; we must positively get rid of them. It will never do to have those young men hanging about; the colonel would do something dreadful, to say the least of it. Why, he would shoot them, and perhaps have a separation, who knows?"

"But then I should be entitled to a maintenance."

"You would, my dear; but unfortunately you well know you have no property, an that, added to an early separation, would put it in his power to offer you and compel your acceptance of a very small sum, which he may pay as he pleases — weekly, monthly, or quarterly."

"I see, ma; but we will run no risk of that kind of thing. Moreover, there would be those girls, they would be a nuisance hanging about the colonel."

"No doubt, and the cause of unhappiness in the extreme. Better to leave all such people; you are a great deal better without them. Why, I tell you what, you will be at no loss of company or acquaintances, you will find they will be sure to spring up; property is sure to enable you to choose those whom you will have, and whom you will not — the reason is obvious enough. Moreover, like loves like, you know, and people with means soon find out people who have none."

"Yes, ma, and those who have plenty; besides, a colonel, and a man of rank and standing — and everybody knows that a colonel in the India service is a rich man — and that would bring us all into the best of society. Only think of my going to Bath, Bristol, and Brighton, in their seasons. Of course we couldn't keep company with people who can't afford to go to some fashionable place at least once in a year."

"Oh, dear, no; certainly not, my dear; but there is no need of our troubling ourselves about that matter; we shall only go when the colonel goes, and we shan't be seen without him, and he'll be a constraint upon them; and, therefore, where they find themselves uncomfortable, they will not come again."

"That will be a very good plan, for it will appear as their own faults; but, at the same time, I do not trust to that upon all occasions; it might fail, and then we should have to take some unpleasant steps to get rid of them, which is certainly easily done, but unpleasant."

Yes, yes, certainly," replied the mother; and then suddenly, as a knock and ring came upon the door, Margaret said, "Dear me, who is that? — I hope none of these people whom I have been speaking about — it will be a dreadful nuisance to all; especially when I am to be married in three days more."

"You needn't be seen, Margaret; I'll see them."

"Do, ma; and I'll go up stairs. But let's hear who it is first, who comes today."

At that moment she heard the door open, and her own name pronounced, and at once knew the speaker, and she said to her mother, —

"Oh, ma, 'tis Miss Twissel, my bridesmaid; what an infliction! but, then, I must see her. She has come, I suppose, to consult me about some new gown, or the way in which she and her friend will have their hair done up on the occasion — nothing more important, I dare say."

"Very well, my dear; they had better come in — send them in pray," she added to the servant. "Oh, Miss Twissel, how glad we are to see you."

"Now, really," said Miss Twissel; "how kind you are, for I am sure you speak the truth. Oh, Margaret, don't you feel all of a flutter?"

"I don't, indeed; I am very comfortable. I hope you are all quite well — don't put yourself out of the way on this occasion; you need not, I assure you."

"Oh, I have got my pa to give us new gowns, and some lace; but I did not mean to tell you that — I and Martha had agreed that that should be a secret between us; that we should not say anything about it to any one; but surprise you on your wedding morning."

"Ah, you have been at a great deal of trouble and expense about this affair, I am sure. You really must not think I wish you to do all this; I really don't know how to scold you enough, for I shall be dressed very plainly indeed."

"Oh, but then you are the bride — we ain't, you know, and that makes the difference; besides which, we have a visitor come up to London to see us."

"Indeed! some young gentleman, I suppose, whose heart you want to run away with, and so have another wedding, and upon your own account this time; and, perhaps, you are helping Miss Martha to a husband. What is he — a physician or a divine?"

"Neither — but, I will tell you, he is only an old man."

"An old man! What a sweetheart you have chosen, to be sure! but, I dare say you have your reason as well as other people. But have you know him long?"

"No, we haven't done so; but, the fact is, pa' and he have had some business together, and they are very much in each others company. He's a man, however, of great rank, though a very odd man to talk to, I assure you, but a man of rank and property."

"Indeed! Oh, tell me what he is — a lord?"

"Well, he is not much short of it; and he is higher than a great many lords, I assure you. Why, he's no less than an admiral — only, I wasn't to say anything about it."

"Oh, will he be with you when my marriage takes place?"

"Yes, he will; and I wanted to know, as he will be much with my father, and as a visitor, shall we be intruding to bring him here to grace your wedding?"

"Oh, yes; by all means," said Margaret, who thought he presence of an old man could in no way interfere with any of her schemes; besides, a man of rank, such as an admiral, would greatly increase the noise of her marriage. Indeed, here was probably a new acquaintance with whom she could be intimate; besides, it was some one of consequence on her side that the great man was to come, and would, she thought, add some luster to herself.

"Well, then, I would not ask him until I had seen you, because it might turn out you would be displeased; and, as I have not done so, I cannot tell you whether he will come or not. He's a strange man, and I won't ask him until the night before."

"Very well; we shall be quite happy to see him. I dare say he'll come, if you tell him who's going to be married. Indeed, if he's likely to come, I'll invite a few friends to meet him; but I won't say anything to anybody about it."

"No; let it be a surprise to them all; and let nobody know whom they are going to meet."

"That will be delightful, certainly — very delightful. What a surprise it will be to them to be introduced to colonel this and admiral that. I declare I long for the day on account of the confusion that some persons will be in."

"I must now bid your good bye; for I've got to call upon my dressmaker, to give her some orders."

"You will stop and take tea with us? Surely you won't run away."

"Oh, but I must," said Miss Twissel, and so said Miss Martha, and after much pressing and refusing, they parted, and left Margaret filled by other thoughts than those she had so recently held.

"Ma'," said she, after a long pause, "do you know what I have been thinking of?"

"No, my dear, I do not."

"Well, then, it is this, that after all, we may as well make a bit of a figure for the last time. That we will have some friends who will figure upon that occasion and no other."

"What makes you think so, my dear Margaret?"

"Why, you see, ma', we are likely to have a distinguished visitor, and we may as well have as many as we can; their number and dresses will look well, and as we shall leave town immediately, I don't see that we shall be at any future time annoyed by their visits. Indeed, it will be retiring from their society after giving them a feast."

"Well, to be sure, I never thought of that," said her mother — "I never thought of it. What shall we do now — how can we provide for so many?"

"Send an order to a pastry cook to provide breakfast for so many, whether they come or not, and then we need trouble ourselves very little about giving them time. If we tell them about the day before, they will have all in readiness for us."

"Well, well — and as for the expense, it will be of no consequence."

"None," said Margaret. "I shall be able to pay that and others, if we owe any. But now comes the job of inviting visitors, and we must only invite those who will make up a show, dress well, and pass off on the occasion for fashionable people."

"Oh, as for that, there are many people who never had a penny in their lives to call their own, may be very fashionable-looking people, and pass for men of a thousand a year, to say nothing of a lord looking like a workman, and the like, which is common enough."

"Then we'll settle it at that point, ma', and you had better superintend the invitations and the other affair — the breakfast, I mean."

"Very well, my dear; you know that I have no objection. I have seen such occasions before, and I well know what they ought to be; therefore you may safely rely upon my judgment in such an affair as that at least."

"And about the selection of friends — visitors, I mean."

"That you may also leave to me," said Mrs. Meredith; "and, depend upon it, I will not invite one party whom we shall have cause to say we are sorry they came; though, you know, every allowance would be made for them by the colonel or admiral, if he come. By the way, I would not tell the colonel a word about it, for sometimes the land service hates the sea service, and the latter often laugh at the former; so it will be safest to say nothing."

"No, ma, I won't — I didn't intend to do so."

Thus both mother and daughter had suddenly changed their views of what was to take place on the day of the intended marriage. They were now resolved they would have as many of their old friends as they could get together upon the occasion, to cause the affair to go off with all the éclat that it was possible; it would be the last ball of the season — that is, it would be the last she ever intended to give them, and that would be the last occasion upon which they would meet.

Her respect for Miss Twissel was augmented by the knowledge that she had an admiral for a friend or a visitor, it didn't matter which. Who could tell what might happen? Mightn't Miss Twissel marry an admiral, as ugly as she was, as well as she should a colonel? but there were many reasons why she should. She, too, might have had some means of entangling his heart; perhaps, after all, she only came there with him for the purpose of showing him off.

"At all events," said Margaret, to herself; "at all events, he is one that we can keep on terms with; and it will look well to be acquainted with some person of rank. I am, at all events, well pleased it has happened as it has."

Mrs. Meredith, on the other hand, appeared to think her daughter's marriage with a colonel, ought to be celebrated by no common rejoicings; that, indeed, the marriage ought to go off with as much disturbance to the whole neighborhood, as it was possible to make.

This could not bet better effected than in the manner we have referred to; namely, inviting a number of persons to come and be present at the ceremony, and to take a late breakfast, and to wish the bride joy, to see her depart, and then to lose sight of her, as she hoped, for ever.

This purpose Mrs. Meredith ably carried out, and she succeeded in inviting about two or three-and-twenty persons together; and any person who had a carriage and would come in it, was sure of an invitation — that was a passport to the marriage feast.

"Well," she muttered to herself, as she reckoned up the number of persons whom she expected to be present upon the occasion — "well, I don't think I have omitted any one who ought to be present, nor have I invited any one who ought not to be here. I shall have a busy day of it — very busy day; but the result is everything; so long as the marriage takes place, and we are really married to an East Indian colonel, why we shall do, there can be no doubt of it."

This was a consolatory reflection. There was but little else, indeed, that could be done — little, indeed. The cook had the orders for the entertainment the next day; they had but little to do in the household with that; indeed, they had extra hands, lest there should be any need of them, as she would not have anything go wrong upon such an occasion, for worlds.

But there was one thing that gave her some satisfaction, and that was, Mr. Twissel had not been to them lately to give any doubtful counsels; ever since she had announced her intention of permitting the marriage to take place, he had not been to express any doubts about the matter; but had been a mere spectator, doing all that was necessary. He had forgotten all objection, and never made one. He was perfectly quiescent; but would now and then look very hard at the colonel, but that was all; he never discovered anything, and all was smooth and pleasant.

Chapter CXXXII.

THE WEDDING MORNING. – DISRUPTION OF HARMONY, AND THE NEW ACQUAINTANCE. – THE CONCLUSION.

*A*ccident, strange to say, had taken our old acquaintance, Admiral Bell, to the house of a lawyer, there to transact some business, as well as to lodge at his house. The fact was, the old admiral hearing that a brother officer was in trouble — one who had shared with him the dangers of the sea and the fight — he came to town to see, himself, what could be done; and finding the affair beyond his comprehension, or, at least beyond his power of personal interference; that, in fact, it required the aid of a third party, and that third person must, of necessity, be a lawyer, he determined to employ the man who happened to be conversant with the circumstances of the case, and this was no other than Mrs. Meredith's friend, Twissel.

However, the admiral's good will towards the race who follow the law, not being so great as his philanthropy, he determined to watch every stage of the proceedings, and to permit nothing to be done without his knowledge, and to see that nothing was neglected.

Hearing from Mr. Twissel the affair that was to take place, a sudden crotchet entered his head, that he should like to be present at the ceremony, and he broached it to Mr. Twissel, who turned to his daughter to ascertain if it were at all possible.

That young lady was desirous of shining among her acquaintants, as one who could introduce an admiral, and who did not like the idea of Margaret Meredith being so find a lady as she now attempted to make herself appear; indeed, she would have been willing to have assisted in raising her some species of mortification; she felt more than true pleasure in the disaster that would be the cause of such feelings. There was a very general dislike to Miss Margaret Meredith, and the truth was, she was much more than usually arrogant and proud, and took all imaginable methods of vexing and mortifying those around her.

But there is little to be said about that; the consent was brought back to the attorney, who felt somewhat elated at it, and communicated it to the admiral, with some remarks upon the kindness and condescension of the persons who had done him so much honor.

This, however, only had the effect of drawing from the admiral, the word, swab, and then he became silent and did not appear to be at all taken aback by the knowledge that an East India colonel was the bridegroom on the occasion, and one of very large property and singular behavior.

The evening before the marriage was a busy one. The young ladies had to arrange and to re-arrange all their finery; and the bride herself had the task of seeing how she became her bridal dress, to do an infinity of other little matters, and to contemplate the change that was about to take place in so short a period. A few hours more, and she would become a wife.

The colonel, himself, did not in the least fall off in his ardor; he was particularly anxious it should, on no account, be delayed after the day fixed. A later day he appeared to have the utmost objection to; indeed, he declared he would do anything if it came but a day or two earlier.

However, this was considered impossible, and the young lady was permitted to have her way, though it was expressly stipulated that it should not be an hour after the appointed time, for he declared himself dying with impatience to call her his own.

"Now, ma," said Margaret, as she sat talking to her mother the night before; "now, ma, I hope you will not give any of these people countenance when I am gone, and throw off their acquaintance; you will be firm on this point for my sake."

"I will, my dear," said Mrs. Meredith, "I will."

"Then, when I come back, I shall know more of the colonel's mind about where we shall live, and how we shall live. He must let me have something handsome; I have no doubt but what he will; he does not appear to be a close-handed man, quite the reverse; and, all things considered, we shall be able to make a very agreeable living out of it."

"Why, yes, my dear, I cannot doubt it; he is, no doubt, a man of property and can well afford us enough, and some sum as pin-money; indeed, he is too liberal now to be otherwise by and bye; perhaps he will keep on this house, and pay for proper domestics, and keep a carriage. What a change it will be for us all, and how the neighborhood will stare!"

"Yes, ma, they will; but suppose we were to reside out of town, we should have our carriage driving into town, as a matter of course, and now and then sleep in town when we made up a party, or went to the theatre."

"Yes, my dear. What time shall you see the colonel in the morning?"

"Not before I am ready to go."

"To church? Well, but you will have some breakfast with him?"

"No, he will be in his own room, I dare say, till late; he will scarce present himself before the time has come to start; you know his habits, he does not get up very early, and I do not expect to see much alteration. At eleven o'clock we are to be at church. We breakfast at nine, you know, so we shall have time."

"Oh, he is sure to be down to breakfast, there can be no doubt about that; indeed, he must be called for the purpose; of course, there must be some deviation form a regular rule upon extraordinary occasions like the present."

"Well, well, there may be; but have you given all the invitations you intended to give? — and have you got any answers to them so as to ensure their attendance?"

"Oh, yes, that is all safe and fixed; we shall have a good many here by half-past eight in the morning, at the latest; but you must contrive to let me have money very soon, or to send me some up, as I am getting very short, for I have laid out a great deal of money lately, and much more than I could, under other circumstances, spare or afford."

"Of course, ma, you will not lose anything by this; I shall take care of you; not a penny that you have laid out but what shall be repaid, and with a handsome return; but do not think about this, it grows late and I must to sleep."

"Do, my dear, and I'll wake you in time in the morning."

*T*he morning came, and some of them were about early. Mrs. Meredith was up, and so was Margaret. She could not lie so late as usual. She had done much, and yet she had so much to do still. It was really astonishing to see what there was to do — no one would have believed it, and even Margaret became surprised.

The morning was now fairly come; the servants were about in the house, and the neighbors were up and about; she could hear her mother chiding and scolding; she could hear the sound of her voice, and she began to believe there was now no time to lose.

The hour of nine was now gone. The knocker and the guests had been heard for the last half hour at the door, and she could hear the voices of the guests below, some of whom spoke audibly enough; then they soon after descended to the breakfast room, which, by the way, was the drawing room, as there was not enough room below.

The colonel, at the same moment, entered the room, and a vast number of congratulations were given and received, form side to side, with the utmost urbanity and good will. The colonel, for the first time, had thrown on one side the green shade which he usually wore, but he looked remarkably pale, though he had still the looks of a hearty and healthy man.

The paleness, which seemed to be constitutional, was very extraordinary; but that was explained by the colonel saying, that he had been so ever since he had the yellow fever, which had had that effect upon his complexion.

There was much rejoicing at the occurrences that were now in progress; everybody praised the viands; everything was of the best and first-rate quality, and there were many attendants, which made it so much the better and the more comfortable, as everybody had an abundance of everything.

Mrs. Meredith now shone in the greatest triumph; there was none so great and grand. She patronized everybody, and appeared remarkably condescending, considering she was the mother of a daughter who was about to marry a retired East India service colonel. There were few who did not understand fully the nature of the condescension of the lady herself; besides, she was the presiding goddess of the feast.

Among those who had been invited was the Miss Smith and Mr. Smith. This was the young lady who had been so terrified at the attack that had been made upon her the first night that Colonel Deverill lodged there, and on that night he was so terribly vexed and disturbed.

Mrs. Meredith had invited them, because they were people of means, and Miss Smith could not now do any mischief, because the colonel was pledged to Margaret too far to retract; and as there were several young females, why, the more the better, because it would divert his attention.

Miss Smith, however, came out of curiosity, and because it was a wedding party, which is the delight and admiration of all young females, and Miss Smith was no exception. Mr. Smith was civil and polite, and hid his internal dislike to the colonel, which he felt and could not account for it; neither did his daughter — she had a great aversion to him, but at the same time suppressed it.

The colonel was courtly and complimentary, and made civil speeches to such as spoke to him; indeed, he never for a moment lost his self-possession; he stood in a less stooping posture than usual, and he was considered a tall, handsome man — a fine man.

"Mr. Twissel," said the colonel, "I am happy to see you — especially gratified to see you — you will be witness of my happiness today — you will mark my progress in this affair, and learn what lesson it may teach. That is the way we should pass through life, Mr. Twissel, is it not? Gain knowledge by experience, and become, in old age, a wise man."

"Why, yes; oh, yes," said Twissel, who felt there was something in the remark that touched him to the quick, and he winced under the smart; but he thought it might have been accidentally given, and the colonel was quite ignorant of his disasters; and yet it was a very home thrust, without any previous introduction to it, that made it all the more uncomfortable, and he merely replied, —

"I am happy to see you, Colonel Deverill, and to see you so happy, and the young lady, who, I am sure, deserves to be happy; in fact, I think you both deserve happiness; I am sure, I wish you every imaginable joy, and it gives me great pleasure in seeing it."

"I am sure you do, sir; but you do not seem to eat and enjoy yourself."

"I am so occupied in witnessing the felicity of others, that I had forgotten it; moreover, I expect a friend to be present who happens to be late; he is quite a stranger to all present, and therefore I wished to countenance him as much as I could on that account."

"Then I will not press you now; perhaps you'll do me the favor of introducing your friend to me when he comes, yourself, and I shall be most happy to receive him."

"Thank you, colonel, you do me much honor; I will accept of your great kindness, and do myself the pleasure of presenting him to you, and to Miss Meredith, whom I hope to see soon changed in name."

"I hope the time will now be very short. What hour is it?"

"Half-past nine," said the attorney, consulting his watch.

"At eleven we must be at the church. Well, if we leave at half-past ten, then we shall be there in ample time; I would it were over and that we were on our journey."

"Ah! you are impatient, colonel," said Margaret, as she came up to him.

"My dear angel!" replied Deverill, bowing, "how could I be otherwise when you are the object of my affections? It is not impatience to leave this good company — quite the reverse. But it is because the change of scene, traveling, and change of air will do you much good, and is, I can see, quite necessary for you."

"I think it will do me no harm," said Margaret; "but here comes ma, who really looks tired."

"Well, my dear, I am a little fatigued, but you know I shall have ample time to recover myself. I shall have nothing to disturb my repose."

"Indeed, Mrs. Meredith!" said the colonel; "I am sure we must alter that; we must find some other kind of employment for you, and not suffer you to remain hidden at home. You have catered so well for us this morning, that I am sure you are a most valuable acquisition to a household; with such a superintendence as yours, we should have everything in the utmost plenty, and at the proper moment."

"Ah, colonel! you are flattering — you are."

"We shall soon show that we are not flattering, I hope," said the colonel. "My dear madam, you are the life and soul of the whole company. What should we have done without you? I hope all our friends here are happy and comfortable. I do not know them well enough to pay them all that attention and respect they deserve."

"Exactly, colonel; they all know that well enough, and are fully alive to the honor you do them in being present in the midst of them."

"Who is that young lady who was looking here just now?" inquired the colonel.

"Who? the young lady with the elderly gentleman by her side?"

"Yes; I should like to be introduced to her," said the colonel.

"Oh! certainly," said Mrs. Meredith, vexed in her own heart that she had invited her and her father, now, for she had no wish that any one present should be future acquaintances; but there was no help for it; she must introduce them, and accordingly she went up, with the best grace she could put on, to them both, to request they would be introduced to the colonel, who desired the honor of their acquaintance.

There was no hesitation, of course, and they at once advance to meet him, and were introduced to the colonel as Miss and Mr. Smith.

"I am most happy to see you, sir," said the colonel; "and the young lady here is your daughter, I can see, by the family likeness she bears to you."

Miss Smith, however, could not repress a convulsive shudder as she looked upon the colonel. It might have been his complexion, or it might have been that his features brought some terrible recollections to her mind; but she could not, for a moment or so, speak.

"The young lady is ill!" said the colonel, who noticed the emotion.

"What is the matter, Clara, my dear?" said Mr. Smith; "what's the matter — you are ill?"

"No, no," said Miss Smith; "it was a — a — sudden — sudden dizziness that came across me. I dare say I shall be better by and bye. I am sorry it should have come upon me now."

"Ah! my dear young lady," said Colonel Deverill, drawing himself up to his full height, and looking gravely, but speaking with the utmost courtesy, "you have nothing to regret respecting the occasion; the illness itself is a matter of regret to us all, I am sure; however, let us hope it will be but temporary, and that you will be able to wish me joy, and my beautiful bride."

"You see, Colonel Deverill, ever since the night she was disturbed by the strange attack of what she believes to have been a vampyre, or something that had the form of a man, and a taste for blood, she has been affected thus."

"Dear me!" said the colonel; "what a shocking thing — a very shocking affair! I think perhaps, the young lady is subject to illness," and he touched his forehead, as much as to intimate an insinuation that the young lady might be somewhat affected in her intellects.

"No, sir; quite the reverse," said her father. "I myself saw a tall, gaunt figure gliding away, which felled me in an instant, and I lay half a minute stunned."

"God bless me!" said the colonel; "this affair is quite romantic! If a German writer had such material by him, what would he not make of it?"

There had been a loud knocking at the door, and some one announced; but nobody took any notice of it. Colonel Deverill did not hear it, but stood talking to Mr. Smith; while Admiral Bell was introduced by Mr. Twissel, who led him towards the group, explaining what had happened.

"By G-d!" said the admiral; "d'ye see how they are crowding about the poor girl? Why, they'd extinguish a fire — if there was one! Why don't you give young woman air? If you don't stand on one side, I'll put a whole broadside into you, as I would into a Frenchman!"

This singular address produced an immediate sensation, and many moved away.

"Colonel Deverill," said Mr. Twissel, "allow me to introduce my friend Admiral Bell to you. Admiral Bell, this is Colonel Deverill. — Eh? — oh! — eh?"

These latter exclamations were uttered in consequence of the extreme surprise depicted on the countenances of both parties. Admiral Bell's surprise was nothing out of the way; but that of Colonel Deverill was a matter of consternation to many of them. He stepped back a pace or two, and then his lips parted, as though he would speak, but he could not; he panted — his eye glared, and his nostrils dilated.

"Shatter my mainmast — upset the caboose — turn my state-cabin into a cockpit, and the quarter-deck to a gambling-booth to the whole ship's company!"

"What's all this about?" exclaimed Mrs. Meredith.

"Oh, that odious man! — who is he? — what is —"

"Why, ma'am, I'm old Admiral Bell; very well known for having beaten the French, and the terror of all vampyres. Why, look at the swab — but you ain't going to get off this time!"

"What is the matter, dear colonel?" said Margaret. "You are ill — speak — what is the matter?"

"Ah!" said the admiral; "let him speak, and he'll tell you he's no colonel, and his name ain't Deverill, or, if it be, it ain't his only name; he is Varney the vampyre!"

"A vampyre!" said Miss Smith, starting up with a shriek; "a vampyre! Good heavens! I was not mistaken, then; that must be the man!" and she sank back in her father's arms.

"What! has he been at any of his tricks again!" exclaimed the admiral, and he made a stride towards him; but Varney — for it was he — avoided him by stepping aside, and placing some other person between himself and the admiral, and then he said, —

"What this madman will say you will not listen to — you — ."

"Madman! well, I'm hanged; call me man!" said the admiral. "I wish I had my sword by my side, and I would teach you how a madman can fight; but you are not going; I have something to say to you first. If he's going to marry that young lady, all I can say is, she will be food for him — she'll never live till tomorrow; her blood will make his pale face ruddy!"

Varney stood no longer; but seeing many around him who appeared to have an inclination to stop his passage, he suddenly made to the door, which he secured for a moment on the outside, and then in another he was clear of the house.

This was no sooner done, than all present, who were staring at each other in mute amazement, and unable to account for what had happened, looked at the new comer, the admiral, who immediately began to relate enough of Varney that made it apparent to all present that he was not what he represented himself to be.

*A*mid the commiserations of their friends, and their jeers, Mrs. Meredith sold all her furniture, and, with her daughter, retired to some little place, where they opened a small shop, to eke out a living by such means. They were unable even to pay many debts they had contracted on account of this marriage, and they were, moreover, ashamed to be seen by their former acquaintance.

Chapter CXXXIII.

A SCENE IN WINCHESTER CATHEDRAL. – THE CATHEDRAL
ROBBERS. – A STORM. – THE VAULTS BENEATH THE AISLE.
– THE FLIGHT OF THE ROBBERS, AND THE RESUSCITATED
CORPSE.

*T*he sun had long deserted the horizon, and the good city of
Winchester had been buried in darkness many hours; while the moon,
though high in her course, was obscured by the hazy clouds that drifted
from the south-west. The gusty winds whistled round the walls of the
cathedral church, producing an unpleasant sensation, with a foreboding
of a coming storm.

The inhabitants of the quiet, orderly town, were steeped in repose,
and a stranger who might by chance have wandered at such an untoward
hour abroad, would not have found one single ray from any window;
save, perhaps, at one or two hotels, which merely keep open till the
London mail passed through, lest any passengers should make their stay
at Winchester.

Save at these places, all were reposing peaceably in their beds; and the
tower of the cathedral frowned majestically upon the tombstones below,
and upon the surrounding buildings, which appeared to peep upon the
limits of the grave-yard; while the fir trees that were yet standing bent
beneath the blast, as it swept across the low walls, by which the cathedral
on one side is bounded.

But the solitary churchyard was not without its occupants, living or
dead; for its sanctity is invaded by the presence of three men, who emerge
from the narrow streets and courts situated between it and the cross,
and then crossing beneath the shade of some object, they stood beneath
the low wall which surrounded the churchyard.

They paused for several moments, and gazed around them in every direction, and up at the houses that were nearest to them; but there was no sign of light or anything stirring in any of the houses adjacent.

"I think all is right tonight," said one of the men to his companions.

"Ay, right enough; there will be nobody near us tonight."

"No," replied a third; "and if the signs of the weather are good for anything, why, we shall have a rough night; and though that is unpleasant, yet it makes interruptions less likely, and success more certain."

"You are right, Josh; we shall have a good job this time."

"There, then, that will do until we are safe; it's no use talking here; if the old watchman comes round, we may have to book it, and then we may not have a chance."

"Ha, ha, ha! as for the old watchman, he is not the fool you take him to be, if you imagine him at all likely to disturb himself on such a night as this; he'll sleep in his box till he wakes and finds it is fine."

"Well, be that as it may," said the other, impatiently, "it is all right now."

"Yes, all right."

"Then just help me over, and I'll get down on the other side, while one of you can get up on the wall and hand the tools down to me."

"Can't you throw them over?"

"I could, but it is not worth while to make any noise, even though we felt sure that it will not be heard. There have been most strange things done in our time, you know, and there is no telling what may happen."

"Ah, the dead may come to life, Josh."

"So they might; and a pig might fly, but, as they say, it is a very unlikely bird."

"Well, then, up with you."

As he spoke, one of the men gave one of his companions a lift up, and with this aid he got on the wall, and then quietly slipping down into the burial-ground, he awaited his companions, one of whom immediately mounted the wall in the same manner, and who received a bag, which he handed down to his comrade, who was in the graveyard belonging to the cathedral.

"Well, is all right?" he said.

"Yes, all right; don't stay up there like a cat on a wall; come down, or you may by chance be seen."

The other two men immediately came over the wall, and they all three collected round a monument that stood up, and here a short consultation took place.

"Now, how shall we proceed?"

"We must get into the vaults somehow or other, if we dig our way in, which I think is much the most easily done."

"What! undermine the building?"

"Scarcely so much as that."

"Well, but we can get into the body of the cathedral, and then into the vaults that way. There is a door."

"Yes, there is a door, but it is so close to the verger's door, that you are sure to awake him."

"I have opened more than one door in my time, and yet I never awoke anybody in doing so; he must sleep wonderfully light."

"Ay, so he may; but in this case the door is so strong that there is no chance of breaking it open, without great inconvenience and noise; there is no room to work in, and, moreover, the verger keeps a little cur always sleeping on the mat close to his door, so that no one can approach without his giving alarm."

"What a brute!"

"Yes; but there is a means of entering besides that."

"Where — and how?"

"In the back of the cathedral there is a large marble slab, on which is carved some letters, that I never could make out; but I'm told it says that somebody lies buried underneath that stone, but I know immediately below are the vaults."

"Well, but the marble you speak of would weigh fourteen or fifteen hundred weight, which would be no joke."

"No, by Jove," said his companion; "we had better by far dig our way in, since we shall have so much difficulty in getting in; we can soon dig out soil enough to let us get down into the vaults."

"Well, we had better set to work at once, lest we lose all chance. If we have a long job, we had better set to work early, as well as stop here, for if we are surprised we shall have to run."

"And the yard will be watched ever afterwards, as sure as we shall have a storm presently."

"So we shall. Work away, Josh; where are the tools?"

"Here they are," said the man, throwing the bag down and opening it; and then he pulled out some tools, consisting of pickaxe and shovels, and a crowbar or two, and several other little materials, which were useful upon such occasions.

"Well, now, where shall we commence?"

"Just at the side here; we are safe to get in somewhere where the wall is weakest, for I believe the vaults are all walled in."

"They must be, to have a secure foundation for such a weight as there must be about it; and, to my mind, we have got a decent job. It's very much like a fortress, and if it was easy to get in this way, we should hear of such things being done much oftener than they are, that is my opinion."

"And a very good opinion it is, too, until another is heard; but it is no use being faint-hearted; the harder the job, the harder we ought to set at it, that's all; but there are some few things not thought of by others, you know, and it is sometimes the hardest thing in the world to think of the most simple."

"There's some truth in that."

The men having found the spot they most desired, they set about digging and picking it up in good earnest; but it was difficult work, and the soil about the cathedral was very hard, owing to the quantity of rubbish that had been driven or trodden into the earth for centuries, either through accident or design, to harden and secure the permanency of the work around. There were many heavy and large stones, as well as small broken stones; also, flint in no small quantity, that every now and then resisted the blows of the pick.

"Well, I'm thinking we have all three worked half an hour, and have not got a foot deep yet."

"We have not got much deeper, certainly."

"Do you think we shall get in tonight?"

"Tonight or never," said the third man.

"You are right, comrade; shoulder your picks and then we shall see what way we can make in another half hour. Who can tell? we may come to a softer soil below; this is only the filling up."

The men again set to work heartily, but they seemed to have no success — they could not make anything of it; it appeared to resist all their efforts; and the sparks often flew from the blows they made with their tools.

The perspiration ran down their faces, and as they paused to wipe their foreheads, they gazed upwards at the clouds. It was heavy, and the wind was blowing fresh, and now and then a heavy spot of rain.

"By St. Peter," said one of them, "I expect we shall have a storm presently. I already feel the heavy drops that fall occasionally; and if one may judge by them of what we may expect, we shall have it heavily."

"So much the better; we shall have less interruption."

"Well, I don't know what you call interruption, but this is a complete stopper; I can't make any impression with the pick, it is as hard as rock; and then comes some of those old walls that are rather harder than granite — you may as well pick at a cart-load of pig iron."

As this was said, the clouds suddenly appeared to open, and such a deluge of rain descended, that the earth seemed to smoke. The drops appeared to be continuous small spouts of water — a shower is too mild a word — it was a deluging, as if some waterspout had burst.

The men stood a moment or two, but it was useless to work; they could not do it, and they rushed to a part of the wall which sheltered them from the fury of the storm that was raging.

"Well, I never saw anything like this before."

"Nor I. Hark at the thunder! There's a flash! Who would have expected that at this season of the year?"

"Not I."

"Nor any one else; but it seems to me as if we were to be defeated tonight. I am sorry we made the attempt, since we are sure to find the yard watched after this, for they will see what we have been up to."

"Yes, it is vexing, but we cannot help this; it is quite impossible to do anything in such weather as this. I do not care about a wet jacket, but I cannot see, and hardly breathe, with so much falling water about me."

"Nor I; but yet I am loath to give it up; Consider the jewelry and money he had about him — it will pay us handsomely."

"Well, it was a strange start of him, at all events. I wonder how he came to be buried in such a manner — how was it?"

"I don't know. All I know is, that the thing was kept secret because it was considered that it would be a temptation to disturb any grave when it was known that he was buried in his clothes and jewelry, and that his money was buried also with him. It was certainly a temptation I could not resist."

"Are you sure?"

"Yes; I will tell you, another time, how I came to know all about it; indeed, I saw him screwed down, and the consequence is, I know that he has the money and valuables about him."

"Then I am sure we had better get into the church itself; we can do more with your slab of marble than on the outside of the wall. And besides that, I do not think that this rain will give over; the hole we have already made is fast filling up with water, and we shall find it impossible to work."

"So we shall. What do you say to getting inside the cathedral?"

"Agreed, my lads; as quickly as you like; for, if we stay here much longer, we shall certainly be drowned. I'm wet through as it is."

"So am I; but never mind, my boys, bright gold and jewels will warm your hearts, and that will keep your outsides dry, or at least you will not feel it. I am sure that I should not if I can but get it."

"Ay, that is all I care about; but, if you get foiled, you may depend upon it you don't feel any the better — you are rather worse, and feel everything more; but what do you say to yon window?"

"That will do if we can reach it: that is my only difficulty."

"That is one that is easily overcome," said his companion, "for I know where the ladder is, and that is just over our heads; all you have to do is to put the point of the crow-bar under the staple to which the chain is fastened that secures it, and then you have the means at once of entering."

"But if we get in and are detected, how shall we get out again?"

"Are we not three to one? If the old verger should come, I think we could make a dead body of him in a very short while; and I cannot tell where you will be if you can't get the better of the old man."

"Well, say no more about it; up with the ladder, and we will get in and chance it. Such a night as this, it would be strange, indeed, if anybody heard us; but, as there is much to be got, why, we can't grumble at the risk."

The three men set to work about wrenching the staple out to which was attached a chain which secured the ladder. That was soon effected, and the ladder placed against one of the lowermost windows, and then one of the men went up, and forcing the window open said, after he had looked in, —

"All right — come up. We have got to a right place."

They all three came up one after another, when the first up crept in at the open aperture, and by means of ornamental work, and a monument that there projected from the wall in a manner that enabled them to descend with ease, and in a few moments more the whole three stood in the old cathedral of Winchester.

At that moment the bell tolled heavily the hour of twelve. The sound was solemn, and it made a deep impression upon the robbers.

"What a dismal, hollow sound that has, to be sure," said one.

"Yea; it sounded like tolling."

"Pshaw!" said one of them; "'tis no matter — if it be tolling, it is not for us, nor for the man we come to visit, so no more old women's fears; if you don't like stopping in this place, you had better set to work and be quick, when we shall have no further need of staying. Of what use is it for you to stare and gape about with white faces, and swelled eyeballs, like so many cats; be men — be active, and use you arms."

"Well, where are we to use them? What are we to do? You brought us here, and yet you do not tell us what we are to do. You know all about this matter, and you cannot, or do not point out where we are to commence."

"Here, then; on the very stone you are standing; set to work to raise this, and then we shall soon find our way into the vaults below, and we shall then satisfy ourselves for our trouble, and be well paid too, I hope."

"I hope so, too, Josh; for, to tell you the truth, I don't ever recollect so uncomfortable a job as that which I am in tonight."

"Well, you ain't got paid all, I'll warrant."

"I haven't got paid at all, yet; but we waste time; lend me a pick. I don't see how I am to get a tool in here. The chinks are all so small, that you can hardly put in the blade of a penknife."

"There is a hole somewhere near the head. There is a small piece of black marble."

"Yes; here it is."

"Well, chip that out, and then you may insert a crow-bar, or pick, beneath the stone, when you will find that it will lift up, and then, by main strength, lift it back, and we may go down."

These instructions were followed out. The black marble was discovered, and then knocked out, when a large crevice was discovered, into which a powerful crow-bar was immediately thrust; and then, by one united effort, they contrived to lift the marble slab up out of its place, though not above a foot, which required a great effort, when it is considered that it was imbedded in cement.

"Well, we shall be able to get it up now, I think."

"Don't be too sure, for we have not got it far — it is enormously heavy, and the lever has done all as yet."

"Well, then, are you all ready? A long pull, you know, comrades, and a strong pull, does the business. Now, then, altogether."

"Heave, ho!" whispered another, and they all three made a prodigious effort. It was not only a strong pull, but a very long pull, for the stone was so heavy, it came slowly and unwillingly upwards, and it was nearly three minutes before the enormous mass stood upright in the aisle.

"Well, I didn't think it would have been done. That's the hardest job that ever I had a hand in, and don't desire to have such another, but yet, hard as it is, it is easier than what we had to do outside."

"Yes, much, and you will soon find it is so. Lend a hand to clear away the rubbish that lies here; there's a trap-door underneath that leads into the vaults; it belonged to the monks of old, of whom it is said it served either for the same purpose of burial, or for a cellar for wine."

"Well, well, there are some things better than wine, I trow, in the cellar, now, if we can find the coffin; there has been no other burial in the vaults since he was buried, so we shall not have much trouble."

"But what are we to do with the stone? If we let it down again, we shall do some mischief."

"We must turn it corner by corner until we get it against the pillars, and there leave it; for if we let it down, it will go down like the report of a gun, and smash all that comes in the way."

This was agreed to, and it was not long before they propped the heavy mass of stone against one of the pillars, and then returned to the place where it had been raised, and began to clear away the rubbish, when a trap-door was plainly observable; and after much labor and force, they contrived to open the door, when there appeared a dark aperture, into which they could not look without some misgivings, for nothing could be seen.

"Well, who's to go down?"

This was a question that no one liked to answer. And certainly no one would volunteer to go below. It was too dark to be inviting, and the men looked at one another as well as they could, for it was total darkness, or nearly so, in the aisle; and below, it was so utterly dark, that it was impossible to make out anything.

"What is to be done now? Have you got the lantern?"

"I have, and matches, but did not think we ought to use them before, lest we attract attention; however, we will have a light now, and should anybody look down, they will think there is a general meeting among the dead."

So saying, he lit the lantern, which threw a light into the vault, and rendered visible a flight of steps that ran up to the opening, but which were invisible in the darkness that had reigned in the place.

"Now, then, jump down, and see where the last coffin is placed; it is easily known from all the others, for I don't think there has been a burial here for many months — the old cathedral is not often disturbed for the reception of the dead, and only when some rich man dies and fancies he may lie more comfortable here."

"Ay, rich men can afford to be buried in a good suit of clothes, and money in their pocket, to bribe St. Peter to open the gate."

"Ha! ha! ha! well said; Peter has the keys."

"Yes, and here we have the coffin."

"Have we? Is this it?"

"Yes; don't you see that it has all the signs of newness about it? There is hardly any dust collected upon it; here we shall find our treasure; the coffin is a strong one, and will, I think, take some trouble to break open."

"Indeed! We shall be choked with the horrible stench which we have below. I can't stand it another minute — I shall be sick."

"Ay, and I too."

"Here, then, I have the lantern. Lay hold of the coffin and bring it up stairs; we can carry it amongst us."

"Ay, anything but remain here — that I cannot do."

"Be quick, for confound me, but such a mass of putrid flesh as there must be here, is horribly sickly. I would sooner be hanged than pass an hour here."

"I'm not so afraid of death as all that. I could manage to live through a night."

"You might, but you would soon find out the ill effects, and die of some fever or other; and that is what we shall have, if we remain here much longer."

The three men then shifted the coffin from its place, and then on to their shoulders, one at either end, and one under the center.

The coffin was heavy — very heavy, and the men were tottering under their burden. They were strong men, but hardly equal to the task of carrying so dead a weight; but yet they never shrank from it, but, with slow and unsteady steps, they gradually neared the stairs that led upwards. They paused. If it was a task before, it was worse now. What more exertion could they make?

"Do you think the steps will hold us?" said one.

"I'm sure I cannot say; and perhaps not."

"I think they are rotten, or partially so; what do you say? How shall we get the body up?"

"There is a rope, is there not?"

"Yes."

"That will do then. I will get that; by its means we may hoist the coffin up to the stone pavement above. I'm almost sick."

"And I too. This place is enough to breed a pestilence in a town."

The smell in the vaults was certainly very strong and very pernicious. The fetid odor that rose from the vaults was especially disagreeable; the smell that comes from the accumulated and putrefying remains of human bodies, is of all odors the most noisome, and, to our tastes, the worst.

Right glad were the men, who had propped the coffin up against the ladder, to get up into the aisle above, to breathe a less impure atmosphere. They gasped again; and one of them climbed up the monument, to get to the open window, at which they had entered, to inhale some of the pure moistened air; and then, after a few inspirations, he returned, at the call of his comrades to aid them.

The rope was procured and secured round the coffin, and one man remained below to guide it, while the two others remained above to haul up the rope, which would bring the body, coffin and all, to the top.

"Well, Josh, how goes the storm?"

"It is blowing over, I think; it does not rain, and it is breaking. I shouldn't wonder if we don't have moonlight after all, and, if we should, we shall have a trouble to get away unperceived."

"You forget what hour it is."

"Hark! there are the chimes."

The four quarters now chimed from the great clock, and sounded solemnly and mournfully in the dead of the night. The iron tongue struck one, and the last sounds of the clock died away before any of the men moved or spoke.

"Well, we have been here an hour, and nearly two hours since our first commencement. It's nearly time, I'm thinking."

"Yes," said the man below.

"Heave ho!" called out the leader of the gang, in a low voice.

The two men at the top hauled at the rope, while he below pushed the coffin up with all his strength, and after a time they succeeded in causing it to rise about a foot, or something less, at each haul, and as it got higher, the man below could the better apply his strength to it, and at length it came up to the top.

Here, however, they experienced another difficulty. It was hard to pull up so high as to enable them to throw its weight on the pavement, and the rope was almost useless as a means of pulling it up higher, and the only one who had it in his power effectually to apply his strength, was the man below. However, after a while, to their great relief, the coffin lay fairly upon the stone pavement.

"A good job done!"

"So say I, Josh; and such another would completely finish me for the night. I might lie down and defy the world."

"How about the coffin — there is no time to rest. I have a small flask of rum in my pocket, which we will discuss as soon as we have broken open the coffin, which I expect is the last hard job we shall have."

"And a hard job it would have been, had I not come provided with a screwdriver — one that is used by undertakers in such work."

"Set to work — good luck to you. I am quite dry, and quite tired too, and the sooner this is over the better. There, the screws come out easily enough, though they are long and hold firm."

"Yes, they go deep; but they have a wide worm, that carries them down or brings them up so quickly."

In a few minutes more the whole of the screws were drawn, and the lid of the coffin was thrown on one side, and the corpse was at once discovered to them. It lay calm and quiet; but yet it was terrible to look at. The living man had been tall — remarkably tall, as well as remarkable-looking.

He was dressed as if for walking. It was strange, the corpse was appareled as if were in life; and this, perhaps, caused the extreme paleness — even extreme for a corpse — to be so apparent that they spoke not, but gazed in silence upon it, until at length one of them said, —

"Put out the light. We have the moon's rays — at least there is enough to enable us to see what we want, and the light is dangerous."

The light was put out, and the subdued light of the moon rendered all apparent enough to the robbers.

The storm had lulled and altogether ceased, while they had been busy in the vaults and getting up the body, and now it was a perfect calm. The moon, though obscured at the moment, promised to shed her rays upon the earth; and as it was at the full, and the clouds clearing off, the probability was that the town would become as light as day.

"There he is," said one of the men.

"Yes; and about as ugly a chap as ever I saw."

"He is no beauty: but he's been a fine man."

"If you mean tall, I dare say you are right; but he's not fine as I take it. He's not quite full enough about the chest and shoulders."

"He's got some fine rings, and a gold watch and chain. Well, there is a good ten or fifteen pounds each, and if his pockets are well lined, why, he will afford us a tolerable good booty."

"Yes; we must not complain. Shall we replace all?"

"It is not possible to do so, either in time to enable us to escape, or to do it so as to escape detection. Besides, there would be no use in it. See how bright the moon is getting. We shall have as much to do as we shall get through to escape being seen. I am sure we shall run a great risk."

"I think so too."

"Well, then, commence proceedings. Ha!"

The moonbeams had fallen upon the corpse just as he was speaking, and he thought he observed a motion in the body.

"What is the matter, Josh?"

"Didn't you think he moved."

"Ha! ha! ha! dead! ha! ha! ha! dead moved — buried moved — ha! ha! ha! Eh? why — oh — it's all fancy; you'll see me believe it, presently. I do declare — well, a man dead and buried — I suppose a week."

"No."

"I think so —"

"Well, it does not matter much how long he has been buried; but he can't move unless you move him. D——n!"

As he spoke he started to his feet, and his hair began to straighten, and his limbs quiver, and yet he appeared to think he might be mistaken; for he endeavored to speak to his companions; pointing to the corpse, he contrived to say,

"I — 'l — 'l take the j — j — jewels; he — he — he moves."

"Eh? Well, I told you I thought so, but you said no, and only laughed at me for doing so; but stand on one side, and let the moonlight come upon him, we can tell better then if he really does move; though, notwithstanding all I saw, I am inclined to believe it is quite an impossibility; but the more light we have the better we shall be able to tell how the mistake arose."

"I thought I saw his eyes move."

As he spoke he moved on the side, as he had been standing between the corpse and the moon's rays, and for the most part intercepted them; but the moment that he did move away, and the rays came full upon the corpse, a shivering motion appeared to pervade it, to the intense horror of the robbers, who could not believe what they saw, but believed they were yet mistaken, though they were too much terrified to speak or even move. They stood gazing upon the body with bursting eyes and gaping mouth, as if they had suddenly become spell-bound by the wand of some magician.

Presently the corpse opened his eyes and glared full at them. Oh, such glistening, lead-like orbs, that froze the very current of their blood; they knew not what to think, but when the body turned on one side, towards the moon's rays, all doubt vanished and the spell was broken.

"The devil, by — !" exclaimed Josh.

Not another word was uttered by either of the other two; but they sprang like emancipated madmen up the slippery sides of the monument, and out at the windows, as easily as a fly can run up a wall. It did not occupy more than a few seconds to enable them to clear the place. Half a minute had not elapsed before they stood shivering by the beautiful old cross, at Winchester.

*T*he corpse in the cathedral, which mysteriously became animated when exposed to the moonlight, turned towards the moon's rays and gazed upon the flying and terrified robbers, who had just exhumed him.

No word passed his lips, and he looked around him for some time in silence, upon the scene before him.

The moon came in at the tall windows of the cathedral, throwing long streams of silvery light upon the stone flooring, and upon some of the monuments that were erected by the pillars, or columns that rise to the roof.

All was silent, all was still — no movement was discernible, save in the form that now sat up, and leaned on his elbow in his coffin; and he but turned his head slowly from side to side, as though he were meditating upon the lovely and solemn beauty of the place.

At length he arose, but he appeared to move with extreme difficulty, and once or twice he placed his hand in the region of the heart, as if he felt something there that pained him, and tottered about; but seemed to recover himself a little after a time, and muttered to himself, in low but distinct tones, —

"I must have been another victim; I am weak, the vital action is languid, and my veins are empty; I must satisfy the instinct of my nature, and another victim must restore me to life and the world for a season."

He looked up towards the window, gave one look around him and on the coffin, while a shudder passed though him; and then, gazing on himself and feeling for his valuables, he slowly clambered up the monument, and carefully got through the window, and thence into the open air, and he finally disappeared from Winchester churchyard.

Chapter CXXXIV.

THE STAR HOTEL, AND THE STRANGER'S ARRIVAL. – A
REMARKABLE COUNTENANCE. – THE ILLNESS AND DEATH
OF THE STRANGER. – A STRANGE REQUEST COMPLIED
WITH.

Some days previous to the scene related in the previous chapter, the
London coach drove up opposite to the Star Hotel, and, as usual, out
came a couple of waiters to see what there was from the metropolis, in
the shape of a passenger, who might become an inmate of the hotel,
and a customer, of course.

"Now, then, Billy," said the guard, a stout, good-humored fellow, to
a very stiff and punctilious waiter, dressed in black, with a white
neckerchief.

"My good friend, my name is William, if you must be familiar,
though I am sure I don't number you among my acquaintances."

"Very good, Billy. I declare you are one of the politest waiters that is
to be found between Portsmouth and London; ay, and more than that,
you are *the* politest. Didn't you say you were educated among a lot of
gals – young ladies, I mean?"

"I never held any discourse, relative to my early days, with you, my
friend; I am not, just this moment, aware of it."

"Ah! I see you are too polite to pass an east wind without taking your
hat off to it; how do they when they have none?"

"Have you anybody for us?" said William, mildly.

"Yes, my pink, I have."

"Who is he, and where is he? I must not waste my master's time; it
is an impropriety I am especially anxious to avoid."

"You needn't be in a hurry, nevertheless, especially as I see he is
fumbling about for small change; but what will you say if I introduce
a customer to you, a good six foot high, and perhaps a little to spare;

and the color of a well scraped horse-radish? Eh? what do you say to that, my primrose?"

William did not know what to say, but, after a moment's hesitation, he said,

"We don't charge our customers by the room they take, or by their personal appearance. A gentleman is a gentleman, Mr. Guard, all the same, whether he have a red face or a white one."

"Well, that's good, Billy; but the chief thing is, after all, of what color is his money, and how he parts with it; eh?"

The guard winked and William's impassive features were lit up with a spark of intelligence and vivacity, which, however, was only transient, and he relapsed into his old state of extreme and unimpeachable gentility.

"Hold your tongue, Billy; here he comes."

At that moment the gentleman pulled down the window, and said to the guard,

"Open the door, if you please; I shall get out here."

"Yes, sir," said the guard, who immediately obeyed the injunction; and a tall, but awfully pale individual descended the steps, wrapped up in a huge cloak, so that but little of his person was seen, or features either; what little there was visible was not prepossessing by any means by the color.

"This is the Star?" said the stranger, inquiringly.

"Yes," said the guard.

"I'll stop here. Are you the waiter?" said he, addressing William.

"I am, sir," said William. "Will you walk this way, sir?"

"Yes; show me into a private apartment — let me have a good fire, for I am exceedingly cold."

William immediately took him into a room where there was a fire, saying, —

"If you please to remain here, sir, we will make you a fire and warm the room; and, as you are cold, perhaps you will prefer this to going into a room without a fire there already lighted for your reception."

"Certainly, I much prefer it."

"Would you like to take any refreshment, sir?" inquired William.

"Not now," replied the stranger, in mild accents.

William left the room, muttering to himself, —

"Well, he deserves to be a prince; he is as mild and gentlemanly as a prince. I vow I never heard any one speak in such a tone, and with so much amiable condescension. What a pity he is so white — at least, that he is so, I only infer from the nose, and part of the forehead and cheeks around the eyes — these being the only parts that I have noticed; he is, indeed, not much unlike, in color, to the guard's vulgar simile — a well scraped horse-radish. I never saw white so opaque and dead before."

While those thoughts passed through the mind of William, he saw that the apartment was placed in readiness for the stranger's reception, and placed himself in communication with the proprietor, and obtained his orders; he then returned to the stranger, and conducted him to his proper apartment, and then awaited his commands.

The stranger gave him some orders, which were at once executed, and then he said, —

"I shall sleep here, of course."

"Yes, sir," said William.

"I am very particular about my beds — I must have my bed well and thoroughly aired."

"Oh, yes, sir," said William; "we always —"

"Never mind, never mind all that," said the stranger, blandly. "Never mind all that; I know what you would say. All your beds are always aired. Well, be it so — I have no desire to dispute it — but I once slept in a damp bed — I fell ill, and have never entirely recovered from it."

"Oh, that makes him look so horrible pale," thought William.

"So you perceive, my friend, that I have cause to be particular, and, therefore, you will excuse me when I inquire minutely into the character of the beds."

"Oh, certainly, sir — certainly, sir."

"Then you will see that my bed is aired, will you not?"

"Yes, sir, I will take care that it is especially aired; and, if you approve of my doing so, sir, I will have a fire lit in your bed-room."

"If you please. If you will do all this, you will greatly oblige me. Are there any females in the family?"

"Yes, sir; the servants," said William, fearing some impropriety was meant.

"Oh, the servants; and no others?"

"None," said William, quite suddenly.

"Oh, yes, that is right — none but the servants. Then my requests will not put you to any serious inconvenience?"

"Not in the least, sir," said William, pleased to find that the females had only been inquired about for fear of annoying them.

The stranger sat up in his room, and appeared to be very ill, and ate and drank but little, though he ordered whatever was requisite for a liberal individual; and, though taken away untouched, yet it was clearly understood he would have to pay for it.

The bed was used and approved of, and the tall remarkable looking stranger expressed himself satisfied to the proprietor of the hotel, who came to inquire if he should desire anything more or different from what was already done.

This was at once answered in the negative, and the proprietor retreated by no means prepossessed in the stranger's personal appearance, which was remarkable to a degree — that was noticed by every one in the hotel.

"Winchester is an old town — a city — sir," said the proprietor, by way of entering into a conversation with his guest.

"Yes, very old," said his guest.

"And the cathedral, sir, has been built in part ever since the Saxon times, and then increased by the Normans."

"Ay, it is very beautiful; one could wish to lie there, it is so calm and beautiful," said the stranger, with a shudder, which he endeavored to suppress; and then he added, "The grave-yard is quiet and retired."

"Yes, sir. You have been in Winchester before?"

"I have," replied the stranger.

Finding any further attempt at conversation likely to appear intrusive, the landlord quitted the apartment with a bow, which was condescendingly returned by the guest, who folded his hands one over the other, and turned towards the fire, upon which he gazed thoughtfully for some time in silence.

The strange and ghastly-looking countenance of the stranger had created quite a sensation among the individuals at the hotel, all of them declaring they never heard of, or saw anything equal to it in all their lives. But what was it? How did it happen so? They had seen dead men, but they had never seen any so ghastly and so fearfully pale.

"He doesn't seem long for this world," said one of them.

"If you had said he didn't belong to this world," said another, "I should almost have been inclined to believe you."

"He does look like a corpse," added an old woman.

"Yes, and what a tooth he has projecting out in front. Upon my word I never saw his like."

"And I," said another, "never beheld such eyes. Why, he is scarcely human. Such eyes as those I scarcely wish to look at again."

"He always appears to me to be in some dreadful agony," said the cook; "he really looks as if he had a perpetual pain in his stomach, and had eaten something that had disagreed with him."

There was some truth in this last assertion, for the stranger always did appear as if suffering from some internal pain — mental or physical, or both — and it was soon seen that he was rapidly losing strength, and could scarcely walk abroad.

The cause of all this none could tell; possibly, it was only a sudden illness, or perhaps it was a long affliction, to which he was used to, and hence the terrible expression upon his countenance, which appeared as if it had never been otherwise, so deep and so settled was the expression of pain.

*T*he stranger appeared anxious to get out, but was unable to do so; he could just walk across the room several times in the day, but was unable to get down stairs; and whenever he attempted to do so, he sunk down, his limbs losing the power of sustaining his weight.

"I can go no further," he muttered to himself, as he endeavored to walk down stairs; "I am lost."

As he spoke, a truly horrible expression came across his countenance, that made William, who came to his aid, step back terrified.

"You — you are ill, sir," he said, in somewhat uncertain accents.

"I am ill," he replied, "very ill."

"Will you allow me to help you up, sir, to your room?"

"If you please," said the stranger, who was endeavoring to rise by the aid of the banisters; and by these, and with William's assistance, he got up; and then, with some difficulty, he reached up stairs — his own bed-room.

"I will send master immediately, sir."

"You need not be in any hurry," said the stranger. "I do not desire his presence."

However, William left the stranger to seek his master; and when he found him, he said, —

"Oh, sir, the strange-looking gentleman in No. 5 is very ill."

"Is he, William? What is the matter with him?"

"I am sure I don't know, sir; he sank down on the stairs just now, and could only get up to his room again by my help."

"Something serious I think, then. I thought he appeared ill when first I saw him, from the expression of his countenance."

"Yes, sir; 'tis very strange."

"Very," said the landlord, thoughtfully. "I'll go and see him; but, in the mean time, you had better send for Doctor Linton, who knows me, and will come at once."

"Yes, sir," said William.

The landlord immediately sought the stranger's apartment, which he entered without any ceremony, and advanced to the bed in which the stranger lay; and, upon his first glance at the occupant, the landlord stepped back in affright, so truly terrible did the countenance of the stranger appear.

"Ah," said the stranger, as he turned his glassy eyes upon him.

"I — I — I have come to see you," stammered the landlord. "I have come to see you; my servant informed me you were ill, sir."

"I am very ill."

"I feared so, and I have sent for Doctor Linton, who will be here immediately."

"It is of no consequence; I believe, I am too far gone to recover."

Another horrible spasm passed across his countenance.

"What does your illness arise from?"

"Decay of the system. I want renovating," said the stranger.

The landlord paused; he didn't understand this at all, for the stranger did not bear the appearance of decay about him. He was tall, and seemingly of the middle age, he thought, and nothing about him to savor of decay, save, indeed, the terrible and remarkable paleness which his flesh appeared to bear; and his system generally, in other respects, bore nothing of the appearance of general decay.

"Shall I send for any one, sir? Have you any friends I could write to for you?"

"None, sir, thank you," replied the stranger, who, however, bated nothing of his politeness, even in his present position.

"Have you any desire to see any one in particular?"

"No one, I thank you."

At that moment Doctor Linton was announced, and the proprietor having introduced him, left the apartment, leaving the doctor and his patient together; the former at once perceived, and wondered at his extraordinary paleness. After a few preliminary questions, he appeared quite puzzled, and said to him, —

"May I inquire what is the cause of this extraordinary complexion?"

"Certainly," said the stranger; "it was caused by damp beds."

"Damp beds," muttered the doctor, amazed, and hardly comprehending what was said, or the nature of the reply; he was at a loss, but did not say so, what was the connection between cause and effect.

"Yes, damp beds," said the stranger.

"Have you ever suffered in this way before?" inquired the surgeon.

"Yes, more than once."

"And you have recovered?" said the doctor, abstractedly.

"I am here," said the stranger, mildly.

"Truly, you are," said the surgeon. "I had almost forgotten that, your case is so singular. Your pulse is very low and irregular."

"It is," coolly replied the stranger; but immediately a kind of spasm shot across him, as he had before exhibited to the landlord.

"Do you feel much pain? — does that often happen?"

"No, only occasionally. I don't think you are at all likely to benefit me, sir," said the stranger, with much courtesy in his manner. "I do not mean any disrespect to you; but my complaint is a fatal one in our family."

"Are you all afflicted in this manner?"

"Yes, all before me died," replied the stranger; "and when it does come on, we have no means of avoiding the end that approaches; there is no medical aid that can be rendered, ever did us any good."

"You are quite an exception to nature, sir," said the medical man, "quite an exception. Your case cannot be beyond the assistance of medicine – if not to cure, to ameliorate – though its nature may not be ascertained; but if we could do so, we could tell you what we might be able to do."

"That has been attempted before," said the stranger, mildly; "and hence it is I am loath to give you needless trouble."

"Well, I will call upon you, and see you again; but you ought to take some medicine. I am persuaded that it is some great and extraordinary derangement of the system – a complete sinking of the whole system."

"Most undoubtedly it is a sinking in the whole system – a sinking which has never yet been stopped by human aid. But you can pursue what course you may deem proper."

"Will you take medicines if I send any?"

"Yes," replied the patient; "I will take them when you choose to send them."

"I will endeavor to send you something that shall infuse something like vitality into the system, that will indeed help you to rally."

"That will, indeed, be doing something more than was ever yet done by any one who attended any individual of our family. I feel I am very weak, and am sinking fast, and do not expect that I shall again have the honor of seeing you."

As he again spoke, the same spasm seized upon him; his frame was convulsed for more than an minute, and his pallid features appeared to give forth expressions which it was impossible to describe.

The doctor paused, and gazed with something like fear and awe upon him. He had never before seen such a case so destitute of facts, nor yet such a man; it was quite beyond his experience; there was nothing like it in all his previous experience; there was no apparent cause for all that he saw. It might be some severe chronic disorder which did not manifest itself outwardly. If this were the case, it was most extraordinary.

But more extraordinary than all was, apart from the medical question, the strange and terrible appearance of the stranger; his paleness – the terrible expression of his features – the strange, and even revolting cast of his eyes, that completely baffled all his attempts to understand them, or to remember anything he had ever heard of, or seen.

The stranger languidly turned in his bed, and then closed his eyes, leaving his medical attendant to his reflections.

"Well," muttered Doctor Linton, as he looked at his incomprehensible patient. "I never met with so fearful a human puzzle before. I never saw such an expression of countenance in all my life; nor did ever I meet with such a case. Had he been one of the fabled monsters of old, the creation of the German mind, he could not have been more unlike a human being, to wear a human form."

As he spoke, he quitted the room, and made his way to the proprietor of the hotel, who was as anxiously waiting to see him, as he was to meet him.

"Well, doctor, what do you think of the patient?"

"Why, I don't know what to think. I never saw such a man before in all my life — I cannot make him out."

"Nor I. I can't understand what he means or what he is."

"Nor anybody else. But he is quite a gentleman; and yet there is something very frightful to be seen in him. I don't know why it is, I don't care about going oftener to him than I am obliged."

"I don't doubt it. There was something in the feel of his hand more like a corpse than anything I ever felt before."

"Indeed — it is a queer affair."

"Do you know him?"

"No, I do not," replied the proprietor. "He has not been here more than two days; and when he entered he had that deadly paleness which he has now."

"Did he indeed. It is, I dare say, natural to him, though it must create an unpleasant sensation, go where he would."

"He must feel it to be so, no doubt; but, at the same time, he could not avoid it. Have you come to any conclusion respecting his complaint?"

"I have not indeed; I will send him some medicine; though, to tell you the truth, I can hardly tell what is the matter with him. His disorder seems to consist of a rapid sinking of the whole system, accompanied by a few minor symptoms, and a spasm, which must be very painful; for it produces an extraordinary effect upon his visage, and his eyes glisten like a piece of tin."

"That's it, doctor. Do you know, I have been thinking for something to which I could liken those eyes to, but could not do it. When do you see him again?"

"Tomorrow, some time; in the mean time I must bid you good day, for my presence is wanted in the Dundrum family."

"Oh, have you any of them for a patient?"

"Yes, two. Good day — good day."

"Good day, doctor," said the proprietor of the hotel, as he bowed the doctor out and then, returning to his own apartment, he wondered, in his own mind, at all that had been said by that learned individual, when William entered his room with a hastiness of manner quite unusual to him.

"What is the matter, William?"

"Oh, sir — I beg your pardon — but the strange gentleman —"

"Eh! — Well! — What?"

"Why, he's dying, and wants to see you, sir."

"To see me, William — and dying!"

"Yes, sir — it's very sudden — but good Lord, how dreadful he looks. He clasped his hands and shook — it made the bed shake and the windows rattle, just as if an earthquake were taking place."

"Goodness me!" muttered the proprietor, who immediately quitted the apartment, and followed William to that of the stranger, who lay in the same attitude as that described by William; but he was evidently endeavoring to repress all nervous emotion, and by the time he was spoken to, he succeeded in this endeavor completely, and lay apparently calm and collected for the landlord's appearance.

"I believe you sent for me," said that worthy, in a subdued tone.

"Yes; I wish to speak a word to you before I die."

"Die!" said the landlord, with a start. "No, no, you cannot mean that — you will get better — you are deceived."

"No, no; do not endeavor to persuade me from believing what I know is the truth. I shall die, and that, too, before many hours."

"If the case is so urgent, let me send to Mr. Linton; he cannot have gone far, and he will return."

"Nay, do not do that; his aid is utterly useless — utterly."

"He is a clever man; but still, if your own feelings tell you that you can't live, allow me to send for a clergyman."

"My friend," said the stranger, "I have settled all that in my own mind. My affairs are all made up, my account is cast, and I shall learn the balance where I am going to. I wish, while I have breath, to beg a favor of you."

"Anything on earth that I can do, I will," said the landlord.

"Nay, I do not desire — all — that — I — I only want you to — to — to — promise me you'll — attend to my funeral."

"All shall be done as you desire."

"My breath — I feel it going. I have money enough about me; you will find in my pocket-book and purse, a certain sum."

"Yes, sir — yes."

"And with that you will have the goodness to liquidate my debt to yourself, my funeral expenses, and place the residue of that sum about my person."

"When you are dead!" exclaimed the landlord.

"Yes; will you promise me — will you swear to see it done?"

"Yes, I will — I do swear."

"See you keep the oath; my breath is going fast — my strength is leaving me — and — and —"

"I will do all." said the landlord again. "Will you have any friend attend your funeral obsequies? It's melancholy, but I am obliged to speak of it to you, because I cannot otherwise know your wishes."

"Do not mind that," said the stranger, turning towards the landlord; "but when I am dead, dress me in my clothes, just as if I were about to walk; let me have all my property and my money — such of it as remains after paying all charges — the remainder cause to be placed about my person — in fact, all that belongs to me; and place — me — and place me — me — me —"

"Where — where would you be buried?" said the landlord.

"Place me," gasped the dying man; "place me in the — the —"

A gurgling noise, succeeded by a sharp rattle in the throat, was all the sound that escaped him, while his glazed eyes were fixed, with a truly horrifying expression, upon the features of the landlord, whose presence of mind appeared to forsake him, and he exclaimed, falling on his knees in affright, —

"Lord, have mercy upon us, what a dreadful affair!"

"Horrible, sir," said William.

"Oh! are you here, William?" inquired the landlord.

"Yes, sir," replied that individual.

"Oh, I'm glad of that; did you see him die?"

"I did, sir. How dreadful!"

"Very; but I am glad you were here because he has made some singular requests about burying him, and in a certain manner, with all his clothes on and his jewels and money about him. Now I should be considered foolish if I did anything of the kind; but I have promised, and as he has no friends, I will do what I have promised."

"It is very good of you, sir; though I think he has been very silly in making such a request; yet you cannot be so considered for performing the wish of a dying man; it is the duty of any one so promising to perform it."

"Quite right, William, quite right; but did you understand what he meant by his last words? I mean, where he wished to be buried."

"I don't know positively, sir, but I think he meant the cathedral — I thought so, at least. I am not sure he said so, but I believe he meant to do so."

"Well, I think so myself; and in the cathedral he shall be buried; but it is a terrible-looking corpse. I'm sure I could not sleep in the same room with him. Poor fellow! What he'll come to at last there is no telling."

"Yes, sir; he does look dreadful."

"You needn't tell anybody we have a dead customer in the hotel, William."

"No, sir."

"Because people might be curious, and wish to see him, and if they were to do so, I am sure they would leave the house."

"So they would, sir. He's a dreadful-looking corpse. I never heard of such a one. What can be the cause of it? — and to be buried in his clothes, too!"

"Ay, and his money and his jewels; that is very strange!"

"Very strange, sir, indeed; and the fewer persons who know of it the better, else the body will not lie very long in its grave. There will be those who would not mind turning resurrection-men for the value of what he had about him."

"So there would be, William; and now I think of it, the authorities of the cathedral shall know nothing about it; for who can tell what fancy they may take concerning it being an unchristian burial?"

"And yet, sir, he paid all his debts like a Christian."

"Yes; and left a remembrance for the waiter."

"There could not be a more Christian act than that, for who could be more Christian-like than to remember the waiter?" and William at once admitted the truth of the assertion, and they both left the room, and instructions were given to William to obtain the proper aid respecting the funeral, and an order was given to the undertaker to come and measure the corpse for its last garment.

All these things were duly attended to, and kept secret, so that a very few persons were aware of the fact that so strange an occurrence had taken place in the good city of Winchester, much less were they acquainted with the precise locality of the very house n which the occurrence took place.

When the morning arrived on which the funeral was to take place, some persons were surprised to behold a couple of mutes standing side by side at the door of the Star hotel, and there had been no previous signs of mourning.

The hearse and one mourning coach, however, was all that attended, into which one solitary mourner entered. There were several others made up for the occasion, to give the cavalcade an uniform appearance.

The body was carried down by eight men. It was very heavy, and the men bent beneath the load they bore, and when it was placed in the hearse, the one mourner got in, and they proceeded towards the cathedral, which was quite close at hand.

A few — very few minutes served to bring them to the goal, and before the entrance of the cathedral they stopped, and out came the undertakers, who contrived, with much exertion, to carry the body into the church; and then, after some preliminary ceremonies, it was conducted into the vaults, where it was deposited, and the burial service was said over it most duly and solemnly, and then left, it was presumed, safe and secure, to abide its final doom at the day of judgment.

But many thoughts prove but the shadow of our wishes, and this seemed but as a mocking shadow; as our readers are aware by this time of what actually took place in the dead of the night.

"In what name was the deceased registered — the burial, I mean?" inquired the clergyman, whose memory, like some of his other faculties, was obscured by age.

"His name was Francis Varney," replied the chief-mourner, who was no other than the proprietor of the Star hotel.

Chapter CXXXV.

A RURAL SCENE BY MOONLIGHT. – THE STORM. – AN ACCIDENT ON THE ROAD. – A NEW AND STRANGE ACQUAINTANCE ACQUIRED. – A DISAPPOINTMENT.

*I*t was one of those pleasant, moonlight evenings that are frequently felt, as well as seen, towards the end of August, that a party of individuals sat in a traveling-carriage, and were proceeding at an easy pace on one of the cross-roads that run from Winchester to Bath, and also from Southampton, the Isle of Wight, between Salisbury – more properly speaking – and Bath.

The evening was lovely: the day had been sultry, and the sun had not been gone down so long but that the heat of his rays yet remained. Indeed, though the moon gave light, yet the radiated heat from the earth, first received from the sun, was so great, that the light evening breeze barely tempered the air.

The party thus proceeding had been spending a few weeks in rambling about Southampton, Portsmouth, and Salisbury, and were now wending their way to the city of Bath. They consisted of but four individuals, – Captain Fraser, his wife, her sister, and younger brother. The latter did not count more than twelve years, while the sister, Miss Stevens, was just seventeen years of age.

Captain Fraser had scarce been married six months, and was upon one of the early matrimonial jaunts which often take place in the earlier part of the married life, when all is sunshine, and the matrimonial barometer might always have the index nailed to "set fair" at such periods.

The lady's sister and brother were residing with her; for their parents were dead, and hence they, the captain and his lady, were their natural protectors.

They were riding in an open carriage, the head parted, and thrown back; and even in this manner they felt the evening air was scarcely, though riding, cool.

"I don't think," said Mrs. Fraser to her husband, "that ever I beheld so beautiful a scene. The time — the warmth of the air — the occasional delicious feel of the light evening breeze — the serene light of the moon; altogether, I never felt so comfortable, or, I may add, so happy as I do at this moment."

"I am glad to hear you say so," said the captain; "it gives me an additional pleasure to find I can please you."

"Now, Fraser, that is too bad of you."

"What is too bad, my dear?" said the captain, inquiringly.

"Why, to say you are glad you can please. That is as bad as to say that it is a very difficult matter; and you know I am very easily pleased, especially when you make the attempt," said Mrs. Fraser.

"Well, we will not quarrel about that, my dear. But I must say, with you, this hour, time, and place are all one could desire, and such as we seldom meet: the scene across the country is truly beautiful!"

"Yes," said Miss Stevens; "it is beautiful, as far as we can see."

"What river is that yonder?" inquired the brother.

"That is the Willey; the same that we saw at Salisbury," said Captain Fraser.

"Indeed! I thought that came from another direction more northerly."

"That was another arm of the same river, and joined this about there, and all the low grounds on this side of yon hills are called the Valley of the Willey; and a beautiful little vale it is, too, fruitful and picturesque."

"How beautiful the moonbeams glisten on yonder water!"

"They do; but not so strongly as they did."

"No. What is the reason of that? The air appears to darken. I have noticed it for some minutes past. Why is that?"

"I suppose it is caused by the evaporation from the grounds and heavy dews, to compensate for the want of rain that usually takes place at this time of the year."

"Then we shall be obliged to shut up the carriage, for the dew is more likely to cause cold than anything else."

"It is so; but we are upon comparatively high ground here; and, moreover, they will not reach us yet; but, here are shawls; you can wrap up if you feel chilly, or you can put on your veils."

"It is yet so warm," said Miss Stevens, "that I should be reluctant to put on any more clothing yet-awhile."

"Do as you please, but do not take cold," said Captain Fraser. "How indistinct the scene becomes around; the river, which we just now saw so plain, is quite obscured, and you can scarcely tell where it is, save here and there, where the doddered willows appear, and which mark out the course of the stream."

"It is so," said the youth. "I can just see the green tops of the trees appear above the thick mist that rises from the river below."

"Exactly; that is the fact."

"And see how it spreads itself over the cornfields and meadows."

"Was that not a flash of light?" said Mrs. Fraser, suddenly.

"Light! I saw no light," said the captain.

"Nor I," said the youth; "did you, sister?"

"No, I did not do so; but it is very sultry, and therefore it is very likely just at this time of the year. How much farther have we to travel before we stop for the night?"

"I suppose seven or eight miles, not more."

"There, that was no mistake, however," said Mrs. Fraser, as a flash of light shot across the heavens, and left not a trace behind it.

"No, there was no mistake about it; nor did I think so before," said Captain Fraser, "only I have not noticed it; but it is harmless — it is what is called summer lightning, and has none of the ordinary results of lightning."

"It will possibly make the air cool," suggested Mrs. Fraser, "and, in that case, we shall have a more agreeable temperature; to tell the truth, the extreme warmth and dryness of the air gives a strange uneasiness to the body."

"Another flash — ah, that's a change in its character."

"Yes; that is the blue-forked lightning, and I am much mistaken if we do not have a sudden change — hark!"

At that moment, a sullen and deep rumbling was heard in the heavens, followed by another flash, and then such a peal of thunder that boomed and rattled through the air in a manner that startled the dull echoes of the night, and made the welkin resound with the fearful sounds that filled the heavens.

"We shall have a fall of rain in another moment," said Captain Fraser; "push on, drive on, and let us get out of this as soon as we can."

"Aye, aye, sir," said the driver, and crack went his whip — the horses increased their speed, and they rattled on at a good pace.

"Had we better not stop and have the hood closed.?"

"No," said the captain; "I can manage that very well, with the assistance of your brother, and we shall not lose time."

Captain Fraser, and the young gentleman alluded to, brought the coach-top up and secured it, just as a heavy shower descended in such torrents that they could scarcely hear themselves speak, so heavily did it rattle upon the leathern covering of the vehicle, and they sat for some time in silence.

Soon, however, the thunder and lightning filled the air with sounds and flashes in a manner that began to create a feeling of alarm in the minds of the ladies, and some uneasiness in the mind of the captain; not upon their account only, but because the cattle might take flight under the circumstances, especially as they were fresh, and had now scarcely run three or four miles; for their stage was a long one before they reached their destination, which was now about two days' easy journeys.

The thunder and lightning appeared to become more and more terrible; the storm, indeed, appeared to increase rather than diminish in intensity; the very center of the storm appeared to be fast approaching, and making the spot upon which they stood the pivot on which it turned; its fury increased, and with it the horses were each moment becoming more and more unmanageable. Though in some measure aware of the fact, Captain Fraser kept his place, fearful lest he should alarm his wife, and at the same time distract the coachman.

Suddenly there was a bright and vivid flash of light, such as they had not seen before, but which illumined the whole place around them, and made everything as visible as if placed in the strongest light imaginable, followed by such a crashing peal of thunder that the living earth appeared to rock again.

It wanted but this to make the horses perfectly ungovernable, and they dashed away at a furious speed along the road.

"Good heavens! the horses have taken fright," said Mrs. Fraser, as she became aware of the speed they were going at.

"They have merely taken fright, my dear," said the captain, unwilling to increase their alarm by informing them of his own; "he will keep them in the middle of the road, and we shall be at our journey's end the sooner, and the more so the better."

They were upon the point of being satisfied, when the jolts of the carriage, added to its eccentric course from one side of the road to the other, attracted so much of their attention that Miss Stevens said, —

"See, captain, how the carriage sways from side to side; we shall all be over in another minute or two — we shall all be killed!"

"There goes the thunder again, worse than your kettle drums," said young Stevens, who appeared to think it rather a joke; "the lightning flashes, too, as if we had got into an electrical machine."

"Do not talk in that way, Charles, for goodness sake," exclaimed his younger sister. "We shall all be killed presently."

"I hope not," said Captain Fraser, "though I admit it looks serious; but all you can do, and the best under all the circumstances, is to remain calm and quiet, and see what happens."

"See what happens! Dear me, captain, what do you think we are all made of that we should sit calm," said Miss Stevens, "and see what will happen, when there may be broken limbs, at the least, if not death?"

"It is the best advice I can give you."

"Had we better not get out — I don't mind trying?"

"Aye, if you wish to run imminent risk of instant and violent death, you will make the attempt; if you remain in here shut up, you have every probability that, if we do have an upset, which is not yet certain, we may all escape with but a little fright, or at most a few bruises."

"Yes, sister; you had better wait for the worst, if the worst must happen, rather than rush into it."

This was sensible advice, and the whole party fell into a deep silence, which was unbroken save by the sounds of wheels, the rattling of the carriage, the rain, and the roar of thunder, enough to employ their minds, and at the same time to keep them in momentary dread of the fearful catastrophe.

Suddenly there was a crash and dreadful jolt; they knew not what had happened, except they felt that the vehicle was turned over.

In a moment more the door was opened, and a stranger lent assistance in getting out the unfortunate travelers.

"Do not be alarmed, ladies," said a strange, but courteous voice. "No further mischief can happen now, beyond inconvenience."

As the stranger spoke, he lifted the two ladies out of the carriage, and placed them in a sheltered position by the body.

"Are you hurt?" inquired the stranger, as he assisted Captain Fraser and young Stevens out of the fallen carriage.

"No, sir, I am not; I thank you for your timely aid. Where are the ladies?"

"There they are; I hope, uninjured."

Captain Fraser immediately ran up to them, and, seeing them in safety, said, —

"I am glad to see you are safe. I was stunned at first by a blow on the side of my head."

"Yes, we are safe; but we have to thank this gentleman that we have been so speedily and so easily extricated from our unpleasant prison."

"I am much indebted, sir, for your aid to the ladies. May I trespass upon your kindness to lend me a little further assistance?"

"I shall be happy to assist you under these unpleasant circumstances; but, allow me to suggest as the first thing, that the cushions be placed under the hedge for the use of the ladies, and what cloaks or coats you have should be thrown over them."

"Right, sir; I thank you."

"If you are deficient in them, my cloak is at their service, though I am afraid that it is almost saturated."

"I have enough here," said Captain Fraser, as he pulled out several articles of that nature; and then he, with the assistance of the stranger, placed them so that Mrs. Fraser and sister were almost, if not entirely, sheltered from the storm.

"Now," said the stranger, "the first thing that can be done will be to right the carriage, and place it in a position where it will receive no further damage."

"But the driver and horses," said Captain Fraser, "I must look after them. Had we better not look after them? He may be dying."

"By no means," said the stranger; "he will do very well; if we place the carriage upright, we shall be able to replace the ladies."

"We can," said the captain, who appeared to be divided between the duties of humanity and the tender anxiety he felt for his wife.

"Exactly," said the stranger; "and permit me to suggest that he has either gone on beyond our aid, or does not require it."

"It is possible."

"And very probable," said the stranger; "but if you prefer it, and think the ladies will not suffer, we can walk on ahead till we come up with them, if they stop before the end of the stage."

"No, no, sir; you are quite right; I will get the carriage up if you can so far assist me; we shall then place the ladies in comparative safety."

"We shall so."

They immediately walked round the carriage, and examined its position, as well as they were able, when, to the captain's great relief, he found that it was still on its wheels, though the body was thrown over on its side.

"How can it have happened?" inquired the captain.

"I cannot well see," replied the stranger; "but you will perceive something must have caught the off-side wheel, and turned the whole of the fore carriage that way, which has left this corner of the body without support; added to which, the speed or momentum it must have acquired in its course, has thrown it over."

"Precisely. I see now how it is; but if we get the body up, it will fall again over on this side, since it has no support."

"Oh, yes, it will remain up, since it has lost all force, all moving power; unless, indeed, any of the straps are broken. We can try."

"Here, Charles," said Captain Fraser, "we shall want your aid."

"Oh," said the stranger, "the slightest assistance is valuable; it is the last strain or effort that may complete the removal. Now, if we can lift it up from this side, we shall soon right it, and then the fore carriage can be forced round, and the ladies replaced, until we can better dispose of them."

The stranger placed his shoulder to the carriage, as well as the captain and his brother-in-law, young Stevens, and thus aided, he soon lifted it up into its old position, and there it remained very quietly.

"Now we had better pull the wheels round."

This was done, and the carriage assumed its former state.

"Well, how could they have got away?" inquired Captain Fraser, examining the axles and the bars; "all appears right."

"They have broken the splinter-bar, and here are the remains of the traces. The splinter-bar, I find, has only lost its hooks, so it will do again. Come, sir, you have less damage to regret than I at first thought it possible you could have escaped with; I am truly glad it is so."

"Thank you, sir; your kindness and assistance has been truly great and efficient; but I have yet to find the poor fellow who drove us."

"We will seek after him; or, I had better ride on to the next town or house where I can obtain assistance, while you will be better able to protect the ladies by remaining with them, and my horse will carry me quickly enough."

"Oh! you are mounted."

"I am; but the ladies wait."

Thus admonished, the captain turned to the ladies, and, with the stranger's assistance, he conducted them back to the carriage, where they were replaced, without any material damage or misfortune of any kind, save what might arise from fright.

"Some one is coming this way," said the stranger. "If I mistake not, they are your runaways, by the sounds."

They listened, and distinctly heard the sounds of horses' feet coming along, with the jingling of harness, that made it pretty certain that what the stranger said was correct, and that it was most probable that this was indeed the man who drove them coming back with the same cattle, or some fresh.

A few moments more decided the speculation, and the man himself rode up, and looked at the carriage, saying, —

"Well, I thought it was upset."

"So it was, but we have righted it now. Has no accident happened to you? But these are the same horses!"

"Yes, sir. When they got loose, or broke away, they went as if they were shot out of a gun, and away they went for some miles, until I contrived to stop them, which was a hard job; however, I thought then, as there was nothing the matter with them or with me, I had better return and see what was become of you, sir, and the ladies."

"Quite right. Do you think they will go quietly in the harness again?"

"Oh, yes — oh, yes, sir."

"Then we will harness them, and go on to the end of the next stage, when we can see exactly what mischief, if any, has been done."

This was immediately put in practice, and they were soon harnessed, the broken straps and traces being mended in the best way time and circumstances admitted, but effectually enough for the present purpose.

"Now, sir," said Captain Fraser, "do you continue this road, or the one we have come? I suppose we must have overtaken you, as you were coming this way."

"No; I was a traveler going in the same direction. I saw your speed from a distance, and, believing your horses to have taken fright, I rode on, and, being well mounted, I overtook you just as the ancient happened."

"Then we may have the pleasure of your company on the road for some distance to come, I hope, sir?"

"As far as the next place to stop at, at all events; for I do not desire to travel further than I can avoid tonight."

"Then I shall be able to thank you more at leisure, and at a better opportunity than at present," said the captain.

"Do not name it; I am too happy to have had it in my power to render you any assistance. Shall I ride on and secure you proper accommodation when you do arrive there?"

"You kindness is very great," said the captain again. "I am much beholden to you; but if we can get as far as we hoped to do, we shall not require it; there will be sufficient for travelers under the ordinary course of events. We shall do very well; and if we should not be able to get so far, we must make ourselves content with whatever chance accommodation we get on the road."

"Then we will journey for that distance in company," said the stranger, as he mounted his horse, which had stood quietly by while the tall stranger rendered the timely assistance he had to them.

They proceeded along now at a cautious pace. The weather had abated, and the rain was now less severe; the thunder only heard in the distance; while the lightning could only be seen in occasional flashes in the distance, in a direction away from them. The clouds began to lighten, and then the diffused light of the moon came and shed a gentle light upon the scene, though it was very scarce, and of comparative little use save it enabled them to see their way all the better.

The roads were good, and they traveled onwards with some increase of speed; and finding none of their amended horse-tackle had given way, they still kept journeying onwards at the same pace.

Time brought them to their destination, and when they arrived at the inn at which they were to stop for the night, they found it had not made much more than an hour or an hour and a half's difference.

When they were fairly housed, the stranger took an apartment to himself. It was while he sat before the fire that Captain Fraser entered his room.

"I must apologize for my intrusion," began the captain.

"Do not say a word on that head, sir," said the stranger; "it is no intrusion — you are welcome. Be seated, if you please; I am alone, and perfectly at leisure."

"I have come to thank you for the service you have done us, and to beg that you will sup with us, and permit the ladies to have an opportunity of thanking their preserver in person. You will oblige us all by accepting the invitation."

"I am much obliged for your courteous offer," said the stranger, who was a tall, dignified man. "I will come after supper, if you please, and shall feel it a great honor, I assure you; but I am so truly sensible that my efforts were more owing to accident than to anything else, that I do not wish to hear anything more of it."

"You must not be so self-denying, sir. We do not wish to put any more merit on your act than we think it deserves; but that much you must accept, if you will permit me to use such a word. Shall we have the pleasure of your company?"

"After supper."

"I will not press you against your feelings; but you will come in after supper, sir? I hope I may have the pleasure of drinking a bottle of wine with you. Will you come?"

"I will, sir, and thank you for the honor."

"May I have the pleasure of being able to introduce you to the ladies by name?" said the captain, with a little hesitation.

"Certainly — certainly. I beg your pardon. I am somewhat forgetful; I forgot I had not passed through an introduction," said the stranger. "Permit me to give you my card."

As he spoke, he handed Captain Fraser a beautifully-embossed card, upon which was printed, in Italian characters, — "Sir Francis Varney."

Captain Fraser took the card and read the name, and then, passing a compliment, he said, that since he could not have his company to supper, then he should expect him when he felt at leisure and disposed to do so.

"My dear," said Captain Fraser to his wife, when he returned to his apartment, "our new friend will not come to supper but will take a glass of wine with me afterwards."

"I am sorry he will not come; though, under other circumstances, I should have been glad of it; but I am sorry on this occasion."

"And why would you have been glad?"

"Because, after the flurry and upset we had, I am hardly fit to see any one, much less a stranger; but he so kindly and promptly rescued us from our danger, that I cannot feel reluctance at any time."

"Yes," said her sister; "and I must say I never heard a voice that sounded so really like a gentleman's — indeed, I could fancy that any one could positively assert that he was a gentleman, only from hearing him speak, without seeing him at all; but, be that as it may, I felt convinced he was such."

"He is very courteous, I must say," said Mrs. Fraser.

"And who do you think he is?"

"I have no means of forming any judgment."

"Well, then, he is Sir Francis Varney."

"Sir Francis Varney! Well, I do not know the name; I never heard the name before that time; but I think there was some one of that name in the time of Queen Elizabeth — an attendant on the Earl of Leicester."

"Are you not joking?"

"Indeed I am not; I have read so."

"And you think this gentleman may be a descendant of his?"

"There is no impossibility nor improbability about it, that I see," said Mrs. Fraser; "but I am the more obliged to him for his timely assistance. I am sure it was fortunate that he was so close at hand."

"Yes, it was very fortunate. Mary, my dear, we shall be introduced to a baronet. It is quite a prophecy of yours in saying he was a gentleman when you only heard him speak. By the way, Fraser, what sort of a man is he?"

"Very singular indeed."

"Singular! Ay — he is very tall."

"Yes, he is tall; but very pale; more remarkable and dignified than handsome; extremely courteous and polite."

"What age is he?"

"Well, I cannot tell; perhaps forty, perhaps not so old by ten years; it is quite impossible to say."

"Dear me, how strange! I think I could guess anybody's age better than that."

"You shall have an opportunity of doing so, then, in an hour or so, when he will come; and I think I may venture upon saying you will be pleased with his dignified politeness, and say he is much superior to most men."

*T*he supper ended, and the wine was produced, and Captain Fraser, his lady, and two young relatives, were seated round a good fire — for the storm had chilled the air; besides, the damp they had stood in rendered such a precaution necessary and pleasant, notwithstanding the day had been sultry; but the change in the temperature was sudden and great — awaiting, with something like impatience, the stranger's arrival.

"He does not appear to come," said Charles Stevens.

"He is not here, certainly; but he will come, no doubt, the moment he is quite sure that we had done our supper, and he had finished his own; perhaps he takes longer than we."

"Perhaps so; but I am strongly tempted to go to him again."

"It might be construed into undue urgency, or something of the sort," said Mrs. Fraser; "and yet he might be waiting for something of the sort."

"So he might," said the captain. "At all events, I will go and see; if he were inclined to do so under other circumstances, he would not take offence under the present."

"Perhaps not."

At that moment the door was opened, and the waiter presented a note.

"A note for me?" said Captain Fraser.

"Yes, sir."

"Who can it be from?"

"From the gentleman up stairs, sir, who came with you an hour back."

"Oh!" exclaimed Captain Fraser.

"He was taken ill, and obliged to go to bed, sir."

Captain Fraser immediately tore open the note, and read as follows: —

"SIR, — I deeply regret I cannot keep my promise to take a glass of wine @Inset = with you, and have the honor of being introduced to the ladies. Favor me so far as to make my excuses to them. It is a great pleasure lost to me on the occasion; permit me to say deferred, rather than lost; and if I might venture to make an appointment, under the circumstances, I can only say that, if convenient, I should be happy to breakfast with you, and then have the honor and happiness I have now the misfortune to lose.

"Sudden and severe indisposition alone have caused me to retire before I had the honor of seeing you, and expressing my inability to attend you. — Yours, obliged,

"FRANCIS VARNEY."

There was a blank upon the countenances of all present. Evidently a deep disappointment was felt by all; but the captain was especially surprised, and, turning to the waiter, he said, —

"Did you see this gentleman?"

"Yes, sir."

"Was he unwell?"

"Yes, sir."

"I mean, was he, or is he, dangerously ill?"

"He was very ill, sir; but I don't know that he is dangerously ill. He suffered much pain, and he was obliged to have aid to go up stairs."

"Did he say what it was that ailed him?" pursued Captain Fraser.

"Not that I heard; though some said he had got the cramp and cold by being too long in the wet."

"Perhaps so — very likely — very likely — that will do. Let me know how he is the first thing in the morning; do you hear?"

"Yes, sir, I will take care."

"Well," said Mrs. Fraser, when they were alone, "I did not expect such a disappointment this evening. However, he makes up for it by appointing the breakfast hour for our meeting; it is the more agreeable, as we shall have had a good night's repose, and shall be the better able to appear to advantage."

Chapter CXXXVI.

THE ALARM AT THE INN. – BED-CHAMBER TERRORS. – A NIGHT SCENE. – A MORNING SUCCEEDING TO A NIGHT OF ADVENTURE.

*T*he inmates of the inn are all fast bound in sleep. The senses of all seem steeped in deep forgetfulness; even the hour of dreams was passed. The storm, which had raged so violently in the early part of the evening, and which had appeared to have gone and a calm succeeded, had returned, and the fury of the blast was only equaled by the deluging rain and the fearful rumbling of the thunder.

But calmly slept the beautiful and innocent Mary Stevens. She was young, and her mind bore no weight of care; when she slept no dreams disturbed her rest, but a calm, death-like sleep sat upon her soul, and steeped it in forgetfulness.

The storm raged around, but she heard it not; she was unconscious of it. Perhaps the disturbance and fatigues of the previous day caused a greater degree of depth to her insensibility, and rendered her mind less liable to slight interruptions. But she slept soundly, and even did not hear the intruder who walked across the floor of her bedroom, and stood gazing on her fair arms as she lay sleeping.

The intruder was a tall man, enveloped in some strange mantle, all white. He stooped over her, as if he listened to the beating of her heart, while his strangely bright eyes, which shone fearfully, appeared to express a horrible kind of joy, too terrible for human nature to contemplate.

He stooped — he placed his hand upon her heart, and felt its pulsations, and a terrible and ghastly smile passed over his features, while a movement of the lips and mouth generally, appeared as if anticipatory of a coming meal.

Then he took the white arm in his hands, and cast a longing look at the features of the maiden, who appeared disturbed by the rude action, and moved in her sleep, and was suddenly aroused from her slumber by a severe pang in her arm, as though some creature had plunged its fangs into her flesh.

She started up, and found herself flung upon the bed with gigantic strength. She screamed, and uttered scream upon scream.

The old inn was filled with sounds of terror and pain. There was a loud knocking heard at the door. Then, indeed, the assailant left his prey to provide for his own safety; but it was almost too late, for the door was burst open violently, as he made for another means of exit, which was the means by which he had entered the apartment; but he was prevented, and, as the first person entered the apartment, he threw him down by placing something in his way. The light was thrown against some furniture, which immediately rose up into a flame.

"Help! help! Fire! fire!"

These were fearful sounds, such as had never before been heard in that place, and the inmates, woke up by the screams from deep slumber, were startled and terrified at these sounds, and springing at once from their beds, echoed the sounds as they run wildly about from place to place.

"Where is the fire? What's the matter?"

"Fire in the young lady's room."

All eyes were directed to that quarter, and in another instant there were several persons rushing to the room, the glare of the fire in which at once attracted their observation, and they rushed to the rescue; among the foremost of whom was Sir Francis Varney, whose bedchamber was not far distant from Mary Steven's. He rushed to the bed, and wrapping the bedclothes round her, he carried her out of the room and the scene of danger, and, as he came out of the room, he inquired, —

"Where is Captain Fraser?"

"Here — here I am, Sir Francis," said the captain, coming hastily forward.

"Then, Captain, Fraser, I resign my charge up to you — you are her proper protector; but I must apologize for my hasty intrusion into her apartment."

"Do not think of speaking in that manner, Sir Francis; we are already indebted to you for our lives, and now we are again your debtor. Your ready aid has twice saved the young lady."

Captain Fraser took Miss Stevens form Sir Francis, and then carried her, as she was quite insensible, to his own room to his wife, her sister, where she was laid upon the bed, and found to be quite insensible.

There was much confusion in the inn — people were running about from place to place, and tumbling over each other in the confusion of thought; and the moments were precious, for many were running about, yet none did effective service, though all were willing enough to do all that could be done by them under the circumstances.

"You had better get some water," said Varney, "as quickly as you can. It is useless to run about and stare at each other. Get all the buckets you can. Be quick about it. There may yet be time enough to save the inn, and keep the fire to the room where it is; but that time will soon be at an end."

Instantly two or three of the men ran down and got a plentiful supply of water, and then, under the direction of Sir Francis Varney, the fire was very soon got under, and the flames were extinguished.

Then came an inquiry how the fire had first appeared.

"Do you know how it happened?" inquired Sir Francis Varney, of the innkeeper, who stood quite mute with astonishment at the scene before him.

"Know, sir!" said the innkeeper. "I don't know anything. I don't know myself. I don't even know where I am, or what's the matter."

"Then I beg to tell you, sir," said Varney, with much suavity of manner, "then I beg to tell you, sir, that there has been a fire in your inn — a young lady frightened out of her senses, and I know not the cause."

"No more don't I," said the landlord, with a short grunt, indicative of wonderment and alarm. "I wish I did. I wonder who set the place a-fire; that's what I wants to know, and why he did it."

"The motive was not a bad one, I believe."

"Not a bad motive, that which causes one man to set fire to and destroy another man's property!"

"Not when it is not only not done with any evil intention, but it was not even done willfully," said Sir Francis.

"Perhaps you saw it done," said the landlord, with another grunt.

"I did," replied Varney; "hearing the disturbance, I hastily threw on some of my clothes, and ran out of my apartment to ascertain what was the matter, and found several others had got here before me, and had burst open the door. The first who entered, had a light in his hand, and fell with it, setting the place on fire, which burned furiously for a minute or more, the hangings being dry and old. I took the young lady out, else I am sure she must have perished."

"Well, I saw you come out with her in your arms, like a salamander; but what I most want to know is, what was it that disturbed my customer? That is of the greatest consequence to me."

"You are perfectly right, my friend," said Sir Francis, with much composure, "to make that inquiry, that being the origin of all that subsequently took place. You are a man of discernment, and must see that the young lady herself can alone give us any account of that."

"True, sir; but I am much obliged to you for the trouble you have taken, not only for the young lady's sake, but for the property you have prevented being destroyed. You have, no doubt, saved the inn, and all it contains."

"That is enough, sir," said Varney, waving his hand, "you have said enough. I am glad I have rendered you a service, and that it has been effectual."

"It has been just the thing," said the landlord.

"Then take my advice. See the place is secure, and send all persons to bed, save, perhaps, a single individual, who might be set to watch the room which has been on fire, and which may have some slumbering spark in it, though I think not; but the quieter the place is, the sooner the young lady's alarm will be over, and then all will be well."

"Certainly, certainly," said the landlord, "it will be better to do so; but here is the only gentleman who can tell us how the young lady is."

Sir Francis Varney turned round, and beheld Captain Fraser coming towards them with a very grave aspect.

"Captain Fraser," said Sir Francis, "perhaps you can tell us what we are so very anxious to learn, and what we have been inquiring about."

"What may that be, Sir Francis?"

"We have been trying to learn what it is that caused the young lady to scream out in such a fearful manner. We have settled the cause of the fire — that has been manifest enough to us all."

"Indeed! I am not acquainted with it."

"It arose from the first person who entered her apartment after the door was burst open, falling over something, and setting fire to the curtains, which blazed up in an instant, and set the whole room on fire."

"Indeed!" said Captain Fraser, almost incredulously.

"Yes, I saw that myself," said Varney, "and I stepped over him as he lay on the ground, and therefore know it; but how is the young lady? Has she recovered from the extreme fright into which she has been thrown?"

"It is a much more serious affair than I had any notion of, Sir

Francis."

"I am concerned to hear you say so."

"Shall I send for the doctor?" inquired the landlord.

"Do — that is what I came to ask you to do; she has recovered once, and has fainted again. I know not what to think. She has a singular wound in her arm. I can't understand that, at all events."

"I did not see it when I took hold of her; though, to be sure, what I did, was done in smoke and flame, and I could not be supposed to scrutinize very closely, had I been so inclined; but what kind of wound is it?"

"I can hardly describe it to you, save it is a bite; and there are teeth-marks plain enough to be seen; though we have no means of telling what kind of creature it was that inflicted the wounds."

"Indeed! I am concerned, for the effect upon the imagination will be very bad; but did she not see, or fancy she saw the object that injured her?"

"It was dark, and the storm raged without; moreover, she was held down by a powerful grasp; and when she attempted to rise, she was flung down, and she could feel the blunted teeth enter her flesh, and the creature appeared to suck her blood."

"Dear me," said Sir Francis, "what a very strange affair! It is fortunate I was obliged to retire early, and I slept the lighter, and was therefore easily aroused from my sleep; but I am proverbially a light sleeper."

"Are you, sir? But what has caused the wound in her arm I cannot tell; it is quite a mystery. She has got a fancy into her mind that it was a human being; but that could not have been the fact."

"I should imagine not," said Sir Francis.

"And then, I know of no animal who could commit such an act: a cat or a dog could not have done it, though a dog might have made the teeth-marks; but a dog would hardly have attempted to suck blood."

"They will do it," said Sir Francis, "that I know to be a fact; and I believe it to be one that is generally admitted by all persons, especially that breed of animals mostly kept, and which have something of the bull-dog in them."

"It may be so; but how could she be held down by one of them? She could not be struck down when she attempted to rise."

"It is not for me to combat the young lady's opinions; but, remember, my dear sir, how terrified, not to say how horrified, she must have been at such an unusual, and, I may add, unheard-of an attack; if you consider such things, and the improbability — not to say what appears to me, the impossibility — you will see plenty of room for mistakes to arise, and give her notions a wrong turn."

"That is very true."

"And besides, I would, if I were convinced of the contrary, endeavor to persuade her of her mistake, unless you can discover the perpetrator of the outrage, when justice demands that such a savage should be severely punished."

"By G-d! Sir Francis," said the captain, "if I could see him, I would shoot the scoundrel! But, then, I am getting angry without a cause; it may not be what she thinks, and then, you know, all one's anger goes for nothing."

"So it does; but, in the meantime, great care and attention is requisite to regain her confidence and serenity of mind."

"Oh, a day or two will make a great difference in these matters, when we come to change the scene."

"Are you traveling far, Captain Fraser?"

"As far as Bath," said the captain.

At this moment the landlord returned, saying to Captain Fraser, —

"I have sent to Mr. Carter, who will be here, no doubt; he is close at hand, and will come in a moment. He's a very clever gentleman, is Mr. Carter. I saw him perform four operations on coach accidents."

"Operations on coach accidents!" said Sir Francis Varney; "a curious matter, that. How did they succeed upon such materials?"

"Oh, they were two broken arms, and three broken legs."

"Indeed! Did they all recover?"

"No; only one got over it."

"Upon my word, a promising member of the faculty to entrust so tender a charge to, under such delicate circumstances. But, landlord, have you any bad characters about your house, or in the neighborhood?"

"I can't say anything about the neighborhood, though I believe it is as quiet and orderly as can be, or usually is. I never hear anything against it, and know nothing against it; and as for them in the house, I can answer they would not hurt a fly, unless provoked to do so; but what I mean is, they are all honest and tried servants."

"Well, that is saying a good deal," said Captain Fraser; "but, have you any dogs about the house — I mean, any large dogs?"

"Ah! dogs! Yes, I have several dogs, and good dogs they are, too."

"Could any of them get into the rooms — the sleeping-rooms? I mean, could any of them get into the room that has taken fire?"

"No, unless the door was opened," said the landlord. "They are not allowed to run about loose here, lest any one should get up in the night and be mistaken for intruders; for my dogs, gentlemen, would take any one they saw moving about outside of a night; but, otherwise, they are quiet, well-conducted dogs."

"Well, you mean to say they could not have got into Miss Stevens's room."

"I do; I am sure of it. They could not, because there were none of them about the house when we went to bed — when the house was shut up at night. However, here is the doctor."

The medical man now arrived, and was forthwith introduced to Captain Fraser, who conducted him to the apartment in which Mrs. Fraser and Miss Stevens were awaiting the coming of the doctor. Captain Fraser, after having introduced him to the invalid, returned to the landlord and Sir Francis.

"Well, I cannot make it out at all," said Sir Francis. "There must be some mystery in it, I am persuaded; and if that could only be discovered, the matter would lose half its terrors to the mind of the young lady."

"No doubt it would do so," said the captain. "The fire and her wound together, have made a deep impression upon her."

"The wound!" said the landlord. "Is the young lady hurt, then?"

"Hurt, indeed! she is seriously hurt. She has received a severe wound in the arm, by some one, or some dog having seized and bitten her seriously."

"God bless me!" said the landlord; "I never heard of such a thing. Somebody began to eat her, I suppose. Upon my word, it would almost make one believe we are in the Cannibal Islands, to say the least of it."

"Here is the surgeon," said Sir Francis, who noticed that gentleman's approach.

"Well, sir," said Captain Fraser, "how is your patient?"

"I fear she is much terrified; and if she were to remain here long, I should hardly like to answer for her health. She has received a very severe shock."

"Her wound — what think you of that, sir?"

"I really can't say anything about it, save that it is a bite; but how inflicted I cannot say. It is very mysterious, indeed; very strange! But, what I look upon as most important in the affair, is the impression it has produced upon her mind; that, you see, may last her all her life, and produce very unfortunate consequences. I do not know that it will be so, but I state what there is a possibility of — or, I may, more correctly speaking, add, — of what there is a great probability."

"I regret to hear you say so," said Sir Francis Varney. "Do you really imagine the young lady has been bitten by any animal?"

"Yes, I do; there are evidences enough to prove that. There is the wound in her arm, and the marks of the teeth quite plain; and she suffers from the anguish of it much; but I shall be better able to say more about it early in the morning, when I call again to see her."

"She will be able to travel, I hope?"

"Oh, yes, she will be able to do that; indeed, I would recommend she should try to do so, as the best means of throwing off all the unpleasant feelings and thoughts upon the occasion."

"Will you call early tomorrow?"

"I will," said the doctor; and then he bade them good evening, and left.

"Well," said the landlord, "I'm amazed at what the doctor says about the young lady. I'm sorry it should have happened in my house; but I hope something will turn up to make it turn out different."

"That I'm afraid is not possible, seeing you have a clear demonstration of what it is now; the mischief has been done."

"I am the more sorry," said the landlord, "that it is likely to prey upon the young lady's feelings, which are to be considered in the case."

"Certainly, certainly; there is where the mischief is likely to spring from."

"However, it is of no use to stand here all night — it is cold. I must get an hour or two's sleep before I get to business in the morning."

"I think so too," said Captain Fraser; "well, I will bid you good night, Sir Francis, and shall expect you in the morning to breakfast."

"With pleasure," replied Varney; and they all parted, each going to his own dormitory, to sleep or to think over the events of the night, as best they might.

Chapter CXXXVII.

*T*he next morning came, and with it came also the usual bustle of a country inn, when strangers are stopping there, especially carriage strangers; as well as the usual coach stoppages, when they change horses, which they did more than once that morning. It was at a later hour than usual when the party breakfasted, and it was somewhat late when Sir Francis Varney entered the room.

"Good morning," said Sir Francis, with great suavity of manner, and in a most courtly tone; "I trust I see you somewhat recovered from the fright you were put to last night."

"Oh, Sir Francis," said Mrs. Fraser; "it was a dreadful fright, indeed; but we have so much to thank you for. To you we owe much, and my sister owes to you a double obligation — you have rescued her twice."

"I am happy to think I have been a fortunate instrument in serving you. I trust Miss Stevens is better than she was."

"I think she is better, Sir Francis; but she desires to remain in her apartment until we are ready to start. Though I thought it somewhat unreasonable, because, if she is to travel, she had better have come out."

"But her rest was disturbed by the accident, and it might have been early before she slept; and an hour's rest and repose might do much towards recovering her," said Sir Francis; "her own feelings are a good guide under those circumstances."

"I think so, too," said Captain Fraser.

"I," said young Stevens, "was awoke by a desperate riot caused by people running about; I did not hear anything of the scream."

"I was awoke by it," said Captain Fraser. "How did you hear of it — how were you awoke?"

"By a loud scream," said Sir Francis; "I was asleep, and when it awoke me, I knew not what it was. I remained for a moment or two in doubt as to whether I had not dreamt, but a repetition assured me that I was not dreaming — and knowing from the sound it was a female's voice, I jumped up, and dressed myself as well as I could; but, before I could do that, I heard people running about, and when I got into the gallery, I heard the door burst in."

"Did any one come out?"

"I cannot say — I saw no one; but the man who first entered the apartment fell down, from some cause or other, and set the bed-curtains on fire — accidentally, of course, but it was the same in effect."

"Did you see any one in the room, Sir Francis?"

"No one at all; I did not even know who slept there; but seeing the form of a human being lying there, and wrapping the bed-clothes, or rather seizing her and the bed-clothes, by grasping with both arms, I carried her out. I used but little ceremony, and the urgency of the case must be my excuse."

"And it is, Sir Francis, though I know not in what way we can manifest our feelings of gratitude to you."

"You may, madam, by saying no more about it; but I shall be delighted to think you have such a good opinion of my services; and the knowledge that they have been useful, that is a gratification to me."

"And one you are well entitled to, Sir Francis," said Captain Fraser.

"How far are you traveling?" inquired Mrs. Fraser.

"As far as Bath, madam, for the benefit of my health."

"We are going to Bath, Sir Francis, as well. I am sure it will be a great pleasure to Captain Fraser, to find that we are to have such a traveling companion — that is, if you can accommodate yourself to traveling in a carriage."

"I can travel as you please. I am mounted, and am used to such traveling, for months at a time."

"Do you travel much at a time, Sir Francis?"

"Yes, I have been a great traveler, for years; not so much as regards distance as to the constancy of my perambulations; for I continue for months together out, riding from one town to another."

"Without an attendant?"

"Always; I never carry a servant about with me; it cannot be done with comfort by any one. You have always proper attendance if you stop at a respectable inn, or hotel; or, if not, if the road you have to travel be a cross route, you cannot expect any additional comfort from a servant, but you are troubled at his not being comfortably lodged; at least, I am, for I have tried it."

"I dare say there is much wisdom in that. I know from experience that a single traveler, who has leisure, and is willing, may enjoy himself better than he could if he were attended by his servant. You are somewhat restrained in your motions, and cannot do as you would please under all circumstances."

"I am fully persuaded of that, from experience; but I shall travel on horseback till I get to Bath, and then I hardly know whether I shall remain at an hotel, or take lodgings for the season — or what."

"What we intend is, to take lodgings," said Captain Fraser, "for a time — as long as we feel inclined — and then to enjoy ourselves."

"Quite right," said Sir Francis; "quite right. I am glad to hear you say so, and I hope it may be of advantage to Miss Stevens."

"I hope so too. Shall we have the advantage of your company *en route?*"

"I shall have great pleasure in having your company so far. It will give me great gratification, indeed; I shall be most happy to bear your company as far as the city of Bath, and shall consider myself the gainer by your society."

"No, we shall be the only party that will benefit by it; but we shall feel greatly your kindness, and I, for one, anticipate much pleasure on the road from your society, and also when we arrive in Bath."

"I feel such will be the case."

At this moment Mr. Carter was announced also. In a few moments more this individual was introduced to them; he was a plain gentlemanly man, who really was a clever man, notwithstanding the fearful account of his prowess and skill which the landlord had descanted on the previous night.

"Well, Mr. Carter," said Captain Fraser, "how do you find my sister — do you think she is any better than she was?"

"I think she is calmer, and much of the first violence of terror is gone; but I cannot say any more — she is still much disturbed."

"Do you think there is anything dangerous in her state?"

"No, sir, I do not; though I cannot hide from you the possibility that there is of her being permanently affected by it — I mean mentally; it may take a deep hold of her, and there will be no getting her free from it, save by judicious treatment."

"You do not consider much, then, of her wound?"

"The arm? Oh, yes; that looks very angry, and has been a very severe bite, and has caused her arm to swell; though I have no doubt about its getting well, still it will be very painful for some days; and, had it been a little more severe, it is possible that some of the tendons might have been injured, or an artery wounded."

"Upon my word," said Sir Francis Varney, "this had very nigh turned out a very bad and serious affair, if not a dangerous one."

"Of that there can be no doubt," said the doctor.

"Well, but, after all, what was it that has caused all this disturbance? What was it, a man or brute?"

"Decidedly the latter," said Sir Francis Varney, "decidedly the latter, be the form of the creature what it may."

"Indeed, you are right, Sir Francis," said Mrs. Fraser; "but she insists it was a human being who made this abominable attack upon her — why or wherefore, no one knows; but she insists it was a man."

"What do you say," doctor?"

"I only know, sir, what the young lady says."

"Do you think it probable?"

"I cannot say I do. I think it most unlikely; though, to be sure, there is nothing in it that is impossible. Had any one felt maliciously towards the young lady, they might have perpetrated the crime; but, in the absence of all malice, I cannot think so bad of human nature as to believe it."

"You discredit it, then?" said Sir Francis Varney.

"I do," said the doctor, "with all due respect to the young lady; but the probability of mistake is so great, and when you consider the terror so natural to the occasion, her powers of observation were limited and liable to error, that I cannot myself believe otherwise than there is a great mistake."

"And what do you consider of the wounds? I mean, do you think it possible they were inflicted by human teeth? Are they of that shape and character that could be inflicted by human teeth?"

"Yes, decidedly; that is, so far as I am able to judge, while the wound is swelled and angry, I should consider them just such as might be inflicted by the teeth of a man or woman."

"That corroborates the young lady's own belief."

"It does, so far," said Mr. Carter.

"Then comes the question of how could it have been done, and by whom?"

"These seem to be questions which cannot be answered. I asked the landlord all that could tend to elicit that information, but with no success; he knew nothing that could throw any light upon the subject."

"Perhaps he knew nothing," suggested Mrs. Fraser.

"Most probably he did not," was the reply.

"I know the landlord to be a respectable, though somewhat eccentric man; and I think him quite incapable of being a party to such an outrage upon any person, much less upon a lady who was stopping at his house."

"Well; however true that may be, yet it is undeniable that this outrage has been committed, though by whom we cannot say, for we do not even suspect anybody. I can't understand it at all."

"Nor I; but, as you observed, sir, the outrage has been committed, and here, too; but, unfortunately, no one is suspected, and justice cannot be done, which, in such a case, ought to be fully and clearly made out, for there can be no palliation."

"None at all."

"I wish," said Captain Fraser, "I had been first in the room."

"Why, sir," inquired Sir Francis Varney, "do you wish that?"

"Because you see, sir, I should have felt that inward satisfaction arising from the fact, that I fancy I might have ascertained whether any one was, or had been, in the room."

"The young lady said there was," said Sir Francis.

"Yes — yes; but then you saw the door opened, and saw no one come out."

"I did not, though, after I had Miss Stevens in my arms, I came away, and then it was possible any one might have got out, though there were others who would have seen them; but still, in the bustle and confusion of the moment, there might have been somebody."

"Yes, there is that possibility," said Captain Fraser; "and I don't see why I should trouble myself about this affair — I mean, by wishing myself there; but I should have done nothing but carry out the body — that would have been my first act."

"No doubt," said Sir Francis; "and what made such an act the more necessary is, the fact that she was in instant danger of death from burning, or suffocation."

"True — true; who would have coolly gazed around him, when there, on the bed, lay the unfortunate victim of God knows what."

"Well, sir, I must bid you good day. I have some patients to visit."

"Not before we square accounts, which is easily done. Let me know how we may stand, sir, and I will pay you at once."

This little affair was soon settled; and the doctor was about to depart, when he said, before he left the room, —

"I have given the young lady directions what to do relative to her arm. She must not use it much; but any medical man who may chance to see it, will be able to prescribe for it; though what I have given I deem almost enough to effect her complete restoration, as far as regards the arm. The shock, the mind and nervous system have sustained, will only be eradicated by time and change."

"Thank you for your advice; that shall be attended to."

The doctor now quitted the hotel; and the landlord entered the apartment with a very serious aspect; and, after making his bow, proceeded to say, —

"I am very sorry, sir, for the occurrence of last night — very sorry, indeed. Indeed, sir, I cannot make it out at all. I have inquired all over the house, and nobody at all knows anything about it, nor can't think how it could be. A good many of them won't believe it at all, though I told them there could be no doubt of it, for the young lady was burnt, and the bed set on fire."

"You may be sure of that, landlord; the young lady has been bitten on the arm most severely."

"And, as for the fire," said Sir Francis, "I saw how that occurred."

"So you said, sir," replied the landlord; "if that fellow as fell down had stood up, why, it wouldn't have set the curtains a fire."

"No, that is true."

"Well, then, he would have been able to have seen what was the matter, instead of his filling the room full of smoke and fire as he did; he hadn't no excuse to tumble down — nobody knocked him down."

"But didn't he hurt himself very badly?"

"Oh, only about two or three square inches, or perhaps a patch as big as your hand, off his chin — that's nothing to such as he."

"Very good. But have you examined the place, to see if anybody could have got in and concealed himself? Was there any possibility of a man's getting into your house, and secreting himself in any part of the bed-room, which would thus afford him an opportunity of doing what has been done?"

"Why, sir, I don't think it likely; and yet these people are so cunning, that you could not, by any possibility, guard against them in any way, especially in an inn. But there is no house free from intrusion of that character; but in this instance they could have had no notion the young lady was to sleep there."

"That is very true," said Captain Fraser, "and tends to show she was not singled out for outrage; but what seems very singular, is, that any one should secret themselves, and that with a view to commit such an outrage."

"That is very true," said the landlord; "but people do very strange things sometimes, and I think the object of any one hiding himself in the house in such a manner as this rascal must have done, was robbery."

"But he met with no resistance, and there could have been no excuse for so cowardly an assault as this complained of."

"There is much truth in that, and yet we don't know what human nature is capable of," said the landlord. "I have known a few things in my time; but the man, or whatever he might be, might have been tempted to make the assault complained of."

"What? Then, landlord, you imagine that a thief who had got into the house, would make an attempt to eat a young lady?"

"Why, as to eating her, sir," said the landlord, scratching his head, "I cannot say that he would. I don't know what his intentions might be, nor do I profess to understand it all. I can't, however, see what can be the motive, save malice and spite; they mightn't care whom they injured, so long as somebody was hurt."

"They must have been very bad."

"Yes, sir; and I wish I had seen them; if I had, I would no more mind chopping them in two than I would cleave a marrow-bone. I truly hope, sir, you won't consider that, however unfortunate the circumstances are, that I am blamable in this affair. I took all the usual precautions in this affair — that is, my house was secured as usual, and the place watched during the day; for we are particular in that respect, knowing that we are very liable to be robbed."

"Exactly," said Captain Fraser; "and though I much regret the occurrence, yet, I tell you, I do not see anything in which I say you are to blame. It is simply a great misfortune, and there ends the matter."

"Thank you. I regret it as much, I am sure, as anybody, because I am very likely to be injured by it."

"You are not to blame. Allow my carriage to be at the door in half an hour, as we shall leave almost immediately."

"And my horse, too, landlord, as I bear this gentleman company."

The landlord departed, and went towards the stables, and gave the necessary orders; while the guests remained conversing on the extraordinary occurrence that had taken place, and much pleased with the courtesy of their new friend.

Many were the speculations that were indulged in respecting the attack upon Miss Stevens; many of them wild, but all wide of the mark, fortunately, for her frame of mind; and then, before they had at all come to any conclusion, or any satisfactory probability, the carriage was announced.

"Well, Sir Francis, I presume you will ride with us?"

"Yes, on horseback."

"I understand so; we shall be much indebted to you for your goodness; but here is Miss Stevens."

At that moment the young lady entered the room, ready attired for traveling, but looking very pale and timid. Sir Francis advanced, and, taking her hand, said, —

"May I have the pleasure of hearing you say the occurrence of last night has done you only a temporary mischief?"

"I hope not," said Miss Stevens; "but, to you, Sir Francis, I owe everything. I am grateful to you for your ready and effectual aid under such trying circumstances. I am sure I never can repay you for your goodness."

"Nay, the task is easier than you imagine," said Sir Francis; "to know that I have saved you, and to see it has been effectual, is repayment enough. I am sure we never feel so much satisfaction and pleasure as when we find our endeavors, however important or unimportant they are, have proved effectual — that we have done what we desired to do — that is ample reward."

"You are so good, Sir Francis."

"We will say nothing about that. None are so perfect but we may see room for amendment; but we will have a truce, I hope, upon this subject, and now converse upon the pleasures of our journey."

"They, I hope, will be very many," said Mrs. Fraser.

"I have every expectation of it myself," said Sir Francis; "the day appears fine, and the sun is high. The storm of last evening has cleared the air of much of its heat; it is cool and pleasant. The country will look refreshed, the fields will be quite gay and pleasant, and the face of nature renewed."

"Well, I am certain it will be a pleasant journey under such a change, for I must say it was very sultry yesterday."

"It was," said Captain Fraser; "the appearance of the earth alone will tell that. But are you all ready?"

"Yes, all," replied Mrs. Fraser.

"Now, my dear Charles, what are you about?"

"I'm looking for my gloves," said the youth; "but I can't find them."

"Never mind them; we shall be off without you."

"I'll come before you have all got into the carriage, so don't wait."

"Permit me, Miss Stevens," said Sir Francis, as he offered his arm, "to have the pleasure of seeing you safe into the carriage."

They young lady accepted of the proffered arm of Sir Francis, though not without something like reluctance, though, why, she could not tell; but yet she did not like to appear to hesitate, and forced herself to do what common courtesy, if not gratitude, demanded she should do. She took his arm, and the whole party were shortly seated in the carriage, and with Sir Francis Varney mounted beside them, they all quitted the inn, where they had experienced such strange vicissitudes of fortune during one night, that it would never be erased from their memories.

Chapter *CXXXVIX.*

THE ROAD, AND THE TRAVELERS. – THE PLEASURES OF DOING GOOD. – THE BEGGAR WOMAN. – SIR FRANCIS VARNEY A PHILANTHROPIST.

*T*he road was pleasantly bounded on either side by hill and dale scenery, while it was itself of a very diversified character; and at one moment they passed through long avenues of trees, at other times a bare heath, without so much as a dwarf hedge; and then well-cultivated country would succeed, studded with handsome villas, and country seats, old half-castellated mansions and halls, where gentlemen lived in the abodes of their ancestors, and felt pride in doing so.

The air was balmy and beautiful – every object appeared fresh, and every tree and shrub looked as though new life had been infused into it; the birds sang merrily, and the whole party were in high spirits.

"Such scenes as these," said Sir Francis Varney, "please me better than the gaieties and follies of the town. I am sure there is much more happiness to be found by a contented mind, than there is in the feverish pleasures of a city."

"There is much truth in that, Sir Francis," said the captain; "but, in my own case, connected as I am with my professional friends, I cannot follow what is the natural bent of my taste; but I find pleasure wherever I go, for I am determined to make the best of all that passes beneath my observation."

"Sweets can be extracted from every bitter, and therefore it is good philosophy to take the bright side of a picture, in all the ordinary relations of life; we are better men and better subjects by so doing."

Thus the distance was soon passed over, and a stage was but the same as a pleasant morning ride; and then an hour or two spent of the heat of the day in quiet in some small, but respectable, inn, with wine and pleasing conversation, gave them a relish for the life they led.

The style of the conversation of the stranger, Sir Francis Varney, was pleasing in the extreme; he was evidently a man of great and varied talents and attainments, and one of great experience, and who had seen much of life.

Two days passed this way, and they had not reached Bath; they were tempted to stop longer by the way than they would have done.

"Tomorrow," observed Sir Francis, "we must reach Bath. About three short stages will place us within its precincts, and then I presume the assembly-room, as well as the pump-room, will occupy much of your attention.

"We shall certainly go there."

"Have you been in Bath before?"

"Yes, but many years ago, when we were quite children, so that I have no recollection of the place."

"And you, Captain Fraser?"

"No, I have not, I am quite a stranger there; but for the kindness of your offer, I should have to trust to strangers, or my own good fortune, to find out those things which strangers usually seek, and those places they usually visit."

"I shall have great pleasure in showing you that which is worthy of your attention. It is now some years since I was there; but I believe, though there may be improvements, yet the place is essentially the same."

"No doubt; cities seldom alter much, unless it be in their suburbs. If the alteration be great, it will point itself out."

"Exactly so."

The party were seated beneath a large cedar tree, which stood in the inn garden, with a table, upon which were spread some wine and biscuits, walnuts, and a few things besides, of a character agreeing much with the place.

Into this garden crept an unfortunate beggar woman, who, espying the party from the road, escaped the vigilance of the waiters and menials who hung about the inn, and entered. She crept timidly towards the party, looking wistfully, but yet fearful of the consequences of the intrusion; for there was a notice in the village, which gave forth fearful threats to them, should they dare to beg for the bread for which they were starving.

Presently, finding the captain's eye fixed upon her, with a beseeching look, she dropped her curtsey.

"Who is that woman, and what does she want?"

All turned to look upon the unfortunate creature, who began her petition by saying, —

"Kind ladies and gentlemen, pity a poor woman who is starving. I am very weary, and am weak with traveling —"

"Eh! what do you do here?" exclaimed the waiter. "Come, come, we don't allow beggars in this place. The high roads, or the Bridewell, are the only places we have in these here parts."

"Do not be in a hurry," said Sir Francis, to the officious waiter. "It might have been right enough to prevent her entering; but now we have seen her, I cannot, if she deserve it, refuse to aid her in her affliction."

The woman dropped a very low curtsey.

"My good woman, where have you come from?"

"From Bath, sir," said the unfortunate creature.

"From Bath, eh? And what took you there?"

"I lived there."

"You lived there; if that were the case, why should you leave a place where you did live, to wander about where you cannot live? That is a bad policy, methinks. What do you say, captain?"

"I think so too, Sir Francis," said the captain; "but that may be only a verbal blunder of the woman; we can't expect propriety in speaking from such people; it would be expecting too much."

"So it would," said Mrs. Fraser.

"I have left Bath for two reasons, sir," said the woman; "one is, I was too unwell to work, and then my rent got into arrears. While I could work, I did pay my way, though living very hard."

"And what was the other reason?"

"Why, sir, I was turned out of my lodging, and having nowhere to go to, and finding nobody would assist me, was compelled to beg."

"What induced you to take this road, my good woman?"

"Because, sir, it will, if I live long enough, carry me to Portsmouth."

"Are you known there?"

"No, sir."

"What induces you to go so far? Speak out and do not be afraid; we have no object in asking you questions, save with the view of assisting you if we find you a worthy object."

"I am going to Portsmouth," replied the poor creature, "in the hope that I may hear from my son, whom I have not seen these many years, and who went to sea about seven years ago."

"You have a son then?"

"Yes, sir, I had one. God knows if I have one now."

The poor woman uttered these words with such sorrowing accents, that all were convinced of the truthfulness of them.

"Speak out and tell us your story. Bring the poor woman some refreshment," said Sir Francis; "her tale may interest us, and give us food for reflection. I am sure one cannot hear the misfortunes of others, without feeling grateful for the luxuries and blessings one enjoys over and above the common lot of mankind."

"That is very true, Sir Francis," said Mrs. Fraser; "and I am sure we ought not to pass those whom we can assist by a trifle, when our means will permit our doing so."

"You are perfectly correct, ma'am."

"Have you no husband?" inquired Mrs. Fraser.

"None, ma'am, none. When I had one, I had a good home over my head. I would not wish for happier or better days to come again."

"What was your husband?"

"A respectable tradesman, who kept a good house and his own servants. We spent such a life as that for nearly fifteen years."

"And how came it to a close?"

"His death, sir, which was brought on by a sudden cold; in a few days he was a corpse. I can never forget that dreadful day. We were living very comfortably and happy. My husband had just at that time entered into some speculations that promised to make a handsome fortune in a few years; and all promised success and happiness, complete and continued."

"How great a change!" said Miss Stevens.

"Yes, miss, great indeed. My husband hearing some news that caused him to be anxious to ascertain its truth, he left home one wet night, and got drenched through; and where he went to, he was obliged to remain in damp clothes, and not being a strong man, he took a violent cold, and inflammation followed.

"After this he had medical advice; but he soon sank, and was pronounced beyond recovery; he died a very few hours after that, and I was left a widow. A few short hours caused a great change in my circumstances."

"What became of the business?"

"Why, that was carried on for a time; but an accident deprived me of that."

"What was that?"

"I will tell you, sir. My son was about fourteen years of age when his father died, and was just able to carry on the business; and I believe we should have done pretty well, because he was a steady youth, and I could trust him; and he looked after the men employed, and I was not robbed.

"However, a severe misfortune awaited me. I thought the loss of my husband a dreadful misfortune; and I believe it was; but in his case he left one behind who could help to maintain me. His loss I mourned; but it did not produce the same disastrous results that the loss of my son produced."

"How came you to lose him?" inquired the captain.

"Why, sir, I had occasion to have some business transacted at Bristol. I could send no one else, though I could ill spare him; but then I was compelled to send him, and did send him. It was to accommodate some terms of sale; and he only knew the affair. He, therefore, went to Bristol.

He was pleased enough, being his first journey; and I could hardly have resisted his importunity, if I had been so inclined.

"He left me, and arrived safely in Britol, and was there a day or two, when, walking about one evening by the water-side, he was seized by a press-gang, and carried out to sea. It was useless for him to complain or to entreat; they would take him, and forced him on board a man-of-war."

"He served his king and country, then?" said the captain. "I honor him, upon my soul; and you are going to learn something of him — if he be dead or alive?"

"Yes, sir; I know this much, he was alive about two years ago, and expected to reach Portsmouth in a couple of years."

"Well, proceed."

"When I heard my fate — the detention of my son — I was thrown on a bed of illness, in which I lay for nearly three months, during which time I was completely robbed, and run into debt; and when I recovered, I had but a few pounds in the world, for an execution had been put into the house, and all was sold.

"Thus was I left without a friend or a soul to comfort me, or any relative upon whom I could call for aid and assistance. I had no right to do so to any one; and after my misfortunes, I found that my former friends deserted me. I found that it was necessary to have the means of purchasing friends, just the same as anything else. I could obtain them for money; but without money I had no friends."

"I was by far too independent to ask for what I felt I was capable of earning. I could live upon little, and I at once left all who had formerly known me, before I attempted anything. I was determined that I would not even ask work at their hands, but get it among strangers.

"Of course this caused me to seek a subsistence in the lowest capacity, and I cared not for it, because it put a still greater barrier between me and my late acquaintances. It was a long time before I obtained any employment, because I was unknown to any one who could recommend me, or who wanted my services.

"This was to be expected; but the first place I obtained work at was through the interest of my landlady; and then I obtained more afterwards, and one led to another, till I obtained a hard-earned but honest living.

"I had a little money by me — some two or three pounds; in case of being out of work, or in case illness overtook me, then I had something to fly to, the workhouse being a place of all others I most dreaded; sooner than go there I would consent to die by the roadside, and I have put my resolution to the test."

"You lost your work?"

"I fell ill for some months; all my little store of money was gone, and my rent grew in arrear. I became more and more deeply indebted, and what food I obtained was given me by others out of charity; but this could not last long, and a soon as I was able to walk, my landlady asked me for my rent.

"I then told her that I had no money, but that, in a few weeks, if I could find food to enable me to get up my strength, I should then be able to work, and I would then pay her off by degrees, until I was out of debt.

"She knew what I had been, and had some thought that I had money, or if I pleased I could obtain it from my former friends, and expected me to make the attempt; but this I refused, and upon my doing so, she, after the first expressions of astonishment and anger, gave me the alternative of doing so or leaving the house.

"I was turned out, and had no refuge. I wandered about, and knew not where to go, or what to do; indeed, I was houseless and friendless — a wanderer without a penny. I could not now obtain work — I could not do it; and my appearance caused people to shut their doors against me, and I wandered about begging.

"This was the first time I ever took what I had not earned, save what was voluntarily given me when I was ill.

"One evening, as I was creeping about, I heard some men conversing about the different vessels that were out at sea, and one of them named the one in which my son was. I instantly listened, and heard one of them say that she was on her voyage homewards, and would be home in a month.

"I had no sooner heard this than I had some hope.

"'I will go,' I said, 'to Portsmouth. I will meet my son, and he will not refuse to support his unfortunate mother. I know his disposition too well to dream of it; and should he be unable to do so, I will beg for him.'

"I slept in Bath that night, and then began to consider how I should get to Portsmouth. It was a long road; many weary miles must be walked over ere I could get there; and as for the means, I must trust to the charity of the passengers. It would not be much more than what I was doing. I could sit on a doorstep and beg; but to walk on the road where there were few or no passengers, I might starve.

"However, I resolved to make the attempt, because I loved my son; and if I could see him I should see an end to my misery.

"I started out about four days ago, and I have got this far; but I have had only bread on the road, and almost despair of being able to reach there; and the charity of people is not enough to support life upon."

"And where have you slept as you came along?"

"Wherever I could, sir; beneath the haystack, or even a hedge."

"Where did you sleep last night?"

"Beneath a haystack about seven miles from this place."

"And is that all you have got through today?"

"Yes, sir, every step; and considering my weak state, I consider it good traveling, and shall feel thankful for even that rate of traveling. You do not know how intensely I wish to get to see my son."

"I have no doubt of it, my good woman, and if I can, I will help you on the road. I think yours is a case that deserves some attention. If you choose to remain here all night and rest, you may. You shall have food till you go, and some food shall be placed in your hands before you go."

"Got bless you, sir," said the poor woman, in tears; "you will, indeed, do an act of kindness to me."

"You will stop?"

"And be grateful to you for your kindness."

"Here, waiter," said Sir Francis.

"Yes, sir," said that worthy, running up.

"Just take this person, and see that she wants for nothing — let her have a bed here and breakfast in the morning, and let me know what the charges are, and I will pay for it — do you hear what I say to you."

"Yes, sir," exclaimed the waiter, who considered the charge as one beneath his dignity; but he was forced to obey, and the woman was desired to follow him, which she did, after thanking Sir Francis Varney for his humanity and generosity.

"*U*pon my word, Sir Francis," said Mrs. Fraser, "you do those things as if they were common occurrences to you."

"Why, madam, I am — and perhaps I ought to abstain from making the confession — one who does not love to come in contact with misery; but then one does not feel justified in turning away from it."

"You must have a deep purse to be able to satisfy all such claimants."

"I cannot do that, if I were inclined, or they were deserving, which many are not, as you no doubt must be well aware."

"Indeed, that is a fact. Very few of the claimants possess the same strength of right to our pity and commiseration. I am certainly struck with the woman's manners, and her artless mode of telling her story."

"Exactly. It bears the impress of genuineness about it."

"So it does."

"And when that is the case, I cannot resist the sense of my duty, which impels me to aid the distressed. But then I injure no one. I have ample means; and, therefore, others may do less, and yet deserve more credit. I have no heirs to come into my property, and I cannot, therefore, injure any one; if I were to give it all away, I should be entitled to do so."

"You are as good, Sir Francis, as you are courageous and fortunate," said Miss Stevens; "I am sure I have every reason to be thankful to you for two preservations."

"Nay, say no more about the past; you say things at which I ought to blush to hear, for my modesty is greater than you imagine; but, seriously, I take more pleasure in it than most people, and that may be a set-off against my disinterestedness, for I am only laying out my money in pleasure and amusement."

"No, no, that will not pass."

"It will, I hope; but permit me to return and see how they have disposed of this temporary protégé of mine."

"Certainly, Sir Francis; don't let us detain you; we shall remain here some time longer, and then we shall leave the shelter of this house."

Chapter CXL.

THE ENTRANCE INTO BATH. – A NEW SCENE. – THE HOTEL AND THE LODGINGS. – THE ATTENTIONS OF SIR FRANCIS VARNEY.

After Sir Francis Varney had left the place where the Frasers were sitting, there was a long silence, in which each of the party appeared to be engaged in meditating deeply upon something or other, and yet each shrunk from expressing them. The first who broke the silence was Captain Fraser, who said, –

"Well, my dear, what do you think of our new acquaintance?"

"I think he is a most amiable man."

"Very courtly," observed his sister.

"Yes; a sure sign of good breeding – of good company."

"He is that," said Captain Fraser. "I never met with one in whom dignity, ease, and complete and unceremonious courtesy were so blended."

"And he appears to be a very kind and amiable man."

"But," said Miss Stevens, "he is also a very strange and a very singular man — a very singular man indeed! I never saw such a man before, or any one approaching him. What a strange complexion!"

"He has a singular complexion, and it strikes me he is well aware of it, and that is the reason why he prefers a country to a town life; and his solitariness, together with his manners, all indicate that his peculiarity in this respect causes him much annoyance."

"I dare say it may," said Captain Fraser.

"I never saw anything so truly terrible!" said Charles.

"Hush! do not speak in that way, Charles; it is ungrateful."

"I hope not; it is merely the truth. I never saw a corpse so pale! Indeed he is just such an one as you might imagine to have started out of a grave with an unwholesome life, and whoever had resuscitated him had forgotten to warm his blood, or to put blood into his veins."

"How very absurd you are, Charles! I am sure Sir Francis Varney deserves better of you than that. You are under a great obligation to him. I feel assured he feels the peculiarity of his complexion — I mean it has an effect upon his mind; and, if we knew the cause of it, it is possible some disinterested action, terminating in evil to himself, has been the cause of it."

"Well, sister, I do not mean to say that you can admire such a visage; but you ought not to say I am ungrateful, for I am not; and, moreover, I never saw any gentleman whom I liked better — his conversation is quite superior; but then, gratitude, surely, does not prevent one noticing so glaring a circumstance."

"Certainly not," said Captain Fraser; "though I fancy it would be better to remain silent upon such topics, if we cannot commiserate them."

"I think you are quite right, Fraser," said Mrs. Fraser; "he deserves respect at our hands, and the less that is said in regard to his misfortunes the better."

"I think the evening is getting very cool," said Miss Stevens; "will you remain here any longer? — I shall return to the house."

"We may as well all go — especially if you feel chilly."

"I do."

"Then come along; tomorrow we shall be in Bath. Come, sister, you must be quite well to share in the gaieties of the place. You know you said you should have the greatest pleasure there — you have been anticipating it all along."

"I did," said her sister.

"Well, but you will do so now. Why should your expectations not be fulfilled? I can see no reason why they should not. Bath is a gay place, and a city apparently made solely for the amusement of those who can pay for them."

"I have been so alarmed and terrified, sister."

"I know that, my dear; but you have had now two days' constant change of scene, and lived, I may say, almost wholly in the open air, so that you ought not now to be very nervous, sister."

"I might have been worse under other treatment," replied Miss Stevens; "but at the same time you can have no idea of what it is to suffer from such an outrage; you cannot conceive anything like it."

"I dare say not; I am sure it must have been dreadful."

"It must," said the captain; "but we will not say anything about a matter so disagreeable and so inexplicable."

"Suppose we go in."

"With all my heart; we shall be in Bath tomorrow, and you will have nothing to fear; how does your arm feel now?"

"Sore, but much of the inflammation has gone down; that I think will soon be well, and then I shall be able to use it as I used to do; I don't think it will leave any permanent injury of evil behind."

"I am glad of it," said the captain.

They now all returned to the inn, while the whole of the party passed the remainder of the evening in company, retiring at an early hour with the view of rising early for the purpose of getting into Bath in the afternoon, or before the evening set in, at all events.

*T*he next morning came, and with it a cloudless sky. They were all in high health and spirits, and sat down to a breakfast that was especially prepared for them.

"What has become of your protégé?" said Mrs. Fraser to Sir Francis.

"I have not seen her this morning. I have not risen long, and I have had no time to spare, but intend to see her before I go, and see that she has means to reach Portsmouth in safety."

"Will you send for her here, Sir Francis?"

"Certainly, if you wish it," said Sir Francis; "I will tell the waiter to inquire if she be ready, and, before she goes, to send her up."

"That will be the best."

This accordingly was done, and in about a quarter of an hour the poor woman came up to the room; there were several alterations for the better in her appearance, and she did not look so careworn and cast down as she had done; she appeared thankful, and refreshed with rest and food.

"You are now ready to start, my good woman?" said Sir Francis.

"I am, sir, thanks to you."

"I wish you all possible success in your mission, and I hope your son may be living, and prove grateful to you, as his mother."

"If living, I am sure he will, sir; and I do not doubt now but I shall be able to meet with him, thanks to your bounty."

"I hope you may. Have they treated you well in the house, below?"

"Yes, very well, sir, and kindly."

"I am glad of it. Have you any food given you to carry you on your road?"

"I have, thank you, sir."

"Then there remains now nothing to be done, but to give you some silver to enable you to provide lodgings, and now and then a lift on the road."

"Thank you, sir," said the unfortunate widow, as she took the silver which Sir Francis held out to her. She could only shed tears of gratitude; and Miss Stevens added some to it from her own pocket.

"You have our best wishes," said Sir Francis Varney. "Go now; we have done all we can for you — good day."

"God bless you," said the woman; "may you never experience misfortune, or ever know the want of even luxuries; you who can give, deserve to have. The poor and unfortunate have few such as you, sir, for benefactors."

"That will do," said Sir Francis. "Good day to you."

"Good day, ladies and gentlemen," said the woman, curtseying low, and then turning round, she left the apartment.

"Poor thing," said Sir Francis, "she has a long journey before her. A temporary aid given to poor people, often lifts them above want, and places them in a decent position in society.

"So it does," said Mrs. Fraser.

"Yet, you see, people disclaim charity, and say private charity is pernicious in its effects. But are there not two sides to any picture? An individual might as well say it was pernicious to take medicine because people sometimes poison themselves with some of the ingredients. Besides that, it does good to the state; for it often prevents such a one from coming to the state, and being a burthen upon society at large. I am really of opinion that much temporary distress might by aid be avoided; while, without that aid, it would, in all probability, become permanent."

"There is much wisdom in what you have said, Sir Francis; though you must be aware that it opens a door to much abuse and reliance upon the charity of others, which can scarcely be credible."

"Oh, yes; I expect there is an abuse of everything; but we do not, from that, argue its total cessation."

At that moment the landlord entered the room, saying the carriage was ready, as it had been ordered.

"Then we may as well at once proceed to the carriage, which is waiting, and we are ready to depart."

"And," added Sir Francis, "I am ready too."

They once more left the house they had slept in, and the carriage again bore them onwards towards the city of Bath, which was now only three short stages from them; and where they could arrive at almost any hour they pleased, if they chose rapid traveling; but this they did not, because it deprived them of much of the pleasure of traveling — the views and beauties on the road.

There were many gentlemen's seats on the road, which called forth comment and admiration; as well as many smaller estates and houses, that were often picturesquely situated, as well as lonely.

At length they came within sight of the famed city; and, each moment they neared it, saw fresh evidences of a large and populous place. However, they stopped not; but the closer they came to the town the faster they went, until they were really within the city.

"Here we are in Bath at length," said Sir Francis. "It is a fine city, and much of fashion and talent may be found here."

"I am glad we have arrived here at last," said Captain Fraser.

"And so am I," said Mrs. Fraser; "for I am almost tired of riding every day. I begin to want rest; I want to stop for a time in one place."

"We get fatigued, even with a change," said the captain, "after a time; and yet our lives are a complete round of change."

"Yes; if you consider the character of time."

They now stopped at one of the principal hotels, into which they all entered, and ordered their dinner; and, while the ladies arranged themselves for the occasion, Sir Francis Varney and Charles walked out into the town, where they amused themselves with looking at the different objects which were presented to the gaze of the stranger. In all these things Sir Francis appeared to be well versed — knew what was now, and what had been formerly.

*T*wo days had passed by, and there had been but little time lost, so far as the visiting of one part of the city and another was concerned, and they gradually became acquainted with and visited the different places of amusement — at least, so many of them as could be visited by them in the time.

Sir Francis Varney was the chaperon; and, as he obtained attention and consideration wherever he went, he was a valuable aid and assistance, and the family had now got quite used to him, and he to the family.

The peculiarity of his countenance or complexion wore off, his pleasing manners producing an effect that acted as an antidote to that, which was likely to cause some peculiar feeling in all who looked at him; but his courtly manners completely took from any one with whom he came in contact the power and the desire to exhibit any dislike or aversion.

However, there was not one among all those who looked upon him who did not look upon him with various emotions; but they were only such as result from a source that acted upon their feelings and tastes, without producing any deep or permanent emotion in any one.

Great care was taken by Sir Francis in dress, and his display was altogether good, but there was no ostentation; his manners were those of a man who was used to the position and sphere above what he even then moved in.

There was no mistake in the matter at all, and the Frasers were well convinced that he was what he appeared to be; and there was, moreover, an evident partiality for Miss Stevens manifested by him, which had already been more than once remarked by the captain and his lady, who tacitly approved of the honor, though nothing was broached on either side.

"Sir Francis appears to be a very gentlemanly man," said the captain.

"Very," said the lady — "very. I never saw one whom I could find so little fault with; indeed, I may say he had none."

"That is a very extensive compliment, at all events," said the captain. "No fault is a thing you can say of but very few people indeed."

"I mean, as far as personal behavior is concerned. Of course I know nothing more; his demeanor appears perfectly unexceptionable. I am sure I never saw any one at all his equal in that respect."

"Perhaps not. He appears to be very attentive to your sister; indeed, I should say he appears to be very partial."

"I think so too. What do you say to Sir Francis Varney, Mary," inquired Mrs. Fraser, "as a lover, eh?"

"I cannot think of him in such a light," said Miss Stevens.

"And wherefore not?" inquired the captain.

"Because I could not bear the idea. I don't know why — I can't tell you; but I could not do so — it would be against my nature to accept of such a lover. It would much pain me to refuse one who had done so much for me; but I could not accept of him."

"Upon my word you appear to feel strangely upon this matter," said the captain; "but I think you might think twice before you answered thus."

"No; think how much I might, it could make no alteration in my mind; for the more gratefully I think, and the more I endeavor to be, yet the stronger would be my repugnance to have such a man for a lover."

"Dear me, Mary! how can you say so?"

"I do indeed."

"Ah, well! girls will be girls; but he has not done you the distinguished honor to ask you, so you must not refuse in anticipation. You may consider the grapes are sour because they hang so high."

"You ask me a question, to which I have given you the best answer I can upon the moment. Besides, we know nothing of Sir Francis."

"We know enough of him, I think, to speak and think with the utmost gratitude of him. Not that that should make any of us overlook the precautions that are usual on such occasions. And as for your opinion, why, that might be amended by time; and I am sure that what we do know of him is enough to cause us to respect him, and to have confidence in him. He has not sought our acquaintance, and that is one guarantee in his favor."

"So it is."

"But all this is useless. Sir Francis appears very sensitive. He is of retired habits and tastes, and, perhaps, something of that may result from the disadvantage under which he lies, which he may feel severely."

"So he might; and, therefore, I would never, if I could help it, make any personal allusion of any character before him, even though I were speaking of some one else, and it had no reference to him, as he might apply it to himself."

"That is quite right, and just what it ought to be."

Chapter CLXI.

SIR FRANCIS VARNEY IN BATH. – THE OLD WOMAN AND HER FANCIES. – THE MURDER IN BATH. – THE TREASURE.

Sir Francis Varney, when he walked out into the city of Bath, appeared to be lost in deep thought, and walked along as if he saw nothing that was going on around him; he was lost in meditation — something weighed heavy upon his mind, and he now and then muttered inaudibly to himself.

Whatever might have been his purpose, he merely wandered about without going to any one place, as if he were in the search for an adventure, rather than having any specific and determinate object. But, after much wandering about, he came near the corner of a street, where he saw two persons conversing together. A stray word appeared to rivet his attention, and he paused, and then stepped into the shadow of a doorway and listened.

"You see, Martha, Aunt Matthew is an old miser. She would sooner see all the world at the last gasp, before she would dream of parting with a shilling. I am sure it is much too bad."

"What is too bad?"

"Why, that she, and such as she, should have so much money, and others, who would work hard, should have none, or even the means of procuring it."

"Yes, it is hard; and yet if those who have it did not keep it, there would be no one who would be worth money."

"That is all very well; but the more money circulates, the more hands it gets into; and that, of course, enriches every one who has for a time the possession of it, for they do not part with it unless they have value for it."

"Well, well, that may do very well; but it does not appear to me to be any business of mine that such an one should beg anything of anybody else; but no matter, she has money enough."

"She is single, is she not?"

"Yes," replied the other.

"Then you may, after all, possess all she has."

"I may, but she is fat and forty; she may live for years, and in the meantime I may be a beggar all my life."

"No, no, not so bad as that."

"And what is worse than all, while she is living, she is decreasing the money she has, and it will yearly get less and less, till, if any comes to me, it will be so small a portion of it, that I am sure there will be but little good come of it."

"Indeed. If she be such a miser as you speak of, I should have imagined that the property, personal or real, would increase under such management as that."

"It would, if she were not living on the principal."

"On the principal — what do you mean?"

"That she lives on the principal, as I told you. She has got some strange fancies in her head, and one of them is, that the banks will break, all and every one of them, from one end of the kingdom to the other."

"What a notion."

"Yes, and that is not all; she believes that all banks will break, so all the public securities will be of no use, but only so much waste paper; and real property will all be seized, and there will be I don't know what universal ruin, desolation, and disorganization."

"What does she do?"

"Why, keeps all her cash at home; and then goes to her strong box and takes out her bright gold guineas, which appear in such abundance, that it would seem as if it could never sensibly diminish; and thus she has been going on for a matter of two years or more."

"Upon my word, what can she dream of? If she go on in that manner, I am sure, too, that she will be a beggar."

"That is certain; but she thinks not, and you can't argue her into any other belief whatever that is contrary to this matter. However, I have no favor in her eyes, because I am her relative."

"And why should that be?"

"Because, bring her relative, she thinks I may be wishing her dead every day she lives; so , you see, if she go on with this feeling about her, she may take a complete dislike to me, and I should never have a farthing left me, even if she died before all was gone, and dissipated."

"Very true. Where do you live?"

"I have been living with my aunt.

"Indeed! And where may that be?" inquired her companion.

"Where — why, don't you know number one hundred and nine, Chapel-street? but I have left there — that is, I shall do so tonight."

"Will you? You are wrong."

"I doubt it, very much — very much indeed."

"What motive can you assert there is, to make it good policy in doing this?"

"She will think I do not care about waiting for her money; and that motive being observed, I am sure it will influence her in my favor."

"Then, you will not go back tonight?"

"No, not at all."

"Well, you know best; but I should. However, I must now leave you, and bid you good day. I must go."

"Good day," said the other, and they quitted the place.

When the two speakers had left the spot, Sir Francis Varney came forth from his hiding-place, and gazed after them for some moments in silence; but when they were no longer in sight, he muttered, —

"Could anything be more fortunate! I am reduced to the last guinea. I have not another pound to pay my way with. Just at a moment, too, when I think I may be successful at last in securing a victim."

He then walked onwards until he came to the neighborhood of the street he had heard the stranger name, and then he paused and approached the house with some curiosity, but passed by it without stopping.

It was a corner house, and a blank wall ran a short way down the street, being the side of the house, and a small portion of ground called a yard; here the wall was lower — here there was a chance of getting over, and here Sir Francis Varney paused a moment, as if examining the place with care and scrutiny.

He looked all around, and saw no one approaching; he heard no sound, and he saw no face in any window that was within sight. It was, moreover, too dark to be seen, and he, without a moment's hesitation, ran a few paces towards the wall, and by a violent effort succeeded in placing one hand upon the summit, and then the other soon followed.

Sir Francis Varney was a man of great agility and strength, and he was not long in drawing himself up to the top, and then he dropped down.

It was fortunate he dropped heavy, and also fortunate, from that circumstance, he fell upon something soft. The good fortune of the occurrences was dependent upon each other. We say it was fortunate he fell heavy, because he fell upon the old lady's yard-dog, an unamiable cur, and prevented an alarm, for the dog was crushed, and unable to utter a single howl before the animal died.

There was now nothing to do but enter the house if the back door was open; but upon trial this proved not to be the case.

This was a matter that required some consideration; the door was not to be forced, and he hoped to get in by that means, but he was foiled; but yet it was something to have possession of the yard, he could hide here; but yet that increased his danger, for if he remained there, he was liable to a discovery, and that, too, before any attempt had been made upon the coffers of the old woman, and no good effected by him.

What to do he could scarcely tell; but after some thought, he determined to attempt the back windows in the parlor, or room above the ground; and to effect this purpose, he would have to get upon a water-butt, and thence to the railings facing the window of the room, and which appeared to have no shutters.

Having once made up his mind, he set about it at once, and was soon on the top of the water-butt, and made good his hold upon the small balcony, and then he drew himself up.

This was a work of some difficulty, because the balcony was very close to the window, and left him no room to lean over; but yet he succeeded, and found to his great joy that the window was only closed without being fastened; he had only cautiously and noiselessly to lift it up, and he could enter it.

This he did at once, and then stood in the room; but all was dark, and he could not hear a sound throughout the house, for he listened many minutes, lest he might be suddenly intruded on by some one, and then there would be no escape from there, and he would possibly lose all.

Caution, therefore, was the order of the day, and he gently closed the window, lest the draught might be felt in some of the other parts of the house.

That was very fortunate, for there was every possibility of a discovery resulting from such a course; for any one, feeling a greater than usual draught, would soon inquire into the cause.

Having got thus far, he opened the door and walked into the passage, and then he heard the sound of conversation being carried on in an undertone; he listened at the door, and heard two female voices.

"Betty," said one.

"Yes, ma'am," replied the other.

"Have you shut the shutters, and locked up all the doors?"

"Yes, ma'am.

"The kitchen-door?"

"Yes, ma'am — all right as can be; nobody can get in, I'll warrant."

"You don't say so?"

"Oh, but I do; the dog's out in the yard, too."

"When you have had tea, I'll have him brought in; he mustn't lay out there, poor creature, to spoil his coat, and catch cold. I'm almost thinking I ought not to let him stay out to this hour."

"He's well enough — he'll not hurt — he's got the kennel to sleep in, and he's plenty of straw; there's many a one about these parts as would be glad of such a bed. I've taken care of him."

"Very well, Betty; sit down to tea, and, when it is over, I'll bet you anything that old Martha Bell will be here."

"Lord bless me, ma'am, you don't say so!"

"Yes, I do; but I won't be at home; she and I have fallen out of late, and I'm not inclined to make up the quarrel, for she won't believe the banks

will break, and you know they will, Betty."

"To be sure, ma'am, they will — I know very well they will; it's quite certain — as certain as the almanac."

"Yes; and, what's worse, she wanted to borrow ten pounds, and that, you know, will never do at any price; she would break, too, and then I should have loss number one, and no one can tell how soon number two might follow."

"He! he! he!" said Betty; "oh, lawks, I shall split."

"What's the matter now — what are you laughing at, silly?"

"Oh, you are so funny, ma'am; I'm sure you'd make anybody laugh — you do joke so, it makes one laugh."

"Laugh! — what is there funny in losing ten pounds, I should like to know? Nobody would laugh at that, I should imagine; I am sure I should laugh at nothing of that sort. If you were to lose ten shillings, I am sure that I should not laugh at you, nor do I think you would, either."

"No, ma'am, I'm sure you would not, and I am sure I should not;

but you do say such things that make me forget all about the money."

"Well, then, go down stairs and fetch some more coals."

"Yes, ma'am," said Betty; and, before Sir Francis Varney had time to slip back and open the door of the other room, the door of the one he was listening at was suddenly opened, and Betty stood before him.

She came out plump, before he had time to step back; and she ran against him before she was aware any one was there; for coming from a room where there was light, she could not see at all in the dark passage.

"Oh, my —"

She had got thus far in her exclamation, when she received a heavy blow from the intruder, which felled her senseless to the floor, and, as quick as thought, he drew his dress sword, and plunged the point through her heart. Not a groan followed — she was dead, and might be said to have died while bereft of sense or motion.

"What is the matter, Betty?" said the woman — her mistress.

No answer was returned, and Varney paused, as if uncertain what to do. He was in some doubt if he should or not go in, or await the woman's approach to where he stood. He had not been seen, or she would have screamed out; and if he went to her she would see him, and have time to alarm people.

He paused, and awaited her coming; but she appeared to defer doing so, and merely said, —

"Betty — Betty, what has ailed you? What can be the matter? You don't mean to say that the tea has got into your head? No, no," she muttered, after a pause; "that can't be the case. She must have been to my medicine bottle, and that has been too strong for her. I shall discharge her. She'll be breaking something or other, and then who knows where that will end — begin by breaking a basin, and end by breaking a bank."

So saying, she muttered something unintelligible to Varney, and then began to rise and walk along the room towards the door.

This was a moment of suspense — the door opened suddenly, and then she stood before Varney, who made a rapid thrust with his sword. This would have been as fatal as that which he had dealt Betty, but the mistress was more fortunate, at the moment, for a steel busk was the means of preventing its taking effect.

"Murder! What do you want! Oh, you wretch — I know you now! Depend upon it you shall be hanged! Murder — murder!"

"One word, and you are a corpse," said Varney.

"Mercy — mercy! Will you spare me — will you spare my life?"

"I will."

"Oh, thank you — thank you! I never hurt you, and I don't think you would me. I am very sorry that I made any noise — but you will spare me?"

"Yes, upon one condition."

"On a condition?" said the woman, tremblingly.

"Yes, upon a condition."

"Tell me what it is you require of me, and I will comply."

"Then," said Varney, after a moment's pause, "show me where you keep your money. I must have money, so give me plenty."

"Plenty of money, did you say?"

"Yes, plenty. I want some. You have money I know — gold — gold in quantity."

"Ha, ha, ha! gold! Oh, yes — gold! Ha, ha! how funny!"

"Funny! Is my sword funny?" asked Varney; "because, if you think so, you may have a small portion of it, which you may consider funnier still."

"No, no; but I have no money — none at all, save a little money I have for immediate expenses. I have but little; for nobody now-a-days keeps money in houses, if they can get any at any time."

"But you have plenty of money."

"I haven't any, upon my —"

"You have. You keep it in the house, you know, because the banks might break, and you would lose all. Now give me some at once, or you are dead as any nail in your house — mark that!"

"Oh, dear! — oh, yes! What would you have of me?"

"Money," said Varney, pressing the point of his sword against her side.

"Oh, mercy! I'll tell you all; but — but you must be satisfied with what I have got, and not leave me a beggar, or kill me because I have no more."

"I will be satisfied with what you have got; but that I know to be much more than I can carry away with me."

"Oh, good lord, you don't know me, or else you would know the reverse of that. A poor lodging-housekeeper is not the person to have much money in the house; but if the truth must be told, I have up stairs my quarter's rent, which I ought to give my landlord. I can give you that, but God knows how he will believe me when I tell him I have lost it."

"You have all your property about you. You have gold in quantities."

"I have not."

"Then take the fruits of your obstinacy," said Varney, in a fury; and, making a savage and sudden lunge at her, he passed his sword through her breast, and with a smothered scream she fell to the earth, where she lay gasping and writhing for several seconds, when a rapid gurgling sound came from her throat, and she died.

"'Tis done;" said Varney to himself; "'tis done, and it would have been as well if I had done it as first; but no matter, 'tis done quietly."

There lay the two bodies upon the flooring, the one in the passage by the door, and the other in the parlor. There was a long pool of black blood, extending from one to the other of the two corpses — they mingled their blood in death, though they held different positions in life. What could be done? there they were, and even Varney could not pick his way without treading in the blood.

He at once entered the apartment, and began to examine the whole place, but he did not find much there — a few odd pounds, and yet he turned everything upside down, to use a common phrase; but yet there was nothing of the sort which he hoped for, and expected to find.

"Can I have mistaken the place?" was his first thought.

Upon consideration, he saw reason enough to make his mind easy upon the score of mistakes in that matter. There was the number and the street, and the old woman, and her conversation answered exactly to what he had heard; and after a few moments' consideration, he muttered, —

"It must be right; there are more rooms than one in the house. I will go and search through the rooms, and if I don't find any, I will set the house on fire. Indeed, I think that will be better done, it will prevent the deed taking light, and as little suspicion may be as well incurred as can be."

This was a thing only thought of to be resolved on; but he cast that aside, and proceeded with his search, and having finished that room, he splashed through the blood, and once more stood in the passage.

"And now for the bedrooms," he muttered.

The candle he held was the only one he could obtain, and he was compelled to walk steadily, lest he should lose its aid by going out; however, he soon got up stairs, and walked into the best bedroom, where he again began to search about for the hidden treasure, but found it not.

"Curses upon the stupidity of the old fool, where does she hide her money? I am sure she has it here, and I wanted to get back without delay. I did not want to be away long, and here I have been, I dare say, an hour."

This was true, and he turned things over and about in great hast; but his endeavors had liked to have been useless, as regarded the discovery, only his eye chanced to light upon a panel.

He started up and pulled away a part the bed-curtains, behind which it was partially concealed.

"Ha! ha! what have we here? What I have been wishing to find, no doubt. This is the secret hiding-place of her gold — the treasury."

However, whatever it might be, it did not appear to be in his power to determine, for he could not open it.

This was, of course, a provoking state of things; and Varney seized hold of each implement that came to his hands, but threw each down again, being unable to effect his object by any means whatever.

He started up suddenly, after making many desperate attempts to break the door open, which, however, were futile, and exclaimed, —

"There are keys to these places, and I am sure the old woman must have them about her, if this place be really the receptacle of her wealth, as I have every reason to believe it is. I will find out, if I can; no doubt, however, I shall find it upon her somewhere — I'll try."

He immediately went down stairs and found the body of the old woman; it was fast stiffening; but the clothes were all sopping in blood, and he turned her over hastily until he found out the pocket; and from that he drew a bunch of keys. They were all bloody, but he did not hesitate about seizing them.

"These will, no doubt, let me into the secret. I shall find my way in, now, and then the house will no longer hold me."

He turned, and quitted the corpse; and, in going upstairs, he saw for the first time that the stairs all bore the imprint of his own foot; he saw they were stained in blood, and were clear, distinct, and well defined.

"It matters not," he muttered; "fire will, and shall efface that; and, besides, if it did not, what care I?"

He ran up the stairs, and again entered the bedroom, and was once more kneeling before the door of the cupboard. The bunch of keys was composed of many, and he tried one after the other, until, after many trials, he came to one, which was of a peculiar make and shape, and which convinced him he was now in possession of the right key.

"I think I have succeeded, now," he muttered, as he put the key into the lock. It fitted very closely into the lock, and then it slowly turned, and he saw the door open; but it only disclosed another door.

"What is the meaning of this?" muttered Varney; "what, is there another door to be found? I suppose some of these keys will fit this as well."

However, he was not compelled to make the search, for the key of this

inner door hung up by one corner, on a little hook, in a niche which had been

apparently cut out on purpose.

This was soon opened, and then came rather a startling sight.

In a small cupboard were packed a heap of human bones — more than bones, for they had yet the flesh dried and sticking to them — the skull was brown and bare, save here and there remained some hair.

"What is the meaning of this?" he muttered, angrily — "and have I troubled myself in this manner for only these few bones?"

It was, however, an apparent fact. There was the place, and it was now opened, and the contents were plain enough — bones! — bones! — human bones! There could be no mistake; and Varney rested his hand on his knee, and gazed intently into the cupboard at the bones, and everywhere else.

He was about to rise, when, somehow or other, he was induced to push the bottom shelf — why, he could not tell; but, when he had done so, he found it give downwards. Yes, the whole cupboard went down; he pushed, and pushed, until the roof was no higher than the floor; then, indeed, he saw a sight that caused him to feel a satisfaction.

"Ah!" he exclaimed, "ah! this is what I have sought, and I will have it — gold! — gold! — aye, here is gold in heaps, more than I can carry."

He stretched forth his arm, and leaned into the cupboard, and then examined the contents, and felt assured that there were several thousands of pounds; the glittering heap before him was what he wanted, and for which he had remorselessly committed such fearful crimes.

"But I must make haste — I must make haste. I shall lose what I have such a certainty of possessing."

So muttering to himself, he put as much gold into his pockets as he could, and carrying a bag under his arm, he re-locked the cupboard. Having retraced his steps below, he replaced everything; while at the same time he carefully examined his person, to see that there were no traces of his deeds upon him; and then, wrapping himself up in his cloak, he left the house, and proceeded towards his hotel.

Chapter CXLII.

THE SCENE AT THE HOTEL. — THE RELATION OF THE CAUSE OF SIR FRANCIS VARNEY'S PALENESS.

W hen Sir Francis Varney reached his hotel, he hurried to his own apartment, and then he called for his luggage; and when that was brought to him, and he was alone, he unlocked a portmanteau, and placed his gold in it; and then, having taken care to dress himself, he again met the Frasers below, at the evening meal.

"I have been strolling the streets for an odd hour," he said, "and find things pretty much as they used to be; I don't see many alterations worth speaking of."

"And yet they say they are improving daily."

"They may be; but only in parts and places; and it does not alter the general plan of the place, though appearances may be benefited."

"Exactly; that, I dare say, may be the case; as, indeed, it is most likely to be the fact, especially when we see that, save in the case of entire new streets, all improvements are effected by individual exertions."

"Exactly; but life and happiness is the result of individual exertions," said Sir Francis; "but yet many shrink from prosecuting a scheme of happiness, lest barriers be placed in their path that would be as injurious to all as they are effectual."

"Indeed, that is often the case."

"I have met with many instances of blighted devotion since I have wandered about over the green vales of England."

"I dare say you have met with some adventures?"

"I have, sir. I have met with many that, perhaps, few men would have ventured into, and ever expect to come out alive; but I have not done so without paying dearly for my temerity."

"Indeed; have you incurred much danger?"

"I have, sir."

"But still it must be pleasant to fall back upon the remembrances of the past, and recall scenes and events that possess interest to your mind."

"It is so. I remember well that, some years ago, when I was in the north, that an occurrence took place that has left a lasting memorial upon me, and one I can never forget as long as I live."

"It must have been a serious affair."

"It was a serious affair — a very serious affair. I was going to Scotland, when, by some accident, the carriage in which I was traveling broke down, and it was unable to proceed, and I took up my abode at the nearest inn; where I determined to remain until the carriage was repaired, which would, it was said, take a couple of days, at the least.

Well, in the evening of the first day, I walked about visiting the different places where I could hope for any pleasure; in doing so, I was wandering slowly down a lane, when I heard voices on before me. The wind blew from them to me, and I heard all they said.

"Then this evening," said one.

"Yes, yes; I consider this the most favorable opportunity than can be taken advantage of."

"Well, then, we had better go at once."

"Yes; now we are on our road there, you see, and we shall be soon there; there will just be light enough to reconnoiter."

"Very well. We can secret ourselves somewhere about the place, where we shall not be discovered, and then we can get into the house at our leisure."

"But we may have to meet with opposition."

"Then, we must resist, too. You don't intend to be taken, I suppose?"

"No, not I."

"What did you intend to do if you were caught?"

"Fight my way out, or, if need be, I can push my knife into the ribs of any one who may be in my way."

"Right. I shall be inclined to do for any one who wants to keep me against my will — you may reckon upon that for a certainty; and if the old man but as much as moves or utters a single cry, I will do for him."

"You don't mean that, do you?"

"I do, and will do it."

"Then I know, and I will do the same. I like to have a pal that will stick by me, and have no nonsense. However, we need not be in a hurry, and just do what is necessary — go to work steadily and determinedly."

"Agreed. We will now go on — strike off to the left here, and we come then to the house. There's only one man servant, but he can be dealt with; and as for the old man himself, he cannot do much."

Then they both proceeded across the fields until they came to some thick wood, when I lost sight of them.

Well, I knew the house they were both going to, and I determined to proceed by another route to the same place.

I followed the lane as far as it would go, and found it led up to the very house which I had heard the men declare their intention of robbing, and possibly of murdering the owners — the inhabitants, I must say, for master or servant alike they would not hesitate in destroying.

I entered the house — the door was open, — after having walked up a broad and stately avenue of linden trees which lined the way up to the hall door. I was for some moments unable to make any one hear, but soon after I heard some one approaching the hall. I paused, therefore, and presently there came an elderly gentleman, with a grave but pleasant countenance, upon whose shoulders fell a profusion of snow-white locks; he was venerable, yet pleasing in the expression of countenance.

He bowed when he saw me, but looked rather surprised.

"I dare say, sir, you appear surprised at my intrusion; but I do not come without a motive."

"I dare say not, sir. But you are welcome; will you walk in?"

"Thank you," I said, "but I have come to put you on your guard against an attempt at robbery, and possibly murder, that is to be made upon your house tonight."

"Indeed, sir. I can hardly believe any one would be so wicked as to do anything of the kind; and yet, I am sure you would not say so if you had not some grounds for such a belief."

"I have," I replied, "and I will relate them."

I then related to him distinctly all that I had overheard in the lane, and the direction the men had taken. He appeared very thoughtful for some moments, and then he said to me, as he led the way up stairs, —

"Will you walk up stairs with me?"

I did as he desired, and followed him up stairs, until he came to a small observatory erected in the top part of the house.

"You say you saw them enter the copse between here and the lane yonder."

"Yes, I did; and I imagine they may be seen if watch is kept in such a place as this; for I am sure they intend to examine the house, as to the means of approaching it, and they expect to find only yourself and a man-servant."

"They would have met but little more, indeed; however, I am forewarned, and I will take care to be fore-armed."

"That is my object in coming to you; to effect this is all I seek; and now I will bid you good evening, for I have got some distance to walk before I can get back to the hotel where I am staying."

"Are you staying at an hotel?"

"Yes," I replied; and I named the place where I was stopping, when he said, —

"You are welcome, if you are pleased to do so, to remain here; I shall be most happy with your company."

"Thank you," I said; "and frankly I must say, I should like to see the issue of this affair, and will accept of your invitation, though, perhaps, I have accepted of your invitation too readily."

"Not at all — not at all, you are heartily welcome; we will sit up and wait for these fellows; when we have beaten them off, we can retire in security to rest, without fear of disturbance."

"Do you see them?" I inquired, as he was looking through a telescope towards the point I had named.

"No, I do not see them yet," he said; "no, no; and yet I — I think I see something now through a portion of the copse — it's difficult to tell what they are about; if they go much further in that direction, they will be plain enough; there — there they are; I can see them both plainly enough."

"Two of them?" said I.

"Yes," he replied, "I see two; they appear to be looking this way; what are they doing now? Oh, I see, they are making for a place of concealment nearer the house. Well, sir, I am much obliged to you — very much, indeed; for you have evidently saved my house from being robbed, and myself from murder — I owe you my life."

"Nay, sir, not so bad as that; the villains might not have been successful enough to have effected an entrance before you were alarmed."

"And if they had, what could I have done? Why, truly, I have fire-arms, but I should have been loath to have used them, and my hesitating might have cost me my life; so I have to thank you for life and property."

"As you please," I said; "but what steps do you intend to take towards your own and your property's preservation?"

"I shall obtain the aid of another, and quietly await their coming; but as I think, from their appearance, they are not mere country people who come about robbing from distress, but men who make a kind of profession of housebreaking, I will have both taken and dealt with according to law."

"It is their deserts," I said, "for a more deliberately planned affair I never yet heard of; and what makes it so very black, is the fact of their early making up their minds to murder any one."

"No doubt," he replied; "but that is an inducement to take them in the fact. I will send for one man, and, what with ourselves, we can secure the villains; we are enough to do that."

"They are desperate," I said.

"But they will yield to numbers," he said."

"No doubt; but there must be a yet greater number; the odds, in my opinion, are not great enough to secure victory. These are desperate men, for they will not be taken, and two to one will not deter them — one, or even two lives may be sacrificed before they are secured, if they do not get off."

"Well, then, you appear to think that we had better obtain more aid?"

"I do," I replied. "At least, a couple of men, if not, three, over the number you first spoke of, if you wish it to be perfectly harmless in its results."

"I should so desire it," he replied.

"Then you'll find that requisite," I answered.

Then I was invited down stairs, and great hospitality shown me by the old gentleman, who was an exceedingly pleasant companion. He was well informed, and a well read man, and was the only inhabitant of that large mansion.

He had been many years a widower, and had but one child, a son, a young man of great promise; he was abroad on a tour, and he was awaiting his return with great anxiety, as he was somewhat longer than he had anticipated.

We sat conversing for some hours. We had a handsome supper, and afterwards some choice wine, and then in came three stout countrymen.

"My friends," he said, "I want you to keep watch and ward tonight in my house, to protect it from robbers."

They agreed to do so, but expressed some surprise at what had occurred, and appeared to believe it hardly possible that any one could have been wicked enough to compass such an object.

However, he told them all I had said, and they were sent below, where they were served with a very good supper, and promised reward, with injunctions not to speak after a certain hour.

This all arranged, I and my host seated before a fire, and with some wine, we passed the time agreeably enough.

"*T*he time passes," said my host, as the clock chimed the hours. "I wonder if anybody is about now?"

"I should think," I replied, "they must be about thinking of what they have in contemplation. I am sure it is a quiet hour in this part of the world, and I should imagine that no human being can be asked about here."

"None, I dare say, save ourselves, and our assailants, if they have not altered their minds, and given up their intentions, or altered the night they intended for the attempt. Who can tell? they may have done so."

"I hope not."

"No; it will be very uncomfortable to be in constant dread, never knowing any night I lay down what I may come to before morning; I may lose my life, and never again see my son."

"Yes," I replied; "but had we better not put out the lights?"

"I will order it to be done."

As he spoke, he rang a bell, and when a servant appeared, he said to him, —

"William, you had better put out all lights, and be quite silent; and if you hear any noise, get out of the way, and remain silent, unless they try to get away and elude us."

"Very well, sir."

"And as soon as you hear them at work, you had better steal up and let me know, as I intend to be present when they are taken into custody, as I have a particular desire to see it done."

"Very well, sir; but you don't know the danger you run. These men are desperate men, and they care not what they do."

"I know all that, William; but hasten down, and see my orders executed."

"Very well, sir," said the servant, who at once left the room.

"These people," said my host, "are not willing that I should run any risk; perhaps they think they will not have so indulgent a master in the next. Perhaps they are right; for I give but little trouble, and my servants are mostly out visiting some of their relatives."

"Indeed. I thought you were somewhat slenderly attended."

"I am. I have two very ill away at this moment, and I have another away on a visit to some relative."

"Indeed; they have an easy life under you."

"It is much the same as not having them at all; and yet, I must say, I have nothing to complain of; my wishes are complied with, and I have all my work done well, and punctually to a minute; and, if they have extra work to do, they never complain, but set about it cheerfully."

At that moment we heard William creeping up the stairs, and my thoughts soon reverted from the contemplation of the calm contentment in which all here appeared to dwell, to the confusion and bustle that was now likely to ensue.

"Hilloa, William!"

"Yes, sir, they are come," said William, in a low voice.

"Where are they getting in at?"

"In at the pantry window, sir. I can hear them unbolting the shutters. They have cut a hole out of it, and they will be clear in another minute."

"Very good. Now do you all keep together, and, at the appointed signal, rush upon them, and bind them hand and foot."

"It shall be done, sir, as soon as they get into the kitchen."

"Very well. I will come down and watch the operations; but don't let them get back again."

"Oh, we'll take care of that."

"Make haste," he said, "and station some of them under the stairs, so that they cannot escape. They must both be taken."

"And they shall."

"Go one. Will you come down with me," he said, turning to me, "or will you remain here till we have secured them? You, sir, are a stranger, and, perhaps, you had better remain here."

"No, not I," said I. "I will go down with you, by all means, and we will see how these fellows behave themselves under these circumstances. Let me see them. I was the first to discover them, and I hope you will not refuse me permission to be present at a *denouement* which I have, in some measure, been instrumental in bringing about. I wish to be present."

"Then follow me," said my host; "we shall not be too soon, for several minutes have elapsed."

I waited not a moment, but hurried down stairs, and found that, as I was going down the kitchen stairs, the robbers were well aware of the fact that they were entrapped; and, in their rage, they fought with desperation, and forced their way out of the kitchen, and through the barrier placed below; and, seeing they would effect an escape, I jumped over the rails, and stood between them and the way out.

I had but my sword, and I drew that, and placed myself in a position, threatening destruction to the first who should attempt to pass.

This, however, was disregarded; and the two men rushed at me, hoping to bear me down, but my weapon ran through the first, when a pistol bullet laid me low, and the man rushed over me."

"Good Heavens! and were you shot, Sir Francis?"

"Oh, yes, and was severely injured; and it was some months before I was cured, the bullet having wounded an artery."

"That was dangerous."

"Yes, so much so, that two surgeons declared that, had I bled another half-second, I must have been dead — that I must in fact have bled to death, and I should never have recovered; for I had, they thought, scarcely half an ounce of blood in my whole body — scarcely sufficient to cause the heart to beat."

"It was a fearful state — where did you remain?"

"I remained at this gentleman's house the whole of the time; he was very liberal, and very generous; I wanted for nothing. He said that, but for the immediate attention of the surgeons, he thought I must have bled to death; he saw me fall, and one of the men, without waiting for orders to do so, ran for a surgeon, and hence the rapidity with which the medical man was in attendance. And, what was worse, I had, in about two months afterwards, to undergo an operation to have the bullet extracted."

"Good Heavens! you had a severe time of it?"

"I had; and I had nearly lost my life a second time, for I lost a vast quantity of blood again; and, ever since that, I have been of the extraordinary pale complexion which you now see."

"I thought it was natural," said Mrs. Fraser, suddenly; but a look from Mr. Fraser told her she had done wrong.

"No, ma'am, it is not, indeed, natural."

"It was not until the loss of blood occasioned it, I presume?"

"No, captain, it was not; it resulted partly from the dreadful loss of the vital fluid which I sustained, and partly from a most violent virulent typhus, which I took in consequence of my looseness of system — that, I believe, did more than anything else towards bringing me to my present position — for, before, I was considered fair and florid in complexion, but my friends hardly knew me, or professed they did not, and I have not see them from that day to this."

"Upon my word, Sir Francis Varney, you have had some extraordinary occurrences in your life. I am amazed at them; indeed I could scarcely believe one person, especially a gentleman of your property and standing —"

"Why, as for that, I can only say that my position and rank here have given me the means to enable me to go through them without any inconvenience, for I have no home or place dedicated to domestic delights; such a life I should be proud and happy to possess, but which I can never accomplish; indeed, I may say, I fear to make the attempt; but, no matter. The prime of life will, in a few years, pass away, and then

I shall be past the desire for a home; and yet Varney-hall in the north, is an ancient, palace-like abode, that would grace a duchess."

"Is that your ancestral hall?"

"It is," said Varney, with emotion.

"And now uninhabited?"

"Oh, dear, no. When I determined to lead the life I do, I could not permit the old place to become ruinous and deserted and, therefore, let it, and those who now live there, are well able and willing to keep the place in repair."

"That is fortunate."

"Well, sir, I hardly know what is fortunate or unfortunate as regards myself; but I have one of my old fits of melancholy come over me."

"Nay, you must battle against them, Sir Francis."

"I have ever endeavored to do so, but I don't know how it is — I cannot, somehow or other, bear up — I feel a terrible depression of spirits."

"I am truly sorry to hear it; but let us hope that the gaieties of Bath will restore you to your wonted serenity."

"I am sure I wish it," said Mrs. Fraser; "but where are we to go tomorrow? — can you tell me that, Sir Francis?"

"To the pump-room in the morning — the library and the assembly in the evening, if you are inclined to do all at once."

"Yes; well, then, suppose we make the attempt; we can but give in if we find it too much exertion, though I am inclined to believe we shall not find it beyond our strength," said Mrs. Fraser.

"Then that is our agreement," said Sir Francis.

"Yes; it is."

Chapter CXLIII.

THE SCENE OF THE MURDER. – THE VISIT TO THE HOUSE.
– THE MYSTERIOUS DISAPPEARANCE OF THE TREASURE.

*T*he next day came; there was much excitement in the family of the Frasers; each one could see the partiality of Sir Francis Varney for Miss Stevens. She herself could not pretend that it was not so, or that she was unable to see it. It was quite plain and evident, and yet it gave her great pain, because she had an unconquerable aversion to him, who was her benefactor, and to whom she owed so much.

This, however, was a strong and inexplicable feeling in her own mind, and she felt that if death or Sir Francis were her only alternatives, she must choose the former. This was from some feeling, from what source it sprung she could not tell you, that appeared to forbid her permitting the approach of such a lover.

It might have been instinct, or it might have been that she had taken a personal dislike to him on account of his complexion; and yet she could not admit so much even to herself as that, and yet it must have had an origin.

She looked at him much more and more each hour, and more and more did she dislike him. At length she felt so much repugnance to him, that, if it were not for the deep gratitude she owed him, she would fly from and not even endure his society, good as that she was compelled to admit really was.

When he offered her his arm in their walk to the assembly-rooms and the pump-room, they were much pleased with the appearance of everything, and with the attentions of Sir Francis, who certainly did all he could to make the party comfortable and amused, he was so well acquainted with every object.

As they returned to the hotel, at which they all remained, they passed the house of the old woman who had been so cruelly murdered the night before. Sir Francis cast a cursory glance at it as they passed, but there was no sign of the door having been opened, and the murder had not yet been discovered; and this arose from the fact that the old woman was an eccentric, and her shutters had remained in that way before; and, therefore, no one took any particular notice of it.

When the party had reached the hotel, Sir Francis said, —

"You will, I presume, attend the ball this evening at the assembly-rooms?"

"We should wish to do so," replied the captain. "Do you intend to go, Sir Francis?"

"I will, captain. It is now some time since I went to such a place, and I think the change will be so great and agreeable, that I will go."

"Then we shall have the advantage of your guidance," said Captain Fraser; "and I hope we shall long have the pleasure of doing so."

"You are very good in saying so, captain; and, if agreeable to yourself and the ladies, I am willing, and shall be happy to bear you company."

"I am sure," replied Mrs. Fraser, "we shall always be happy with Sir Francis Varney's company, and thank him for his condescension — shall we not, sister?"

"Yes. I am sure I shall be much obliged to Sir Francis for this, as well as many other services he has done us."

"Do not talk in this manner," said Sir Francis, — "do not speak of the past, Miss Stevens; it is the present I would wish you to think of; at the same time, I desire only to be accepted, because I may not be thought intruding."

"Dear me, Sir Francis, how you talk! Really, I am afraid we have said something to give you displeasure, or my sister, here, has misbehaved herself; if so, I shall really take her to task for so doing."

"You will be acting unjustly if you do. But permit me to leave you for a short time. I have some matters to transact. I expect a remittance of money to this place, for I usually appoint some particular town or city, for I do not consider it safe to carry any great amount of money about me; it gives such temptations to robbery and violence that, traveling as I do, from place to place, I am especially liable to such attempts."

"Certainly, you are."

"Then I will bid you good evening, for the present," said the baronet, and he left the room.

When Sir Francis left the apartment in which he had been with the Frasers, he walked to his own apartment, and taking a large cloak and a small portmanteau he had purchased, he made his way to the very house where he had the night before committed such a double murder.

Before he reached there, however, he put the cloak on, and when he approached the house, he found the street entirely deserted; then hastily stepping up, he put the key into the key-hole, and at once opened the door and walked in.

He paused a moment or two, and then went down the passage a few feet, until he came to the body, for which he felt with his foot.

"Ah!" he muttered; "I see all is right — quite right; here is the body — nobody has been here to disturb it."

He took out materials for obtaining a light, and then he pushed past, and walked up stairs, until he came to the bed-room, where he again opened the strange receptacle of gold and bones; but, as he did so, what was his amazement to find a small packet of paper lying down, but all the gold gone!

He started up in an instant, and laid his hand upon his sword, but at the same time he appeared riveted to the spot, and paused in this attitude for more than a minute.

Then, recovering himself, he gazed round slowly and carefully from side to side, as if to assure himself he was not trapped. But hearing no sound — nothing stirring from any quarter whatever, he began to think there might be some mistake in his vision.

"Surely — surely," he muttered, "no one could have come in, and, seeing the bodies, possessed themselves of the money, and then walked out. They would surely have given the alarm; besides, any one who had entered would never have gone further than the bodies.

"It is impossible," he muttered, and he again stooped down to examine the cupboard from which the treasure appeared to be abstracted. But there was nothing to be seen, save the bare boards; no signs of the treasure remained. This was a strange and mysterious disappearance of what could not have gone without human means.

"How did they get at it?" he muttered; "the place was locked, and in the same order as I left it; there is no getting into such a place without unlocking or forcing open the cupboard, or, I may say, chest, for this is a strong place; it is not broken open, and I have the key."

Varney paused for several moments, and then he picked up some paper, which was folded up, and seeing it was written upon, he thrust it into his pocket, and again looked into the treasure coffer, but all was gone.

"D — n!" muttered Varney, furiously stamping his foot, as if at that moment only he had become perfectly aware of his disappointment. "What can be the meaning of this? But this is no place for me; some one has been here, and the murder is known. I must quit it — eh?"

At that moment there came such a peal at the door with the knocker, that made the house appear as if it were a pandemonium of noises and echoes, which followed the first stunning sounds that filled the place.

Varney started and listened.

"Ah," he said, "they have tracked me here. What can that mean? Have they, indeed, laid a trap for me? Do they think I am caught? But, no — no, I am too fast; they know me not, nor can any one have traced me here, for they know not where I came from, and — but there, it is useless speculating; they may have laid a trap to catch whom they could, or they — ah, they have seen the light, and the house being shut all day, they now want to see if anything is the matter; but I'll warrant all is safe and clear; there is nothing known, and all I have to do, is to get away."

That was very true; all Sir Francis had to do was to get away; but it was somewhat more difficult to perform than he had any notion; for, as he came out into the landing, he found there was an unexpected obstacle in his path. As soon as he attempted to descend to the back parlor for the purpose of getting out of the back window, he found the door had been burst open by the impatience of the mob who stood below, and the door not being very strong, the shoulders of those who were nearest were sufficient to force it open.

In a moment the passage was filled with the crowd, the foremost of whom tumbled over the body, and were up in a moment.

"Good God!" exclaimed one, "here is somebody lying down in the passage."

"It is a corpse," said another.

"The woman's murdered," said another, "Get a light — get a light, and let us see what is the matter. Here is a dead body — a light — get a light, can't some of you?"

"Well, I suppose we can; but what of it? I expect it can't be done without giving anybody time to do it in; if you think it can, you had better do it yourself, and perhaps you'll begin now."

However, there was a light produced, and that put an end to the altercation, and silence was immediately restored, when they saw the congealed blood, and the body lying in it; and then one, on pushing his way into the parlor, exclaimed, —

"And here's the old woman, she's dead and cold."

"She's murdered!"

"Yes, there's no doubt about that, poor creatures; and no one at hand to lend them any assistance. What a horrible affair!"

"Yes, horrible; but who's done it? There are rooms up stairs; they had better be searched; let's go up at once."

"Aye — aye."

Sir Francis waited not a moment more; he had heard enough to convince him his only chance was to escape while he could, for if they once seized him under such circumstances, he would not be able to escape again, and he immediately rushed to the back window; but there was no balcony there; he could not get out there, so came to the landing, and just reached the short steps that led to the roof, and there, had scarcely got the trap-door unbolted, when the heard a voice say, —

"Up stairs, lad — up stairs. I hear somebody there trying to get out — up stairs, lads, and follow him — up stairs."

There was a shout, and then all rushed up stairs, and Varney had scarcely got into the loft, when some one called out, —

"I see his legs — he's got into the loft. Up the steps."

"Hurrah! hurrah! up the steps, my boys; follow me," said one man, as he got on the landing, and ran to seize the ladder; but Varney saw the necessity of preventing immediate and hot pursuit, lest he should be recognized and followed to the hotel, when that would be death to his hopes.

Just as the man had reached the ladder, Varney lifted it off the hooks upon which it hung, and flung it back against the man, who fell back, and he, with the fallen ladder, created a dreadful confusion amongst those who were coming up stairs, many being knocked down, and the remainder retreated, thinking that at least there were a battalion of murderers.

This gave Varney time to get to the roof, and he then crept along several house-tops, without being discovered, though he could hear the shouts and hum of the mob, as they gathered round the house he had left.

Then how to get out of his present position was a question he was not well able to tell. He must let himself out through some of the houses, and to do that without raising a hue-and-cry, was a question he was not able to solve. Once or twice he thought of letting himself down from the outside; but this he gave up as being impossible, for destruction to himself would be the instant result.

"I must get into one of these houses, and remain concealed," he thought, "till the dead of the night, and then I could get through the house without any trouble, or fear of detection — but then the Frasers. I must not disappoint them."

This last consideration appeared to determine him, for he immediately crawled to one house that appeared to be the best calculated for his purpose, and he at once entered it by means of a small window that belonged to an attic. In this room was to be seen only a bed, and a few chairs, and a table.

All was silent, no one was moving; he stepped up to the bed, but was somewhat startled to find it occupied by some odd-looking human form, wrapped up in a curious and uninviting manner.

"Ah!" thought Varney, "I didn't think to have found any one in possession of this place so early; but they sleep, and that is enough."

He had scarce said so, when a voice said,

"Nurse, nurse — confound you, why don't you bring my posset? Do you hear, cuss you? here have I been kept here for two hours without my supper, and what you gave me last night had no rum in it. How's a man to get well, and kept upon short allowance? I tell you it cannot be done, not at any price. Will you bring me my grog posset, or won't you? You inhuman wretch, to keep an old sailor upon short allowance of grog and won't give him any except in the shape of a posset!"

This was pathetic, but Varney paid no attention to it, and gently glided out of the room. When he quitted the apartment, he descended the stairs, and then he came to the passage or hall, when he was met by a stout female.

"Whom do you want?" exclaimed the fat female.

"Madam," said Varney, "are you aware of the calamity that has befallen you?"

"No, sir. What — what is it?"

"The lunatic in the top room has in a fit of malignity set the upper part of your house in flames. You had better take care of yourself."

"Oh, my God! the house is on fire!" said the fat woman. "Oh, mercy, mercy! Fire! fire! fire! The house is a fire."

Varney turned round and opened the door, just as several people were rushing out of their rooms at hearing these alarming exclamations.

"That will do," muttered Varney, as he closed the door behind him, and then walked hastily towards the hotel, to which, however, he did not go quite straight; he went a little on one side to avoid meeting the crowd, as being an unpleasant mass of human creatures which are singularly unpleasant to meet with, leaving them to secure themselves and find the murderer, if they were able to do so.

Chapter CXLIV.

THE ASSEMBLY. – SIR FRANCIS'S FIRST OVERTURES TO MARY STEVENS. – THE BREAKFAST SCENE. – AND THE HONOR DECLINED.

Sir Francis Varney, as soon as he reached his hotel, changed his habiliments, and sought the Frasers, whom he found ready for the assembly, and somewhat fearful he was not coming; but he easily excused himself on the score of illness, and then they persuaded him to remain at their abode, and they would all do so too; but at the same time Sir Francis insisted that his indisposition was but temporary, and he would rather visit the place, as it was a ball night.

Thus persuaded, they agreed, and the five of them proceeded to the assembly rooms, where they amused themselves as fashionable people usually do. They danced, and were highly delighted with the place, which was certainly of a very superior description, contained the very *elite* of the Bath visitors, and appealed to advantage.

The wealth and beauty to be found in the room would have caused many a heart to bound with rapture, whether it was the miser's or the lover's; for both could there find that which gladdened them most, gold and beauty – wealth and youth; each could gloat his eyes on that he held dearest.

"Did you ever witness a scene like this?" said Sir Francis Varney, as he led Miss Stevens to a seat, and handed her refreshments. "Did you ever behold one in which was collected so much beauty and youth?"

"There are many happy faces," said Mary Stevens.

"And hearts, too, I hope," said Varney.

"I hope so, too," replied Mary.

"There are several here who have never been to a ball before; 'tis their *debut* in life, and a fine and lovely commencement it is; and if all their future years should be such a round of pleasure and gaiety as this, they needs must be happy."

"I am sure they must. People here seem to wish to make each other happy."

"And if they strive in heart, they must succeed in doing so, and in making themselves happy too."

"No doubt they do."

"And you, Miss Stevens, would you not make yourself happy when you make others happy?" inquired Sir Francis Varney.

"I certainly do feel happy when I am an instrument in the hands of another doing good, and seeing it really gives others happiness."

"That is one of the noblest ends of life."

"And one which you, Sir Francis, have pursued to some purpose. You ought to be happy, if any man can claim happiness."

"I am, in one respect; but when there is a great void in life, which has to be filled – when that void is in the affections, can it be surprising that sorrow and grief are there?"

"I cannot give you an answer, because I have no knowledge of such an existence; had I, it would be otherwise; but I cannot say yea, or nay."

"Well," said Sir Francis, "it is so; that void is in my heart; and, before I saw you, I felt it not; but now," he paused, "but now I feel it – feel it deeply, and I shall ever do so unless – but I hardly dare say more – my heart will never again know sorrow, and never again feel tranquil. Wants and wishes have sprung up which, until now, have never presented themselves in the shape of possibilities, much less probabilities, and which now are realities."

"This is a strange conversation, Sir Francis."

"It is, Miss Stevens, and I feel it to be so; but, unfortunately, I have a certain difficulty to overcome, which, perhaps, accident, more than courage, will enable me to break through. But, to speak plainly, before I saw you, the whole world was alike to me; I cared not for one more than another; but, now the world has new charms, I have new hopes and wishes. God knows if they are to be dissipated, like the morning mist before the glories of the rising sun. Love has made sad havoc in my heart; and to love and despair is the bitterest lot humanity can fall into. Man can bear all that adverse fate may entail upon him; but that saps at the foundation of the superstructure, our love of life, without which, society could not hold together; and, with disappointed love, there is no love of existence."

"Indeed, Sir Francis, I regret to hear it."

"Will you prevent it?"

"I cannot now answer you any such question, if I were inclined to do so – I have not the power. See, Sir Francis, there is another set."

"Will you dance?"

"No; I do not think I will dance any more tonight; but I shall be glad to rejoin my sister and brother."

"I will lead you to them, with pleasure; but will you allow me to name this matter to Captain Fraser?"

"I have no right to dictate to you, Sir Francis," said Mary, with evident embarrassment, "much less would I do so, or endeavor to do so to one to whom I owe so much; and yet I fear it will be fruitless."

"There, yonder, are your friends."

As Sir Francis spoke, he pointed to another end of the room, to which he was leading her, and which was occupied by many of the most fashionable and beautiful; they also had to pass down a lane of fashionables who were occupying seats, having been fatigued by dancing — many not having danced at all, but come to keep watchful and Argus eyes upon the sons and daughters whom they brought with them.

These, at least, noticed them — all eyes were fixed upon them, and Sir Francis, certainly with an air of triumph, led the beautiful Mary Stevens towards her friends, who were gazing at them with attention.

Mary thought herself somewhat awkwardly situated, and knew not how to release herself; and also felt that any attempt of the kind would really be as ungracious as it would be ungrateful, and so resigned herself.

A few yards more, and then she was once again in the company of her friends, but not released from Sir Francis, for he seated himself by her side with the ease of one who was well accustomed to their society, and of those around him.

"Well, Sir Francis," said Mrs. Fraser, "you have not been unnoticed in the ball-room. You have created quite a sensation; your dancing is superior, and your tall figure has set you off."

"You mistake, Mrs. Fraser; the object of such general attention was no other than your beautiful sister — my fair partner."

"Don't make her vain."

"That, indeed, would be a misfortune; but she has such an excellent capacity of mind, that she runs no danger of such a misfortune; but even were it not so, there would be much excuse."

"You are flattering, Sir Francis."

"Not I, I assure you. How do you find yourself?"

"I am getting fatigued. My recent journeys must plead an excuse for my weariness at such a time and in such a place as this."

"I am not surprised at this, considering how you have been riding about for many days past. Would you choose to retire tonight, and remain later on another occasion?"

"I think," said Captain Fraser, "it may be as well. What do you say, my dear?"

"I am quite willing."

"And so am I," said Mary. "Indeed I would much sooner we left early — if midnight can be called early."

"It is much past that hour now."

"Then I think we are decided upon going."

"Very well," said Sir Francis; "then I will obtain a carriage for our use, and then we shall retire to our homes."

"If you please, Sir Francis."

Varney then rose, and went out for the purpose of procuring what was wanted, and, by the aid of a little silver, he soon obtained what he desired, and then returned to inform his friends of the success of his mission.

They then left the ball-room, and proceeded at once to enter the carriage, which was so placed that they could at once enter without any inconvenience; and they soon gained their hotel, and, after a slight repast, they separated.

*I*t was late next morning when Sir Francis Varney entered the room in which he usually took breakfast with the Frasers; but, though late, he only met Captain Fraser.

"I am afraid, Captain Fraser," said Varney, "I have kept you all. Perhaps the ladies are gone out?"

"No, no; they have not yet come down. Indeed, had you been in five minutes earlier than this, you would not have found me here."

"Well, I know not the reason, but I slept well myself. To be sure," said Sir Francis, "I did not fall readily to sleep, and that may account for it."

"Indeed! and do you not sleep sound?"

"Usually — I may say, generally; but sometimes some reflections keep the mind actively employed against one's own wishes."

"They do so, Sir Francis. I have myself found that to be the case; but I am sorry my female folks do not come down."

"Nay, nay, Captain Fraser, do no wish that on my account. I am rather pleased they are not down than otherwise."

"Indeed, Sir Francis!"

"Yes," replied Sir Francis, " as it leaves me an opportunity of saying a few words to you, Captain Fraser, upon a subject that concerns myself nearly and deeply."

"You amaze me, Sir Francis."

"I had hoped you might have had some guess at it, Captain Fraser, as it would have helped me through my task; for my heart almost fails me when I think of the possibility of want of success — my want of nerve is not habitual."

"I can depose to so much, Sir Francis; you showed courage, and nerve, where courage and nerve were most wanted."

"Ah, well, Captain Fraser, If I had been brought up to your noble profession, I should have been better able to make an impression; but I will do my best; but the subject is a grave one, as it relates to my feelings toward your sister-in-law, Miss Mary Stevens."

"Indeed, Sir Francis!"

"Yes, Captain Fraser. I, who have passed through so many ordeals of beauty, have at last been compelled to bow before the shrine of beauty. I am a devoted and humble admirer of Miss Stevens's charms and virtues."

"Well, Sir Francis?"

"I now beg your permission to visit her, and be accepted in your family in the character of one who ardently wishes and desires to become a member of it by means of an union between myself and that young lady."

"Personally, Sir Francis, I have the greatest pleasure in hearing you say so much."

"Then I am likely to be fortunate."

"So far as my approbation, and my consent are concerned, Sir Francis, you certainly are successful; but, according to the vulgar proverb, as one swallow makes no summer, so one individual's consent is not decisive where two are required to concur."

"Certainly, Captain Fraser. I was not wishing to put the young lady aside; but having your consent, I may go on to endeavor to obtain the happiness I so much look forward to — but I may count upon your good offices?"

"You may, most certainly."

"And your amiable lady?"

"Yes, I think I may say she will unite with me in using all due means of aiding you in your wishes — but here she is."

At that moment, Mrs. Fraser entered the apartment, and advancing to Sir Francis, offering him her hand and saying, —

"Sir Francis, how do you do this morning? I am afraid I have kept you — ah, I see you are alone with Captain Fraser — where is my sister?"

"Mary has not yet come down," said Fraser.

"Ah, we are both late, I think."

"I am, madam; but you have come at a right moment."

"Have I? Why do you reckon it so?"

"Because I was just at that moment speaking of you, and here you are; so that I can speak to you, which is much better."

"Well, so it is — but what is it about?"

"You amiable and lovely sister."

"Ah, that is what you men always say — it is just what Captain Fraser said to me."

"Then may I hope for a like success?"

"I don't understand," said Mrs. Fraser, doubtfully."

"Why, I was saying to Captain Fraser, if he could obtain your aid in my behalf in an attack upon your sister's heart. I have been unable to hold out any longer — I am deeply and desperately in love."

"Well, that is a very dangerous disorder, and I must see what Mary can do to console you in your affliction."

"You will indeed deserve my best thanks if you will do so; and, should success crown our efforts, how deep a debt of gratitude will mine be to you."

"How much are we not yours already?"

"But my whole happiness will be through your efforts."

"Oh, no, no; remember, you said but just now it was my sister you meant to wed, and not me."

"Good God! how could you imagine I had any such profane thought?"

"Ha! ha! Sir Francis, I must see what I can do with Mary; but, she comes — another of the *dramatis personae.*"

Mary Stevens at that moment entered the room, and felt most abashed at finding all eyes riveted upon her without speaking, and she advanced towards the fire, having made an inclination to Sir Francis, saying, as she came down, —

"I fear I have been the means of keeping you waiting. I am sorry you did so; but I was really not aware of the hour."

"Nor were we," said Mrs. Fraser; "and it appears we have all been late, save Sir Francis, who, like a true knight, has been at his post, I don't know how long before I came down myself."

"Nay, don't you listen to any charges, Miss Stevens. I have been here but a very short time, though I ought to have been here earlier."

"It is fortunate then you did, Sir Francis, and I am relieved of the charge of detaining breakfast to an unusual hour."

"It matters but little when it is had, so long as it is to be had when it is wanted. What say you, Sir Francis?"

"I believe that the grand object of all our wishes and wants, is to have what we want when we want it. An eastern potentate could not be better served, or more powerful, or richer, than to be able to say so much."

"You are his equal."

"I am in some things certainly," replied Sir Francis; "but I want an empress, and thus, you see, I am dethroned and rendered powerless by a few words."

"You can obtain even that."

"Not exactly; for she whom I might choose might refuse to become mine; then, I am a weary wanderer upon earth's surface — I am no longer one among men; but a mere existence, moving about without filling any allotted position."

"This is very doleful, Sir Francis," said Mary; "if you say much more, you will spoil your appetite for breakfast."

"Mary, that is a cruel cut, you did not mean it, I dare say; but it is a sufficient rebuke. I must come to plain speaking, and at once hope you recollect the subject upon which I spoke to you in the ballroom last night."

"I do, Sir Francis; it would be affectation to say I did not."

"Well, I have sought Captain and Mrs. Fraser's permission to endeavor to win those smiles and good wishes, that I so much desire should be mine."

"You can never deserve less than good wishes from me," said Mary Stevens; "you cannot have less, I am too deeply indebted —"

"There, now, pray permit me to interrupt you. I must not hear any more of that; I did my duty on that occasion —"

"Occasions!"

"Well, occasions; and I hope no gentleman, having the power, would have done otherwise; and if so, I have only done what others would have done under the same circumstances — a very ordinary act indeed."

"You are making less of it than it deserves, were it only for our sakes."

"I see you won't entertain my wishes seriously; but, recollect, what is sport to you is death to me — the affections of a blighted heart cannot weigh lightly when the evil is consummated."

"Do not think, Sir Francis, I wish to evade or to slight any wishes you may form; as far as I am concerned, they are a great honor to me; but I am yet too young, and averse to anything of the kind yet to feel justified in seriously entertaining such matters as those you allude to."

"That, indeed, must be a mistake; you are not too young. Let me hope that you will not refuse to allow me the satisfaction and pleasure of your company; that would indeed be a greater misfortune than could otherwise happen to me to be deprived suddenly of that, I assure you."

"Certainly I cannot feel otherwise than gratitude to you, Sir Francis, and derive that pleasure in your society which others feel, and which all your friends must experience; but we will say no more upon this subject, except that I have given as serious and positive an answer as I can."

There were many other observations made during breakfast-time to much the same effect, but it is unnecessary to record them, and the breakfast passed off as pleasantly as possible, under the circumstances.

Chapter CXLV.

THE TWO SISTERS. – MARY STEVENS'S DISLIKE OF SIR FRANCIS VARNEY. – AN USELESS SUIT. – DISUNION.

*T*here was much stir in Bath next day on account of the murder that had occurred, and everybody spoke of it. The papers were filled with it, and it was thought to have been the most barbarous murder that had ever been committed, and most active exertions were being made to discover the perpetrators of this horrid deed. All sorts of conjectures were being made as to who the murderer might be, and his object in becoming one. Gold, of course, was assigned as that.

There was something terrible in the fact that this should have occurred just as the Frasers had arrived in Bath – it was startling, they thought, though they could of course have no connection with it whatever.

While the examinations were being proceeded with, Sir Francis Varney appeared out in the streets as seldom as possible; not that he had any fear of recognition, for that was impossible; but, at the same time, he would not run unnecessary risk, while so much was to be won.

The days passed, and many very pleasant hours were spent, and the gaieties of Bath were enjoyed to their fullest; while Sir Francis was their great friend everywhere, for, somehow or other, Sir Francis obtained the precedence go where he would, and they shared it with him.

He pressed his suit with much ardor, and Mary Stevens appeared each day less and less inclined to accept of Sir Francis Varney for a lover. She felt a greater and greater repugnance to Sir Francis, who, however, pressed her more hardly and more assiduously than ever.

However, Captain Fraser and his lady were sensible of the advantages of such a match to themselves and to Mary, for they could not believe that one so courteous and brave could do otherwise than make any lady happy; the first objection would wear away in the person of such a man as Varney; they therefore espoused his cause warmly when they found that Mary was averse to the match.

"What can be you objection, Mary?" inquired Mrs. Fraser.

"I cannot tell."

"Surely it cannot be an insurmountable objection," said Captain Fraser, "since you do not know what it consists of. You cannot have a very definite idea; and possibly a little explanation may set the matter to rights."

"I know well enough what it means."

"Do you, dear? Why not tell us?"

"I will. It consists of a strong dislike to Sir Francis. I cannot tell you why; but it is a very strong and yet distinct feeling."

"What can it arise from?"

"That I cannot explain."

"If you could, we should be able to come to some conclusion respecting it; but at present it appears like a blind, causeless antipathy, and, against one so well calculated to make any female happy as Sir Francis Varney, is so extraordinary that it really exceeds belief. I cannot express my regret and astonishment."

"I cannot understand it."

"I am sorry for it."

"And more like ingratitude, Mary, than I though you capable of. There are two occasions upon which you stand indebted to him for your life. He risked his own greatly on the last occasion."

"I am truly sorry it should happen so, sister."

"Well, then, Mary, amend the error; for if it were an ordinary affair, common dislike might pass very well; but towards such a man as Sir Francis Varney it is decidedly wrong. Indeed, when I recollect the horrors of that night — when I remember the flames and smoke, and saw you wrapped up safely from the effects of the fire, while he was exposed to every breath of hot air —"

"Hush! I recollect it all; but it makes me shudder."

"Can you, then, regard such a man with cold dislike? Upon my word, I am shocked at your baseness."

"Sister, sister, you are too severe — too severe."

"Only just, Mary — only just."

"More than just. Do not turn persecutor."

"I would not; but this conduct of yours make me feel strongly — very strongly, and I can hardly face Sir Francis Varney and tell him that one who belongs to me can treat him in such a manner."

"Does love always spring from gratitude?"

"It is useless to ask such questions, Mary, or I might retort by asking if such services as his always produced dislike. But Sir Francis is no ordinary man. Suppose you do not love him, which might be explicable;

but then you have no other love; you are fancy free, are you not?"

"Yes, yes."

"Well, then, you have no motive for dislike, though you might be indifferent. In such a case, I should not have thought it possible that there could have been less than gratitude, and the warmest esteem for his services and his own good qualities; for he has as good qualities as a man can have."

"Yes, sister; but that dreadful night has left such an impression upon my mind, that I cannot, dearest, do what you desire — I mean I cannot love Sir Francis Varney."

"What! not love him because of the remembrance of his services?"

"You quite misunderstood my feelings upon that occasion. I can never feel grateful enough for the rescue from the horrible monster who attacked me while I slept at the inn. I can never forget that moment of horror and terror. I cannot even to this day make out the object of the intruder. It was not robbery, and it could not have been any ordinary attack, for it was not carried on in the usual manner. To seize any one by the arm, and suck the blood from their veins, appears to me to be a proceeding quite unaccountable in the ordinary course of things."

"It was very strange."

"Yes; and, stranger than all, it has given me a perfect horror of man in general. I cannot abide the thought of being married at all; indeed, I won't, and I hope that is enough."

"Upon my word, my good sister," said Captain Fraser, half angry and half jestingly, "you would almost make me believe you were desirous of taking the veil; but you cannot have any reason for taking such a strong antipathy to male creatures. You must know very well that, because you have got a fright in a country inn, that all the abodes of men in the world are not filled with goblins, spirits, and the like, and wicked ogres, who are only waiting to eat up young maidens."

"It was no jesting matter to me."

"I do not say but what it was a frightful reality; but, at the same time, such terrible occurrences as these cannot be supposed to happen every day in one's life; indeed, one in a long life would be a terrible frequency which is never known, and I think you might dismiss the subject from your mind, as an inexplicable event, unpleasant and unprofitable to recall."

"But it has been too terrible and too mysterious for me to ever forget; and, least of all, could I do it in so short a time."

"Well, I do not expect you could forget it immediately; but, at the same time, I cannot see how it could affect your opinion of your preserver. Indeed, it is a strange perversion of intellect, not to say a degree of ingratitude, that it is difficult, if not impossible, to understand or believe."

"Well, I can say no more," said Mary.

"That is very resigned and easy on your part; but what we are to say to Sir Francis Varney I am sure I cannot tell. It appears to me that you have a childish dislike to him — one for which you can allege no reason, and, therefore, improper. I wonder what he, or any impartial person, could think of it, if they had all fully and carefully explained to them."

"I am sure I do not know; but it is usually sufficient, in a case of this kind, to say one cannot love the party, and to escape from what becomes an infliction, or, in time, a persecution."

"But this is not such a case as you would appear to imagine. There is no persecution, and Sir Francis only desires that you will permit him to attempt tot obtain your good will."

"But knowing he cannot obtain that — speaking in the light you mean — it becomes a serious annoyance to me to think I should always be attended by a person who, on the score of having done me some services, expects me to listen to his addresses, and to accept him as a lover. It is becoming a slave, indeed, when one must not exercise one's discretion in a matter that so nearly concerns the happiness of my future life."

"You are making mountains out of mole-hills, Mary."

"I have not taken the same view of this matter that you have," replied Miss Stevens, "and therefore you quarrel with me. I think that a great deal too bad; I did not believe you would have quarreled with me upon such a subject — one that concerns me so much, too, as this."

"Exactly; it does concern you, and it concerns us also, and that is the reason why we feel warmly upon the subject. Your want of motive is so apparent that it quite concerns us — we are completely staggered. What it can all end in I am sure I cannot tell; but Sir Francis must think us an ungrateful set, or at, least, he must believe you are actuated by the worst and most ungracious caprice, and capable of great ingratitude."

"I am sorry for it; but for all that, I cannot consent to marry Sir Francis Varney. I know not why, but I do."

"You really ought to be ashamed of such an admission, for I am sure he does not deserve such treatment."

"I am compelled to admit that to be true."

"Then why, in the name of Heaven, should you let prejudice surmount reason — and reason that you acknowledge ought to be paramount? You know your folly, and yet you persist in it. Was there ever such folly? Come, Mary, come, you must give up this kind of nonsense; you must act as I have always believed you would; you must meet Sir Francis in a proper spirit, and the result will no doubt be that you will banish all these idle fancies."

"I should be glad to do so, for they make me very unhappy."

"Well, well, they are calculated to do so, and when you have cast them aside, your own happiness and that of your friends will be much increased."

*T*here was much stir in Bath on account of the murder, and the papers were filled with terrific descriptions of the scene, which some even went to the trouble and expense of producing sketches of, which, what with being badly drawn, badly copied, blotted, and printed, and being as unlike the original as possible, gave the inhabitants and strangers not a very vivid idea of the place.

When, however, the details were adverted to they were terrible enough; and when Sir Francis Varney entered the apartment in which he usually dined, he found his friends were full of the discussion.

"Have you seen anything of the murder, Sir Francis?"

"No, sir," replied Sir Francis.

"Well, there is a dreadful affair happened. How horrible to think — they might not have been discovered at all, but for the neighbors breaking the doors in."

"What is it all about, captain?"

"Why, two old women were murdered a few nights ago, and they have but just been discovered; the papers are full of it."

"What, the murderers? Well, that was a quick discovery."

"No, no; I mean it was not discovered at all, as it is supposed, till at least four-and-twenty hours after the deed."

"Dear me; how was that?"

"I cannot tell, except the old woman was an eccentric, and her shutters had been closed before for a whole day; but there were no other signs of life about the house the whole day, which alarmed the neighbors much, and they began to take precautions towards the evening to force the door, when a tall, peculiar-looking man was observed entering the house by means of a key."

"They observed that, did they?"

"Yes; he was seen quite plain."

"It will be fortunate, if he should have been the murderer, because they can identify him."

"Undoubtedly they can."

"I am glad of it," said Varney.

"Well; he was seen to go in, and then to go over the house, because there was a light seen to travel up stairs, and stop there some time; and then they knocked for admission, but not being answered, they at once forced open the door, and they all rushed in, but were horrified to find themselves tumbling over the dead bodies of the old woman who kept the house, and her servant."

"Ah! it must have been a startling thing, certainly."

"Well; they stopped a moment or two — as was most probable at such a sight — and then they ran up stairs, believing the murderer was there."

"And was he there?"

"He must have been so, because they heard him get up to the roof, and they followed, but were baffled, because he threw the ladder down, which caused them some confusion, and during that the murderer contrived to escape."

"Well; it was quite a field of adventure; but it is to be lamented," said Varney, "they were not successful in their endeavors to catch the murderer; but what is the alleged motive for the deed?"

"They say that she had some strange fancies, and that, among others, she had all her money in the house — her capital, upon which she lived, without any fear of exhausting it. That was known to some one or other, and got whispered about, and it is presumed that for this purpose the poor woman was murdered."

"How horribly barbarous! but ain't there any suspicion upon any one, because it is usually the case?"

"There is, I believe."

"And upon whom does it fall?"

"Upon a relation of her own, who has not been seen for some days, and who had been know to have spoken with impatience at the old woman's life, and the mode in which she spent her money."

"That speaks for itself," said Varney.

"So it does; but they have not taken him yet."

"I hope they will, I am sure; because the whole affair is so truly horrible!"

"So it is. Will you go to the theatre tonight; there is no ball — we can have an excellent box?"

"What do you say, my dear?" said Captain Fraser to his lady.

"I am willing. Are you agreeable Mary?"

"Yes; I am quite content with your decision."

"Then we are all agreed to the proposal. There will be a celebrated actress from London there, and I hope we shall find the entertainment well worthy of our patronage — indeed, I have little doubt of it."

Chapter CXLVI.

THE EFFECTS OF PERSEVERANCE. — SIR FRANCIS VARNEY
AND MARY STEVENS. — AN EVENING PARTY AND
CONVERSATION.

*T*he evening was spent agreeable enough at the Bath theatre; Sir
Francis Varney having taken the greatest pains to ingratiate himself with
Mary Stevens so much and so delicately, that she could not but feel
ashamed at her antipathy towards him, and certainly did all she could
to get the better of it, and succeeded in some measure in doing so.

They all returned home in very good humor with themselves and
everything. Captain Fraser and his lady were completely predisposed to
look upon Sir Francis Varney as one of the first men in England for
rank and breeding; even Mary Stevens was compelled to admit she never
saw any one whose demeanor was to be more admired more than his.

The next morning they all assembled at the breakfast-table, and were
all full of lively images and thoughts of the preceding evening.

There was much more of cordiality and intimacy than had been felt
among them before; for Sir Francis Varney's courtliness gave way, and
he became almost as one of the family. Mary looked upon him with
something like wonder, to see how agreeable a man could be whom she
disliked.

One or two days more passed in this manner; and the dislike of Mary
Stevens to Sir Francis, if not less, was at least not so active or violent;
but she received him as an old friend.

That much emboldened Sir Francis, who again resolved he would
speak to her, and that in the presence of her brother and sister, hoping
by such a proceeding he should be able to overcome her dislike or fears
by his own efforts, aided by Captain and Mrs. Fraser, who would create
a diversion in his favor.

"I wish not," he said, "to be importunate; but, in a matter that concerns one's future hopes and wishes — one cannot well slumber over them — I wish to become one of such a family as that into which I find myself so strangely and accidentally introduced, though I fear I have failed to make myself as acceptable as I could wish."

"No one could think Sir Francis Varney otherwise than acceptable," said Captain Fraser; "your services to us alone would be enough to endow us all with the most lively gratitude and admiration, were you only to appear amongst us with no other qualification; but you add those which evidently make any gentleman an ornament to the circle he may grace with his acquaintance and friendship."

"You take a favorable view of all that you see, Captain Fraser."

"No, no; I merely speak what I think upon a subject which I have had, I may say, some experience. I have myself had some dealings in the world; my profession puts me forward, and I may repeat what I said."

"No, no, I will not suffer you to do that; what I wish to do is, to impress, if possible, my fair friend here with favorable sentiments towards myself. I am not as some of the young men of these times, who win by the violence of their suit, which they urge with all the haste of violence to attack and storm the citadel."

"That is a very good plan, Sir Francis; why don't you yourself pursue such a system? It must carry the citadel by assault."

"No, no," said Mary, "you will not do anything of the kind. Was that the way in which you yourself acted? If so, I am sure I pity my sister; for what can she hope for when she was taken in such a violent manner?"

"Oh, no, no; Fraser was the unfortunate victor, who was taken prisoner in the moment of victory."

"Yes, that is the fact; I was taken prisoner; but I have since been appointed governor in the enemy's country."

"Ha! ha! ha! well, that is a fortunate issue to your adventure. I would that mine were as fortunate — I love, and yet fear to say so."

"Fear never won a fair lady," said Fraser; "so don't be afraid."

"What does my fair enemy say her?"

"I have said so much upon the subject, sir, before, that I was in hopes I should not have had any occasion to say more."

"I am sorry to hear you say so."

"Why, it is a pity to render a matter that is settled uncertain, without the prospect of anything being gained by it."

"So it is; but I hope that is not the present case, Miss Stevens. My petition, I hope, is not rejected merely because it has suffered so before. I cannot but hope, though despair for ever stare me in the face for it; but perhaps devotion and heartfelt love may make some impression upon you, and soften the rigors of a heart that cannot, I am sure, feel any pleasure in the distress of another."

"No, no, Sir Francis; you only do me justice in saying so much. I can, indeed, feel no pleasure in such things. You may rely upon it, gratitude alone would prompt me to comply with any request you might make at once and cheerfully; but you must admit that this is a question that alters the complexion of other matters, and what might be proper under other circumstances, cannot be expected under this."

"Nor am I so unreasonable as to expect anything of the kind. Now, Miss Stevens, you much mistake Sir Francis Varney if you think him capable of such meanness. I wish you to act from your own unbiased judgment, and, however painful the result, yet I would in silence put up with your decision. But still I hope you will not act imperatively — that you will look upon my suit with, at least, not a harsh and averse spirit. Have some compassion upon one who is entirely at your mercy."

"Come, Mary, do not act unkindly."

"I — I do not know what to say. I — I cannot give any other answer."

"Nay, I won't hear of such a thing, Mary," said Mrs. Fraser; "now or never. I will not say that you must not be mindful of the past; but you were never ungrateful, that I know. You cannot be otherwise than happy."

"You embarrass me."

"Miss Stevens, let nothing weigh with you, save your own happiness; that is my object, and my own at the same time."

"Say yes, Mary."

"I — I cannot."

"Will not! What objection? What on earth could you wish for more?"

"Do not press me."

"I should be sorry to do so at such a moment, were it decidedly your desire not to give an answer now; but I do beg you will not let me linger longer than necessary. Indeed, I find I cannot exist in your society and be deprived of the hope that I may call you one day mine own."

"Do, Mary, say yes — say yes!"

"Will Miss Stevens give me leave to suppose that there may be a time when I may be rewarded for my patience? I will not press you for a plain answer now, but give me some token that I am not to remain unhappy."

"Come, Mary, come — Sir Francis gives you every indulgence."

But Mary was obstinate some time longer, until Sir Francis, in a transport, pressed her hand, and placed it to his lips; at the same time she suffered her silence to be construed into a consent to his wishes.

"**W**ell, Sir Francis," said Captain Fraser, "let me congratulate you in having subdued the enemy, and you, Mary, in having such a conqueror. I protest it was a hard fought battle, and one that I could not tell who would prove triumphant."

"I feel well assured you may congratulate me, Captain Fraser. I congratulate myself, I assure you; therefore you may do so to me."

"I do heartily."

"Thank you; I shall be happy. But what are the tactics for the night?"

"What are we to do?"

"Yes, precisely."

"Oh, suppose we have a nice party among ourselves. We can amuse ourselves, I dare say. I am fatigued myself, and care not to go out tonight. We have all gone out so lately that it will be a change and a rest."

"So it will," said Miss Stevens. "I am really glad that we shall have one night, on which we can retire at early hours."

"Are you willing, Sir Francis, to spend a dull evening?"

"It cannot be dull, at all events, in such company. I shall be happy to remain with you, indeed. I feel that a quiet, happy evening is a thing that would be very acceptable to me, at least; but still I can do as you please."

"Then we'll have a quiet evening among ourselves."

"Have you heard anything more about the murder that took place the other day?"

"No," replied Sir Francis. "Have you?"

"I have," said Mrs. Fraser.

"What have you heard?" inquired Sir Francis.

"I will tell you," replied Mrs. Fraser. "You recollect that the nephew had been suspected of having murdered the two women, and committed a robbery afterwards."

"Yes, yes; I heard so much."

"Well, they have taken the nephew now, and he has been examined before a police-constable, and will be again examined in another day or two."

"Indeed! they have made quick work of it. How can they suspect he had any hand in the affair?"

"I believe they knew he had been very poor, and had been very impatient for the old woman's death, that he might have it all. Now, such a line of conduct was bad, and has caused persons to suspect him; and, also, the fact, that he has got a quantity of gold about him, for the possession of which he cannot account."

"Ay, that seems bad; but what kind of excuse can he give for the possession of such treasure – he is surely not silent?"

"Oh, dear, no, he is not silent. All he says, however, is, that his aunt gave it him to leave the country with."

"That is strange – very singular."

"It is, and that is why they disbelieve it; besides; he had made no preparations for his departure, that have yet been discovered – besides, his shoes were evidently soiled with human blood, and the footsteps in the passage and on the stairs — at least, some of them, were exactly of the same size."

"That is a strong proof."

"So it is; but there appears to have been an accomplice, for there are other footmarks of a different size, much larger and longer."

"Dear me," said Varney; "didn't you say there were many people who ran up stairs after the man, who got away?"

"Yes; to be sure."

"Well, some of them might have left a foot-print."

"Well, I suppose they might, and yet they must have reasons for saying that these footsteps were those of an accomplice; perhaps they were fresher than the others, or it may be they have a different appearance from the more recent ones."

"It may be so."

"However it may be; it is quite certain that he has done the deed; whether he had any help or not, he, at least, will be punished."

"No doubt he ought to suffer for such a deed; it is that which gives security to the rest of society."

"But it was a dreadful thing. A murder committed by a friend or relation is, I think, more heinous, if possible, than when committed casually, by ordinary murderers, whose sole crimes are murder and robbery."

"To be sure; when any tie that can bind one individual to another is broken, who would have taken precautions against such as those whom we value; but he was ungrateful, and killed his benefactress — for such she had been."

Chapter *CXLVIII.*

THE WEDDING MORNING. – THE PROGRESS OF JUSTICE, AND THE DISCOVERY OF THE MURDERER. – THE DISSIPATION OF A SCENE.

*T*he days flew by, and the aspect of affairs insensibly changed. Sir Francis Varney gradually drew over the scene such an appearance of candor and disinterestedness, that the Frasers were delighted with the prospect of such an alliance, and they left no means of propitiating and influencing Miss Stevens in his favor; and they succeeded to a certain extent in stifling all expressions of dissent, and brought her to a state of passive obedience.

She had nothing to allege against Sir Francis but her dislike to him, and even that she felt was weaker, and the more she exerted her mind, the weaker such impressions appeared to be; a convincing proof to her that it was a mere blind, reasonless prejudices which it was her duty to throw off, and she exerted herself to do so.

Thus it was she became passive in the hands of her friends; and Sir Francis Varney had the satisfaction of seeing that he was about to pick up a bride at length. His pleasure knew no bounds, and his eyes glistened in a manner, that once or twice Mary recoiled from him in terror, and she had nearly revived her fist feelings against him.

However that might have been, he saw his error, and he conducted himself differently afterwards; for he too well knew the effect it must have upon the artless and beautiful young girl, whose affections he cared not to win, so that he stifled her objections, and obtained her hand – her heart was not with him an object.

"I think now," said Captain Fraser to Sir Francis, when they were alone – "I think, now, Sir Francis, that we ought to come to some understanding."

"I shall be but too happy, Captain Fraser, to do so, in every sense of the word, and upon every subject we can have in common."

"Then we shall have no difficulty in this affair."

"I hope not, I assure you."

"Well, then, Sir Francis, you desire to marry into our family?"

"Most unquestionably; my heart and fortune are at the disposal of Miss Stevens. I care for nothing else but her — fortune, Captain Fraser, is no object to me; I do not care for a single penny piece. I have enough for myself."

"Money is not happiness itself," pursued the captain.

"I believe it — I feel it."

"And yet Mary is not penniless; she has her dower, though by no means a large one; yet she has one."

"Then let the whole, whatever it may be, be safely, securely made over for her own use, and that of her children."

"It is generous — very generous of you, Sir Francis; and your generosity much embarrasses me, and I hardly know how to proceed with a little matter which I deem a part of my duty to perform."

"Do not let me be an hindrance to you; I am sure I should regret it much; besides, the more we know of each other, the greater confidence we have in each other, provided our knowledge is of that character that will increase our respect."

"You are quite right, Sir Francis."

"Well, captain, I hope what you are going to say, will not give me cause to feel myself less happy than I am."

"I hope not; I believe not; but what I was about to say is a very ordinary and common occurrence on an occasion like the present."

"Well, let me know all about it, and then the murder will be out."

"Good. We have but little more than personal communication with each other, apart from our respective homes; and we do not know much of each other in the ordinary acceptation of the word. I wish to know something relative to your private affairs."

"I really cannot do so, unless you travel northward with me."

"Indeed — indeed —"

"Stop. I can give you corroborative proof; I have none direct about me; but I can do that much; but perhaps it will not do."

"Quite enough. I am satisfied — if you can give me corroborative proof of what you say, and that without premeditation, it will be still stronger and more valuable."

"If you think so, what do you say to those two letters, Captain Fraser?"

"Two letters."

"The one is from my gamekeeper, and the other is from my bailiff, who has to overlook my property, and advise me of what was being done on the estate, and the state of my financial affairs."

"They will do, sir, I believe."

As Captain Fraser took the two letters, he looked at the post-marks, and saw that they were plain and readable, and the date: they had been correctly described by Sir Francis Varney — they came from the north, and one was a business-like letter from the bailiff, and one quite in keeping from the head gamekeeper, both of whom mentioned many local and petty matters, that fully bore out all that was to be expected from them.

"And do you keep up an establishment of this character, Sir Francis?"

"I do. I can afford it, and I do not like to turn the knaves adrift on the world, who have, ever since they have been born, looked for abundance from the soil that produced them; and I don't think I shall be justified in having the hardness of heart to turn them off."

"You are a kind and good master."

"I wish to be so."

"And when, Sir Francis, do you intend to return there?"

"I am glad you ask the question. I should like to take my bride there to spend the honeymoon. I wish now to leave other objects, and to get back as soon as the ceremony is over. There I should like to take her; it would be a rare and splendid life to lead in the old gothic mansion — as much like a castle as anything I can describe; but an ornamented castle, of course, for I don't mean high walls, and no windows."

"Certainly not."

"But will you assist me in obtaining her consent to a speedy union; and, that effected, we will whirl off for the mansion, and you can follow us at leisure. The union will, I hope and believe, be most happy."

"I hope so. I trust and believe it will."

"In the meantime, any more information or proof you can desire shall be obtained for you. Do not be backward upon this head."

"I am quite satisfied, Sir Francis."

*T*hus Sir Francis Varney had succeeded in hoodwinking Captain Fraser and his wife, and had now entirely subdued all shew of objection, and had so far succeeded as to obtain a quiet and tacit consent to all he desired.

The interview described was reported to Mrs. Fraser and her sister, and was considered liberal and satisfactory, and the marriage was spoken of as likely to be immediate, which brought forth no remark from Mary, and the matter was considered as nearly settled; the day only was to be appointed, and that could not be very distant.

One morning as they were seated at breakfast, and that after the day had been fixed at a greater distance of time than Sir Francis Varney liked, the subject of the murder was again brought up, and Mrs. Fraser said, —

"There is nothing more about the murder now — is there?"

"No," replied Sir Francis; "not that I have heard of. I believe the unfortunate man will be tried one of these days — he stands committed."

"Stop," said Captain Fraser, "here is something in the paper."

"What is in it?"

"Something more about the murder."

"What is it?" inquired Sir Francis. "I am anxious to learn if they have done anything more, for I was sick of it, and wish to know when such a horrible tragedy will end — the sooner it is past and forgotten, the better."

"That is true; for knowing a man is lying waiting for the hour to arrive when he shall die a violent death, is truly terrible."

"So it is. They seem to say there is some clue to another person, of a most remarkable appearance, who escaped through another house, and deceived the inmates by describing a fire that was up stairs."

"Indeed! How strange," said Sir Francis.

"Yes; they say they will not publish more, lest it defeat the ends of justice."

"Something else sprung up, I suppose?"

"No doubt. But here is something more: the prisoner will be tried in a few days, and, if condemned, executed in a very short time."

"Then I wish that one happy marriage would come off before that time. I am sure Mary will be wretched, and I cannot be so happy as I could wish to be."

"Then postpone it for a few weeks."

"No, no, no; that would never do; hasten it. Besides, we should have to pass through all the wretchedness consequent upon knowing a man — a murderer, it is true, and perhaps two of them — that is waiting to die."

"I think myself," said Captain Fraser, "that we might, with advantage, leave Bath before the trial takes place. It would certainly be more comfortable."

"So it would," said Mrs. Fraser; "and, to tell the truth, I begin to get tired of this place, beautiful as it is. In fact, I want to get to your mansion in the north."

"Not more than I do, madam," said Sir Francis. "Will Miss Stevens permit me to persuade her to shorten my period of probation, to escape some of the disagreeables we have mentioned relative to this unhappy affair?"

*T*he wedding morning was arrived. Sir Francis Varney had not been sparing of his ill-gotten gains. He willingly made some handsome presents to Mrs. Fraser and Mary Stevens; jewels were the form he gave them in; and Sir Francis himself took care to display no small degree of ornament, and yet he appeared to be a man, who, though wearing and having the best of all, still wore but little ornament.

But the occasion made the change in his habit. And now the post horses are ready at the door — ready to bear them northwards. They are at the church. Sir Francis, and Mary Stevens leaning upon his arm, come before the altar, and the friends of the bride were on either side of them. The clergyman was about to read, but asked first, if any knew any causes or impediment, &c., to the marriage.

No answer was returned; when there was some bustle at the other end of the church, and the clergy man paused to ascertain its character.

In a moment more there was a motley group of persons making towards the altar; and foremost among these were two or three peace officers, and after them a woman, dressed in many clothes, which added to her natural obesity.

"Ah, that's him — that's the wagabone that said my house was on fire when it warn't; that's him as frightened me so, that I'm quite thin through it."

"Shiver my timbers, and they begin to creak a bit now — d — n the gout! — but that's Varney, the vampyre! Who'd a thought he would always be turning up in this way, like an old mop as nobody can use?"

Varney turned to the clergyman, and begged that these mad people might be turned out, and, after the ceremony, he would meet any proper accusation at a proper time and place; but he showed his anger so strongly, that Mary shrank from him; while the two officers demanded him as a prisoner.

The clergyman yielded; and Sir Francis, striking the officer near him down, made a rush at a side door, and escaped.

The fact was, there had been more than one doubt about the murder; and Sir Francis had been followed to the hotel the night of the murder by one of the waiters, who came up behind him. They took his shoes, and found they were bloody; and all things being traced home to him, it was agreed to capture him at home; but he had left for the church, when the officers followed him. Old Admiral Bell, who was gouty, happened to see him pass, and determined to unmask him, which he did.

Chapter *CXLIX.*

THE MURDER IN THE WOOD DEL NOTTI. – A NEAPOLITAN SCENE.

*T*here had been a great heat during the day, even for the sunny shore of Naples. Not a cloud had been seen all day, not a breath of air had been stirring; all was golden sunshine – all was fair; the very sea glittered like molten gold, and the heat was oppressive in the extreme – so much so that even the Neapolitans themselves stirred not out of doors, but sank listless and sleepy on the couch, fanning themselves, and endeavoring to create an air that would give some slight refreshment.

Even the sea was calm – the very waves lashed the shore lazily, and appeared to partake of the general weariness that came over all nature – all things that moved.

There was no soul stirring in the villas that were seen dotted about the environs of Naples, most of them like palaces, surrounded on every side by gardens and fountains, walled in, and secure from the intrusion of a stranger.

There was one of great magnificence adjoining the small wood Del Notti, that reared its stately structure on a slope looking towards the sea, though at a mile or two's distance, but close adjoining the wood.

The gardens were extensive, and abutted on the wood, which was a cool and shady spot at most times, and if such a one were now to be found, it would certainly be found in the wood Del Notti.

The trees grew tall, and spread their branches out until they interlaced each other so completely, that when the foliage was on them the light rarely found its way to the earth, save in a dim and diluted form.

Here there might now and then be found some of those who had been overtaken by the heat of the day, or who from choice preferred the coolness of the woods to the walls of their houses. Here, then, reposing beneath the great trees, might occasionally be found a few individuals who slept in coolness and shade.

Near the wall of the villa where the wood ran were some tall black trees, mostly fir and cedar; there beneath one of the latter lay a tall, gaunt-looking man, who, notwithstanding the weather, was wrapped up in a cloak of large dimensions, and sable color.

There was something strange in that man's appearance; above all, the cloak which he wore was a thing so much out of place, that none other than himself could or would have worn it. What was his motive none could divine, were it not for the concealment of his person, which seemed likely enough.

His slouched hat was bent over his eyes; his face was scarcely distinguishable between the collar of the cloak and the hat, though he lay on his back motionless, and without heeding aught that neared him.

It was true, there did not exist any reason why he should take any heed, seeing that at that point no one ever came. It was a spot that was not frequented, having a bad name, which usually deters people from trusting themselves in such a place.

However, the stranger lay motionless, and apparently without fear. Perhaps it was the long two-edged sword he wore, that gave him his security; at all events, he lay there in silence, and almost motionless — quite and entirely so, save the motion in breathing; and his eye now and then turned in a particular direction.

The hours rolled by, and no one approached, till the sun sunk towards the ocean, there to bury himself till another morrow appeared.

The heat of the high noon was past, and the shadows of the trees reduced the light in the wood to a twilight; and the stranger arose and stood beneath the shadow of a tall one, while he appeared to be listening for some sound which he appeared to expect from some particular quarter of the wood.

The hour of noon is some hours past; and with it a gentle sea breeze begins to fan the heated shores, and here and there might be seen some of the inhabitants creeping about in the shady places.

The stranger listened, and from the quarter to which he appeared most to direct his attention, he heard sounds proceed. These were those made by persons walking over the dried leaves and sticks which lay scattered about from the effects of the storms that sometimes visit even these pleasant shores.

"She comes!" he muttered, and his eye glanced round, and he grasped the hilt of his sword. "She comes! but does she come alone?"

He paused, and again listened.

"She comes not alone — another is with her; but no matter; she shall come. I have the means of security here. But, above all, I need *her.*"

He paused again, and listened, but quietly drew his sword, which was long and sharp, and stood beneath the tree, while the voices and sounds slowly approached, until they came quite distinct and audible.

"And so," said a man's voice, but in a low key, "the marchese is not well."

"She is quite indisposed."

"I was about to say I could hardly feel it in my heart to regret it."

"And why could you be so unfeeling?"

"Because, by dear Fiametta, had she been well, you would scarce have got away from her this evening, and I should have had but little of your sweet company."

"I admit that; but were you not selfish in desiring it?"

"Yes, I was."

"And are you not ashamed to say so?"

"No, I am not, Fiametta. I can acknowledge anything that concerns myself and you; for I must admit a great deal of selfishness in this matter. I love you tenderly, and that puts all the world beside us. I think nothing of any one save you, and for you I would sacrifice the whole world."

"I am fearful of you."

"And wherefore should you be fearful of me, fair one? Am I not willing and ready to fight and die for you? I would not fear the summons of death this moment, if I knew that I could save you but one hour's pang."

"I hope," said Fiametta, leaning on her lover's arm, "I hope that you will never be called upon for so sad a sacrifice. I am sure I should never know an hour's happiness if I thought there was a possibility of it."

"I do not think there is any possibility of that happening. But, Fiametta, when do you hope for an end to this slavery? Can't you leave the old marchese? — she is anything but kind to you, and would marry you to one of her poor relatives; and unless you marry with her consent, you will never be rewarded for the many listless hours you have passed, night after night, at her bedside."

"But she will reward me when she dies."

"What an age to wait!"

"Surely you cannot grudge her life!"

"I do not, only so long as it is a term of imprisonment for you. If you would leave her, and come back with me, I will make you happy. You shall have a happy home, and form new ties, and new affections."

"I have not got so tired of the old, that it is necessary to change them; but I cannot leave the marchese. She is almost alone — no one goes near her to do her a good office, and I am her only friend."

"And yet she won't give you liberty."

"She says I am too young, and, if you must know all, she says I am too pretty to be trusted in everybody's company."

"I must admit there is much of truth in that, and yet I cannot see its application in this instance, as far as I am concerned."

"No; that is not to be expected from you, you know; but this must be admitted, that she speaks of men in general. Besides, she says, if I have patience to await her death, she will handsomely endow me."

"Upon my word, I think the old woman only wants to lease her life a few years longer, or, I should say, wishes to live forever."

"How can you make that appear?"

"Thus — when you are waiting for people's deaths, you never do succeed in hearing of their dying within any reasonable space. It gives them new life, and the spirit of opposition and obstinacy is created within them, and they won't die."

"For shame."

"Nay, you will find, Fiametta, that we shall both grow grey-headed in waiting for the happy moment when you and I are man and wife. Do not stay, then, any longer, leave here, and come with me; we shall be happy, and defy the world."

"But look what a dowry I shall lose."

"Never mind about that. Such a dowry would not make you young again, nor would it recall many years of past service and attendance upon her. You must know how very precarious such a life must be. It may so happen that you may forfeit all you have deserved through some fancy of this old woman. She may take it into her head to insist upon your marrying her poor cousin there. You know, if you were to displease her, she might very easily leave you nothing for your pains."

"I admit all that; but it amounts to nothing, because she has said as much that she would never force me, only she wished me to marry him, as being a worthy man and one who would act justly to me through life."

"Justly through life! What a sound! It sounds but little of love. Justly, indeed! I would I could act no otherwise to others, but to you, Fiametta, I should as soon think of forgetting you as merely acting justly. I love you; I would, at this moment, lay down my life for you."

At that moment they neared the stranger, who was standing silently and motionless, with his sword concealed beneath his cloak, but eagerly watching them, and devouring every word they uttered; and, by degrees, they drew nearer and nearer.

"I am sure it will be wise to wait awhile. I am sure the poor old marchese will not live long. She cannot eat and drink, save with great difficulty. I am sure we shall not have long to wait."

"I am willing to abide by your wishes, Fiametta; but it cannot be well to wait for an age — it cannot be well to wait till we are old."

"I know that; but —"

Fiametta screamed, as her eye fell upon the stranger, who rushed out upon them, with his sword drawn. This gave her male companion time to defend himself, by, in the first instance, jumping aside.

"Mercy! mercy!" screamed Fiametta.

Her lover drew his sword, and put himself upon his defense, saying, as he parried the first thrust of his enemy, —

"Villain! what mean you? Is it robbery you would attempt, or murder alone? Will nothing but shedding blood satisfy you?"

The stranger made no reply, but pressed on furiously, and with great strength and skill, for two or three minutes, when Fiametta's lover, by changing his ground, contrived to elude so desperate an assault upon his life.

Fiametta, however, believed her lover was getting the worst of it. She screamed out for help several times, but none came. However, it caused the stranger to press his adversary more quickly, and to hasten his own movements, for he was quite desperate and furious; but this laid him open to the assaults of the other. But, so fierce the attack, and such was the strength exhibited, that Fiametta's lover was compelled to give ground.

"What is your object, villain? — speak!"

But the stranger spoke not, but furiously threw himself upon him, and endeavored to beat down his guard, which his great strength and height almost enabled him to do; but as the other gave ground he was obliged to follow him, and then his foot caught against some of the tangled roots that grew out of the earth, and threw him forward; and his adversary, not slow to profit by it, and rid himself of so dangerous an enemy, stepped forward and received him upon the point of his sword.

"A good deliverance," said the lover, drawing his sword out of the body as it fell to the earth — "a timely deliverance, truly."

He wiped his forehead, for the perspiration streamed down his face; the day was warm, and his exertion great.

"Oh, Jose," exclaimed Fiametta, "what a horrid man!"

"A brigand, I suppose."

"But he said nothing — he asked nothing."

"No, he meant murder; there is no doubt of it, now, in the world; but I never saw such an ill-looking wretch before."

As Jose spoke, he kicked the hat and cloak off which the brigand wore, and which remained partially on. There was a ghastly wound in his breast where Jose's sword entered and let out the life of the stranger.

He was very tall, but thin and emaciated; his features remarkable, and he wore some straight, straggling hair, that was disordered, and fell over his forehead and face of more than marble paleness.

"Well, I never met with such an encounter before, and I never met with such an ill-looking villain," said Jose. "Come away, Fiametta; we need not say anything to any one about the affair. I will not come here again, though it may be needless to take the precaution, seeing that none could be brought to match this fellow in villainy and ugliness; at least, it is so to my mind. Come away."

Wiping his sword on the cloak of the fallen man, and sheathing it, he took the hand of Fiametta, and drawing it through his arm, left the spot.

Chapter CL.

A MAIDEN'S MIND DISTURBED. – AN EASY WAY OF PROMOTING COMFORT OF CONSCIENCE. – THE MONK.

*T*he spot was deserted, and no soul came near; but the body lay, with its ghastly wound, all sopping in its gore. It was a fitting place for such a scene as this; no sound was heard, and the lazy hours turned slowly over, till the shades of evening came on apace; the light grew dim, and darkness increased; but there the dead body of the tall, remarkable-looking stranger lay, without motion. It was cold and bloodless – death had long since deprived it of its last spark of animation.

*J*ose and Fiametta quitted the neighborhood of the deed of darkness as quickly as they could, and it was many minutes before either of them spoke, so filled were their minds with the reflections natural to, and consequent upon, the strange occurrence that had just before fallen upon them.

At length Fiametta broke silence, by saying, –

"Oh, Jose, what a dreadful thing has happened!"

"Truly, it had like to have been a dreadful affair; but it don't matter now, he's settled, I believe."

"Yes; but you have killed a man."

"Truly, my dear Fiametta, I have killed a man, or devil, I don't yet know which; but that man would have killed me if I had not done so."

"Yes, he would; but how dreadful."

"So that being the case, it is, in my opinion, a very good job he is dead; a very good job, indeed; he will be safe where he is."

"But still," said Fiametta, crossing herself, "how dreadful it must be to be slain thus; with all one's sins upon one's head."

"What would have been my fate?"

"As bad, and to me it would have been worse by far; but still it is really dreadful to think that there should be a soul thus sent to heaven without so much as the good offices of a priest."

"He would have killed me without giving me time for repentance. He would have forced me to leave a world in which I have all happiness yet to know; a world which I am by no means prepared to quit."

"Truly no, Jose, nor I; but what a state for this man to be in; he is so much the worse prepared than even you, because his end was bad; now, you had no evil intention."

"None — none."

"You did not know even that you were in danger from him."

"I did not, Fiametta, else I had never brought you there. I cannot understand what brought him there — what he wanted, or why it was he made such a desperate attack upon me; my life was aimed at."

"It was, Jose; but have you no private enemy, whom you believe capable of such a deed as this? Surely — surely it cannot be done, save from some motive."

"That is the thing that most puzzles me; I cannot understand the motive. I know him not; I have no enemy who would hire an assassin; but there let him and his deed lie buried in oblivion."

"He has no burial."

"He deserves none," said Jose.

"But, dear Jose, do you not think we ought to give him one."

"Are we his executors or heirs?"

"God forbid! — but we saw him die, and not for his sake, but for the sake of human nature, do not let us leave him unburied like a dog. He may not deserve it, but he has answered all his offence."

"Yes, yes; I admit he has been punished — he paid to the uttermost all he owed me, and I gave him a receipt in full. He will never make another demand upon me; we have quite done with each other, I believe."

"I shall never forget the horrible sight; it will haunt me day and night; I shall not be able to banish the terrible features from my mind. I shall, in truth, pass a sad life; I wish this had never happened."

"Why, so do I, dear Fiametta; but, surely, you do not accuse me of wrong, in having, to save my life, killed this man. I was compelled, forced to do it; it was either his life or mine; and, the truth to tell, I never was in such peril, from any single sword, in all my life, and but for the lucky accident that laid him open, I had not been here with you, but where he now is."

"Thank God for your deliverance, Jose; but — but what a revolting thing to remember, that in the wood Del Notti, there lies a corrupting mass of humanity, over which loathsome insects crawl; a thing that had once been a living soul like ourselves; but now, alas! what is he?"

"But, Fiametta, your grief appears misplaced; you mourn this stranger as if he was near and dear to you. Do you know him?"

"Not I," said Fiametta, sorrowfully.

"Then what have you to grieve about, Fiametta? Tell me truly. You have nothing to blame yourself with. I do not feel I have acted wrongly. Say what it is that causes you so much sorrow."

"I grieve to think that the body of that sinful and wicked man lies unburied, and that no masses have been said for the repose of his soul."

"If that be all you require to set your mind at rest — though the villain deserves it not — I will see that he is buried and masses said for him."

"Will you, indeed, Jose?"

"Upon my conscience, I will see your desire executed."

"Well, then, Jose, yonder lives a holy monk. He is a pious and good man, and will, I am sure, do all that is required — watch and pray by the body till midnight, and continue there until the sun shall illumine the wood."

"Be it so, my dear Fiametta — be it so. We will go to the holy man and tell him of our distress, and will reward him; and then I will see you in safety, and return to conduct him to the spot where you know we left the body. I would the villain had come by a less noble death than falling by the sword."

"It will be a danger that will never be forgotten by me," said Fiametta.

"Nor by me," replied Jose. "What that man meant I cannot conceive. But then there can be but one answer to the question — he meant robbery; nothing else could have tempted him to draw his sword upon me."

"But why did he not demand your money at once?"

"Because he might meet with what he has met; and he took me at a disadvantage, and, of course, gave him a better chance of killing me, and running less danger in doing so. I am not, therefore, surprised at it."

"Here is the holy father's residence. He is poor — very poor; but, withal, he is very good. He is a holy man."

"Then he will serve our turn the better; for it would, in my opinion, take something more than a saint to pray out of purgatory such a soul as his must be. It must wing its way through space very much like a bat."

"Hush, Jose — hush! Not a word about that. Here is the holy man's abode. Shall I enter with you?"

"If you will, Fiametta — if you will."

Fiametta stood by her lover's side while he knocked at the holy man's door, and, after a pause of about a minute, a deep voice said, —

"Who is it that knocks at my door?"

"'Tis one who needs your service, good father."

"Enter," said the monk, and a bolt was withdrawn. The door opened, and Fiametta followed her lover into a hovel, or rather a bare room, in which was nothing, save some straw in one corner, and some few clothes; besides which there were one or two articles of necessary use and convenience, but they were very few indeed.

"Well, my son, what wouldst thou? Dost thou require mine aid to bind thee to this maiden, and she to thee?"

"I do indeed wish so much, but she is not willing."

"Not willing! Then wherefore dost thou come to me?"

"You see, holy father, as we were walking in the wood Del Notti, which I dare say you well enough know —"

"I do, my son."

"Well, I was talking to my companion, heedless of danger, nor dreaming any could be at hand, when my attention was attracted to a spot on the right of me whence a man rushed out upon me, with a drawn sword, and attacked me."

"I should not have had time to see him, much less time to draw and defend myself, but for the scream of her who was by my side. I looked where I saw her look, and saw him advancing, and had time to spring back and draw."

"Did you kill your opponent?"

"As it fell out, good father, I did. He rushed on and pressed me so hard, that I had no alternative. My life was in great danger, and I could not rid myself of my enemy, or preserve my own life, except at the expense of his."

"Did you slay him?"

"I did."

"Another soul ushered into eternity," said the monk, gloomily. "How long will it be before the wickedness of men shall cease to bear such fruits?"

"But, holy father, I did but act lawfully in saving my life. It was only the law that nature has implanted in us, and can hardly be called wickedness, since Heaven itself gives us the power and impulse."

"Hold thy peace, my son, thou knowest nothing of these matters; therefore I say hold thy peace, and let me know what it is you desire of me."

"That you will say masses for the repose of his soul, and give him

Christian burial. I do not like — we do not like such a portion of humanity to remain where it is; we would it were not entirely neglected, or deprived of burial rites."

"It is but just of thee, my son; but I have known many who would have neglected it altogether, and permitted the body of one of God's creatures to lie and rot like a dog. My son, you have done well, and I will, for your sake, do mine office."

"Nay, holy father, I cannot permit thee to do it wholly without giving the church some due, and here in this purse you will find all I have."

"I take it, my son, not for my own sake, but for that of the church, to whom belongs all that is offered her."

"And this, too, holy father," said Fiametta, giving a small purse; "take that, and for my sake do what may be done by those on earth for those who have departed from it by a violent and sudden death."

"I will, daughter."

"And now, holy father," said Jose, "if you will, I am ready to take you to the spot where fell this man."

"I will follow, my son," said the monk, concealing his two gifts beneath his garments, but rising at the same time — "I'll follow thee."

They all left the place, but went a circuitous route, to enable Jose to leave Fiametta in safety at the marquise's villa, where she resided in half dependence, being a distant relative of hers.

Jose led on the monk until he came to the spot where the stranger fell, and where he yet lay just as he had fallen — a ghastly corpse.

"Here, holy father, you see the caitiff, a treacherous villain, who has now been paid for his villainy — for, perhaps, a life of villainy."

"Perhaps so, my son. He does not appear to have been formed by nature when in one of her most kindly moods; but yet it might have been she impressed his character upon his features as a warning to the rest of mankind."

"It was so, most likely; but you see he is slain. Fiametta would never have known peace again unless the body was watched through the night by some holy man, and prayed for. That is what is desired, holy father; and now I will leave you to your task, bidding you adieu, and wishing your office a prosperous one, and a pleasant night to watch by."

Chapter CLI.

THE WATCH BY THE DEAD MAN'S SIDE. – THE DEAD ALIVE.
– THE DEATH-STRUGGLE, AND THE MURDER OF THE
MONK.

*T*he monk gazed after Jose for some moments, until he had vanished from his sight; even then he continued gazing upon the vacant space that he lately filled, as if meditating in his own mind, and quite unmindful of the present. At length he turned and gazed upon the clay-cold corpse before him.

There it lay in all its hideousness – all its horrible reality. The slouched hat was knocked off in the fall, and the face was exposed to view.

"Ave Maria!" muttered the monk, telling his beads. "I never before saw so unfavorable a looking creature. I pray Heaven he may have been better favored in grace than in features – that he may make a better appearance spiritually than bodily. I would I had had time to speak with him before his spirit fled, for I misdoubt me much of his salvation – but I will not charge him with unknown sin."

"That," he muttered, after a pause, "might, indeed, be quite unnecessary, seeing his appearance and his deeds – at least the only one I know of is of a like character; were it otherwise, I would be loath to doubt him; but two such proofs are enough to damn the best spoken-of being in all Christendom."

He paused again; examined the features of the dead man, but could not appear at all satisfied with the success of his ministry.

"I would sooner have had some poor, but honest corpse to watch by," he said as he gazed upon the long white visage of the dead man, whose leaden eye appeared fixed upon him; "I would," he continued, "much sooner have had some early flower cut down before its prime – I could have wept and prayed for him, then; but this, alas! was but full-grown iniquity, I strongly fear — it cannot be otherwise."

The monk sank down upon a tree.

"Alas! what a sinner I am, for uttering such a thought — nay, I am worse for conceiving such a thought, and expressing it must be heinous. To have such a one would be to cut off the most worthy, instead of looking at the destruction of the full grown sinner in all his pride and moral deformity, as being the full extent of the length he was permitted to go by Devine wisdom and intelligence. He has filled his measure of iniquity, and the Lord hath cut him off in the midst of his sins."

The monk now devoutly crossed himself, and muttered several of his Ave Marias and paternosters, and prayed in bad Latin for some time, nearly an hour, when he appeared to think he might be indulged in a rest from his theological labor, and that his mind might refresh itself.

The monk arose and paced about the body for some minutes in solemn and deep wonder at the place chosen for such a deed.

A number of fresh thoughts now rushed through his mind, as he assigned all possible motives for the deed that had been done, or attempted to be done; and, also, for the choice of spot; but this speculation was more curious than useful.

Time passed by, and the hours rolled on, and darkness came on apace. A heavy atmosphere seemed to hang over him, and the light gradually faded away, and the moon showed no light on that night.

"It is dark," muttered the monk, "but the Lord is my light, and darkness has no fears for me. I am in the discharge of my ministry, and am safe. The dead man lies quiet and still — no sound comes thence."

He listened, but no sound; not the rustle of a leaf could be heard; not a breath of air stirred. All was silent and still; no one sound disturbed the stillness of the night — all was quiet.

"It is a night of death," said the monk to himself — " a night such as might be supposed to exist if the last man had ceased to live."

There was a weight in the air that appeared stronger, and had an effect upon the monk, and made a gloomy feeling come over him.

"What ails me?" he said to himself. "I am not strong and confident as I am wont to be — the reverse; I am doubting, and very sad. Yet why should I be sad — I, a minister of religion? I, at all times, am prepared to die, or ought to be.

"And yet there is the clinging after life, as in all; but I am mortal, as other men are. I have not all the motives for life they have. I am alone in the world. I am but a pilgrim, whose stay is short, and who leaves behind him nothing to remember, and no one to remember me. It is better it is so than otherwise."

The monk paused again, and approached the trunk of the tree, upon which he sat in deep meditation for more than an hour, without altering his posture, or uttering a single word. a whole hour passed thus.

"Now," muttered the monk, as if waking up from a profound meditation, "man is here but in a state of probation. If he were not, what would be the explanation of the checkered course he runs, what the use of all the various stages he goes through during a long life, and then to drop into rottenness at last?"

"Why are we educated and improved, if for any other purpose? Why should we spend years in improving ourselves, only to be deprived of the jewel at last, and to have it not only taken, but destroyed.

"No — no; it is for better use."

The monk's mind was evidently disturbed in regard to some speculation which had been suggested by the solitary moments of his watch. At such times, all the strange and inquiring thoughts that could be devised by man usually arise and enter his mind, and strange doubts and fancies will supervene, when all other thoughts have been banished, and they take their place.

Man's mind is always liable to these fanciful intrusions, and will remain so, while there is a single important assertion or circumstances existing, incapable of positive and mathematical demonstration.

When all shall be clear, and when there shall be no longer any play for the mind — any room for imagination — any possibility of conception left, then doubt may be cleared up, and an unanimity might be raised upon such a structure that never would be raised under any other circumstances whatever.

But, as this is not likely to happen, human doubt will exist, more or less, to all; we shall none of us be freed from that great cause of all the calamities of races. But to proceed with our narrative.

The monk looked around him. He could, however, see nothing, save the few trees near him, but beyond that he was unable to see. There was a strong mist up — one that limited vision, and left no room for any other object to shine through, and diversify the scene.

"I would," muttered the monk, "that the morning would come. There is no light; the moon is hidden; no rays penetrate the dense air; and all the while the air is close and muggy, Not a star out, or luminary visible."

He looked upwards, and found he could see the spot where the moon was striving to force its rays through some thinner stratum of the clouds; but it was doubtful, and the monk, of very weariness, began to count his beads and to repent his paternosters, between whiles and alternately, until he grew weary.

It wanted yet an hour of midnight, and the night would not be passed for many hours, and the monk thought that the nights were long.

"It is cold," he muttered; "but yet 'tis not midnight. 'Tis the moisture with which the air is loaded, and thus it is cool more rapidly than it could have otherwise happened; but it matters not to me — if I were to lose my life, I shall only be called home in my ministry; therefore it matters not. I am in the discharge of my duty, and shall have the reward appropriate to the service."

A slight breeze sprung up, and in a short time the mist was cleared off, and not a cloud was to be seen on the horizon.

There might be seen the moon rising slowly and majestically, while a gentle and diffused light shed its influence throughout the wood. Of course its direct rays could not enter until it had risen to its full height.

"Ha!" said the monk, "now I shall be relieved of some of the terrors of my watch; it will cease to be so tedious and so long; but, no matter, I am content, quite content. Soon I shall be able to see the body, and then I will close its eyes. I had forgotten to do so before; but it is time enough."

"Pater noster," again began the monk, until he came to the last word, by which time the light was enough to enable him to discover the body plainly; then he knelt down by its side to pray, and gazed on its features.

"I see its eyes are glaring wildly – aye, no wonder! no wonder! he met with a sudden, painful, and violent death.

"Poor erring mortality! what an end to come to; but, alas! what can men expect? He who lives by the sword will die by the sword."

The monk closed the eyes of the dead man, and pulled the cloak, which lay open, over him, and then leaned back against a tree, and shut his eyes for a moment; but they did not remain long shut, for some fancied noise drew him out of a train of speculation he was indulging in.

"He moves not!" he muttered.

However, he knelt down by the side of the body, and began to repeat his paternoster again, and for a few moments shut his eyes, as if he had no service for them, and continued his prayers without intermission.

The moon's rays now came with their full effulgence, and the forest appeared like some enormous piece of lattice work; for the moon's rays were able to penetrate the leaves and branches of many of the trees.

The moonbeams at length fell upon the body of the dead man, and he got slowly up until he rested on his elbow with his face towards the moon; and the monk, who yet remained kneeling, was still praying with his eyes wholly shut.

"Ha!" groaned the stranger.

The monk stopped in his prayer, started, and opened his eyes, which were fixed, in an extremity of terror and horror, upon the apparition before him – he was entranced, and had no power to remove his eyes.

"Ha!" said the figure, slowly rising to a sitting posture, but, at the same time, immediately facing the unfortunate and wretched monk, who was prostrated by fear.

"Ha!" groaned the figure, by a strange effort.

"My God – my God!" exclaimed the monk, save me – save me!"

He endeavored to rise, but shook so much he could not do it, for the figure kept its horrible eye fixed upon him, and he shook violently; but after a while he contrived to say, scarcely audible though,

"Avaunt, Satan, I command thee."

The figure heeded it not, but took some ominous proceedings, by laying its hands upon the monk's shoulder; but this had the effect of releasing him from his spell, and he sprang to his feet, exclaiming, –

"The Lord of Hosts aid me!"

The figure replied not, but rising without taking his hand off, a deadly struggle ensued between the two, which lasted some minutes. The monk, being driven desperate, resisted with great strength; but he had one to deal with, whose strength was far beyond his, and he felt himself gradually sinking, till, after another effort, which ended in a wild shriek, he was forced on his knees.

In this posture the strange man seized him by the throat, which he compressed, and thrust his knees into his chest, until the unfortunate and wretched man was quite dead and senseless.

Chapter CLII.

THE DEVIL A MONK WOULD BE. – THE DEMAND FOR ADMISSION INTO THE CONVENT OF ST. MARY MAGDALENE. – THE FORTRESS AND THE MONK.

*I*t was some minutes before the stranger, who had so newly risen from the dead, let go of the grasp he had of the monk's throat. He held him firmly by the throat by both hands; but as he stood grasping him, his face was turned upwards towards the moon's rays, which fell upon his breast and features, insomuch that he appeared to gain strength at every breath he drew.

But what a ghastly face he wore; what a death-like paleness spread over his forehead; the horrible looking eyes appeared to throw back the light of the moon, much the same as its rays are reflected by glass.

The unfortunate monk was partially kneeling, his back forced against the trunk of the tree, upon which he had been sitting, his face turned upwards, and his eyes almost bursting from their sockets, while his hands convulsively grasped those of his enemy; but his strength decreased as that of the other increased; his cowl fell off, and his bare head was exposed to the moonlight.

There was a death-like pause, and the figure slowly released its hold upon the throat of the monk and stepped back a pace or two to look upon his work. The monk's body retained the posture given to it by the efforts to extinguish his life, and appeared as though his muscles had rigidly set in death, but the trunk of the tree itself was a sufficient support.

"Dead!" muttered the figure; "dead!"

Again he moved about, and went into an open space, where the moonlight came uninterruptedly, without any barrier, and from this spot he surveyed the hideous work of his hands.

"Dead – dead!" muttered the figure.

This was undoubtedly true; and yet there remained the body of the monk, which, but for the turn of the head backwards, and its face upwards, it might be easily supposed that he had died in the attitude of devotion or supplication; but, as it was, it was evident by what means he had come by his death.

"I must have a victim," muttered the stranger; "am I always to meet with the pangs of death but to renew such a life on such term! Never to obtain a renewal without the pangs of death; and why? because I have not been able to obtain the voluntary consent of one that is young, beautiful and a virgin; I might then for a season escape the dreaded alternative."

He walked round and round the body of the monk for some time, and then he came and sat down by its side upon the trunk of the tree, and appeared lost in contemplation; but at length he looked at the body, saying, –

"Ay, ay – I have a plan. The church has furnished many a victim – let it furnish me with one. The church will furnish the sacrifice, and will give me the means of obtaining the offering. Well and good; it shall be done."

He arose, and walked about the body once more, and then approached it; having apparently made up his mind, he came to it, saying, –

"I will become a monk, too, of the most holy order of St. Francis; yes, that will serve me well enough. I will take his cassock, it will serve my turn, and be a ready introduction to the religious world. I am the good monk Francis myself. My learning and sanctity is great; it will carry all before it, and I shall be in great request. It will indeed be strange if there be no fruit upon such a tree. I am sure I shall deserve it."

He seized the body, and pulled off the monk's clothing, and quickly appareled himself in it, leaving the body as if fell by the side of the tree; and, having thrown his own clothes on one side, he drew the cowl over his head, and, seizing the staff he brought with him, he was about to leave the spot; but a sudden thought occurred to him, and he turned back, and began to rummage among the pockets of the monk.

"These churchmen, I have heard, never travel without something of value about them, and his gold, if he have any, may as well be mine as any one else's who may be passing this way."

He found the two purses that had been given him by Fiametta and Jose, and some that he had beside; moreover, there were some letters and papers, which he put into his pocket, merely observing, –

"These will enable me to pass for the character I assume successfully. I am and will be a monk. I will shrive and confess poor deluded souls, and send them on their eternal journeys."

A ghastly and hideous smile crossed his face; and having burdened himself with what he thought necessary, or worth while, he quitted the spot.

*T*here were two convents, or nunneries, near the city of Naples, at some short distance apart from each other.

One was the convent of St. Mary Magdalene, and the other was the convent of St. Cecilia, about a mile and a half apart, or perhaps more – some said a league; and so it was by the road, but not in a direct line.

It was late one evening, when the great bell of the convent of St. Mary Magdalene gave warning from without that some one demanded admission. The superior of the convent, a woman far advanced in age, and somewhat proud of her character, and not a little disposed to personal comfort, was much annoyed at the sound which gave some promise of trouble.

"Well," muttered the portress, as she rose from before a fire, and tottered towards the gate, looking through the iron grating for the object that disturbed her in her meditations and her devotion to the good things that Providence had furnished her with, – "well, what do you want?"

"I am a poor traveling broth of the order of St. Francis; I am benighted, and I wish for a lodging and food."

"Friend, brother of St. Francis, this is at a later hour than that at which we open our gates to strangers."

"They little think at Rome," said the monk, "that, to obtain a shelter, we have to get to the gates of a holy house before a certain time; and those who most need shelter, because it is less to be had, must wait and perish in the cold."

"The gates are shut."

"I see it."

"And the abbess has got the keys."

"Will she not give me shelter and food?"

"I may not ask her."

"I must, then, remain here outside the walls until the morning, and then I will wend my way back to the holy city, where I will say their messenger could not obtain rest and shelter at the convent here."

"Do you come form Rome?"

"I do; and do you refuse to tell your abbess an unworthy brother of holy St. Francis is here, and waiting for admission?"

The portress made no reply; she was by far to indignant to make any answer, and yet too fearful to refuse to do his bidding; for he spoke in a peremptory tone, that indicated an authority beyond what was usual in his appearance.

She, therefore, found her way to the lady abbess, to whom she began with every expression of submission and respect.

"My lady," said the portress, "there is one without who wants to come in."

"Well," said the abbess, "we can't let him in."

"I told him so," replied the portress; "but you would hardly credit it what he said about a holy pilgrim from Rome, stopping outside the gate all night, and returning to the holy city and speaking of our inhospitality."

"Did he," said the abbess, "say so much?"

"He did."

"Then let him in," said the abbess.

"Let him in!" said the portress, in an ecstasy of surprise, opening her eyes very wide, and repeating the words "Let him in."

"Yes; do as we bid you," said the abbess.

"Yes," replied the portress, "certainly; whatever our holy superior orders, it is for me to obey. I do your bidding."

Away went the holy portress to discharge her spleen in privacy; and, at the same time, unable to account for the orders given her, she returned to the portal, and having unbarred the gate, she drew the bolts and turned the lock, and opening the door, stood for the monk to enter.

"Come in," she said. "What do you mean? — do you not want to come in?"

"Am I free to enter?"

"Wherefore do I hold the gate open — for pleasure?"

"No, sister," said the monk, "through anger, I believe; but if you can find it in your conscience to be angry because I am at the door and give you this trouble, what will be the feelings of St. Peter, who keeps the gates of Heaven, when you present yourself thereat a hungry being and erring sinner; but peace be upon this place."

"Amen," said the portress.

At that moment one of the nuns came from the superior of the convent, saying, —

"Holy father, when you have rested and refreshed yourself, our worthy abbess will be glad to converse with you."

"I am even now at her commands," said the holy man.

"Will you not taste food, and rest yourself?"

"I never tire or need food, when I have aught to do that in any way concerns our religion."

"But, holy father, the body needs refreshment."

"It can be supported upon spiritual food alone, if the Lord wills," said the monk, crossing himself most devoutly.

"You must have great gifts, holy father!"

"Not I, but he that sent me," said the monk, solemnly.

"Will you follow me, holy man, and I will lead you to the abbess, who will be right glad to speak with you?" She wishes to speak to one lately come from the holy city; you can tell her news of the holy father."

"I can, my sister."

"Then, come this way," said the nun, who immediately led the way to the abbess, and the monk followed her closely, till he was lost sight of by those in the waiting-room.

Chapter CLIII.

FATHER FRANCIS'S INTERVIEW WITH THE ABBESS OF ST. MARY MAGDALENE. – THE OBJECTS AND WISHES OF THE HOLY FATHER.

*A*fter passing through a few passages, they entered into a room which had the appearance of a waiting-room, in which were placed chairs and seats; but they did not stop here, for the sister approached a door, at which she knocked, and paused a moment; but a voice from within desired her to enter; and, beckoning the monk to follow her, which he did, they both entered a comfortable room in which the abbess was seated.

"Here is the holy father," said the sister, "who demands lodging and refreshment; but he will take nothing until he has done all that may be required of him."

"Holy brother," said the abbess, "the traveler needs rest, and he that is hungered requires food. Will you partake of our hospitality?"

"I was told you desired to converse with me, and I could not let my ministry wait while I, like a glutton, ate and drank."

"No, brother, it was not for such a purpose I sent for thee, but to hear what news thou hadst from Rome, whence I heard you have come."

"I have come thence."

"But will you not take some refreshment here – it shall be brought thee, if thou wilt have it, or in the buttery, which you please."

"Whichsoever you please, sister," said the member of St. Francis.

"Then let some of the best be brought, sister, for the good man; and stay, I ate none at the last meal, which I may amend now; let me have a small moiety of a pasty, and a small trifle of cold venison."

The sister departed, and the abbess opened a small cupboard, from which she took a bottle and two glasses, of goodly dimensions, considering the fact that the place was inhabited only by females.

"Pronounce a blessing upon us, holy father," said the abbess. "This has been tasted by no unhallowed lips; it was a present from a holy lady to me, to take myself, and to offer to such as I deemed worthy of it — and you, holy father, I believe are worthy."

The worthy monk pronounced the required benediction, and drank as fine a glass of real Burgundy as ever went down consecrated lips.

"Thanks, worthy sister, thanks."

"Brother, I am glad to be able to give it thee; it gives me more pleasure to do so than thee to drink. I'll warrant me, that never has such wine passed through the merchants' hands, because he would never have parted with it at a price that would have made it procurable in a place like this, for we are, holy brother, poor, very poor."

"The people who live in these parts are, I fear, not so godly as they should be, to let a house like this want."

"There are many nobles."

"And they ought to pay handsomely."

"They do, I am thankful; but I should like to be able to offer the poor, diseased, and helpless men, better sort of diet than I do."

"It ought to be in your power when the rich and great are so close around you here. You ought to have rich penitents."

"But few of the rich are penitent, brother."

"Naples I was told was a sink of iniquity. I did not expect to find it in reality such as I have heard it described. But, sister, we must be thankful that we have what the times will afford; but, at the same time, when he enemy is thus about, we must be up and doing, and preach salvation to them."

"But they only answer by sending invitations for Sabbath balls," said the unfortunate abbess, in great dolor.

"That must be looked to. They must be chidden."

"And then they withhold their hands from works of charity — from doing any good deed to us — and we have no gifts and offerings."

"But that ought not to be any motive. When they see you in earnest, they will not resist any longer; they will, as they must, give in."

"Ah, holy father! you don't know the Neapolitans; they are the most sinful set of men that you ever met with."

"The holy father must know of this; he must be informed of the character of these bad people — of these facts. It is a melancholy state of things, which is a disgrace to a Christian country, and must be amended."

At that moment the nun returned with the refection for the monk and the abbess, who cast a longing glance towards it.

When this was laid on the table, the abbess gave a signal that there was no need of the further attendance of the servitor, who quitted the room, leaving the abbess and the monk to enjoy each others society at leisure.

Some minutes elapsed before either spoke, which time was spent in mastication of no ordinary morsels, being some of the most delicious meats that could be obtained for a religious house of this character, and they were usually supplied with the best of everything that could be had.

"Holy father," said the abbess, "the fare is poor; but I hope it will relieve those calls which imperious nature demands you to satisfy."

"Yes," said the monk; "I am well satisfied."

"Permit me to press upon your notice those venison pasties; they are made by Sister Bridget, who never made an indifferent one in all her life."

"I decidedly approve of Sister Bridget's skill," said the monk. "She is no doubt a worthy woman, and a woman fit for her station."

"I would not have another to do her duties for a trifle, save as a penance," said the abbess. "I will, at all events, retain her while the convent will give her a place of shelter."

"Very right, sister — very right."

"But what news from Rome, brother?"

"Little, save the holy pontiff has been very ill."

"I heard as much; and by many it is presumed that his holiness will be translated, if he should not be better soon."

"No: his holiness is safe, as far as it is possible for any human being to be. God preserve him long!"

"Amen!" said the abbess, devoutly.

"But have you no penitents, holy sister?"

"I have several, but they are all in the way of performing their penances, save one, who is somewhat refractory, holy father, and I know not what to do with her. She has no respect for those in authority."

"Is she one of the order?"

"No, a neophyte."

"How is it, then — what brings her here?"

"She is sent by relatives who are afraid of a disgrace, and will not give her any chance of committing their family to such a disgraceful marriage. She at one time pledged herself to take the vows, but now has some objection to do so."

"On what grounds does she refuse?"

"Because she thinks she shall not be happy."

"Absurd! Where is she?"

"We must have been compelled to secure her, for she has made more than one attempt to escape, and I have reasons to believe that these efforts have been aided from without."

"'Tis a serious offence — a very serious offence to those concerned, and would inevitably lead to a terrible example, if they were detected."

"No doubt; and we should feel it our duty to make every exertion to punish any one who makes an attempt to violate the sanctity of our house."

"It must be so, sister."

"Yes, certainly; and I have secured the maiden, who, if she be brought to their mind, will largely endow the convent."

"That ought to be seen to."

"I am, as you may imagine, holy father, anxious that the young maiden should become a member of our house. Who can tell," muttered the abbess, half aloud, "but she may become a chosen vessel by which much good may be effected?"

"She may," said the monk. "I am from Rome; you may examine the these credentials which I have with me. I will take the charge of this refractory sister of yours, and will pursue such a course as will bring her round to your way of thinking."

"And the endowment?"

"Will still belong to your house, to which it will be given. I have no object, sister, save the welfare of the church; reward I seek not, save what may be given in the good words of the wise and good."

"You are deserving of all praise, holy father. I was not thinking about the endowment, holy father, because, you see, it will not belong to me, but to the church, and this house in particular, for the use of the poor lambs here, over whom I am appointed shepherdess; so I have no feeling in the matter beyond what I ought to have in the spiritual welfare of our fellow sinners."

"I have no authority to interfere in aught else."

"I see, holy father," said the abbess, "you are a wonderful man, and such a one as will do much good."

"I will make an attempt to do good, sister."

"And I will make bold, holy brother, to say you will be successful; though, I venture to say, with humility, that I have tried everything with the unfortunate young woman, which appears to aggravate the evil, rather than give any promise of the future."

"So I might expect."

"You will pursue a different course?"

"I may; but it must depend upon circumstances. If I find it necessary, I must have some place of security, where no one can have any communication with her, save when I shall order it, or deem it proper she should be so confined."

"Certainly; very right."

"Moreover, if I find she needs such severe measures, I shall not let any food be given, save what is given by me, or in my presence, which, of course, amounts to the same thing."

"Exactly, holy father."

"And," continued the monk, "I will not permit this holy house to be insulted by a recusant, for I am quite resolved that no heretic shall baffle the ministers of religion."

"Oh, very improper; it would be indeed, not only an aggravation, but a decided loss to the church, which would damnify it to that extent."

"Undoubtedly," replied the holy man, "undoubtedly; and with your aid I hope to be able to make one good effort, and I pray heaven it may be attended with grace."

"I trust so; and now, holy brother, what may I call you?"

"You will see by these presents I am called Father Francis, of the order of St. Francis; and unworthy brother, who has, perhaps, beyond his gifts, obtained the praise and good wishes of his holiness the Pope, who has been pleased specially to send me forth on a traveling commission, to report to him and to stay where I thought my services might be required."

"Holy father, we may have you stay here some time, I hope, and your favorable report of our poor endeavors; they are in the right direction, and carried on with the right spirit; but we are all weak and erring mortals, we cannot always be as successful as we would wish, and in this matter we have been unsuccessful."

"You have done all that could be expected; there are some matters that will not yield to the weaker vessel, but which would yield to the stronger; therefore you have nothing to blame yourself with; but you are to be commended for what you have done."

"Thanks, holy father; I would not be willingly found wanting."

"Nor are you, sister, according to my poor judgment."

"And when will you see this neophyte?"

"I will see her on the morrow; and in the meantime I must be chargeable to you for board and lodging, if you will so far grace me."

"Name it not, holy father; I have nothing here but what is yours; and when you choose to retire, there will be the best traveler's bed ready for you."

"Straw and sackcloth are good enough for me," said the monk, ostentatiously.

"But it concerns our housekeeping, holy father, and our hospitality too. We must not let you lodge thus. I pray you, for our sakes, permit us to do what the credit of the place will permit us to do in the way of entertainment."

"Be it even as you will, sister; it does not beseem me that I should contend for matters like these — be it so; I will retire."

"It grows late. I will summon Sister Agatha to show you your dormitory."

Accordingly, Sister Agatha was summoned, and the monk was, after another delicate libation of rich Burgundy, led to his room.

Chapter CLIV.

THE CELL OF THE NEOPHYTE. – THE INTERVIEW. – THE
UNEXPECTED TURN GIVEN TO THE AFFAIRS AT THE
CONVENT OF MARY MAGDALENE.

*T*he morning broke, and the matins were duly performed at St. Mary Magdalene.

This was what happened every day in the week included, for the convent was always alive to the performance of its duties from the dawn of day until sunset and after; but it was their business — a business from the toil of which they rested not on the Sabbath.

But then it happened that there was no labor; it was all easy-going, straight-forward work, and was a mere pastime, that only occupied the lips and ears; for not half of it was understood, and the other half had long since ceased to produce any impression upon the stagnant minds of the mewed-up sisterhood.

However, there was not lack of comfort, especially for those who held any of the good offices in the convent. The holy Father Francis was met at table by the abbess, who was great and gracious to him.

"Will you inform the sisterhood, holy sister, of my stay here, lest it bring any scandal upon your house, the well-being of which is to me of importance."

"I have already done so. I anticipated your wishes on that point, holy father — in fact, I did it on my own account, too, for we live in evil times — in very evil times."

"We do, sister."

"So that being done, you have but to express your wishes; for of course they are the wishes deputed of the pope."

"Certainly — certainly; it could not be otherwise."

"I knew," said the abbess; "and now I wait for your wishes; let me know them, and I will answer for it, that nothing that is desired by his holiness through you shall meet with any other than the most profound attention and willing obedience."

"You are a worthy superior, and if Heaven please to permit me, I will not fail to let his holiness know of all this devotion and obedience; and, not less, your regularity and religious observances; he will be well pleased, I am sure."

"Thanks, holy father."

"Nay, 'tis justice. But I would now see your unworthy guest."

"The probationist? Yes, she can be seen. She has had her food given her for breakfast, and will be ready to receive you."

"I am ready, then. In the meantime, what is her name and designation?"

"Her name is Juliet, and of a noble house — that of the famous Di Napotoloni."

"Indeed! 'tis very strange."

"She desired to marry against her friends' wish, who would not hear of the iniquity that was desired to be perpetrated."

"I will see her, then. I may be able to do some good."

"You cannot fail."

"I do not know. The race is not always with the swift, nor the battle with the strong; but I will essay to try."

"If you will come this way, holy father, you shall be admitted into her cell. Shall I remain, or shall I return?"

"I will be alone, for I will confess her, and bring her mind to a calm state. Then, when I have her confidence, I will begin the object in view, and then we shall find whether there is any probability of that system being successful."

"Certainly; but if not?"

"Why, we must adopt more energetic means, and these we must continue to pursue until there is an end of hope, or life; for when coercion is once begun we must continue it on without intermission."

"No doubt — no doubt, holy father."

"Have you any others who are in a very similar state to this unhappy being?"

"None, holy father, none; but this is her door. She will be sulky, or spiteful, as the humor may be; but, at the same time, she will not spare me, because I have, as you see, thus confined her to this place as a punishment."

"You have done right, sister, quite right — there is no blame."

The abbess opened the door, and at the same moment they both entered the dungeon in which the unfortunate young female was thrust by the aid of paternal authority, sanctioned by religious usage, and a presumed right they had over her actions.

"This, holy father," said the abbess, "is the unfortunate female whose case I told you of as being so desperate, that there is no remedy left but that to which we never resort, save in an extremity, and upon no other occasion whatever."

"I see, sister — I see; but I hope one so young has not been entirely won over to the enemy. I trust she will not strive against those who strive for her."

"This holy man," said the abbess to Juliet; "this holy man has traveled from St. Peter's, at Rome, and has come to examine, with the sanction of his holiness the Pope, the state of our spiritual existence. See that you give good account of yourself."

"What the lady abbess has stated to you," said Father Francis, "is no more than the truth. I am so come, and for such a purpose. Prepare, therefore, to confess, and tell me freely what it is that troublest your soul. Confess, daughter."

The monk drew a stool towards him, and having sat down, he waved his hand towards the abbess, who stood by, saying, —

"I will hear her confess; we must be alone."

There was an instant movement on the part of the abbess, and she quitted the cell of the lady, placed the key of the door on the inside, and left them alone.

"Daughter," said the monk, after awhile, "daughter, what is this I hear of you?"

The unfortunate young woman fixed her eyes upon her questioner, and took them not off him during some minutes; and a shudder seemed to pass through her mind.

"I have spoke to thee," said the monk.

"You have," answered Juliet.

"Then answer me."

"I cannot. I know not what has been said."

"Could you not guess?"

"I might, holy father; but what can that be to such as you? You must know that I have been put here according to the abbess's orders."

"I do know so much, daughter. What more have you to say?"

"Simply, that I know not what I am thus confined here for."

"Since you know it not, I will tell you. You have disobeyed the abbess's orders — that is what you are now punished for — 'tis a heinous offence."

"I am not yet one of the order, holy father; and, therefore, the abbess has no right to do this; and if she did not know that my friends were her abettors, she dare not do it; 'tis a grievous injury, and a deep and shameful wrong. Instead of religion being, as it ought to be, the safe-guard of the poor and weak against the rich and powerful, it is a means of oppression against those who have no power."

"These are hard accusations, daughter."

"They will bear the proof, however, and that fairly. Where have I taken the vows? — where am I the sworn sister? — tell me that, holy father."

"I have come for another purpose, daughter; you have been undutiful to those whom nature and God gave control over you; and you have desired to live disgracefully; surely, these are things that deserve punishment, for they are great moral crimes."

"I cannot see any such, holy father."

"I am afraid your soul is in an unclean state, daughter. There is no hope for you until this is amended; depend upon it, you can never prosper while you set at naught the desires of those who rule you."

"But they have no right to force me to an alternative that my soul revolts at."

"You cannot mean you revolt at becoming one of the holy and chaste sisterhood here? — that must be a libel upon your chastity."

"Holy father, it is not the age, nor under the circumstances, at which such a proposal can be made with any chance of success; for I am quite confident that I am born with better prospects than those which now threaten me. My father and mother had no right to send me here; they led me to believe I should inherit a fortune, and now they desire I should enter a cloister."

"And you have given them cause to change the original intention they had concerning you; you are disobedient, that is enough."

"But, holy father, there is a power stronger than a father's or a mother's — a power of which the church approves. What would you more?"

"What power?"

"The divine command which says, we shall leave a parent and fly to the arms of him whom we have chosen to become our husband."

"The devil can quote scripture when he has any object in view. But, Juliet, you are carried away by the strength of your own passion. This is a disgraceful marriage, and one you should not contract — one that would never be sanctioned by them."

"It might be so — that is, unsanctioned by them; but there is no disgrace in being married to a young officer who loved me."

"And whom you mean really to marry?"

"Yes."

"And you would, in fact, marry any one who would offer himself, instead of being a nun?"

"I would sooner die — and I will, by slow starvation — sooner than become one of this or any other order."

"I see — but who was this young man?"

"Jules di Maestro."

"How strange — how passing strange!" said the monk, changing his tone from one of severity to one of sadness and sorrow.

"Why, what ails you, holy father? Has anything happened?"

"I know not, my daughter, whether to feel most sorrow or most anger; but your case is one that requires some care. Whether to tell you all, or whether to conceal a part, or — or — in fact, to tell the whole and trust to your goodness."

"What do you mean — what do you mean? Your manner distresses me. I cannot understand you at all — speak, for the love of Heaven!"

"I can hardly do so, unless, by a solemn vow, you promise secrecy."

"I swear," said the hasty and impatient Juliet.

"Then listen."

"I do — I do. For Heaven's sake, keep me no longer in suspense!"

"Well, then, Jules di Maestro and I concocted a plan together, which we were to execute with the view of getting you out of this convent, so that you might both quit the kingdom of Naples, and get into some of the free states."

"Oh, dear Jules! and did he really take so much trouble about me — did he really mean to do so much? I can never be grateful enough to him."

"Why, you remember his last attempt?"

"I heard of it; but it did not succeed, But it must be two months ago."

"It was. We both were present."

"Both! You?"

"Yes; I was present, and wounded in the affray, though not so bad as poor Maestro."

"Hurt! but he has got over that, else you would not come here from him to plan another escape, which I see you have. I am truly sorry for his hurts; but he is, no doubt, well again."

"Stay — stay — you are much to sanguine."

"He has not forgotten me?"

"No; but you must permit me to speak. I am quite sure that had you heard the whole of the affair, you would not speak in this strain; for had I known that I had to tell you unwelcome news, I would not have undertaken this affair, even urged as I have been by him and your beauty."

"What mean you?"

"Why, that Jules is dead. He died within a few days after the last attempt that he made to rescue you from your captivity."

"What, do I hear aright! Jules dead! Great God, impossible — quite impossible! Nothing so dreadful can be real."

"I am sorry to say it is so," said the monk; "very sorry."

"But how did it fall out?" asked Juliet, who appeared to be too much stunned to feel anything acutely; "tell me how."

"When we made our last attempt to get you out, it failed; for we were both compelled to defend ourselves, and to fly before a numerous body of men. I should have got clear of them, but I saw that Jules was made prisoner, so I charged and rescued him from their hands."

"It was nobly done of you."

"Then, you see, I got some marks that I could not help; there were too many; but poor Jules got mortally wounded."

"Heaven be merciful to him!"

"I hope so; but he was not killed immediately. I got him quite away without any one being able to tell who he was, but that was an effort that cost me much. I took him away, as I said, and I sat by his side when he breathed his last breath."

"And what said Jules?" inquired Juliet, as she shed many bitter tears. "What said he? did he not curse her who had caused him such an end?"

"No, no; Jules did not; he wept when he knew his wounds were mortal, not because he was to die, but because he must leave you here, and you would be for ever ignorant of his fate; that is what most affected him, I assure you."

"Ah! he was of a noble, generous nature."

"I, however, promised him that I would see you, and let you know how the matter had stood with him; and he gave you his last blessing, and desired me not to tell your family that he was dead, as it would be a triumph for them; at the same time he wished, if possible, I could supply his place to you in his stead."

"No, no," said Juliet; "no, no; that can never be. I loved Jules, and can never love any one else, and will never try. No, no; Jules and Jules only, will I live for!"

"But he is dead."

"Then for him will I die, too; he died for me, and I will for him."

"But his last words were to me — 'Go and see Juliet, tell her truly how I died, and what my last wishes were. Those I have formed with the full belief that they are for her benefit. I know how she is placed — without a friend, and in danger.'"

"Yes, yes; now I have no one to help me."

"You have me, if you choose."

"Not at the price you spoke of."

"But you know not how clearly he expressed himself upon the matter; he knew the life you lead then — what it will be by and by — you know the starvation which you will have to feel, and, perhaps, be built up in a wall after all."

"Oh, God!"

"He said, 'See, and tell her you have nearly lost your life in serving me, and in serving her; that I am under an obligation to you for saving my life more than once. Thus, Juliet is the last word I pronounced, and the last I thought of — but if I had a legacy to leave you,' he said, 'I would leave her, and die happy if I thought you would enable her to escape. Marry her, and keep all the world at defiance — then, indeed, I could be happy — almost as happy as if I lived to be in your happy position.'

"'I will,' I replied; 'I will endeavor to obtain her escape.'

"'Will you swear?'

"'I do swear,' I replied; 'and at the same time I will risk my life, and lose it, if she will accept of me for a husband; but I cannot for less.'

"'You have said enough,' he replied; 'I am satisfied.'"

"And he died?" said Juliet.

"Yes; he died; but I have been long enough. I will see you again before another day is past, and then I will learn your determination. Do not let my cause be rejected because I have not urged it forward as I could have done; but the truth is, it is an honest one, and it will speak for itself. Farewell for the present; be secret and silent. They think me monk, for I have assumed this disguise, at the peril of my life, which will be taken with cruel tortures if I am discovered."

There was a pause, when the monk resumed again, —

"If you can consent to become my wife by this time tomorrow, I will endeavor to free you from bondage."

"Why purchase the motive to a good action?"

"I do not do so. I only purchase a right which, if risk of life, and all that man hold dear, be anything, why, you will not think me a Jew in the bargain. Think, lady, think upon what I have offered you."

"I do think; but 'tis a hard bargain for me to lose my liberty either way."

"Nay, you gain it, for you would be my mistress. But, hark! here comes the abbess. I must bid you adieu."

"How fares the penitent?" inquired the abbess, entering.

"I cannot gain either a satisfactory or an unsatisfactory answer to your inquiry. I will, however, see her tomorrow again, and if I find she is obdurate, perhaps the shortest way will be an application to the inquisition."

"Think of that, daughter," said the abbess, leaving the cell.

"Think of that," added the monk, "as your means of leaving the cell — of escaping. Farewell, daughter. Benedicite."

Chapter CLV.

THE NUN'S ATTEMPTED ESCAPE FROM THE CONVENT OF
ST. MARY MAGDALENE. – THE PURSUIT AND THE
DISCLOSURE. – THE ESCAPE OF THE PRETENDED MONK.

*T*he next day all Naples was alive to the fact that a holy man had been murdered in the wood Del Notti – a holy brother of teh order of St. Francis, who was much respected by the good people of Naples.

Jose and Fiametta both attended before the municipal authorities to give the required information they had give the monk gold to remain by the side of the dead man whom Jose had killed.

There was a general terror throughout Naples, for no one was aware of how the matter had fallen out, nor how the enormity would be punished, and who would be the sufferers in the present case.

The officers of the state were in active search after the perpetrator of so wicked a deed – as well as the officers of the inquisition.

*T*he next time Father Francis called at the convent, he went straight to the lady abbess, and said to her with some earnestness, –

"I am sorry to tell you, the more I reflect upon the conversation I had with your neophyte Juliet, I have some strong doubts about the course I originally thought of pursuing towards the young person."

"In what respect, holy father?"

"I thought of pursuing a mild course towards her."

"I have done it, and failed."

"The reason I think is not that she is hardened, but that she simply does not believe we will proceed to the extremity that we have threatened."

"I think she is hardened, holy father."

"Time alone will show; but I have altered my plans respecting her."

"In what respect, holy father?"

"I think I will begin to strike terror into her soul, and at once shew her the reality of my intentions, with respect to what I shall subject her by way of punishment for her resistance to her religious superiors."

"Very good, holy brother; I think it the plan that will most likely succeed the best; if she be terrified, she will be obedient."

"And to that end," said the monk, "I have ordered the alguazils of the inquisition to be here in half an hour's time, when she will be carried there, and subjected to the first process of torture."

"You will not hurt her?"

"Not much."

"Just enough to teach what powers you can exert."

"Yes, just so. Now, when they come, let me know, and, if she consents to go, all well and good; and, if she do not, we must use force."

"And how long will you keep her at the inquisition?" inquired the abbess; "because, eventually, the parents will claim her of me."

"About three weeks, at the farthest; but, if the parents are troublesome, name the inquisition, and say holy brother Francis, from Rome, will come and confess them, and make some inquiries concerning their belief and faith in the church."

"I will, holy father."

The monk now returned to the cell where the unfortunate Juliet was confined, and, on opening the door, he found her in tears.

"Juliet," he said, "I come again."

"You are here;" she replied, "I see."

"And I am here with all the means of escape; you have but to say the word, and you are free and at liberty."

"I cannot – I cannot."

"You cannot. Do you love life – do you love liberty?"

"I do."

"And yet you choose the cold, bare walls of a cloister, to a life of happiness and love; to a life that is made for such as you."

"I cannot love you."

"I love you; that I have risked my life for you more than once, is true; my persecution is another proof of that."

"It may be so."

"Then why not consent? you have no alternative that can interest you more, or that will offer you more happiness."

"I cannot so soon forget Jules."

"Nay, we will not quarrel about that; I cannot expect you. I am not unreasonable, because I know so well the circumstances of the case. All is haste and confusion; there is no time for thought or preparation – all lies in self-preservation; say at once you will have me; I will endeavor to gain your love and esteem afterwards; our happiest days, our courting-time will come after our wedding."

"It cannot come."

"But will you choose the horrors of the inquisition rather than wed one who would give life and fortune to you?"

"Who speaks of the inquisition?" inquired Juliet, terrified.

"The abbess spoke to me about it when I came here last time, and said she had your father's commands to deliver you over to them."

"I'll not believe it."

"I entreated her not to do so, but to leave it in my hands, and I would undertake to communicate with the inquisition, and bring their officers here today."

"And have you?"

"I have brought those who will counterfeit them, and carry you off. The plan is matured. Will you leave this place, wed me, and be a happy woman, or remain here to be tortured and disfigured by the tortures of the inquisition — perhaps to die in their hands?"

"Horrible!" said Juliet, with a shudder.

"Think on this and on that."

At that moment a tremendous uproar occurred in the convent, and a ringing of bells. The pretended monk started, and listened attentively.

"They come," he muttered — "they come!"

"Have they discovered you?" inquired Juliet.

"I know not — I care not if they have. Will you quit the convent, and leave Naples with me? Will you become my wife? You see what I have risked for you. I wait but your answer: they are coming."

Before any answer could be given, the door was thrown open, and the abbess, followed by a troop of soldiers, entered the cell, and, among them, the vampire monk saw his late adversary, Jose, and his love, Fiametta.

"There is the murderer," said Jose, pointing to the monk, whose cowl had fallen off; "and he is the man whom I believed I had killed."

"Oh, yes, it is the same horrid face!" said Fiametta.

"The murderer of Father Francis?" said the abbess.

"I know not how it was done; but I told Father Francis to watch and pray by the dead body, and see it decently buried, and he said he would do so. I gave him gold, and left him at his watch and his devotions."

"And he is dead now — his cassock and papers torn from him."

"Seize him, comrades!" said the officer.

At the sound of the officer's voice, Juliet looked up, and beheld her lover, Jules di Maestro, whom she was told had been killed. She sprang up, saying, —

"It is all false, then. You are not slain — you are still living — and you did not send this man to marry me?"

"I — who — Oh! Juliet, have I found you?"

"I am here, dear Jules. Take me hence — take me hence!"

"I will not do so now; but I have their majesties' favor, and will take care you shall be released from this vile durance."

"And that man —"

"Ay, look to your prisoner," said the officer.

But there was no prisoner to look to. He had slipped off his cowl and cassock, and left the convent, leaving all present immersed in their own affairs. The abbess was indignant at the imposture, and would not risk Jules's appeal, on behalf of Juliet, to the king, and at once consented to her release and immediate marriage; and at the same time Fiametta consented to wed Jose, so that all was forgotten, save the murder of the holy Father Francis, and the resurrection of the vampire monk, who was, in reality, no other than Sir Francis Varney, who was no more heard of in Naples, but supposed to roam about the world at large.

www.ingramcontent.com/pod-product-compliance
Lightning Source LLC
Chambersburg PA
CBHW060427030726
47495CB00003B/770